BROKEN
HOME

BROKEN HOME

ROBERTA KRAY

sphere

SPHERE

First published in Great Britain in 2011 by Sphere

A CIP catalogue record for this book
is available from the British Library.

Hardback ISBN 978-1-84744-440-0
Trade Paperback ISBN 978-1-84744-441-7

Typeset in Garamond by M Rules
Printed and bound in Great Britain by
Clays Ltd, St Ives plc

Sphere
An imprint of
Little, Brown Book Group
100 Victoria Embankment
London EC4Y 0DY

An Hachette UK Company
www.hachette.co.uk

www.littlebrown.co.uk

For Janelle Posey, a treasured friend

Prologue

It was almost six o'clock and the tube was full to bursting. The carriage was hot and sticky, humming with the stink of sweat, of overly powerful perfume and damp coats. As the human cattle truck rocked along the tracks, bodily contact was impossible to avoid. Arms brushed against arms, thighs against thighs. No one paid Connie any particular attention. Dressed in the bland uniform of an office worker, and with a pair of ugly glasses perched on her nose, she was just another weary commuter on her way home.

Connie Tomlin was always careful in her choice of victim: they were usually men, the type who wore designer suits and flashy watches, City boys with more money than sense. The younger ones were the best; cocky and careless, they were usually too busy posing or eyeing up the talent to notice her deft fingers relieving them of their wallets. It was surprising how many suckers kept them in their back pockets. She already had three in her bag from her previous journeys. Plenty of credit cards, she was sure, not to mention a fair wad of cash. She hadn't had time to check them out yet. Hopefully it had been a lucrative couple of hours.

Connie had already chosen her next mark: he was a twenty-something male sporting a Rolex and a February suntan. He was holding on to one of the straps attached to the ceiling of the carriage, and his jacket had risen at the back. She smiled. This was going to be easy. The silly sod hadn't even bothered to do up the button on his pocket. That wallet was simply calling to her!

Connie glanced around to make sure no one was watching. The commuters who were sitting down all had their noses in newspapers, magazines or books. The ones who were standing were all studiously avoiding each other's eyes. That was the law of the tube: never meet another's person's gaze if you could possibly avoid it. It was a law that had served her well over the past couple of years.

This, she decided, would be her last job of the day. No point in pushing her luck. Anyway, her feet were sore from all the standing around in her cheap high heels. She wiggled her toes. What she needed was a hot bath, some soothing music and a good strong drink. She'd pick up a bottle of voddie on her way home, and later, when Pony came round to pick up the credit cards, she'd buy a bit of weed off him.

Sometimes Connie worked with the other girls, but today she was playing it solo. As usual she was standing by the doors – always useful for a hasty exit – and she waited until she knew they were close to the station. When the train gave a jolt and everyone lurched forward, she made her move. She was carrying her coat over her arm, and from beneath its cover her hand snaked out to whip the wallet from its resting place.

She had the usual adrenalin rush as she waited to see if he'd realise. It was a heady mixture of excitement and dread, the biggest kick she'd ever known: better than drugs or alcohol or sex. Her heart was thrashing as she waited for a reaction, but the man continued to gaze straight ahead, utterly oblivious.

There was no indication that anyone else had clocked her either. She breathed out a soft sigh of relief. Once again she'd got away with it.

Connie didn't feel guilty as she stepped briskly out on to the platform. Why should she? You had to take care of yourself in this city; no one else would do it for you. The flash git probably earned more in a day than most people did in a week. He didn't give a toss whether she lived or died and so she didn't care that he mightn't have quite as good a Friday night as he'd originally been planning. And it wasn't as if she'd stolen all his worldly possessions. In fact, she was doing him a favour, teaching him a useful lesson about securing your valuables when travelling on public transport. He'd never make the same mistake again.

As the train pulled away from the platform, Connie made her way up to Liverpool Street station, crossed over the forecourt and went down to the Ladies'. Rummaging in her bag, she found the change she needed to get through the turnstile. Once inside, she picked out a cubicle at the far end and locked the door behind her.

First she took off the glasses and placed them in their case. Then she removed the mousy-coloured wig and folded it neatly into her bag. She shook out her long dark brown hair and ran a comb through it. Using a compact mirror, she applied mascara to her lashes and put on some lipstick. Finally she turned her reversible raincoat inside out and put it on so that the blue side was showing. No matter how convinced you might be that you were free and clear, it was always worth taking precautions.

Next came the bit she looked forward to most. Please God, let it have been worth her while. After pulling down the lid of the toilet, Connie perched on the edge and took the stolen wallets from her bag. Her smile widened as she slipped out their contents. Four hundred and twenty quid in all, a fistful of credit and store cards – including one Gold American Express – and a bit of loose change. Yes! She couldn't complain about that little haul. It was a damn sight more than she'd get tending bar or flipping burgers.

She could have dumped the wallets in the bin, but Lana had taught her to be careful. You could never tell when the bins were going to be emptied, and if some cleaner happened to remember you leaving the cubicle . . . There were other bins of course, but then there were CCTV cameras to be wary of; the streets were full of them these days. There were fingerprints to worry about too. Connie never wore gloves when she was working – your fingers had to be free and nimble – and so every wallet, if it was being disposed of, had to be properly wiped. It was easier to take them home and do it there. She put the cash and cards in her own purse and dropped it, along with the empty wallets, back in her bag.

The only time Connie ever felt a pang of guilt was when she came across photos, especially of kids. On those occasions she told herself that no one with any sense would carry around the *only* copy of a picture. But it still niggled, taking the edge off her pleasure in the other spoils.

Before leaving, she checked the floor to make sure she hadn't dropped anything. Then she stepped outside the cubicle and went through the process of washing and drying her hands. A few minutes later she rejoined the bustle of the forecourt. The trains ran every twenty minutes at this time of day, and there was already one waiting on the platform. She jumped on, and after a quick walk through the compartments found an empty seat by a window.

It was only a short journey from here to the East End borough of Kellston. She settled down, happily anticipating the hours ahead. No more work for her today; she was going to have a well-deserved drink and chill out in front of the TV. Tomorrow,

4

as usual, she'd go up West with Lana and cruise through the crowds. There were always good pickings on a Saturday.

About six months ago, she'd discovered a tiny gold cross and chain tucked into a pocket at the back of a black leather wallet she'd lifted in Piccadilly. There had been over eight hundred quid in the wallet, the best result she'd ever had from a single lift. She should have thrown the cross away, or given it to Pony to get rid of, but she hadn't. Something had held her back. Connie wasn't religious, she wasn't even particularly moral, but she'd still baulked at passing this particular item into the grasping, nicotine-stained fingers of Pony Adams. Lana would kill her if she ever found out. One of the first rules of the game was never to hang on to anything you thieved – well, nothing but the cash. Connie didn't wear the cross, but sometimes, if she was feeling down, she'd take it out of the box she kept her special things in and hold it in the palm of her hand. It was like a good-luck charm that always made her feel better.

Connie only ever wore one piece of jewellery. Lifting her fingers to her neck, she touched the silver locket that nestled at her throat. She thought of her mum and dad, both dead now. The locket had been a gift for her tenth birthday. Scenes from the past rose up in her mind, but she quickly pushed them down again. That time was over. There was no going back.

It was dark and still raining when Connie got off the train. At the exit to the station, she turned right, in the opposite direction to the high street and its fancy shops. Tanner Road was a five-minute walk away. Because of its location, sitting right on the edge of the local red-light district, property was more affordable than in other parts of Kellston.

Even in this rather dubious area, Connie never worried about walking around on her own. She glanced to her left, along the length of Albert Street. Some of the girls were out already, loitering near the kerb, puffing on cigarettes while they scanned the passing cars for likely punters. She knew most of them by sight, skinny regulars touting for trade. She shivered, not from the cold, but from the knowledge that she could quite easily have been standing there beside them. If it hadn't been for Lana, for the twist of fate that had brought them together, she too could have been desperate for her next fix and willing to do anything to get it.

She pushed her hands deeper into her pockets and hurried on, not wanting to dwell on what might have been. She was young and had her whole future ahead of her. The bad years, the ones she didn't like to think about, were behind her now. Her life might not be perfect, but at least it was tolerable. She smiled. No, it was better than that. She had a warm place to sleep, food to eat and friends she could rely on.

When she reached Tanner Road, Connie stopped at the corner and went into the shop. Jamal was standing at the counter, his arms crossed over his chest, staring up at the TV. The news was on, some politician gazing earnestly out of the screen, spewing out the usual slimy lies.

'Hey,' he said, giving her a nod. 'You all right, love?'

'Not bad, ta. Give us a bottle of voddie, will you, and a bottle of red wine. That Merlot stuff if you've still got it on offer.' Her eyes scanned the shelves behind him. 'I'll have a pack of fags too. The usual. Oh, and some Rizlas, the green ones.'

She watched as Jamal carefully put her purchases into a carrier bag. He was a plump middle-aged man with wily dark eyes in a heavy face. A small brown mole lay just above the left corner of his upper lip.

'You should watch yourself out there. Another girl almost got it a couple of nights ago. Left her for dead, the bastard did.'

'I know,' Connie said. 'I heard about it.' Gemma Leigh was the third working girl to have been violently assaulted that month. The first had been in Hoxton, the second in Bethnal

6

Green. And now it was Kellston. The attacker was clearly concentrating his attentions on the East End. She glanced up at the TV. 'Any more news on her?'

Jamal shook his head. 'Still in intensive care. And you shouldn't be walking around on your own. It's not safe.'

'It's early yet,' Connie said, suppressing a shudder. She didn't want to think about that poor girl lying in the hospital, or what her assailant had put her through before dumping her in an alley near the Mansfield Estate.

'First there was that business with the funeral parlour, and now this. Where's it all gonna end, huh?' Jamal slowly shook his head again. 'That's one sick bastard out there. Men like that . . . they should string 'em up, get them off the streets for good.'

Connie turned up the collar of her coat. It was warm in the shop but a chill had just run through her. It wasn't only Gemma's fate that was making her skin crawl. Any mention of that funeral parlour gave her the creeps. The business had been closed down a couple of months ago after a young man had been killed in the basement. The story had hit the headlines, been splashed all over the front of the papers, because Toby Grand hadn't just been murdered – he'd also been meticulously embalmed.

Jamal spread his hands on the counter. 'Anything else, love?'

'That's it, ta.' Finding her head full of the kind of images that only ever gave you nightmares, Connie quickly got out her purse and paid. She wanted to get home, to close and lock the door behind her. Grabbing the carrier bag, she mumbled a hasty goodbye, and left.

Back on the street, she headed towards the flat. The cops were keeping quiet about the more disturbing details of the attack on Gemma Leigh, but Lana had heard rumours from the girls, tales of disgusting brutality and torture. She'd recited the details over breakfast. It was an attempt, Connie knew, to scare the hell out of her. *And what if it's him?* Lana had said, peering at her over the rim of her mug. *Danny Street's a psycho and everyone knows it. Stay away from him. You want to be the next poor cow on his list?*

Connie felt her stomach twist. Maybe Lana had a point, but nothing was going to stop her from searching for the truth. She might be playing with fire, but how else was she going to find out what had really happened to her dad? There were some risks that simply had to be taken. She was halfway down Tanner Road, hoping that the bottle of vodka might help her get back in Lana's good books, when she heard the sound of heavy footsteps behind her.

'Stop there! Police!'

Connie stopped dead in her tracks, her brown eyes widening with alarm. She remembered the empty wallets in her bag, the stolen cards in her purse, and her heart began to race. *Damn, damn, damn!* Should she try and make a run for it? But she didn't stand a chance of escaping in the high heels she was wearing. Turning, she stared at the man behind her – and suddenly realised who it was. A wave of relief flowed over her. Raising a hand to her chest, she heaved out a groan. 'You rotten sod! I thought . . .'

He grinned. 'Jesus, that's one face you've got on you there. If I was the filth, I'd arrest you just for looking so guilty.'

'Good thing you're not, then. What are you doing here?'

He frowned, pretending to be offended. 'Now what kind of a welcome is that?'

'The best you're gonna get after scaring the bloody life out of me.' Connie finally gave him a smile. 'Shouldn't you be at work? I thought you usually . . .'

'Yeah, I've got to get back. I just wanted to run something by you if you've got ten minutes. It's to do with that stuff you were talking about the other day.'

Connie looked towards the flat, where a light was shining from the living room window. Someone was home. 'Okay. But we'd better not do it here.'

'How about I buy you a drink? You look like you need one.'

'And whose fault is that? God, you could have given me a heart attack.' She raised her free hand to her chest again. 'It's still going like the clappers.'

'Sorry, love. Shall we go to the Fox? I've left the car there, so I can drop you off after.'

'Okay, just a quick one then.' The Fox was a large, busy pub near the station with a car park round the side. Most of the local streets were permit parking only, or so jam-packed that it was impossible to find a space. They started walking back in the direction she'd come from, but as they turned on to Station Road he stopped.

'Not that way,' he said. 'It's quicker to cut through the lane.'

Connie hesitated. She could see Railway Lane from where she was standing, a thin, straight alley, bordered on one side by a ten-foot fence and on the other by a series of abandoned station buildings. Had she been alone, she wouldn't have considered walking down it. It was long and shadowy, lit only by a thin orangey light escaping from the end of the platforms.

'What's the matter?' he said. 'Scared I'll get the urge to jump you when we're halfway down?'

She narrowed her eyes and laughed. 'I'd like to see you try.'

They were ten yards in when Connie, who had taken hold of his arm, felt his whole body stiffen. It was the kind of flinching that made her glance automatically over her shoulder. There was no one there. There was no one ahead of them either. She looked at him. 'What's the matter?'

His mouth, which had been smiling a moment ago, was now tight and grim. 'Nothin'.'

'Yes there is.'

9

'You want the truth, hun?' He stopped walking, shook off her hand and glared down at her. 'As it happens, I have got a bit of a problem – a problem with you, that is.'

Connie was aware of the sudden change in his voice, of its ominous overtones. His expression had altered, becoming hard and cold. Jamal's warning flashed into her head. 'What do you mean?'

'What I mean,' he said, leaning down to bring his face closer to hers, and lowering his voice to a whisper, 'is that I know *everything*. You think I don't know what you've been up to?'

'I haven't . . . I don't understand. I don't—'

Connie didn't have time to finish her protestations. He grabbed hold of her shoulders and pushed her back hard against the fence. She felt the force of his shove resound down the length of her backbone. Wincing with the pain, she tried to fight him off. But it was too late. He had her firmly pinned.

'You know what you are, love? You're a bitch! A fuckin' lying bitch!'

'What are you—'

Connie had barely opened her mouth before she felt his hands move to grip her throat. The carrier bag slipped from her fingers and fell to the pavement. She was aware of the clatter of the bottles on the concrete. Had they smashed? Even as the thought entered her head, she realised how ridiculous it was. She had more to worry about than a couple of broken bottles.

His voice was now a menacing hiss. 'And do you know what happens to bitches like you?'

Clawing at his hands, Connie desperately tried to free herself. She could barely breathe. His fingers were tightening round her windpipe. She struggled, but he was too strong for her. His voice, full of hate, full of venom, was the last thing she heard before her knees buckled and she crumpled to the ground.

Chapter One

Hope was standing by the sink when the doorbell rang. She paused for a second, in two minds as to whether to answer it. She wasn't expecting anyone, and her friends knew better than to call round unannounced. Then the sound came again, another two sharp rings. She sensed, although she wasn't sure how, that the caller wouldn't stop until someone eventually responded.

With a sigh, she flapped the excess water off her hands and dried them on a towel. Then she strode through to the hall and yanked open the door. There was a man standing on the other side. He was in his late thirties, about five foot eight, lean and thin-faced. She scowled at him, certain that he was about to try and sell her something – gas or broadband, politics or God. Well, whatever it was, she didn't want it.

'Yes?' she said sharply.

'Hope Randall?'

It briefly crossed her mind to deny it, but some fundamental streak of honesty – or maybe simply the fear of being found out – prevented her from going through with the deception. Instead she gave a small, barely perceptible nod.

'I'm sorry to disturb you. My name's Flint. I was wondering if I could have a word.'

Hope glared back at him. 'What about?' Just one mention of favourable energy rates or the love of Jesus and she'd be ending this exchange pronto.

The man hesitated, screwing up his eyes. 'It's a bit, er . . . delicate. Could we talk inside?'

'No,' she said bluntly. Although the small resort of Albersea was hardly renowned for its mad rapists or sweet-talking conmen, Hope had no intention of inviting a total stranger into her home. She'd lived in London for eight years before coming back up north, and had developed a healthy suspicion of anyone she didn't know.

'But you are Jeff Tomlin's daughter? I've got the right Hope Randall, haven't I?'

Hope stared at him, suspecting now that he might be some kind of debt collector. He didn't really look the part, although never having met one before she wasn't entirely sure what they *did* look like. He was casually dressed in a pair of faded blue jeans and a navy blue jumper. His face was pale, fine-boned and clean-shaven. It was a pleasant, almost sculpted face, only marred by a small kink in the centre of his nose, as though it might have been broken once. A lock of pale brown hair flopped over his forehead, and although he seemed friendly enough, there was something determined about his cool grey eyes. His accent was southern but she couldn't exactly place it; neither coarse nor refined, it occupied that vague middle ground in between. He was holding a supermarket carrier bag in his left hand.

'Who?' she said, playing for time. She had a bad feeling growing in her guts and was beginning to wish she'd never answered the door.

'Jeff Tomlin,' he repeated patiently.

Hope knew very little about her biological father, other than that he was (according to her mother) 'trouble with a capital T'. He'd left before she'd even been born and she had no idea of where he'd gone or what he'd done next. And she hadn't been interested either. His name might be on her birth certificate, but that didn't make him anything more than a casual sperm donor. It was Lloyd Randall who was her real dad, who'd always been there for her.

'I don't have any contact with him,' she said firmly. 'And I don't know where he is. If it's money you're after, you've come to the wrong place.'

'This isn't about Jeff, or money,' he said. A frown appeared on his forehead. He glanced briefly down at his shoes before looking up again. 'Christ, you don't know, do you?'

Hope, although she rarely thought about her father, felt an unexpected tremor run through her. She could tell from Flint's expression what was coming next. 'Is he . . . ?'

'I'm sorry,' he said, with what seemed like genuine concern. 'I presumed you'd have heard. It was years ago.' He paused as if doing a swift calculation in his head. 'About twelve, I think.'

Hope wasn't upset. How could she be? She'd never even met her father. But she did feel something. It was a kind of bewilderment, along with a growing resentment that now she'd never get the opportunity to tell him exactly what she felt about men who abandoned their children, who couldn't or wouldn't face up to their responsibilities. She wondered if her mother had known that he was dead. Well, it was too late to ask her now. Fay Randall had succumbed to cancer over six months ago. To cover up her confusion, Hope put her hands on her hips and kept her voice sharp. 'So what are you doing here? What do you want with me?'

'It's about your sister.'

'I don't have a sister.'

As if she was being deliberately pedantic, Flint's voice assumed a slightly caustic edge. 'Sorry, your *half*-sister then.'

'I don't have—' Hope stopped abruptly, suddenly realising that she had no idea whether she had a half-sister or not.

'Connie? Connie Tomlin?' As he looked at her, Flint's face twisted. 'Ah, you didn't know about her either. She was never sure. I mean, she knew about you, but . . .'

'What do you want with me?' Hope said again.

'Your help,' he said simply.

'With what exactly?'

Flint hesitated again. He glanced over his shoulder at the house across the road, instinctively aware perhaps of the twitching curtains. Hope followed his gaze. She still hadn't readjusted to the inquisitiveness of her neighbours, especially the likes of Edith Barry. In London, people had kept their distance – she'd liked that – but here there was always someone in your face, watching everything you did. It had bothered her when she was a teenager, and it still bothered her now.

'Are you sure you wouldn't rather do this inside?'

Hope thought about it, but then shook her head. 'No. I'm sorry. I'm busy.'

'I'm a friend of Connie's,' Flint said. 'She's disappeared. I'm trying to find out what's happened to her.'

'I don't see what that's got to do with me.' Hope knew it sounded cold, callous even, but she didn't give a damn what this stranger thought of her. She was still trying to deal with the grief of losing her mother and had no room in her heart for anyone or anything else.

'You're her only living relation,' he said harshly. 'If you don't care about her, who will?'

Hope raised her eyebrows at the vehemence of his reply. She thought of suggesting that *he* clearly did, but instead she asked a question of her own. 'How did you find me?'

14

'It wasn't hard,' he said. 'Connie mentioned where you lived. She didn't have the exact address, but she knew that you'd grown up in Albersea. I got the details from the electoral register. To be honest, I thought it was a bit of a long shot – you could have moved away years ago.' He gave a small smile. 'But here you are.'

Hope could have told him that twelve months ago he wouldn't have been quite so lucky, but she wasn't prepared to furnish him with any more information than he already had. It made her feel uneasy being tracked down like this. 'I'm sorry,' she said, 'but I don't see what use I can be. As you already know, we never met.'

'You could come to London and help me search for her.'

Hope barked out a startled laugh. 'What?'

'Why not?' he said.

'Don't be ridiculous!'

Flint gave her a long, steady look, his gaze travelling over her face. Suddenly, as their eyes met, something unexpected happened. It was as if a connection had been made between them, a spark ignited. His lips parted a little. 'There's nothing ridiculous about it. I want to find out what's happened. Someone out there knows more than they're saying. You could help me get to the truth.'

Hope's breath caught in her throat. What had just happened there? A faint blush had risen to her cheeks. 'No,' she said, shaking her head. 'I can't.'

'Can't or won't?'

Hope couldn't work this man out. He had an unpredictable quality, one moment sympathetic, the next provocative, as if he were trying to goad her into some kind of reaction. 'Both,' she said firmly. 'I'm sorry, but you've had a wasted journey. I don't want to get involved.'

'You're already involved. You're her sister.'

'No,' Hope said again. Eager to be rid of him, she took a step back and prepared to close the door. 'Now if you wouldn't mind, I really have to get on.'

Flint gave a light shrug of his shoulders. 'Okay, I get the message.' He lifted the carrier bag and offered it to her. 'Here are some of her things. Her landlady gave them to me. Connie's been gone a while now and she didn't know what to do with her stuff. There's not much, just a few bits and pieces, but I thought you might like to have them.'

'I don't,' Hope said, shrinking back.

Flint, ignoring the response, put the bag down by her feet. 'I'll be here for a few days. I'm staying at the King George on the front. My number's in the bag. Give me a call if you want to talk.'

Without another word, he turned and walked away. Hope watched as he sauntered down the street, his hands deep in his pockets. He had a graceful sort of walk, smooth and light-footed, utterly devoid of any male swagger. Quickly she transferred her attention to the bag, and frowned. Why had she let him leave it? But it was too late to give it back now; he'd already disappeared around the corner. She picked it up, went inside and slammed the door behind her.

She flounced through to the living room and threw the bag on the sofa. She wasn't sure why she was feeling so angry. The past few minutes had had a surreal quality that she was still trying to come to terms with. She felt disoriented, upset. Part of her distress was down to her privacy being invaded; ever since her mother's death, she'd done her best to avoid unnecessary contact with other people, to keep her barriers in place, but Flint had just crashed straight through her defences like some invading army.

What right did he have to come here, to tell her that her father was dead, to ask for her help in finding someone she'd never known? She stared resentfully at the carrier bag. So she had a half-sister. So what? Her reckless biological father could have spawned an endless number of kids. Was she expected to feel responsible for them all? But maybe, mixed in with her anger, was just a tiny bit of guilt. The missing Connie Tomlin, whether she liked it or not, was still connected to her.

Hope walked over to the window, folded her arms, and looked outside. It was a bright September afternoon, but cold, with a brisk, chill wind sweeping off the Irish Sea. If she opened the window she'd be able to smell the salt on the air. It was only a five-minute walk to the beach, and she was tempted to take a stroll, to get out of the cottage and let the wind whip away her bewilderment. There were so many thoughts buzzing around her head, she couldn't think straight.

She sighed as she gazed down the street. The trees were at the start of their magnificent transformation, their leaves turning from green to gold, to russet and bronze. She drank in the colours, grateful for the distraction. She wasn't sure what she was still doing in Albersea. Her intention had always been to return to London, but after her mother's death she had felt so numb, so bereft, that she hadn't been able to summon up the energy to pack her bags and leave. And then there'd been her stepfather Lloyd to consider. He'd descended into a deep depression, barely talking, barely eating. She'd been scared that he might do something stupid, but he was past that stage now, wasn't he? She wondered if she should call him, tell him about the visit from this man called Flint, but decided not. The last thing he needed was reminders of the past.

Hope knew that she ought to be getting back to work – there was a stained-glass panel waiting to be finished – but still she stalled. Glancing over her shoulder, she glared at the carrier bag. The damn thing wasn't going to go away. And until she looked inside, she wouldn't be able to concentrate on anything else.

Chapter Two

Hope sat down on the sofa, and after a short hesitation pulled the bag towards her. She realised, as she peered tentatively inside, just how little she'd asked Flint about the missing girl. (She still couldn't think of Connie Tomlin as her sister.) Like how old she was, for example. Probably younger than herself, but by how many years? And how long had she been missing? Long enough, she thought with a shudder, for her landlady to presume that she wasn't coming back.

Hope had already felt from the weight that there wasn't much in the bag. Perhaps Connie was the kind of person who always travelled light, who never accumulated things. Or perhaps she simply hadn't been able to afford much. That was something else Hope hadn't asked about. What kind of a life had this girl led? She shook her head. She wasn't getting involved. She couldn't afford to. She'd satisfy her curiosity and then return the bag to Flint. Not in person – she had no desire to see him again – but by taxi. The driver could drop it off later in the foyer of the King George.

Now that she'd decided what she was going to do, Hope took a breath and reached inside the bag. The first item she drew out was a small brown bear. It was obviously old, with one ear missing, and the stuffing poking out from a split in the seam. A legacy, presumably, of Connie's childhood. She stared at the bear for a moment. Its black eyes seemed to gaze entreatingly back at her. Before she could start attributing human emotions to this ragged piece of fur, she smartly put it to one side and delved inside the bag again.

This time she retrieved a bundle of cards tied with a piece of frayed pink ribbon. Slipping off the ribbon, she opened the first one. *To our darling daughter on her tenth birthday, love Mummy and Daddy.* She opened the next one. *Happy Christmas, love Mummy and Daddy.* She quickly flicked through the rest. They were in reverse order, going back to when Connie was a baby. Hope, despite her determination to remain dispassionate, couldn't help being curious as to why the cards had apparently stopped at the age of ten. And then she suddenly remembered what Flint had told her: Jeff Tomlin had died about twelve years ago. But surely Connie's mother had still given her cards, still celebrated her birthdays? Or had something happened to her mother too?

Hope paused for a second, disturbed by this notion. She couldn't help but recall her own privileged childhood: the parties she'd been given, the expensive gifts, the beautiful birthday cakes. She had been raised in a happy and harmonious family home, a house that had been full of joy and laughter. Perhaps Connie had not been quite so fortunate.

Hope frowned, but then shook her head, refusing to embark on a guilt trip. Whatever Connie's circumstances had been, they were nothing to do with her. She had no reason to feel bad. Before any more doubts could worm their way into her thoughts, she reached inside the bag again and pulled out a piece of folded paper. This had Flint's name and mobile number written on it. She threw it on to the coffee table.

Next she retrieved a half-full bottle of perfume. It was a brand she'd never heard of, and she gave it a sniff before squirting a little on the back of her hand. It had a soft, rather subtle smell. Why did that surprise her? Perhaps because it was the kind of scent she might have chosen for herself.

The next item was a black address book. She turned over the pages, noticing the large, almost childlike handwriting. Most of the sections were empty; Connie probably kept the numbers she needed on her mobile phone, and that would have been with her when she ... Hope screwed up her face, not wanting to dwell too much on Connie's fate. She hurriedly snapped shut the book and laid it down beside the perfume.

The final item she pulled out was a hinged oblong metal box, about eight inches by five. The lid was enamelled with a symmetrical pattern of blues and reds. She placed the box on her knees and opened it. Inside, on top, was a birth certificate. She unfolded it and quickly read the details: Connie's parents were Jeff and Sadie Tomlin – Hope was faintly surprised that anyone had actually got her father down the aisle – and she'd been born in Shoreditch, London. From the date, Hope worked out that Connie was now twenty-two, five years younger than herself. She thought back to the collection of cards – so they *had* stopped at around the same time as Jeff Tomlin's death.

Underneath the birth certificate were a couple of photographs. The first was of three girls sitting on a sofa – well, two girls of about twenty and an older woman in her late forties. Hope stared at the girl on the left, a girl with long, straight dark brown hair exactly like her own. Although their features were far from identical, there were some similarities: the same oval face, the same thick-lashed brown eyes. Their mouths were different, though. Connie's was wider, more generous, as if she was often quick to smile. Clearly she didn't share Hope's natural reserve. Hope wondered if the older woman was Connie's mother, Sadie, but as she flipped it over, she saw written in that large, rather clumsy writing, *Me, Lana and Evelyn.*

Before she could start to ponder on what it meant to see her half-sister for the first time, she moved on to study the second picture. This one was old, badly creased and slightly out of focus. One corner was missing and the remaining edge was tinged brown, as if the photo had been in a fire. It showed a little girl of about three years old standing in a yard, holding the hand of a man. He was tall and broad-shouldered, but Hope couldn't see his features clearly. She turned the photo over. *Me and Daddy* was carefully inscribed on the back in red felt-tip. The words, even though they weren't entirely unexpected, sent a tiny shockwave through her. She turned the picture back again and stared intently at his face. So this was her blood father. Was it also the person she'd inherited most of her features from? Her mother, Fay Randall, had been a typical English rose, fair-haired and blue-eyed, but Jeff Tomlin had, perhaps, possessed the same brown eyes, the same dark hair, even the same slightly faltering smile as herself.

How had he died? Yet another question she hadn't thought of asking Flint. They were starting to accumulate. But that didn't mean she was going to see him again. Her mouth set in a firm, straight line. Absolutely not. The past was gone, irretrievable. There was no point in raking it all up.

The only things left in the box now were a few cheap bangles, a man's gold wedding ring, some flimsy earrings and a little gold cross and chain. That was the lot. Hope gazed at the items gathered beside her on the sofa. Not much to show for a life. She wondered vaguely what had happened to Connie's clothes and make-up – perhaps her landlady had disposed of them.

Slowly, Hope put everything back in the bag. The tattered teddy was the last to go in. His small black eyes gazed sadly up at her. Her resolve, as she stared back, began to waver. Perhaps

Flint had been right. If she didn't care about what had happened to Connie, who would? No sooner had the thought entered her head than she pushed it away. 'No,' she said tightly to the bear. 'I don't care what you think. I'm not getting involved.'

Chapter Three

It was the second time Hope's hand had slipped as she was scoring the glass. 'For God's sake!' she hissed. It was five o'clock, and she was still trying to finish the panel ordered by Mrs Hopkins. Progress, since Flint's unexpected visit, had been painfully slow. Normally she loved her work, loved the feel of the glass, the vibrant colours, but this afternoon she just couldn't concentrate. If she wasn't careful, she'd make a mistake and ruin the whole damn thing.

She put down the cutter and moved back, taking a breather. She looked around. Her current makeshift studio had been converted from the old garden shed. It didn't compare to the lighter, more spacious studio she'd had in Spitalfields, but it did have two advantages: one was that it was within walking distance of her own back door, the other that it was free. She'd organised heat and electricity, installed a long workbench and put up half a dozen shelves. It wasn't perfect, but she'd worked in far more trying conditions when she'd been a student.

Her eyes alighted on the sheets of glass carefully stacked in the corner, and she automatically smiled. She worked mainly with the antique variety, more expensive than the machine-made but, in her opinion, worth the extra cost. It was Lloyd who'd first introduced her to the beauty of stained glass. She'd only been a child then, about eight years old, but she could still remember being entranced by some of the names he'd recited: streaky, crackle, flashed, Baroque, fracture and streamer. Even now, repeating them to herself, she experienced the same inner thrill.

She was standing by the window and could see the small two-bedroom cottage Lloyd had bought before he'd married her mother. Since then he'd been renting it out. Hope had moved in when her mum had got sick and had been living there ever since. It was a pretty whitewashed building, partly covered with ivy – the perfect place to retire to, but perhaps not entirely suitable for a twenty-seven-year-old woman still brimming with unfulfilled ambitions.

Hope turned away from the view, stepped forward again and gazed down at the panel. It was for a porch window and was the last in a flurry of orders she'd received after the local paper had published a piece about her. They'd included a few photographs, illustrations of her work, and this one, with the tall pink flamingo at its centre, had proved especially popular. She was glad of the orders, but felt faintly uneasy about them too. Did this mean she was planning on staying in Albersea? The more commissions she took on, the less likely she was to leave.

Her stomach gave a lurch. She was worried about becoming trapped, sliding back into a way of life she had fought so hard to escape from. She had once seen London as her salvation, a chance to free herself from the constrictions of a small town, but now she was almost afraid to return. Since her mother's death, everything had changed. She'd lost her determination, her drive and most of her confidence. In the city you had to fight to be noticed, to stand out from the crowd; here, when it came to her work at least, there wasn't so much competition.

Thinking of London reminded her of Alexander. She felt that familiar painful squeeze in her chest. They'd been together ever since he'd turned up at her college to give a lecture on Caravaggio. Tall, handsome, cultured and amusing, he'd been her idea of the perfect older man. She'd fallen head over heels for him, and embarked on a roller-coaster ride that would last for two years. She wondered now whether she hadn't been searching for a father figure, someone to fill the gap that Jeff Tomlin had left. Lloyd had been a good stepfather, kind and patient, but she'd always been aware that he was a substitute for the real thing.

As the image of Alexander lingered in her mind, she sighed. Well, so much for love. He'd dumped her a few months after she'd come back to be with her dying mother. Not that she'd expected much else; he wasn't the kind of man who could do long-distance relationships. Although it still hurt, the rational side of her was glad that it was over. She'd invested too much time and emotion in something that had been doomed from the start. She had made the same mistake as so many women before, believing she could change him, that she would be the one to make him want to commit.

She still had lots of friends in London, though. Or did she? It was surprising how quickly you could drift apart from people. As the weeks, and then the months had slipped by, her contact with them had become more irregular. Preoccupied with her mother, she had neglected emails and ignored phone calls. Of course she still had friends here, people she'd known from school, but most of them had partners and small kids. A part of her envied their settled, comfortable existence, but another part railed against it.

Hope frowned, suspecting she was starting to feel sorry for herself. She could hardly complain about her current situation. Solitude was what she'd chosen; it hadn't been forced upon her.

If she wanted something different, it was up to her to make the change. She thought of the carrier bag, still sitting on her sofa. Why hadn't she sent it back to Flint? All she had to do was pick up the phone and order a cab. Tomorrow, she told herself. But why put it off? In her heart, she knew exactly why – she was still undecided as to what she intended to do next.

Chapter Four

Hope, dressed in a black polo-neck sweater, black trousers and a black wool coat, walked briskly along the front. She'd tied back her long hair to stop the wind from blowing it across her face. Last night she'd finally made the call and arranged to meet Flint at eleven o'clock this morning by the entrance to the old pier. She was already ten minutes late. Lloyd had rung her on the landline just as she was on her way out and she hadn't wanted to hurry him. They'd had a chat, talked about this and that, but she hadn't mentioned Flint's visit or her forthcoming assignation.

Hope felt guilty about the deceit but didn't want to cause unnecessary worry. She didn't want Lloyd to imagine that now her mother was dead, she was reaching out towards the ghosts of the past. He might start to think that she didn't consider him as real family. Anyway, it wasn't worth making a fuss over. She was only going to talk to the man, to find out more about Connie. She wasn't committing herself to anything, least of all to some madcap scheme of going back to London with him.

Flint was already there by the time she arrived. He was in the same blue jeans and sweater as yesterday, only this time he was wearing a brown leather jacket. As she came up beside him, he turned his cool grey eyes on her and smiled. She felt a tiny jolt inside, but couldn't explain exactly what it was. He didn't bother with any of the usual niceties, didn't say hello or even ask her what had made her change her mind, but glanced away and said instead, 'What is it with piers? They seem to be in the habit of burning down.'

Following his gaze, Hope stared out towards the blackened skeleton. It was over six years since the blaze, but funds still hadn't been found to start any major restoration work. 'I've no idea,' she said.

'Something to do with that perpetual battle between fire and water?'

Hope gave a light shrug, unwilling to embark on an abstract debate with him. 'Or just sheer carelessness.' If she recalled correctly, the fire had been started by an unfortunate spark from a welding iron. She gestured towards the beach. 'Do you want to walk?' She suspected he'd been intending to conduct their meeting in a nice warm café, but had no intention of pandering to his southern ways. Even though she had chosen to come – he'd hardly twisted her arm – she still felt a simmering resentment. After all, if it hadn't been for his unexpected and unwanted appearance on her doorstep, she would be at home right now, concentrating on the unfinished panel and happily oblivious to the existence of a half-sister.

As if he guessed what was going on in her head, that smile played around his lips again. 'Sure. Whatever's good for you.'

They strolled a little way along the front and then cut down on to the shore. The tide was way out, the sea only a distant glimmer on the horizon. They weren't alone – the beach was rarely empty – but their only other company was an elderly couple walking a dog, some teenage kids kicking a football around, and a guy with a metal detector. The golden-brown sand was hard and rippled; she could feel the ridges through the soles of her shoes. It was littered with the usual flotsam and jetsam, bits of rotting wood, old tin cans and tangles of seaweed.

Hope was the first to speak again. 'I've only come to talk, nothing else. I'm not making any promises. Is that clear?'

'As crystal,' he said.

There was something close to mockery in his voice, but she let it pass. If she wanted information, she couldn't afford to be too touchy. 'So tell me about Connie.'

Flint hesitated for a moment, as if gathering his thoughts together. He gazed out briefly towards the sea before turning to look at her again. 'I first met her about fifteen years ago. She was just a kid then. I was working with Jeff and I got to know the family.'

Hope was tempted to ask what her father's work had been, but refused to give in to her natural curiosity. She was here to find out about Connie, no one else. 'Go on.'

'Sadie – that was her mother – was a great woman, lovely, but she went to pieces after ... after Jeff died. She simply couldn't cope. I stayed in touch for a while, but ... Well, let's just say that she wasn't the easiest person to be around. She developed all kinds of problems: depression, booze, drugs, and that's only the highlights. It took her a couple of years, but she finally managed to kill herself. Connie was about twelve, I think. There were no other relatives on the scene so she was taken into care.'

Hope flinched. There were five years between the two of them, so she would have been seventeen then, attending high school, and with nothing more pressing to concern her than the latest gossip and whether to spend her allowance on CDs, clothes or make-up.

Flint gazed out towards the horizon again. 'If you're wondering if I feel guilty, then yes, of course I do. The truth is that by then I'd stopped seeing Sadie, stopped calling her even. She was getting too difficult to deal with. I walked away and left her to it.'

'I wasn't thinking that. She wasn't your responsibility.'

'She was Jeff's wife. And Connie was his daughter. I should have made more of an effort.'

Hope, still battling with her own conscience, offered him a reasonable excuse. 'You can't have been that old yourself.'

'Old enough,' he said. 'And Jeff was a mate, a good one. He deserved better – they all did.' He gave a long, bitter sigh. 'God, I didn't even know that Sadie was dead until three months after it had happened. She'd cut herself off from the old crowd, moved to another area; it was only by chance that someone heard about it and told me. If I thought about Connie at all – and to be honest I didn't, not that much – I just presumed that someone decent had taken her in. It was easier to think that way, to not have her on my conscience.'

Hope could understand what he was saying, and it went some way towards explaining what he was doing here, but just because he felt guilty didn't mean that she was obliged to follow suit. And she still wasn't sure if everything he was saying was true. Her natural suspicion told her to be cautious. She kept silent, and after a while he continued.

'Connie was nineteen by the time we met again. She'd been chasing up some of Jeff's old friends, and one of them suggested my name. She thought I might be able to help.'

'In what way?'

'She wanted to know about her father's death.'

'I don't understand.'

Flint screwed up his face, pushing his hands deep into his pockets before he looked at her again. 'Sorry, but there's no nice way of putting this: Jeff didn't die from natural causes. He was murdered, shot through the head.'

30

Hope gasped. Whatever she'd been expecting, it certainly wasn't that. The revelation briefly took her breath away. She stopped dead in her tracks and stared at him. 'Why would anyone ... I don't ...' Unable to find the right words, she ceased trying.

'There were rumours that it was some kind of gangland hit, but the cops never discovered who did it. Connie, understandably, found that hard to live with.'

High above them, a gull gave a screech. The sound seemed unnaturally loud, and Hope jumped a little. 'Why?' she finally managed to splutter out. 'I mean, why would anyone want to kill him?'

'That's what Connie was desperate to find out. She was asking questions, digging around for information. That's why she came to me. She thought I might know something.'

'And did you? *Do* you?'

Flint shook his head. 'Nothing useful. Unless Jeff and I were working together, we kept quiet about what we were doing. It was better that way. And yeah, we both came across some dodgy characters from time to time, but he never gave any hint that he might be in trouble. If he'd been seriously concerned about anything, he'd have told me. I'm sure of it.'

Hope was still thinking about that gangland connection. She knew she had to ask the question, even though she probably wasn't going to like the answer. 'So what was it he did for a living?'

Flint hesitated again, his eyes growing wary.

She met his gaze and gave a rueful smile. 'I take it this is something else that I'm not going to like too much.'

He looked down and for a few seconds dug his heel into the sand. When he glanced up again, his mouth was twisted at the corners. 'Your mother hasn't told you anything about Jeff?'

'No,' she replied, 'other than that he was trouble.' Still

shocked by his earlier revelation, and trying not to show it, she was speaking more out of bravado than anything else. 'And I get the feeling you're about to prove her right.'

He gave a snort. 'From what I've heard, she wasn't too bothered about that when she was with him. Fay might not have approved of what he did, but she never objected to spending the money. You should ask her about it.'

Hope glared at him. 'I wish I could, but she died six months ago.'

He winced before his head went down again. 'God, I'm sorry. I didn't realise. I shouldn't have ...'

Hope turned away from him. She didn't care about his embarrassment. And she didn't want or need his sympathy. When she'd gathered herself enough to look at him again, her voice was cool and steady. 'So are you going to tell me what my ... what Jeff did for a living?'

Flint pushed back his shoulders, looked her straight in the eye and nodded. 'He was an artist, and a damn good one at that. He should have been able to make a decent living, a legitimate living, but he couldn't. He never got the breaks he needed to really succeed. They say talent will out, but that, if you'll pardon the expression, is just a pile of shite. If you don't know the right people, don't have the right background, you're buggered.' He stopped, took a quick breath and then went on again. 'There are, of course, a few working-class artists who've made it big, but they're the exception to the rule. They've succeeded despite the odds, not because of them.'

Hope could hear the frustration in his voice and wondered if it was purely to do with Jeff Tomlin. Perhaps there was something more personal about this particular diatribe. She glanced sideways, her eyes settling briefly on the guy with the metal detector. He'd stopped to investigate some hidden treasure and was poking about in the sand. Flint carried on talking.

'The whole scene made him angry. Maybe he wanted to prove a point, I don't know, but he started painting forgeries, and excellent ones at that. He didn't go for anything big – we're not talking Rembrandt or Picasso here; more middle-of-the road stuff, Victorian watercolours, that kind of thing. He could churn them out and feed them through to dealers and auction rooms in different parts of the country without rousing any suspicion, or too much attention. He'd started getting into Russian art too – there was plenty of Russian cash sloshing around, and those guys liked to think they were buying a bit of the old country's heritage. It could be that he sold a painting to the wrong person, someone who realised it was a fake. No one likes being taken for a fool.'

Hope's head was starting to spin. Even putting aside the fact that her father had met such a grim end – and that wasn't easy – she was still trying to come to terms with the fact that he'd actually been an artist, albeit a somewhat renegade one. For some reason she'd always presumed that her own interest in art had come exclusively from Lloyd. That it hadn't made her feel confused and curiously defensive too. 'Look, why are you telling me all this?'

'Why not? You've a right to the truth, haven't you? Anyway, if you want to know about Connie, you need to understand her background, where she came from, how her mind worked. I mean, that is why you're here, isn't it?'

But Hope hadn't expected to hear anything like this when she'd set up the meeting. It was all too much to take in. 'You said you used to work together sometimes. So is that what you do too? Are you an artist, a forger?'

'No, I never had his talent. Not in that direction. I'm more of a fixer. I sourced the materials, brushes, canvases, et cetera. Anything he needed, I'd find it for him. And I put him in touch with ... well, let's just call them interested parties, people who

33

had connections to private collectors, or dealers who sold abroad.'

Hope found the matter-of-fact way he talked about it thoroughly disturbing. His morality, it appeared, was as severely flawed as her father's. 'I could go to the cops with what you've told me. Get you locked up.'

Flint gave a small, tight laugh. 'Oh, I don't think so. It's not as though you've got any actual evidence. And would you really want the whole world to know that your daddy was a crook? It might not do much for your own prospects.'

'Are you trying to blackmail me? Because if you are—'

'Christ,' he said. 'Don't be so touchy! I'm just saying it like it is. You can walk away any time you like, forget we even had this conversation. You're not under any obligation, and I'm hardly about to go shouting the truth from the rooftops.' He paused. 'So do you want me to go on?'

Hope glared back at him, then simply lifted her shoulders in a light, angry shrug. She knew that she was being unreasonable, but somehow she couldn't stop herself.

'Okay,' he said. 'Let me tell you about Connie. She was in care – not a happy time – until she was sixteen, and then she got a place in a hostel. After that she found a grubby little bedsit in Hoxton. For the next three years she drifted in and out of badly paid jobs, mixed with the kinds of people who were never going to do her any favours, and began the slow descent that would probably have landed her in the same morgue as her mother if she hadn't had the good fortune to meet Lana Franklin.'

Hope remembered the photograph she'd found in the metal box. 'So who is she, this Lana?'

'Lana's a dip. Connie was working with her up until she disappeared.'

Hope frowned. 'A dip?'

34

'A pickpocket,' he said.

'Yes, I know what a dip is,' she said curtly. 'I'm just ... just surprised that Connie was doing that.'

Flint pulled a face. 'There are worse ways for a girl like her to make a living.'

Hope felt a light flush rise to her cheeks. 'A girl like her?'

'Yeah, a girl who's been through what she has. Those years she spent in care, and the ones that followed, weren't exactly a bed of roses. Connie's smart and funny, but she's kind of screwy too. Nothing can eradicate the misery she went through. It's going to be with her for ever. Plus she didn't get much of an education. Her prospects weren't exactly the brightest in the world.'

'Whereas being a pickpocket is one rung on the ladder to ultimate success.'

Flint slowly shook his head. 'You really don't have a clue, do you? As if you've ever wanted for anything in your life ... '

Hope heard the contempt in his voice and reacted to it. 'You don't know anything about me. So I've got a few principles; why's that so terrible? I'm hardly in the minority when it comes to thinking that stealing off other people isn't the right way to live.' And although she believed in what she was saying, she was also aware that she sounded like a small-town, stuck-up prig.

'Hey,' he said, 'there's no need to take it personally.'

But he *was* passing judgement, and perhaps rightly so. Connie hadn't had the same choices or the same advantages and could quite easily have ended up on the streets. Hope couldn't help thinking about her own much happier time in London. She'd had no idea while she was there that she had a half-sister living in the same city, a girl who must have been in desperate need of help. She took a moment to gather her thoughts together and then said, 'If Connie knew about me, why didn't she try and get in touch?'

Flint looked at her. 'Because she didn't know how. And even

35

if she had, she probably wouldn't have bothered. After Jeff died, Connie didn't come too high on the list of her mother's priorities – and if Sadie wasn't interested in her, then what were the chances that you would be? She wouldn't have wanted to be rejected again.'

'I wouldn't have—' Hope stopped abruptly, aware that yesterday she had done exactly that. But she would have behaved differently, surely, if Connie had approached her directly.

'Anyway,' he continued, 'I doubt if Sadie painted a pretty picture of your family – if you'll excuse the pun. After Jeff died, she was off her head for most of the time, day *and* night, and what she told Connie was probably tinged with more than a hint of bitterness. Sadie couldn't stand your mother and wouldn't have shown much restraint when it came to passing on those feelings.'

Hope was confused. 'Sadie knew my mother?'

'Sure. Sadie was Jeff's girlfriend before he met Fay. He left her for your mother – and then went back to her when he got dumped.'

'No,' Hope insisted, 'he dumped my mother when she got pregnant.'

'From what I heard, it was the other way round.'

'Well then you heard wrong.'

'Or maybe you did.'

It had started to rain, a thin drizzle that fell on their heads and shoulders and made tiny pockmarks in the sand. The old couple had gone and the kids were starting to drift towards the promenade. Hope noticed the metal-detecting guy looking up at the sky. She automatically glanced up too. Great dark clouds had gathered overhead. Flint was mistaken, she was sure he was, but now wasn't the time to be debating the point. 'So when did Connie go missing?'

Flint hesitated before he answered. 'In February.'

It was now almost the end of September. 'That's seven

months,' Hope said, astounded. Her stomach shifted at the thought of what that might mean. 'If it was so easy to find me, why has it taken you so long?'

'I've been ... how shall I put it? Indisposed. A small misunderstanding over some forged passports.'

Her eyes widened as she realised what he was saying. 'You've been in jail?' She remembered what she'd said earlier about getting him locked up, and her cheeks coloured again.

'If I told you I'd been stitched up, would that make a difference?'

'Were you?'

'Well, grassed up might be a more accurate description. I think someone wanted me out of the way, didn't want me asking questions about Connie's disappearance.'

Hope had never met anyone who'd spent time in prison before. She scrutinised him whilst pretending not to, her gaze sliding over the plains of his face. There was nothing, absolutely nothing, to indicate where he'd been. What had she been expecting? Some kind of defining mark, perhaps.

He must have noticed her expression, because he smiled back and said, 'Don't worry, it's not catching.'

Hope smartly transferred her gaze to the ground. 'Do you think Connie's dead?' she blurted out. 'I mean, if she's been missing for this long ...'

'Or just running scared. She could be hiding out somewhere, keeping her head down.'

Hope raised her eyes again, suspecting that was wishful thinking. 'Has it been reported to the police?'

Flint stared at her. 'Course it has. But to the cops, she's just another missing girl from Tanner Road.'

'I don't understand,' Hope said, not for the first time.

'That's where she lives ... lived ... with Lana and Evelyn. It's Lana's flat, but she rents out a couple of rooms. It's in Kellston, close to the red-light district. So far as the cops are concerned, Connie's just another hooker who's decided to move on to pastures new.'

'But she wasn't . . . *isn't* a hooker. And even if she was, that doesn't give them any right to ignore her disappearance.'

'Spoken like a true liberal,' he said.

Hope frowned at him. 'And what's that supposed to mean?'

'That you haven't a clue as to how the real world works.' His voice had slipped into its more caustic mode. 'Thousands of people disappear every year, just walk out of their homes and never go back. Some of them are ill, or confused, or running away from a problem they can't face, and others are just plain sick of their lives. The cops have got limited resources. If someone doesn't want to be found, it's unlikely that they will be.'

'So what are the chances of finding Connie?'

'It doesn't matter what the chances are; it's the trying that's important.' He paused for a moment. 'But maybe someone like you wouldn't understand that.'

'You don't know anything about me!' she retorted.

'Enough,' he said.

'You think?'

Flint dug his heel into the sand again. 'What I think is that you've already made a decision as to what you'll do next, and nothing I can say or do will change your mind.'

Hope, still annoyed by his comments, huffed out her reply. 'There's plenty you can say and do. Like how exactly I can make a difference. Even if I did come to London, why should anyone talk to me? If she's been missing for this long, it's going to be a waste of time, isn't it?'

'If you say so.'

'I thought you wanted my help.'

'I do, but only if it's given willingly. I'll understand if you don't want anything disrupting your tidy little life.'

Hope glowered back at him. He knew nothing about her life. How dare he judge her like this? But as quickly as the anger flared, it died back again. He was just trying to play her, to manipulate her feelings. 'Don't take me for a fool,' she said.

A hint of a smile played around the corners of Flint's mouth again. 'Okay, I'll tell you how you could help. No one need know you're Connie's sister. Or that we've ever met. You can mix with her crowd, talk to her friends, see what you can pick up. They may not be as cautious with you as they are with me.'

'But they don't know me from Adam. They're going to get suspicious if I start asking questions.'

'Not if you're subtle about it.' Flint gave her a glance, as if trying to figure out whether subtlety was in her repertoire. 'And Lana will help. She's the one person we *can* trust. You can stay with her; she'll show you the ropes, introduce you to the right people.'

'You mean in Kellston?'

'What's the matter?' he said. 'Not upmarket enough for you?'

'I didn't mean that. I just wasn't expecting . . . ' She shook her head. 'Forget it. It doesn't matter.'

'Look, you've got some big decisions to make. Why don't you go home, think about it and give me a ring when you've made up your mind.'

Hope suddenly found herself eager to put some distance between them. She needed time alone, time to absorb everything she'd learned today. 'I'll do that,' she said. 'And if I say no?'

'Then I'll carry on without you.'

'Even if you're not getting anywhere?'

'That doesn't mean I have to stop trying.'

Hope wasn't sure how much she liked him, but she couldn't fault his determination. As she was about to go, something else occurred to her. 'I don't even know your first name.'

'Michael,' he said, 'Michael Flint. But everyone calls me Flint.'

She nodded. 'I'll call you.'

'I'll be waiting.'

Hope turned and walked away. She'd just reached the promenade when the heavens opened and the rain came bucketing down. Pulling her umbrella from her bag, she quickly put it up. She looked back to see Flint still standing on the beach. He was the only person left; everyone else had run for cover.

Chapter Five

Chris Street stood in the bathroom and stared morosely into the mirror. He was still a couple of years off forty, still theoretically in the prime of life, but he didn't like what he was seeing. He reckoned the last nine months had added at least ten years to his face. The frown lines on his forehead were deep, his skin was even more sallow than usual, and his eyes were red and sore from lack of sleep. And he had plenty to be sleepless about. It was all falling apart, the whole bloody business. Everything was in freefall and he was the only one who seemed to give a damn.

He glanced at his watch. It was almost midday. He hadn't got back from Belles until close on five, and by then he was too hyped up on caffeine to even think about going to bed. Although the club closed at two, he'd had a mountain of paper-work to go through. Licences didn't get renewed by themselves, or booze ordered, or receipts properly filed. There had been those dodgy passports to be sorted too. Sometimes he wondered if the girls were worth the bother.

With a groan, he ran his fingers through his dark, almost black hair, convinced that it was receding slightly. He leaned his face against the glass of the mirror, grateful for its coolness. It wasn't just the business that was causing him grief; his personal life was in ruins too. It was six weeks now since Jenna had left. She'd given him an ultimatum – either we move out of this house together, or I'm going on my own. He'd thought about it, but not for long. Leaving his father and brother alone was tantamount to putting two wild tigers in a cage and waiting for them to tear each other's throats out. He just couldn't do it.

Chris showered and shaved, and then got dressed. As he approached the kitchen, he could hear the sound of arguing. His heart sank. Couldn't he even have his breakfast in peace? As he opened the door, he knew he was walking straight into another family row.

'Are you completely fuckin' stupid?' Terry Street was trying to shout at his son. His voice, ever since he'd been shot in the throat, had a peculiar rasping quality.

'*Me* stupid? Shit, man, you don't even know what day of the week it is.'

Chris stared at them both. Danny was standing by the sink with his hands on his hips. He had that pinched, tight-lipped look and his eyes were blazing. His father wasn't a pretty sight either. Unwashed and unshaven, he was sitting at the table with a bottle of whisky in front of him. It was nine months now since he'd got out of nick, but he was still knocking back the booze like it was going out of fashion. And once he'd had a skinful, he'd be straight on the phone to that Kathleen bitch, trying to find out where his daughter had gone. Chris still couldn't get his head round the fact that the redhead who'd worked at the old funeral parlour was actually his sister. He had no interest in his father's bastard child, and she clearly had no interest in any of them either. She'd taken off as soon as she could and hadn't left a forwarding address.

'What's the hell's going on?' Chris said.

Terry jerked his thumb towards Danny. 'Your fuck-brained brother here wants to put the screws on the girls, slap 'em around a bit, get 'em back to work.'

'There's no need for that,' Chris said sharply. He had no general objection to the use of violence – it was as good a way as any for getting what you wanted – but you had to know when and how to use it. Danny had always been too quick with his fists; punch first and ask questions later. That volatility could be useful on occasions, but this wasn't one of them.

'While they're sitting on their arses, we're losing money,' Danny said. 'Someone's gotta sort it out.' He glared at Terry, the contempt clear on his face. 'And he's too fuckin' pissed to find his way to the bathroom, never mind make a decision.'

Chris raised a hand, trying to calm things down. 'It's okay. It's under control.' The East End attacks had stopped for a while, but had recently started up again. Two girls had been viciously assaulted in the past couple of weeks. They were both still in hospital, and even when they got out – if they got out – they had the kind of injuries that meant they wouldn't be working again. With a madman on the loose, the other girls were naturally nervous. 'They'll settle down before long. Believe me, their need for a fix is gonna drive them back faster than any threats you can make. I'm putting Solomon on Albert Street.' Six foot six of solid muscle should provide them with some reassurance. 'He'll keep an eye on things. In a few days' time it will all be back to normal.'

'A few days?' Danny sneered. 'And how much is that gonna cost us?'

'Not half as much as losing them completely. If we're not careful, they'll just sod off, find themselves somewhere safer to work. There are plenty of other streets to walk. Kozlov's sniffing around, looking to pick up anything he can. Is that what you want? You want to push the girls straight into his welcoming arms?'

'I'd like to see him try – or them, come to that.'

'Yeah, right.' Chris reached for the kettle, jabbed at the switch and pulled a jar of instant coffee out of the cupboard. If Jenna had been here, there'd have been fresh coffee in the percolator. He could have made it himself but couldn't be bothered to wait. He needed a caffeine fix and he needed it quick.

Danny glared at him. 'What's the matter with you? You growing soft in your old age?'

Chris tried not to rise to it. His younger brother could be a pain at the best of times. His head was banging and he rubbed at his temples. 'You ever heard of the subtle approach?'

Terry snorted into his glass. 'He doesn't know the meaning of the word.'

'Jesus,' Chris said, 'can't the two of you even try to get along?' But that, he knew, was a pointless request. There was no way to turn the clock back. Too much water had passed under the bridge. Too many accusations had been made, too many things said and done for the status quo to ever be properly re-established.

'Look at him!' Danny hissed. 'He's a waste of goddamn space.' He took a threatening step towards his father, but Chris grabbed him by the elbow. A low growl came from under the table. Danny's bull terrier, Trojan, was lying by Terry's feet. Chris looked down. A pair of cold, angry eyes stared back up at him.

'What's that fuckin' dog doing in here? How many times have I told you? I don't want it in the kitchen. I don't want it in the house.'

Danny yanked his arm away. 'He's not doing any harm. And he's better company than some I could mention.'

Terry leaned forward, his whole body stiffening. 'At least I'm not a fuckin'—'

Before he could finish the sentence, Chris interrupted. 'Enough!'

he snapped. 'Can't I even have five minutes' peace? Jesus, it's like living in a war zone.'

'Whatever,' Danny said. He yanked his arm away and grabbed his jacket off the back of a chair. 'I'm off.' He gave a quick whistle and the dog jumped up. As they slouched off together, Chris was glad to see the back of them. Danny was getting on his nerves, and that brute of a dog gave him the creeps.

There was a long silence after they'd left. Chris busied himself with the kettle. He didn't want to look at his father, didn't want to see the expression on his face. He knew exactly what his father had been about to say before he interrupted him. Ever since that crazy funeral parlour woman had murdered Toby Grand, there'd been ugly rumours flying around about Danny's part in it all. But what she'd accused him of couldn't possibly be true, could it? No brother of his could be that twisted. He shuddered even to think about it. Eventually he turned and looked at his father.

'This can't go on. I'm sick of it, sick of it all.'

'That boy needs to learn some respect,' Terry said. His voice was slightly slurred. 'You have to sort him out.'

Chris could have said that that was Terry's job, not his, but he didn't have the energy to embark on such a conversation. Anyway, even if he had been tempted to talk to Danny, his pleas would have fallen on deaf ears. The esteem in which Danny had once held his father had long since disappeared. Chris understood how his brother felt. Twenty-six years it had taken for the truth to emerge, for all the secrets and lies to finally be exposed. His own initial anger, however, had softened over the past nine months into something more akin to a pitying contempt.

He sat down at the table and sighed into his coffee. Terry was staring determinedly at his mobile phone, as if by the sheer force of his will he could make it ring. It had become an obsession with him, this need to find Iris O'Donnell. Perhaps it was his only way of justifying his actions. If he could force his daughter back into his life, then some sense could be made of everything else.

'What about us?' Chris had wanted to shout at him on more than occasion. 'What about your sons? Don't *we* matter?' But he was always too proud to go there, too anxious about sounding like a jealous kid.

Had Lizzie still been alive, things would have been different. Chris had never had much time for his stepmother – she'd been a greedy, grasping whore – but she'd been savvy too. He had to give her credit for that. She would never have allowed for this slow disintegration of the family. He still didn't know if his father had arranged to have her killed, although it seemed more than likely. He'd had ten years in jail to think about everything she'd done, his resentment festering like an infected sore.

Those two deaths, within weeks of each other, had changed everything. They'd exposed a kind of rottenness, a creeping decay that maybe nothing could stop. As Terry poured himself another generous shot of whisky, Chris scowled. 'And how's that going to help?'

Terry glared back at him. 'What the fuck's it gotta do with you?'

Chris gave a shrug. When he'd had a few, his father could flip in a matter of seconds: sarcasm could turn to rage, passivity to violence. 'Nothing,' he said.

'Yeah, *nothing*,' Terry said. 'That's all you're fuckin' good for. You're just like the rest of them, a fuckin' pile of shite.'

'Don't start on me.' Chris could have said more, like how the hell was he supposed to hold it all together, but he bit his tongue. He could feel his father itching for a row, but he wasn't prepared to give him the satisfaction. How had it all gone so wrong? Once the name of Street had been enough to strike fear into the most hardened of criminals, but now Terry was rapidly becoming a laughing stock. It was only a matter of time before it all went down the pan.

Chris still loved his father, but he had long since ceased to feel any pride in him. Terry had become weak and pathetic, reliant on alcohol and pills to see him through the day. Chris took a gulp from his mug, wincing as the hot black coffee burned the roof of his mouth. He was doing all he could, but it still wasn't enough. Reputation was everything, and theirs was in shreds. And it wasn't just general opinion he had to worry about. That Russian bastard Kozlov was circling like a vulture eager to peck the flesh off the corpse.

Terry snarled at him. 'If you're so pissed off, why don't you get the fuck out of here?'

Chris nodded. Christ, if he had any sense, he'd do exactly that. He *should* get out of here, not just out of the house but the whole bloody country. Grab his wife and passport, empty his account and go abroad. Why not? The Costa del Sol had a damn sight more to offer than the lousy dump of Kellston. But as he looked again at his father, he knew why he wouldn't, why he couldn't. Some ties, no matter how twisted, could never be cut.

Chapter Six

Hope couldn't say for certain when she'd made up her mind. It might have been that moment when she'd looked back to see Flint standing alone on the beach, or it could have been when she'd come home and searched again through the metal box. Holding Connie's tiny gold cross and chain in the palm of her hand, she'd suddenly become aware that she didn't really have a choice. Or if she did, it was only between being a decent person and a bad one.

As she stood on Lloyd's doorstep, she replayed the phone conversation she'd had with Flint last night. Had she expected to hear some expression of gratitude, or even relief, at her decision to join him, it hadn't been forthcoming.

Flint had left a long pause. 'Are you sure?'

'What do you mean, am I sure?'

'Well, are you actually committed to this? Do you really want to find out the truth, or do you just feel obliged?'

Hope, annoyed by his attitude, had been tempted to retort, 'Stuff it then,' and hang up and leave him to it. Instead, she'd taken a deep breath and replied, 'I thought you wanted me to come with you. If you've changed your mind, you only have to say.'

'I haven't. I just need to be sure that you fully understand what you're doing. Some of these people, the ones you're going to have to mix with, aren't exactly your law-abiding types.'

Hope could have stated that he appeared to fall into that category himself, but had wisely decided that it was hardly the time for cheap digs. 'Are you telling me it might be dangerous?'

'Connie was asking questions about the murder of Jeff Tomlin. She was talking to gangsters, to lowlifes. Now she's gone missing. No, I'm sure it's not the slightest bit dangerous.'

'There's no need to be sarcastic.'

'I wasn't—' he'd begun, but then abruptly stopped. 'Sorry. I just have to know that you're taking this seriously, that you've really thought it through.'

'Of course I have,' she'd said firmly, although in truth she hadn't thought much further than agreeing to the proposition. And in many ways that *had* been down to a sense of obligation, to a faint but distinctive feeling of guilt. Connie, after all, was her half-sister, and someone had to care about her fate. However, as the full implication of Flint's warning had started to sink in, it had been accompanied by a wave of uneasiness. But it had been too late to back out then. Her pride wouldn't allow it.

'Okay. Well, I've got the car with me. I'll pick you up tomorrow morning. If we leave about ten, we should miss the rush-hour traffic.'

Hope, not expecting to go so quickly, had been taken aback. 'Tomorrow? Friday?'

'No point hanging around. The sooner we get on with it, the better.'

'But that's impossible. I can't just drop everything. I've got stuff to do.' She still had to complete the Hopkins panel. If she worked flat out, she could probably get it finished and delivered by Monday. 'You go. I'll follow on. I'll get the train on Tuesday and give you a call when I get there.'

'Or I could wait.'

'There's no need,' she'd said.

There had been a distinct hesitation on the other end of the line, as if he doubted that she'd ever get the train at all. 'All right, but let me know what time it gets in and I'll pick you up from the station.'

Hope was still thinking about what she was planning to do – and wondering if she had made the right decision – when her stepfather answered the door.

'Hey,' Lloyd said, bending down to kiss her cheek. 'How are you?'

'Good, thanks.' Even now, after all this time, she was still faintly shocked by the gauntness of his face, by the amount of weight he'd lost since her mother had died. She smiled quickly. 'I come bearing gifts,' she said, hoisting up the warm white carrier bag.

Lloyd sniffed, his lips curling into a smile. 'Is that a Thai duck curry I can smell?'

'Got it in one.'

'Ah, my favourite.' He stood aside. 'You'd better come in then.'

She followed him along the hall and into the kitchen. It still felt odd coming to the new flat, rather than the house she'd grown up in. She understood why he hadn't been able to stay there though; every room must have reminded him of her mother. And the flat, on the second floor of a modern three-storey block, was nice enough. The rooms were spacious and it overlooked the park. There was even a balcony where he could sit out when the days where warm enough.

'So,' he said. 'You come bearing gifts. Could there be a whiff of bribery and corruption in the air?'

Hope took the foil containers from the carrier bag and laid them on the counter. She glanced up at him. 'Am I that obvious? No, don't answer that. Actually, you're right. I'm off to London on Tuesday, just to catch up with some friends.' She felt guilty about lying to him, but what was the alternative? She could hardly tell him the truth. 'You don't mind, do you?'

Lloyd pushed his wire-rimmed glasses back up his nose and smiled. 'You don't have to worry about me.'

But of course, she did. She couldn't help herself. 'I'm not sure how long I'll be gone for. A week or two. I'll call you, though. I'll keep in touch.'

'I'll be fine,' he said. 'You have to get on with your life. We both do.'

Together they dished out the fragrant curry and rice, then took the plates through to the living room and sat down at the table by the window. Hope glanced out at the park. The rain was holding off and a few local office workers were sitting on the benches eating their sandwiches. She picked up her fork and started on the food. 'I can always come back if you need me for anything.'

'Hope,' he said patiently, 'I'm sixty years of age. I think I can just about manage on my own.'

'I didn't mean . . . I was only . . . ' She made a vague flapping motion with her hand. 'I wasn't suggesting that you couldn't cope or anything.' In truth, she *was* still concerned for him, for the toll the grief was taking on his body. Sixty wasn't old these days, but over the past six months he appeared to have shrunk, to have curled in on himself like a wounded animal. His cheeks were hollow and the deep-set eyes behind the glasses were clouded with sorrow.

'As it happens,' he said, 'I have some news of my own. Do you remember that gallery we talked about opening?'

When he said *we*, Hope knew that he meant himself and her

mother. 'I remember. On King Street, right?' It had been a project they had all been excited about, but Fay's terrible and terminal illness had put a halt to the plans.

'Well, the property's come up for sale again. I've been thinking that I might go ahead with it.'

'Really? Are you serious?'

'There's no need to sound so surprised.'

'No, I'm pleased,' she said. 'Really I am. It's a great idea.' There was a thriving arts and crafts scene in Albersea, and plenty of prospective buyers for the work. Close to both Liverpool and Manchester, the resort was a popular place to live. In addition to the well-off retirees, there were plenty of high-income commuters too.

'It's early days yet, but if it all goes ahead we could exhibit some of your work there.'

Hope laughed, relieved that Lloyd finally had something positive to focus on. It made her feel less guilty about going to London. 'Wouldn't that be viewed as nepotism?'

'If I can't indulge in a little nepotism in my own gallery, I can't see the point of owning it.'

Hope laughed again. How old had she been when Lloyd had come into her life? About seven or eight years old. She'd never called him Dad, and yet he'd been more of a father to her than Tomlin ever had. His kindness, love and support had been a constant while she was growing up. And when she'd been older, when she'd reached those tempestuous teenage years, he'd been the voice of reason, a calming influence, as she'd embarked on a battle of wills with her mother.

Hope remembered those times with an inner sigh. She had loved her mother but hadn't always liked her. As a child, she'd hero-worshipped the tall, slender woman who lit up every room she entered. Fay had been so beautiful, so exuberant, so full of life. But later, Hope had begun to see another side; she'd also been selfish and superficial, overly concerned with appearances, with status and money.

Lloyd, however, had accepted Fay's character without complaint or reproach. His love for her had been absolute, all-consuming. He had neither judged nor criticised. Was that why her mother had chosen to marry him? Or had it been more to do with the size of his bank balance? Lloyd had owned a small art gallery in Liverpool – a gallery he'd sold as soon as Fay had become ill – but the income from that had always been irrelevant. He came from a wealthy family and had inherited enough money for them all to live in comfort.

'It's great news,' Hope said. 'It's what she would have wanted.'

'Do you think so?'

Leaning forward, Hope laid her hand briefly over his. 'Yes, without a doubt.' She pondered, as they continued to eat, on that saying about how opposites attract. Her mother, who hadn't a creative bone in her body, had always been drawn towards artistic types. The numerous parties she'd thrown at the house in Trafalgar Street had been filled with painters and sculptors, writers, even the occasional film director. Suddenly Hope felt an almost overwhelming urge to ask Lloyd about Jeff Tomlin – surely her mother must have talked about the father of her child? – but she quickly forced back the impulse. This wasn't the right time.

As if sensing that she had something on her mind, Lloyd said, 'Everything is all right, isn't it?'

Hope nodded. 'I'm just glad that you're going ahead with the project. I'll help out when I come back. I could do with some gainful employment.'

'Only if you want to,' he said, although he looked pleased by the offer. He paused and glanced down at his plate. 'And thank you for lunch. It was very sweet of you.'

Hope was instantly assailed by guilt, a feeling that seemed to be occupying a disproportionate amount of her mind at the moment. If only she could tell him the truth, ask for his advice, but she couldn't. 'No worries,' she said lightly. 'And you're right, about what you said earlier. We do have to carry on. We have to look towards the future.' Even as the words slipped from her mouth, she was aware of how false they were. In a few days' time she'd be off to London, raking up the embers of the past. She could only hope that whatever she discovered wouldn't come between them.

Chapter Seven

Driving along Albert Street, he makes sure he doesn't slow, doesn't draw any undue attention to himself. He's not worried about the CCTV cameras; the damn things never work. No sooner are they repaired then they're immediately vandalised again. The council is fighting a losing battle and it knows it. No, it's only the girls he's concerned about. They're going to be more wary than usual, more alert to every car passing by. They'll be checking out the drivers, clocking the familiar faces and wondering – oh yes, they're bound to be wondering – if the attacker is someone they already know.

So it's a risk coming down Albert Street, but one he feels obliged to take. It's something to do, he thinks, with tempting providence. He watches the girls out of the corner of his eye, amused – even aroused – by passing so close. Knowledge is power, and they know nothing. He slaps the palm of his hand on the wheel and laughs. Ignorant whores, the lot of them.

There are fewer of them out on the street than usual. In the wake of his latest attack, it's only the desperate ones who are taking the risk. He could choose a victim right now: the bleached blonde with the thigh-high boots; the dark-haired girl with the fag in her mouth; the older tart trying too hard to look ten years younger than she is. He doesn't have a type. He doesn't need one. It's what they represent, not how they look, that's important.

He knows what people are saying, what the papers are saying: that he's a madman, that he hates women, that he won't stop until he's finally killed, but they're only partly right. His lips twist into a thin, mocking smile. The truth is that he's the only one who sees things clearly: it's the women who are the destructive force, who cheat and seduce, who are the killers of all hope. He only does what he does because he has to.

He likes the girls to beg, to plead – although it's God's forgiveness that they really crave. He can't grant them absolution for their sins, but he can allow them to suffer, just as Christ suffered on the cross. He can grant them that one small favour. It's more than they deserve, but he has a generous spirit, a genuine desire for their filthy souls to be saved.

Chapter Eight

Hope looked up from her BlackBerry and glanced out of the train window. The landscape rushed by in a blur. They were about twenty minutes from Euston and her nerves were starting to twitch. She looked back down at the screen. She'd been searching the internet for art fraud, doing some research, and now her head was full of the subject.

At the beginning of the twentieth century there had been Han Van Meegeren, a Dutchman and a successful artist in his own right. According to the information she'd pulled up, he'd turned to forgery after the art world had mocked his second exhibition. His fakes had made him an incredibly wealthy man, but he'd eventually been exposed. He'd died of a heart attack in prison.

Then there had been Eric Hebborn, a cockney born in 1934 who'd won a scholarship to an art school in Rome. Finding his work unappreciated by contemporary critics, he'd begun to copy the Old Masters – artists like Rubens, Van Dyck and Jan Breughel – and the fakes, believed to be originals, had sold for thousands of pounds. In 1984 Hebborn had confessed to the forgeries and boasted of how he'd managed to fool the so-called experts of the art world. His fate had been as unhappy as Van Meegeren's: in 1996 he'd been found in a street in Rome with his skull caved in.

Hope breathed out a sigh. Art forgery, it seemed, was not entirely good for the health. And Jeff Tomlin, had he lived to tell the tale, could have borne testimony to that. She had tried Googling his name but nothing had come up. There must have been reports of his murder in local if not national newspapers, but before she started to delve further, she would need to find out exactly when and where he'd died.

The middle-aged man sitting beside Hope shifted in his seat, and she automatically pressed herself closer to the window. She was surprised by how busy the train was. It was midday, hardly the time for commuter traffic, but the carriage was packed solid with people in suits. Dressed in a pair of old blue jeans and a cream jumper, she was suddenly aware of the chasm between them: they were probably all going to London on business, to make deals, to have meetings, whereas she was going to ... to do what? No, that was something she didn't want to think too much about at the moment. She glanced down at her clothes. Her suitcase was on the luggage rack above her head. She hadn't been sure what to bring with her, what kind of garments were suitable for mixing with dips and gangsters, and in her uncertainty had packed far too much.

Hope turned her attention back to her BlackBerry, slightly tilting the screen so the man beside her couldn't see what she was studying. John Myatt was the latest artist she'd been reading about. Another British forger and one who'd been active in the late eighties, early nineties. He'd been prolific, churning out more than two hundred paintings – all forgeries of works by famous cubists, surrealists and Impressionists. Hope couldn't help but feel a sneaking admiration for the sheer cheek of the man. But there was something else about him that interested her. He'd had a business partner called John Drewe, who'd managed to sell the paintings through auction rooms like Christie's and Sotheby's. Drewe had been an expert at creating false provenances, even to the extent of pretending to be a researcher and doctoring index notes at the Tate and the V&A.

Hope immediately found herself thinking about Flint. He'd been responsible for shifting Tomlin's fakes, hadn't he? Which meant he must be a pretty convincing liar. She realised that she couldn't be sure whether anything he'd told her was true. She pressed her cheek against the window and frowned. What did she really know about him? Very little. And yet here she was on her way to meet up with him again.

As the train pulled into Euston, Hope found herself taking long, deep breaths. Her nerves were beginning to resurface, but it was too late to change her mind now. Perhaps she had made a mistake in not telling Lloyd what she was planning to do. London was the kind of city where a person could disappear without a trace. And Connie, she remembered with a shiver, had done exactly that.

She fought against the temptation to call him. All she'd be doing was transferring her own fears and anxieties. And that, after everything Lloyd had been through, was the last thing he needed. Especially when he finally seemed to be looking towards the future again. No, she couldn't, *mustn't* spoil that for him. In a week or two she'd probably be home – in her heart, she wasn't really convinced that she'd find out anything useful – and he'd be none the wiser as to what she'd actually been doing.

Having made the decision, Hope got to her feet, retrieved her case from the overhead rack and made her way off the train and on to the platform. She was quickly absorbed into the crowd of passengers. She saw Flint before he saw her. He was standing a few feet away from the gate, not scanning the faces as she might have expected, but gazing idly up at the ceiling with his hands deep in the pockets of his brown leather jacket. She had a few vital seconds in which to study him. He wasn't conventionally handsome, not the sort to turn heads, but there was something about him. His grey eyes were slightly hooded, his lips wide and finely formed. Sensual was the first word that sprang to mind. She instantly pushed it away.

'Hi,' he said, as he dropped his gaze and she came into his line of vision. 'Good journey?'

Hope nodded. 'Not bad.'

Flint stretched out a hand, almost as though he was intending to shake hers, but then took hold of the suitcase instead. 'Here, let me take that.'

'It's fine,' she said. 'I can manage.' There was a brief ungainly struggle before she managed to wrench it back. She wasn't quite sure why she was so insistent. It was to do, perhaps, with maintaining some tiny element of control over the situation. She didn't want to feel indebted to him for anything – not even carrying her suitcase.

Flint withdrew his hand and smiled. It was a smile she'd seen before, bordering on the indulgent, the kind of smile a tolerant parent might use towards a spoiled and temperamental child. 'You didn't change your mind then.'

'I'm here, aren't I?' She was aware, even as she spoke, of how snappy she sounded. But worse than that, almost petty, as if he'd forced her to come here against her will. And that wasn't true. She'd made her choice and there was no point in being resentful about it. 'Sorry. I didn't mean to be . . .'

He gave a light shrug of his shoulders. 'It's okay. If I was you, I wouldn't be too happy either. You must be wondering what you've let yourself in for. But if it helps, I think you've made the right decision. I really do.'

Hope nodded again. For all her uneasiness at being back in

Flint's company, she was still pleased to be in London. This was where she'd always felt most at home. As they crossed the station forecourt, she drank in the atmosphere, the hustle and bustle, the crowds, the buzz that was almost like an electric charge. God, she'd missed the place. Life might be pleasant enough in Albersea, but it lacked the noise, the pace, not to mention that endless thrill of possibility. Anything could happen in London. But no sooner had the thought crossed her mind than she found herself stressing again. Wasn't it that 'anything' she had to worry about?

They went down to the car park, Hope bumping the suitcase clumsily behind her. Flint's dark blue Audi was parked near the exit, and they were out on the street in a couple of minutes. As they joined the line of traffic, her eyes drank in the familiar landmarks. For some reason she found herself thinking about Alexander. Perhaps it wasn't that surprising; he'd often come to meet her at the station after she'd been home for a family visit. She tried to push him out of her mind; their relationship was over, and rightly so. Even without the trauma of her mother's illness, it would never have lasted. He hadn't been the type to settle for one woman, and she wasn't the type who could share the man she loved with anyone else. But no matter how rational a slant she tried to put on their split, there was no getting over the heartbreak.

'You all right?' Flint asked.

Hope hadn't said anything for the last two or three minutes. 'I'm fine. Just getting readjusted. It's been a while since I was here.'

'You know London?' he said.

She suddenly realised that Flint wasn't aware that she'd ever lived in the city. So far as he was concerned, she was just a small-town girl who happened to be related to Connie. She was tempted to play him along, but then changed her mind. 'I was here for eight years,' she said. 'In Islington. I was at college from when I was eighteen, and then ... then I stayed on for a while.'

'So you know Kellston? You've been there before?'

Hope shook her head. 'No. I used to have a studio in Spitalfields, but that's as close as I got.' In truth, Kellston was a part of the East End that she'd always been wary of. She'd heard too many stories about the level of crime, the number of assaults and muggings, to have any desire to go there.

'A studio?' Flint said, after a short pause. 'Does that mean you're an artist too?'

Hope gave him a sideways glance, her eyes narrowing a little. 'I'm not a painter if that's what you're thinking. I work with stained glass.'

Flint grinned. 'Hey, I was only asking. I'm not lining you up for the next master forger.'

Hope wasn't so sure. Flint was the type, or so she imagined, to always be on the lookout for the main chance. Still, he'd be disappointed if he thought she could knock out a few Vermeers in her spare time. She might be Jeff Tomlin's biological daughter, but she hadn't inherited his talent on the painting front.

'Can you make a living out of that?' Flint asked.

'Just about,' she replied shortly. Although of course without the free accommodation in Albersea, it would have been a struggle. When she'd been living in London, she'd had to take temp jobs, secretarial stuff mainly, to pay her rent and make ends meet. She didn't bother sharing this information with him. It wasn't any of his business. Instead she said, 'So what's the plan?'

'Good question. Not sure if I have one at the moment, other than getting you acquainted with the people Connie knew.'

'I still don't see why they're likely to tell me more than they've already told you.'

'Because when you ask, they won't suspect any ulterior motive. So far as you're concerned, Connie's just a girl who used to live in the flat. She's disappeared and no one knows where she is. Women have a natural curiosity about these things.'

'You mean they like to gossip.'

Flint grinned again. 'Did I say that?' He stopped at a red light and tapped his long fingers lightly on the wheel. 'They're always going to be wary of me. They know I was helping Connie to dig around in the past. They're too scared to open their mouths in case someone else finds out they've been talking. The "someone else", that is, who murdered Jeff Tomlin … and was maybe responsible for Connie's disappearance too.'

All of which served to remind Hope of the danger she might be putting herself in. She swallowed hard, hoping her uneasiness wouldn't be conveyed in her voice. 'But what about Lana?'

'What about her? She wants Connie found, but she's not prepared to stir up any trouble in the process. In her line of business she can't afford to make enemies. All it would take is an anonymous tip-off to the cops and she'd be looking at a five-year stretch. And Lana, believe me, has no desire to spend the next five years sharing a cell with some predatory dyke.'

What he was basically saying, Hope thought, was that no one else was prepared to put themselves on the line. Although with Connie still missing, that was hardly surprising. 'So it's down to me, then.'

The lights changed and Flint edged the car forward again. 'Down to *us*,' he corrected her. 'I'll be with you every step of the way. Well, perhaps not every step, but you get my drift. All you have to do is try and jog a few memories. Anything could be important, any little detail.'

Hope thought he was clutching at straws but kept her opinion to herself. 'So what name am I going to use?'

'Your own,' he said. 'It'll be easier. It's not as though anyone's going to link you with Connie. You've got a different surname; you even come from a different part of the country. She told me that she never talked about you to anyone, so it should be safe enough. Yeah, the best thing is to keep it simple. That way you don't get caught out in any stupid lies.'

Hope nodded. 'Okay, but what's my reason for being here?'

Flint thought about it for a moment. 'Well, you're right, we do need a cover story, so I figure something along the lines of you having got yourself in a spot of trouble up north and having to lie low for a while. Lana's prepared to say she's an old friend of Fay's, and that's why she's putting you up.'

'What kind of trouble?' Hope said.

'I don't know. Maybe you crossed someone you shouldn't, or picked the wrong person to lift a wallet from.'

Hope's brows shot up. 'You want me to pretend to be a dip?'

'You got any better ideas?'

Off the top of her head, she hadn't.

'You can say what you like,' he continued, 'but it has to be connected to something dodgy or you won't fit in. No one's going to accept you, or confide in you, if they think you're a stuck-up middle-class prig who's going to stand back and judge them.'

Hope shot him a look, wondering if that was how he saw her. 'Right,' she murmured. As she gazed out through the windscreen, she suddenly found herself thinking about her mother, regretting all the bad times and wishing they hadn't argued so much. Fay had loved London too, although she'd never come back here after leaving Jeff Tomlin. She'd returned to Albersea, to the place she'd been born – just as Hope had done.

'As it happens,' Flint said, 'you'd make a pretty good dip. No one would ever suspect you.'

Hope wasn't sure whether that was meant as a compliment. She thought not. He was probably suggesting that she looked too boring, too strait-laced, to be considered any kind of threat. Changing the subject she said, 'So who else lives in Lana's flat?'

'Only Evelyn at the moment. She's a nice kid, really cut up

about Connie. The two of them were close. Lana's tried talking to her, but if she knows anything, she doesn't know she knows it, if you get what I mean.'

Hope nodded. She remembered the photograph she'd found in the metal box, the picture of the three of them sitting together on the sofa. She hadn't taken much notice of the third girl, her attention being concentrated on Connie and the woman she'd initially thought might be Sadie Tomlin. 'And is Evelyn . . . is she in the same line as Lana?'

'Yeah,' Flint said. 'Lana's got a small crew, a group of girls she works with regularly. Waifs and strays mainly, all from the same God-awful backgrounds. Lana takes care of them. She's like a surrogate mum.'

Some kind of mother, Hope thought, who sends her kids out stealing. She was tempted to say it out loud, but didn't. There was no point in adding to Flint's already substantial list of reasons to despise her.

'Connie met up with someone a few weeks before she disappeared,' Flint said. 'It was someone from the past, a bloke, but she wouldn't tell me his name.'

'Why not?'

'I'm not sure. I could be wrong, but I think she found out something important, a clue as to why Jeff was killed. She was on edge, but kind of excited too. When I pushed her, she clammed up, said she needed time to think things through. Maybe she was just trying to protect me. If this guy had given her a lead, she might have felt it was too risky to pass it on.'

Hope wondered if that was true. Perhaps Connie had had another reason for wanting to keep the information to herself.

Flint gave a sigh and shook his head. 'Or maybe she just didn't trust me.'

Hope looked at him, surprised to hear an echo of her own thoughts. 'Why shouldn't she?'

'Why should she? Her father was murdered. Just because I used to be a friend of his doesn't put me out of the frame. In fact, statistically speaking, it's more than likely that he *was* killed by someone he knew.'

There were a few seconds of silence.

'But in case you're wondering,' he said, 'no, I didn't have anything to do with it. I'd hardly have come looking for you if I had. And if I was a cold-blooded killer and Connie was on to me, I wouldn't want her found.'

'I suppose not.'

Flint glanced at her. 'You could try saying that with a bit more conviction.'

Hope gave a thin smile. She didn't believe him capable of murder, but that didn't mean she was about to wholeheartedly put her trust in him either. It was too early for that.

Caution was what was called for here, and caution was what she was good at.

Chapter Nine

The traffic was running reasonably well and they were soon on Old Street. Flint glanced at his watch. 'We're almost there. We've got half an hour before we're due to meet Lana. How about I give you a quick tour of the area?'

'Sounds good,' Hope said.

He took a left, and wound around the back streets. 'As you probably know, Bethnal Green lies to the east and Shoreditch to the west. Okay, we're coming on to Kellston High Street now.'

Hope stared out of the window. It was a high street much like any other; a long, wide thoroughfare flanked by a few spindly trees and numerous shopping outlets. The people were the usual mixture too, men and women of all races, creeds and colours. The only thing that surprised her was that it wasn't as run-down as she'd expected. In fact some of the shops looked quite upmarket.

Flint gestured with his hand. 'That's the station to the right. Lana's flat is only a five-, ten-minute walk from there. There's no tube, but there's a decent rail service that takes you into Liverpool Street. And plenty of buses, of course, if you need to get to the West End.'

'You're beginning to sound like an estate agent.'

He gave a mock grimace. 'And that's a bad thing because . . . ?'

Hope was about to reply when she turned her head and caught sight of some iron railings and a flash of green. 'Oh, was that a park we just passed?'

'Nothing quite as grand, I'm afraid. It's the local green. The perfect place to walk your dog, rest your weary feet or buy your drugs – crack, brown, dope, anything you fancy so long as you've got the cash.'

'Delightful,' Hope murmured. She made a mental note to stay well away. The next thing she noticed was a restaurant with a row of white circular tables on the pavement. Most of the tables were occupied. It was one of those pleasantly warm September days when the sky was a clear blue and the sun was out, the perfect conditions for an al fresco lunch. She'd had a sandwich on the train but was beginning to feel hungry again. She thought about suggesting they stop off, grab a bite to eat, but then changed her mind. He might misinterpret the suggestion, start imagining that she didn't mind spending time with him. No, that wouldn't do. She had to keep her relationship with Flint on a strictly business type of footing. She had to maintain some distance between them.

As if sensing her discomfort, he said, 'You all right?'

'Fine,' Hope said, a bit too brightly. She stared out of the window. Beside the restaurant was a smart-looking jeweller's, and next to that a designer clothes shop and a couple of bars. 'It reminds me of Islington. You know, the part around Angel tube.'

'You mean the smart part.'

Hope bristled. Was there some kind of underlying criticism in his comment – as if the only kind of place she'd be familiar with was a smart one – or was she being oversensitive?

'That's Market Road to your left,' he said. 'It leads down to the square. As the name suggests, there's a market there on . . .

on Saturdays, I think. Maybe Wednesdays too. And there's a cinema.'

'I doubt I'll be here long enough to take advantage of either.'

Flint shot her a look, his grey eyes faintly accusatory.

Hope immediately regretted the comment. It made her sound like she was planning to leave as soon as possible. And although that was to some extent true, she didn't want to come across as only going through the motions. 'I mean, I haven't come here to go shopping or to catch a film, have I? That would be ridiculous. There are more important things to be concentrating on.'

Flint pulled another of his faces, as if he wasn't convinced by the answer. He nodded towards his right. 'That's Cowan Road. It's where you'll find the police station, should you ever feel the need to visit.'

'From what you said at Albersea, they haven't been too helpful to date.'

'No, and I don't suppose that's changed since Connie was reported missing. Anyway, they've got enough to occupy them at the moment. I don't know if you've heard, but there's been a number of assaults over the last nine months, all on working girls in the East End.'

'You don't think Connie could have been—'

Flint shook his head, quickly interrupting. 'No, this bastard likes his victims to be found. And he doesn't kill, or at least he hasn't yet. He just enjoys inflicting pain.'

Hope had a bad feeling in her guts. What if Flint was wrong? Instinctively she shifted down in her seat, hunching her shoulders. The idea of Connie being harmed in any way made her feel nauseous. She'd never thought much about having a sibling before, but now that she knew a half-sister existed, her desire to meet her, to talk to her was growing with every day that passed.

The Audi, caught in a snarled-up line of cars, edged slowly forward. As Hope gradually focused on their surroundings again, she realised that the landscape had changed. From the relative prosperity of the earlier part of the high street, they had progressed into a much greyer area. Here, at the northern end, were the more typical signs of East End poverty and deprivation. Walls were covered in graffiti, the pavement was strewn with litter and most of the shops were boarded up. There was even an undertaker's, Tobias Grand & Sons, that had closed down. Hope raised her brows. 'I didn't think funeral parlours ever went out of business.'

'That one has something of a history. The guy who ran the place was called Gerald Grand. His son was murdered there last year. I don't suppose it does much for trade.' His lips curled into a smile. 'Still, I guess he chose a handy place to get himself killed.'

Hope frowned. She wasn't in the mood for Flint's black humour, or his flippancy. She was still thinking about Connie and what might have happened to her.

The traffic started moving again. Flint took a right turn, drove a hundred yards up the road and pulled up beside a gateway. 'And this is the Mansfield Estate, a credit to 1960s British architecture. Peachy, isn't it? And somewhere to stay clear of if you've got any sense. You'd be lucky to walk ten paces without getting mugged – or worse. Just promise me that you won't ever come here on your own.'

Hope gazed up at the three tall towers, bleak grey constructions with rusting balconies. How anyone could think that such buildings were fit for habitation was beyond her. She felt a stab of pity for all the poor souls who were forced to try and survive in such wretched conditions. 'So whereabouts do you live?' she asked, realising that she didn't even know this simple fact about him.

'Oh, I never stay anywhere for long. I like to move around.'

70

'But at the moment?' she said, refusing to give in to his evasion. 'Does it matter?'

'Yes.' She turned to face him, to look directly into his eyes. 'Or is there a reason why you don't want to tell me?'

He grinned. 'Boy, have you got a suspicious mind. Okay, if it's that important, at the moment I'm living in St John's Wood.'

'Very nice.' She wasn't that familiar with the area but did know that it was a far cry from the depressing grey towers of the Mansfield Estate. 'Not exactly slumming it, then.'

Flint didn't rise to the bait. 'So if you ever feel an over-whelming urge to see me . . .'

Hope couldn't envisage a situation where she might actually feel any kind of urge to see him, but she still wasn't prepared to let him off the hook. He had her address in Albersea, and he knew where she'd be staying in Kellston. Surely, in return, she had every right to know where she could find *him*. 'So how does this work exactly? I just go there and whistle, right?'

He gave a light laugh. 'Or you could try the phone.'

'Or you could write down your address.'

'If it makes you happy.'

Hope was about to say that happiness had nothing to do with it when she became aware of a kid standing by the gateway. He was a skinny youth, about fifteen, with a baseball cap pulled down over his forehead. He was staring hard at Flint. 'Does that boy know you?'

'No, the little bugger's just waiting to see if I'm stupid enough to leave the car here. He's hoping Christmas might have come early.'

Hope's initially good impressions of Kellston were starting to fade. The whole area was beginning to depress her. 'Let's go. I've seen enough.'

'You ready to head over to Lana's, or do you want me to take you back to Euston?'

71

'What do you think?'

He gave her another of his trademark grins. 'Only asking.'

Flint did a fast three-point turn. As he drove back along the high street, he was quiet for a while, and then he nodded towards a café called Connolly's. 'You see that caff? It might be a good place for us to meet up. I don't think Lana would appreciate me making too many visits to the flat. Someone might notice and pass on the information to an interested party.'

Hope wondered if he was being paranoid, or just sensibly cautious. 'Is that likely?'

'Like I said earlier, Lana's prepared to help out, but only to a point. The one thing she doesn't want is to be associated with me. And bearing in mind where I spent most of the last six months, I can't say I blame her.'

Hope was reminded of the fact that he'd been to prison. For possession of fake passports, or so he claimed. What if he'd been lying? What if he'd been inside for something completely different. What if—'

'You've got that worried expression on your face again. Don't worry, I'm not about to sell you into the white slave trade.' Flint turned into Station Road, drove about a hundred metres and then pointed to his left. 'Although if I was, this would be the place to do it. Albert Street. It's where most of the working girls hang out. Another place to avoid. Well, unless you're short of a few bob, in which case—'

Before he could expand on the subject, Hope cut him short. 'Thanks for the tip. I'll bear it in mind.'

'No problem,' he said.

Tanner Road, their destination, was only a couple of streets further up. It consisted of two rows of large detached Victorian red-brick houses, and although it was clear that the area had once been prosperous, the buildings had long since fallen into disrepair. Paint peeled from doors and windows, gutters hung from roofs, and the front gardens – if the concreted-over expanses of ground could be described as such – were mainly filled with rubbish bags, abandoned furniture and the carcasses of rusting cars. Hope felt a sadness rise up inside her. These would once have been family homes, residences to be proud of, but now the clusters of bells in the front porches spoke only of multiple bedsits, of cramped divided rooms and endless loneliness.

Flint pulled up outside a house that was a little less neglected than the others and switched off the engine. 'You ready?'

'As I'll ever be,' Hope said. Before she could change her mind, she took a breath, got out of the car and shut the door. She could feel her heart beginning to beat faster. As she stood on the pavement looking up at the house that was going to be her home for the foreseeable future, she felt a shiver run through her. What was she doing? This was the start of something, the beginning of a journey, but where it was likely to end she had no idea at all.

Chapter Ten

Flint got her suitcase from the boot of the car, and this time Hope didn't bother trying to wrestle it from him. They walked down the drive together and stood in the porch. He pressed the bell for the top floor. It was a couple of minutes before they heard the clatter of heels from inside.

Lana, a tall woman dressed in a smart navy suit, opened the door and stared at Flint. 'Oh, so you made it then.'

'Hello, Lana,' he said. 'Good to see you too. This is Hope. Hope, this is Lana.'

Hope was about to stretch out her hand, to say it was nice to meet her and thanks for letting her stay, but Lana, without so much as an acknowledgement, had already turned away and was heading back up the stairs. Hope now had a feeling of discomfort to add to all her other anxieties; she clearly wasn't welcome.

They went up the two flights in silence. As Hope looked around at her surroundings, her heart sank. The plaster on the old magnolia walls was crumbling, there were holes in the lino, and part of the banister was missing. It had that peculiar odour that so many communal hallways possessed, a mustiness combined with the smell of old cooking. She had a sudden yearning for her clean, pretty cottage in Albersea.

The door to Lana's flat was open and they followed her inside. Hope, having prepared herself for the worst, was pleasantly surprised. The flat was a conversion, occupying the entire second floor of the house, and was well proportioned, high-ceilinged and spacious. There were two large windows in the living room, and the sunlight flooded in.

'I suppose you want tea,' Lana said, with the kind of barely disguised weariness that people reserved for unwanted guests.

Flint nodded. 'If it's not too much trouble. Where shall I put the case?'

'Just leave it there.'

Lana disappeared, presumably to go to the kitchen. Hope continued to gaze around. The walls were painted in one of those soft shades of white, the carpet was pale green, and there was a moss-coloured leather sofa with two matching chairs. A tiled Victorian fireplace provided a centrepiece for the room, and above it was a wide-screen plasma TV. There were lots of plants, and a vase full of lilies gave off a strong pervasive scent. Some people hated the smell – a reminder perhaps of funerals – but Hope had always liked it.

'Not quite what you expected?' Flint said.

Pretending that she didn't have a clue what he meant, Hope sat down on the sofa and gave a small shrug.

Flint went to stand by one of the windows. 'Lana's a smart cookie. She bought this place years ago when Kellston was a real dump. She reckoned it was the next up-and-coming area, and she was right.' His eyes roamed around. 'Even in the current economic climate, it must be worth a lot more than she paid for it.'

'It's very nice,' Hope said, although she wasn't overly keen on its proximity to the red-light district. She got to her feet, went

75

over to join him at the window and lowered her voice. 'But she doesn't want me here, does she? I don't see how this is going to work.'

'Don't worry about Lana, she's always cautious with strangers. Once she gets to know you, it'll be fine.'

'I wouldn't be so sure.'

'Just give it a few days, yeah? See how it pans out. If you still think it's a waste of time, you can easily move out again. We'll think of something else.'

Lana came back with three mugs of tea and a bowl of sugar on a tray. As she laid the tray on the coffee table, Hope took the opportunity to examine her more closely. She was in her late forties, with dyed red hair and a figure that had probably once been voluptuous. Now her breasts looked too heavy and she was developing a paunch around her stomach.

'So you're the sister,' Lana said, finally addressing her. Her blue eyes seemed faintly accusing.

'Hope Randall.'

'Come over here then. Let's take a look at you.'

Hope did as she was told.

Lana put her hands on her hips and looked Hope up and down with the kind of disappointed expression a judge of pedigree dogs might use at Crufts. 'I don't know,' she sighed. 'We'll have to do something about the hair.'

Hope self-consciously lifted a hand to her head. 'What's wrong with it?'

Lana, ignoring her completely, glanced at Flint. 'You're right. She has got a look of Connie about her. And that won't do. It won't do at all. If anyone starts to suspect . . .'

'They won't,' Flint said. 'You can sort it, can't you?'

'I suppose,' Lana said, although not with any degree of enthusiasm. 'Maybe blonde. What do you think? And some decent make-up would help.'

'Sure,' he said. 'Do whatever you have to.'

Hope looked from one to the other. 'Er, I am in the room, you know. Don't I get a say in any of this?'

Lana's red lips puckered into disapproval. 'I've already told Flint, I'm only prepared to do this on *my* terms. It's my neck on the line if it all goes tits-up. You can clear off back to wherever you've come from, but I have to go on living here. If people think I've been lying to them . . .'

'Okay, okay, I get it,' Hope said.

'This is Kellston, love, not some northern backwater. The people round here act first and ask questions later.'

Hope didn't like Lana's abrupt manner or the way she talked to her. She took a few deep breaths, trying to stay calm. 'I said I understood, didn't I? And I'm not a complete idiot, so there's no need to treat me like one.'

Flint, worrying perhaps that Hope was about to change her mind and demand that lift back to Euston, quickly intervened. 'Ladies, *please*. We're doing this for Connie, right? Maybe, for her sake, we could at least try to sort things out in an amicable fashion.'

Like two hostile cats, the women glared silently at each other. If Hope could have walked away from it all she would have, but her instincts were fighting a losing battle with her conscience. Flint was right. For Connie's sake she had to give it a chance. Guessing that Lana was probably the type who could never be seen to back down, Hope swallowed her pride and made the first move. 'I'm sorry. I do appreciate your situation. I understand the position you're in, and I'm grateful . . .' She glanced at Flint. 'We're both grateful for your help. I'll do whatever it takes to make this work.'

Lana seemed partially pacified. She gave a small nod. 'Let's have that tea, then.'

They were about to sit down when Flint said, 'You know

what, thanks for the offer but I think I'll skip on the brew. I'm sure you two have lots to talk about.'

Hope could hardly believe what she was hearing. He couldn't just clear off and leave her alone with Lana. She tried to catch his eye, but he didn't, or wouldn't, meet her gaze.

'I'll call you,' he said, and was out of the door before Hope could say anything to stop him.

'That's men for you,' Lana snorted. 'A spot of trouble and you don't see them for dust.'

Hope, still annoyed by his hasty departure, gave the tea a brisk angry stir. 'Have you known him long?'

'I don't know him at all, not really. Connie mentioned him once or twice – an old friend of her dad's, she said – but I didn't meet him until she went missing.'

'But you trust him.'

'Trust him?' Lana barked out a laugh. 'You must be kidding.'

Hope was surprised by her answer. 'So why are you doing this?'

'For Connie, of course.' Lana sat back and folded her arms across her chest. 'If there's any chance of finding out what … Well, the filth don't give a toss, and it's not as though she's got anyone else to worry about her.' At this point, she threw Hope a hostile kind of look. 'That poor kid deserves better. Someone has to make the effort.'

'I didn't even know she existed until last week,' Hope said defensively. 'And I'm here now, aren't I. I'm trying to help.'

Lana huffed out a breath, as if that wasn't exactly anything to celebrate.

'And Flint cares.'

'Does he?' Lana gave another snort. 'God, I suppose he dragged out that touching sob story about how guilty he felt when Connie got in touch with him again, about how sorry he was to have walked away from her and Sadie in their hour of need.'

Hope felt a light blush rise to her cheeks. She recalled standing on the beach at Albersea, listening to that very explanation. And she'd swallowed every word of it.

'Oh, don't worry,' Lana said. 'I'm sure he was very convincing. But Mr Flint, whoever he is, has his own agenda. Just remember that and watch your step.'

'So he's using me. Is that what you're saying?'

'He's using the two of us – or at least he's trying to. But that works both ways. So long as I find out what I want, I don't give a damn about his reasons.'

'But how do you know?' Hope said. 'I mean, how can you be certain that he isn't being straight?'

Lana slowly shook her head, as if the answer was obvious. 'Because I've met a hundred men like him before, dear. And none of them have been the sentimental type. But that doesn't mean we can't all work together. If he's prepared to go digging up the past, and to accept the consequences, then who am I to stand in his way.'

'But Connie must have trusted him,' Hope said. No sooner were the words out of her mouth than she recalled how Connie hadn't been prepared to tell Flint about the man she'd talked to. 'Well, to some extent.'

'Yeah, but Connie didn't have the brains she was born with. I warned the silly cow. I told her she was asking for trouble, mixing with that lot.'

'That lot?'

'All those bloody lowlifes that Jeff Tomlin knew. That stupid father of yours – no offence, love – was up to his ears in it. And whatever it was he was involved in, it got him killed. You can't sup with the devil without paying the price.'

'You think she's dead too,' Hope said softly.

Lana's face suddenly twisted. She blinked hard, tears coming to her eyes, and stared down into her lap. 'It's been seven months. Connie wouldn't have left without saying goodbye, even if it was only a phone call. And she didn't take anything with her.'

It was the first time Hope had seen anything other than cynicism in Lana's face. It made her seem, if nothing else, a little more human. She was tempted to come out with one of those blandly encouraging kind of comments, something along the lines of how they mustn't give up, that there was always a chance – but there was little point in offering up false hope. Lana was probably right. If the two of them had been close, Connie would have found a way to contact her. 'I'm sorry,' Hope murmured. She left a short respectful silence and then added, 'So where do we go from here?'

As if she'd revealed too much of herself, Lana's face instantly hardened again. She stood up, pushed back her shoulders and stared down at Hope. Her voice assumed its more familiar tone. 'We need to make sure you're sorted before the girls get here. That's if you still want to go ahead with this.'

Hope didn't see how she could back out now, even if she wanted to.

Chapter Eleven

Chris Street was rapidly coming to the conclusion that he'd have been better off staying in bed. Since waking that morning, he'd experienced nothing but grief, and now things were getting even worse. He glared across his desk at the short, swarthy man who'd just delivered the latest piece of bad news.

'You must be kidding,' Chris said. 'That's way above market rate.'

'That's the deal, Mr Street. Take it or leave it.'

Chris did a fast mental calculation. 'At that price, there's barely any profit.'

Mendez shifted in his chair, crossing his legs. He lifted his heavy shoulders in a shrug. 'Better than no profit at all. If you don't wish to pay, you can always buy elsewhere.'

But that, as Chris was more than aware, was easier said than done. Finding another supplier, especially at short notice, would be a nightmare. The Colombian cartel that Mendez represented was both reliable and efficient – and the next consignment of coke was due in a few days' time. 'For fuck's sake,' he retorted angrily, 'how long have we worked with you? Fifteen years, twenty? And now you're trying to screw us over.'

Mendez, as if wounded by the remark, laid his hand gently against his heart. His heavy dark eyebrows came together in a frown. 'Ah,' he said softly, 'that is not the case, Mr Street. I hold your family in extremely high regard. If it was down to me . . .' He left an exaggerated pause. 'But sadly, it isn't.'

'So what the hell's going on?'

Mendez's gaze slipped to the floor for a moment. When he looked up again, his brown eyes were cautious and yet full of guile. 'You didn't hear this from me.'

Chris nodded. Aware that he wasn't going to like what was coming, his guts gave an involuntary twist. Bad news seemed to gravitate towards him these days. 'You have my word.'

'An offer has been received, a very generous offer.'

'Go on.'

'The gentleman in question is prepared to pay a more favourable price for the goods. I think we can safely say that he wishes to . . . to dispose of the competition.'

That was when Chris suddenly saw the light. 'Christ, it's that Russian bastard, isn't it?' His hands instinctively clenched into two tight fists. Andrei bloody Kozlov was trying to squeeze them out. By offering to pay over the odds for the drugs, he could effectively cut off their supply. Well, either that or force them to operate at minimal profit, which wouldn't do much for their cash flow. Of course it wouldn't stop them from going elsewhere, and paying less, but that would take time to organise, to negotiate, and even when another deal was done, Kozlov could pull the same trick again. He clearly had the kind of capital that Chris could only dream about.

'The money's on the table,' Mendez said. 'And my bosses aren't the type to . . . how do you English describe it . . . to look a gift horse in the mouth.'

Chris knew he was being backed into a corner. He was tempted to tell Mendez to shove it, to stuff his deal up his bloody arse, but the satisfaction would only be temporary. If he didn't pay the inflated price, they could end up with nothing to sell. And that's when Kozlov would step in to fill the gap. So although it took an effort of will, Chris held back from venting his frustration on the man sitting in front of him. Instead, he said coolly, 'So much for trust. I won't forget this.'

Mendez lifted his shoulders in another of his leisurely shrugs. 'As you say, we've worked together for a long time. That's why we're offering you the opportunity to match the offer. Business is business, Mr Street, but there is some room for loyalty too.'

Like fuck, Chris thought. All the cartel was doing was max-imising its profits, and hedging its bets. Waiting to see who emerged from this conflict with their brains intact. 'Once he's driven out the competition, Kozlov won't be willing to pay those prices any more.'

Mendez gave a slow, sly smile. 'True,' he said. 'But by then the money will be in the bank – and he will still need a reliable supplier. It might not be us, but even if it isn't, we can always find another buyer.'

Chris couldn't argue with that. No matter which way it went, the cartel would come out on top. He sat and stared at Mendez. Out of the blue, it occurred to him how little he knew about the man, even after all these years. He had no idea where he lived, whether he was married, or had kids. He didn't know how old he was, what his likes or dislikes were, what he did in his free time. Their relationship had always been strictly business, but even business associates usually got to learn something about each other.

Perhaps reading the silence as a signal that the meeting was over, Mendez got to his feet. 'I'm sure you'd like time to think it over. Let's say twenty-four hours. Will that be satisfactory?'

Chris stood up too. He did his best to keep his voice neutral. No matter how angry he was – and he was angry as hell – he knew it was best not to go burning any bridges. Good suppliers, even if they were prepared to stab you in the back, were hard to find. 'Fine. I'll let you know.'

Mendez stretched out his hand. 'I sincerely hope we'll be able to continue working together. It would be a shame, after all these years, to let this get in the way of such a long and ... pleasant partnership.' He gave a slight bow of his head. 'Please pass on my regards to your father.'

Chris forced out a smile. He would rather have shaken hands with a snake, but business was business. Mendez's fingers were remarkably dry and cool; if the man had felt any anxiety at all in delivering the news, it wasn't apparent. Of course only someone with a death wish would mess with the cartel – their revenge would be fast and fatal. Chris wasn't afraid of much, but he knew how those shitheads operated.

After showing Mendez out, Chris returned to the office, and sat back down. He slammed his fist on the desk and swore loudly. It didn't change anything. The beat of the music, although muffled by the heavy door, was beginning to give him a headache. The midday session at Belles was still in progress: the girls were dancing, and the in-house dealers were taking advantage of all those clients – and there were plenty of them – who wanted a little extra thrill before they went back to work in the City. By this time next week, if he didn't accept Mendez's offer, they would have a lot of disappointed punters on their hands.

Chris stood up again and began to pace around the room. What to do? It was a good thing he'd got rid of Danny, or things would have really kicked off. There was no controlling his brother when he lost his rag. And taking it out on Mendez wouldn't achieve anything; he was only the messenger. What was most worrying, and this was a fact Chris couldn't ignore, was that the cartel obviously saw Kozlov as a better long-term prospect. Why else would they have done this? They thought the Streets were finished and were quietly forming new alliances.

He wondered what Lizzie would have done about it all. It was the first time since his stepmother's death that he actually missed her. She may have been a bitch, but she'd been smart with it. On a good day, she could outwit the Devil himself. After her murder, he'd tried to clear the office of everything of hers, but sometimes he still came across the occasional eerie reminder, a short scribbled note or a lipstick in a drawer.

Thinking of Lizzie reminded Chris of everything that had gone wrong over the last nine months. His father's release, after ten years in nick, should have been an opportunity for the family to reaffirm its authority over the East End, to stand together in a show of strength, but instead the very opposite had happened. The cracks had started to show almost as soon as Terry's release papers had been signed . . . and now the three of them were slowly tearing each other apart.

Terry still thought that his authority was cast in stone, that he only had to click his fingers and everyone would jump. But those times were long gone. He was a dinosaur, out of touch and living in the past. And Danny? Chris shook his head. Sometimes he wondered if he knew his brother at all. All those rumours about him, all that ugly gossip, hadn't done much to help the family's reputation. In their line of business, secrets and lies were par for the course, but people would only accept so much. There was a thin line between respect and disgust, and once that line was crossed . . .

Chris poured himself a stiff whisky and knocked it back in one. If things carried on as they were, Andrei Kozlov wouldn't need to lift a finger; the devious Russian bastard could just sit back and wait. He refilled his glass and drank this one more slowly. He'd been left, or so it felt, with the unenviable task of captaining a sinking ship. Already the icy water was lapping round his knees. Unless he acted, and acted fast, it wouldn't be long before he'd be putting on a life jacket and playing out the final scenes of *Titanic*.

Chapter Twelve

Benjamin Tallow crouched down by the sofa, covering his face with his hands. He could feel the thumping of his heart, and his breath came in short, fast pants. What was he going to do? He knew the question was crazy even as he asked it. There was nowhere to run, no back door, no means of escape. The light from the window squeezed between his fingers, and he quickly shut his eyes, as if by making the room disappear he could make the problem leave with it.

The doorbell went again, a longer ring this time. An impatient ring. Then the rattle of the letter box.

'Benjie?' the voice called out again. 'I know you're in there. You've got ten seconds. Open this door or I'll kick the fuckin' thing down!'

It had been a mistake to turn the music off like that. A dead giveaway. He should have known better. But it had been an instinctive, knee-jerk reaction and there was nothing he could do about it now. He reached for his phone, but who could he call? Not the cops. If he called the law he'd be branded as a grass, and anyway, they were never in a rush to get to the

Mansfield Estate. He'd have drawn his last breath well before any patrol car cruised leisurely through the gates. And who else was there? None of his so-called mates were going to get involved in something like this. He felt a sudden stab of loneliness. Dropping the phone, he curled up into a ball and bit down on his knuckles.

'Ten, nine, eight . . . '

Benjamin listened to the voice with a growing sense of dread. He should have made himself scarce, laid low until this whole mess had blown over. He should have jumped on a bus or a train and got the hell out. Too late for that now. Could the bastard really kick the door in? Maybe not. It was pretty solid, and the bolts were pulled across. But he could easily smash the front window and get in that way. It wasn't as if anyone would try and stop him. Even if the neighbours heard the noise, they'd do sod all about it. No one on this estate was stupid enough to get mixed up in someone else's troubles.

'Seven, six, five . . . '

Benjamin wrapped his arms around his knees. There were only two choices left: he could sit tight and wait for him to break in, an option that wasn't likely to enhance his visitor's already less than friendly mood, or he could face it out and try to explain. But you *couldn't* talk to men like him. They didn't want to listen. They weren't interested in excuses. He pressed his hands against his ears, trying to block out the countdown.

'Four, three, two . . . '

A sudden burst of adrenalin shot Benjamin to his feet. Shit, anything was better than sitting here helplessly. 'Hold on,' he yelled. 'I'm comin'.' He ran through to the hall and dug in his jacket for the small silver flick knife he always carried when he was out and about. Quickly he shoved it into his back pocket. Then, with his hands starting to shake, he dragged back the bolts on the door.

'You took your fuckin' time,' Danny Street said, barging in. He kicked the door shut, grabbed Benjamin by the elbow, and propelled him into the living room. 'Where's my money? It's Tuesday, for fuck's sake.'

Benjamin shook his head. He opened his mouth, but nothing came out.

Danny Street let go of his arm and stared at him, his dark eyes flashing with anger. Then he leaned forward and hissed into his face, 'Where's my fuckin' money, Benjie?'

Benjamin could smell something metallic on Danny's breath. It made him even more frightened than he already was. He swallowed hard, and tried again. This time he managed to speak, although the voice didn't sound like his. It was small and croaky, a stranger's voice. 'I-I ain't got it, Mr Street.'

Danny frowned for a second, and cocked his head to one side as if he hadn't quite heard properly. Then with a single fluid movement he grabbed hold of Benjamin's arms and shoved him back against the wall. His hands went up to grip his throat, his thumbs pressing into the soft flesh around the Adam's apple. 'What do you mean, you ain't got it? What you playin' at?'

Benjamin felt the force of the blow travel down his spine. He struggled to catch his breath, and had to force the words out through parched lips. 'I-I were jumped, Mr Street. It ... it weren't my fault. They took the cash, and the ... the gear too. There were two of 'em. They had a gun.'

'You just handed it over?'

'They were gonna shoot me, man!' Benjamin wailed. 'Please don't hurt me. I'm sorry. I'm really sorry.' But he knew, even as he begged, that he was making matters worse. His whiny pleading would only reinforce Street's suspicion that he had something to be punished for.

Danny Street's grip tightened around his throat. 'Or maybe

you just sold the gear,' he hissed. 'And kept the cash, eh? Is that what really happened?'

Benjamin tried to shake his head, but it was caught in a vice-like grip. He could feel a warm, slimy stream of snot leaking from his nose. It hurt to talk, but he mustn't stop now. A beating was on the cards – there was no chance of avoiding it – but how bad that beating was going to be could still be up for negotiation. 'No,' he mumbled. 'No. Honest. I wouldn't do that. I'd never do that.' He left a short, scared pause. 'Not to *you*, Mr Street.'

Danny Street stared deep into his eyes for a few seconds, and then abruptly released him. 'Nah,' he agreed. 'You wouldn't fuckin' dare.' Turning, he began to pace around the room, his arms swinging by his sides, his big hands clenching and unclenching. He was muttering something under his breath.

Benjamin, although relieved to be rid of those fingers round his throat, didn't move from his position against the wall. He'd got a temporary reprieve, but it wasn't over yet. He shifted warily from one foot to the other, fighting against the impulse to make a run for it. Street had closed the front door but he hadn't locked it. Could he outsprint him? Over a long clear stretch perhaps, but not within the confines of the hall. Street would be on to him before he'd even got the door open.

Danny Street continued with his pacing, and his indecipherable monologue. Occasionally he stopped and glanced to his left as if an invisible companion had made a response. For a moment his brow would crunch into a frown, and then the pacing would resume. Up and down, up and down. Sometimes he kicked out at a chair, a table leg, or the base of the tattered sofa.

Benjamin was following his every movement. He winced each time the steel toe of Street's boot made contact with a piece of furniture. It was a warm day, and he was overly aware of the stuffiness of the room, the stink of old fag smoke and the smell of the lager he'd been drinking that morning. His guts were churning, and a taste like bile had gathered in his mouth.

Eventually Danny Street came to a halt right in front of him. 'So who was it, Benjie?'

'They was f-foreign,' Benjamin stammered, terrified at finding himself the focus of attention again. 'Polacks or summat. You know the ones. They're always hanging round the place.'

Danny Street narrowed his eyes. 'Kozlov's crew?'

Benjamin rubbed nervously at his throat. He wasn't sure, but he nodded anyway. 'They did Jimmy Keyes last week, got him with a knife. Almost cut his arm off. He could 'ave bled to death. They don't mess about, man. They don't ask twice. I was scared. I was—'

Danny was scowling as he leaned in, placing his hands either side of Benjamin's head and pinning him against the wall again. He thrust his face forward until their lips were almost touching. His voice was hardly more than a whisper, but its tone was full of menace. 'More scared than you are of me?'

Benjamin knew that he'd said the wrong thing. Shit, why hadn't he kept his stupid mouth shut? 'N-no,' he said quickly. 'I didn't . . . I didn't mean—'

'So why did you give them my fuckin' gear?'

Even before Benjamin could begin to formulate an answer that wouldn't make the situation worse, a backhand blow caught him on the cheek. He felt a stinging pain, and then a warmer sensation as the blood began to flow. The sharp-edged gold rings that Danny Street wore weren't just for decoration.

'You see, Benjie, that's just fuckin' disrespectful. You do see that, don't you?'

Benjamin closed his eyes for a second, offering up a prayer to a God he had never believed in. *Help me, Lord. Please help me.* There was no reasoning with someone as deranged as Danny

Street. He was mad, crazy. He lowered his head, trying to protect his face against any further attacks. 'Y-yeah. I'm sorry, Mr Street. It won't . . . won't 'appen again.'

'Too true it won't.'

The next strike was a low one, a blow so ferocious that Benjamin yelped and sank to his knees. Cradling his balls in his hands, he tried to catch his breath. But Street wasn't going to give him any time to recover. The knee came up fast and hard. It caught Benjamin on the jaw, and sent him sprawling. And then Street was on top of him, astride him, spewing out obscenities. .

Benjamin could see the rage in Street's eyes. It wouldn't be long before his fists started flying again. Panic swept through his pain-filled body. His mind began to race. Street was out of control, on another planet, and this wasn't going to stop until . . . No, shit, he couldn't allow that to happen. He was only nineteen. He was too young to die.

'A lesson! A fuckin' lesson! That's what you pathetic little scrotes need. Kozlov? Kozlov can go fuck himself. This is my fuckin' patch, not his. No one messes with Danny Street!'

As the frenzied diatribe continued, Benjamin managed to raise his right hip slightly off the ground. It gave him just enough room to reach into his back pocket and pull out the knife. If he was fast enough, he could get him in the back, in the kidneys. He had to do it. What choice did he have? To just lie there and wait for the inevitable to happen? Danny Street was about to make an example of someone – and that someone was him. He had to defend himself. Now. He had to do it now. He gripped the handle of the knife, feeling the coolness of the metal against his fingers. Then he found the button, and heard the tiny, distinctive click as the blade was released.

But he wasn't the only one who heard it. Or maybe Danny Street had simply sensed the sudden tensing in the body beneath him. Whatever the reason, he twisted smartly away as

Benjamin stabbed wildly at his spine. The blade missed its target completely and only caught the back of Danny's hand.

For a second, Danny Street looked bemused, as if he wasn't sure what had happened, but then an understanding suddenly blossomed in his eyes. He stared at the wound, at the trickle of blood that was seeping between his fingers, and released a long, low growl. 'You shit! You filthy little shit!' Grabbing hold of Benjamin's wrist, he slammed it down against the floor. The knife fell on to the carpet, and Danny quickly snatched it up.

Benjamin lay paralysed with fright. His limbs had become limp, useless. All the fight had gone out of him. If only he'd been faster, if only he hadn't answered the door, if only . . . but it was too late for all that now. The full weight of Danny Street was back on top of his chest. He was completely at his mercy. Even as the thought sprang into his head, he knew it was a joke. Mercy? Crazies like Danny Street didn't know the meaning of the word.

Danny bared his teeth and bent down towards his face. 'What did they do to Jimmy Keyes?'

It was a question Benjamin hadn't been expecting. His teeth were chattering as he tried to find the right answer. 'W-what?'

'You heard.'

'I told you.'

'Tell me again!' Danny demanded.

It took Benjamin a moment to splutter out a reply. He didn't know where this was going, but wherever it was wasn't going to be good. 'They . . . they jumped him. Over by the Haslow. In the alley. They had a knife.'

'And?'

'I dunno.'

'Course you do, Benjie. What did they do? What did they do to his arm? Come on, spit it out. You know you want to tell me.'

Benjamin stared up at him before lowering his eyes. He was overly aware of Danny's groin, of the bulge that betrayed his perverted excitement. He tried not to look. He tried not to think about all those rumours he'd heard, all those ugly stories about the dead girl at the funeral parlour. 'They . . . they tried to cut it off.'

'Only tried?' Street hissed. 'Perhaps they need someone to show 'em how to do it properly. What d'ya think, Benjie?' He pressed the sharp tip of the blade against Benjamin's bare shoulder. 'How long d'ya think it takes to saw through an arm? All that muscle. All those tendons and the rest. Not an easy job, huh?'

Benjamin's eyes widened with horror. There were some things, perhaps, even worse than death. He felt the knife slowly piercing his flesh. 'Nah, please!' he begged. 'Please, Mr Street. Don't do it. Please don't do that.'

But Danny just smiled down at him. His eyes were bright, gleaming with sadistic pleasure.

'I'm sorry, Mr Street. I'm sorry.' He knew it was a waste of time, but he couldn't stop himself. 'I won't ever . . . please. . .' He had a sudden vivid memory of his mother wearing a dress patterned with red blossoms. She was standing by the sink with her feet apart and her hands firmly planted on her plump, flowery hips. *Mark my words, Benjamin Tallow, the way you're going you'll end up dead in a gutter.* He closed his eyes and began to cry, great heaving sobs that racked his entire body. His limbs began to shake, his chest to rise and fall.

Danny Street grasped his chin with his left hand. 'Shut up! Just shut the fuck up!' He shifted forward a few inches. Then he laughed. It was a nasty, hollow sound. 'You know what, Benjie boy, even niggers get a break occasionally. Today's yer lucky day. I can't be arsed. You're not worth the fuckin' effort.'

If Benjamin relaxed, it was only for a second. No sooner had

94

he exhaled a single breath of relief than he felt the knife move to the corner of his lip. In an instant he realised what was happening. He tried to shift his head away, but couldn't. He opened his mouth to protest, to beg, to plead, but it was already too late. The blade was slicing quickly and deeply through the flesh, cutting a path towards his jaw. A hot, searing pain burst across his consciousness. It seemed to go on and on and on. His right leg jerked up and then fell back against the floor. A scream rose to his throat but couldn't escape; Danny's cold, clammy palm had clamped down over his face.

A whisper curled its way into Benjamin's ear. 'Something to remember me by, kid. Every time you look in the mirror.'

After a while, Danny Street stood up and wiped the blood off the back of his hand. He looked down at Benjamin Tallow with the same level of interest he'd show towards a piece of garbage lying on the pavement. Then he carefully examined his clothes. There were bloodstains on the cuff of his white shirt and he glared at them with growing annoyance. A good shirt ruined. It was a bloody waste. Why did people have to wind him up so much? He pulled down the sleeve of his jacket, covering the offending stain. And then, without so much as a backward glance, he left the flat, closing the door softly behind him.

Chapter Thirteen

Hope stood and stared at her reflection in the bathroom mirror. A girl she didn't recognise, a girl with long gold-streaked hair and wide black-lined eyes, gazed back at her. She was like a stranger to herself. Lana had whisked her off to a small salon in Hackney, where Hope had spent the last two hours in hairdressing hell, watching while her once dark brown locks had gradually been transformed. The pungent fumes from the dye still lingered in her nose. And after that ordeal was over, Lana had taken her shopping, and then brought her back to the flat and started on her face.

'So what do you think?' Lana said.

'It's very . . .' Hope struggled to find an adequate response. In truth, she felt something close to dismay, but that was hardly a sentiment she could share. The whole look, including the strappy, cleavage-showing pink vest Lana had insisted on her buying, made her feel like a wannabe WAG. 'It's certainly different.'

'You see?' Lana smiled widely, as if this was an entirely good thing.

Hope smiled weakly back. 'Thank you.' How had she let herself get talked into this? To prove a point to Flint, perhaps. She wondered what Lloyd would say when he saw her next. Unless she could get her hair fixed before she went back to Albersea, he'd wonder why she'd undergone this sudden change of image.

'The others will be back in half an hour or so,' Lana said. 'I've already told them you'll be staying here, and why. We don't need to go over the story again, do we?'

'Of course not.' During the afternoon, Lana had given her the lowdown on the three girls she currently worked with, and also a protracted lecture on what Hope should and shouldn't say to them.

Lana gave her a doubtful look. 'I mean, if you start asking endless questions about Connie . . . '

'I'm not going to do that. I'll be careful, I promise.'

'Make sure you are.' She gave Hope one final glance in the mirror, and nodded. 'Okay, you'll do. I've got a few calls to make, so why don't you get unpacked? I've put you in Connie's room. It's the one at the front, at the end of the hall.'

After Lana had gone, Hope remained in the bathroom. She was still trying to get accustomed to her new image. Tentatively she ran her fingers over her head, and down the length of her freshly coloured hair. At least the makeover had achieved one positive result: Lana's original antagonism appeared to have slipped into something closer to tolerance. They weren't exactly bosom buddies, but they weren't at loggerheads either. It was a start.

After a while, Hope retrieved her suitcase and made her way along the hall. She entered the room and looked around. It was a decent size, with one large window. The walls were painted cream, and the carpet and curtains were a deep shade of blue. There was a double bed with a pale blue duvet, a dressing table, a chest of drawers and fitted wardrobes. She put down the case and slid open the doors to the closet, almost expecting to see Connie's clothes hanging there, but apart from a few wire hangers, there was nothing.

There was something sad, ominous even, about the empty space. Hope experienced a sudden tingling sensation. She spun around, but no one was there. Nervously, she touched the nape of her neck. Was there such a thing as ghosts? No, it was just her imagination playing tricks. After all, it *was* odd, even slightly surreal, to be standing in the room of a half-sister she'd never known.

She went over to the window, folded her arms across her chest and looked down on the street. She wondered how often Connie had stood here, staring at the very same view. There wasn't much to see, only the shabby houses opposite, a single almost leafless tree and the occasional passer-by. It was a quiet street, or at least it was at this time of day. It might be a different story when the local pubs closed for the night.

She sighed and turned away. What had Connie been like? Flint had told her a little, but not enough for her to have any clear idea. Her eyes alighted on the two framed pictures on the wall opposite the bed. One of the pair she instantly identified as *Forest Bird* by Paul Klee, but the other, although it had similar colours and was in the same geometric style, was unfamiliar. Her heart gave a tiny leap. What if the second one wasn't a print at all, but one of Jeff Tomlin's more ambitious forgeries? She walked over and peered closely, almost pressing her nose against the glass. No, it was definitely a print. Disappointed, she went and sat down on the edge of the bed.

Apart from the two pictures, there were no other personal items in evidence, and maybe even the prints weren't Connie's. The room was rented, so Lana might have chosen them, although Hope couldn't really see Klee as being to her taste. But then she didn't know much about Connie's taste either. All she had to go on were the contents of a small metal box and her own gut instinct.

She stood up again and began to unpack, thinking even as she did so that most of the clothes she'd brought with her would never get an airing. The various shirts and sweaters all seemed too bland, too conservative for the world she'd just entered. Maybe she'd hit the high street tomorrow, see if she could pick up a few items more in keeping with the remodelled version of Hope Randall.

It was getting on for six when Hope heard the front door open and close. She hurried out of the bedroom and along the hall. There was a young woman standing in the living room, peeling off a stylish grey coat. She was small, about five foot two, and was probably in her early twenties. Dark-haired and pretty, she had a Mediterranean look about her, Spanish perhaps, or Greek. As she caught sight of Hope, she smiled.

'Hiya. How's it going? I'm Evelyn.'

'I'm Hope.'

'Just let me deal with this lot,' Evelyn said, reaching into the depths of a capacious leather handbag. 'I won't be a sec.' She went over to the table that stood between the windows. There were two bowls sitting on top, one red and one green, and there was a tiny clatter as she dropped a handful of credit cards into the green one. She reached into her bag again, pulled out half a dozen wallets and put these into the red bowl.

Hope tried not to stare. She was simultaneously shocked and fascinated by the matter-of-fact way Evelyn dealt with the stolen property. Flint had told her what the girls did for a living, but somehow Hope had expected it to be hidden from her.

After a moment, Evelyn turned to her again. 'Lana told us you were coming. You'll be safe here. No one will say anything.' She paused. 'Oh, and I'm really sorry to hear about your mum.'

Hope smiled weakly back. She was uncomfortable at what

99

she'd just witnessed, and on top of that she now felt an additional awkwardness about her mother being brought into it.

Evelyn, mistaking her embarrassment for something more emotional, bit down on her lip. 'Oh, I shouldn't have said anything, should I? I'm always putting my foot in it. Jackie says I should be gagged.'

'No, really,' Hope insisted. And now she felt bad about making Evelyn feel bad. The girl's sweet, open face looked genuinely stricken. 'It's okay, honestly. Don't worry. It's fine.'

'Are you sure?' Evelyn took a few steps forward, swiftly enveloping Hope in a hug. Her thin arms wrapped themselves tightly around her. 'There's no need to be sad. We'll take care of you.'

Hope, who wasn't used to such extravagant displays of emotion, was surprised, even alarmed by the embrace. She felt her body stiffen and had to force herself to relax. 'It's fine, it's fine,' she repeated, patting Evelyn lightly on the back.

After what felt like an eternity, Evelyn eventually let go. She looked up at Hope and smiled again. 'We're going to be friends. I know we are. I'll show you around. Have you ever been to London before? Is there anything you want to see? What do you like doing?'

Hope, if only temporarily, was saved from Evelyn's well-meaning interrogation by the reappearance of Lana. She'd changed out of her suit and was now sporting a pair of casual mauve joggers, trainers and a white T-shirt. 'Hello, love. I thought I heard someone come in. Good day?'

'Not bad,' Evelyn said. 'I've just been saying hi to Hope.'

'That's nice,' Lana said. She wandered over to the bowls and peered inside. Seemingly satisfied with what she saw, she gave a small nod. 'I thought we might get a takeaway, have a quiet night in. It'll give Hope a chance to get to know everyone.'

'Lovely,' Hope said, feeling the nerves begin to flutter in her stomach. Evelyn, she suspected, took people at face value, but the others might not be so trusting. All it would need was a few careless words and her cover would be blown. *Concentrate*, she told herself. *Don't say anything stupid.* If she kept her cool, there was no reason for anyone to disbelieve her story.

But ten minutes later, her worst fears were realised when the second member of the crew arrived. She was a sharp-faced girl in her mid twenties with cropped brown hair and wary blue eyes. Her gaze instantly settled on Hope. It was a far from friendly scrutiny, and Hope felt all her worries resurface.

'This is Jackie,' Evelyn said. 'Jackie Woods.'

Hope shifted on the sofa, and produced one of her brighter smiles. 'Hi there.'

Jackie, who clearly subscribed to Lana's less effusive style of welcome, didn't smile back. Instead she continued to stare at her, a cold, assessing kind of stare. 'So you decided to come, then.' She spoke with a strong Essex accent, and her voice had a hard edge to it.

'Of course she did,' Evelyn said. She was sitting beside Hope, with her bare feet curled under her. 'Why shouldn't she?'

Jackie shrugged her shoulders.

'Don't mind her,' Evelyn said to Hope. 'She's just got the hump 'cause you've got Connie's room. She was after it herself.'

'But I won't be staying for long,' Hope said. 'It's only for a while, nothing permanent. I won't be—'

'How long a while?' Jackie interrupted rudely, as if she couldn't wait to be rid of her.

Lana came into the room and glared at Jackie. 'For as long as she likes. And while she's here, we're all going to make her feel welcome, aren't we?'

Jackie pulled a face, her thin lips twisting. 'God, I was only asking. Nothing wrong with that, is there?'

Hope, not wanting to be the cause of a row on her very first night, tried to calm the waters. She was still attempting to work out whether Jackie's attitude towards her was personal, a kind of instant antipathy, or if she was simply peeved about the room. 'That's okay,' she said, looking over at Jackie. 'Probably just a week or two.' And then, sensing that Jackie wasn't the type to be impressed by anyone who didn't stand up to her, she added rather caustically, 'If that's all right with you.'

Evelyn sniggered.

Jackie gave a grunt, and headed towards the table. 'Whatever.' As her hand reached into her bag, she suddenly paused and looked over her shoulder.

'Oh, don't mind Hope,' Lana said. 'She's seen it all before.'

For the second time that evening, Hope watched as the spoils of the day were emptied into the red and green bowls. She tried to appear nonchalant, as if she was no stranger to such activities, but privately she wondered how it worked. Did the girls get to keep all the cash they lifted, or did Lana take a share? Did the credit cards get pooled? Presumably they were passed on to a third party. Hope glanced over at Lana, who was sitting in one of the armchairs perusing a takeaway menu – a modern-day Fagin trying to decide what kind of noodles to order.

'Are you staying to eat?' Lana said to Jackie. 'I'm going to phone up in a minute.'

'Sure,' Jackie said. She took a seat in the leather armchair closest to Hope. She pulled a pack of cigarettes from her bag, lit one, breathed out a long stream of smoke and immediately started in on the questions. 'So where do you come from, then?'

'Crosby,' Hope said nicely. 'Have you heard of it? It's near Liverpool.' She'd decided it would be wiser not to mention Albersea. If things went wrong (and she didn't want to dwell on what those things might be), there was no point in leaving a trail that would lead straight back to her own doorstep.

'So why do you talk like that?'

'Like what?'

'Well, that's Scouse territory, ain't it? And you ain't no Scouser.'

'She said *near* Liverpool,' Evelyn piped up, 'not in it.'

'Same difference,' Jackie said.

Lana, wary of the direction the exchange was taking, flapped the takeaway menu in the air. 'What's everyone having, then?'

But Jackie wasn't going be so easily distracted. Keeping her gaze on Hope, she said, 'So what's this bother you've got yourself into?'

'None of your business,' Lana said sharply, before Hope could even begin to reply. She tapped the side of her nose with her forefinger. 'Just keep this out of it, right?'

Jackie scowled, and switched her attention to Lana. 'How exactly did you and her mum get to know each other?'

'It was years ago. Fay used to live in London. We worked together. We were mates.'

But Jackie still wasn't satisfied. 'You've never mentioned her before.'

'Why should I? It was a long time ago. We kept in touch but we didn't see much of each other after she went back up north.'

'You've never mentioned *her* either,' Jackie said, jerking her chin towards Hope. 'She turns up here out of the blue, and we're all expected to—'

'It's not out of the bloody blue,' Lana snapped. 'What's wrong with you? I told you last night that she was coming.'

'I meant *before* that.'

'Because it's none of your damn business. And if you don't like it, you don't have to hang around. You know where the door is.'

There was a short, uncomfortable silence.

Jackie leaned forward and crushed out her cigarette in the ashtray. 'No need to bite my head off. I was only saying.'

'Well don't.' Lana pursed her lips, and threw the menu into Jackie's lap. 'Now can you pick something, and quit with all the stupid questions.'

Jackie pulled another of her faces. 'Just showing an interest. Nothing wrong with that, is there?'

Lana stared at her.

Jackie glared back for a moment, but then lowered her head.

Hope was aware of a bristling tension between the two women. She wasn't sure if it was down to her presence in the flat or something else entirely. Perhaps they had other unresolved issues. Well, whatever the cause, she would have to be careful. Jackie was clearly itching for a fight, and she looked like the type who wouldn't fight fair.

Chapter Fourteen

It was another hour before Hope got to meet the last member of Lana's crew. They were just finishing the food, their plates clattering down on the coffee table, when Sharon arrived at the flat. She was laden with grocery shopping, and panting a little from the walk up the stairs.

Lana got to her feet as she came into the room. 'You need to cut back on those fags, love, or you'll be dead before you're forty.'

'Yeah, yeah,' Sharon said dismissively, although not with any obvious irritation.

'You want a brew? I was about to put the kettle on.'

'Nah, I only popped in for a minute. Mick's got the kids so I'd best not hang about.'

Lana, who had bent over to collect the plates, lifted her head and frowned. Her voice had a worried edge. 'I thought he was okay with them.'

Sharon grinned at her. 'It's not the kids I'm worried about. It's Mick. They'll be running rings round the poor bugger by now.'

While this exchange was going on, Hope kept quiet. After

her earlier run-in with Jackie, she wasn't sure what kind of a reception to expect. She threw the woman a few quick glances, trying not to stare. Sharon Blunt was in her late twenties, with short fair hair cut in a bob. Despite the smartness of her clothes, and the designer sunglasses perched on top of her head, she had a decidedly frazzled air about her.

Sharon dumped the bags on the floor and rubbed at her aching arms. 'God, that bleedin' tube. I was stuck on the stinking Central line for over twenty minutes this evening, going absolutely nowhere. Packed solid it was. I could barely breathe. And even when the damn thing did get going again, I ended up next to your friendly neighbourhood pervert. I swear his knob was poking into my hip all the way to Liverpool Street.'

Jackie laughed. 'Don't be so bloody selfish, Sharon. You probably gave him the only thrill he's gonna get this week.'

Sharon laughed too, and then looked over at Hope. 'Hiya,' she said. 'You must be ... er ... '

'Hope,' she said helpfully.

'Sorry, hun. Lana told me, but I'm rubbish at names. Always forgetting. Anyway, nice to meet you. You settling into the madhouse okay?'

'Just about.'

'Well, don't let Jackie here give you any grief. She can be a real cow when she puts her mind to it.'

'Oh, ta very much,' Jackie said.

'It's a pleasure.' Sharon went over to the table and emptied out her handbag, just as the other two had done. She glanced over her shoulder as Lana returned from the kitchen. 'I'm going to leave this lot and run. Are we meeting up tomorrow? I've got to take Aaron to the dentist, so it'll have to be after eleven.'

'How about Victoria,' Lana suggested. 'The bus station at twelve? We could grab something to eat first.'

'Yeah, that sounds good.'

Had Hope not known better, she would have thought she was listening to two friends making arrangements for a pleasant afternoon out. As it was, she was more than aware of what they were actually planning.

Sharon hoisted her handbag back on to her shoulder, and picked up the two bags of groceries. 'You gonna come, Jackie?'

'Sure.'

'What about you, Ev?'

Evelyn gave a tiny shake of her head.

'Ah, come on, it'll be a laugh. I hardly see you these days.'

Evelyn shook her head again. She laced her fingers together, stretched out her arms and then dropped her hands back on to her lap. A low sigh slipped from between her lips. 'No, I don't fancy it. It's not the same without Connie.'

Sharon smiled kindly at her. 'Yeah, I know, hun. But she wouldn't want you to ... you know, be on your own all the time.'

'I'm all right.'

'Well, if you change your mind ...' Sharon was heading for the door when she suddenly stopped and put down the bags again. She rummaged in her handbag, pulled out her purse, took out a twenty-pound note and passed it to Lana. 'Here, this is for Pony. And tell him if he tries to palm me off with the same crap as last week, he'll be sorry he was ever born.' She must have caught Hope looking at her, and guessed it was a dis-approving look, because she laughed and said, 'It's only for a bit of puff, hun. I don't do the hard stuff.'

'Oh, I wasn't ...' Hope tried to shrug it off, pretending that it didn't bother her. At the same time, she made a mental note to try and stop her moral judgements from reaching her face. If she wasn't more careful, she'd give the game away before it had even started.

Sharon laughed. 'Don't worry about it.' And then, with a cheery wave, she was off. 'See y'all. Have a good night.'

As soon as she'd gone, Lana pulled on a pair of thin latex gloves, the type that dentists used, and started sorting out the bowls on the table. She wiped the empty wallets clean of any prints, dropped them into a carrier bag, tied it up and placed it inside another bag. Then she started on the cards, wiping them too before snapping them into piles as efficiently as a croupier. She wrote some figures down on a piece of paper, wrapped elastic bands around the separate piles and slipped the cards into her pocket.

Hope felt a flutter of panic rise into her chest. God, she was sitting in a flat full of stolen property. There could well be drugs on the premises too. What if the police came? How would she explain that she hadn't been involved? Would she be arrested along with the rest of them? She had a horrible vision of being placed in handcuffs and shoved into the back of a car.

'How about you? You up for it?'

Hope glanced over at Jackie, not sure what she was talking about. Her head was still spinning with the kind of scenarios she'd only previously witnessed on TV police dramas. 'I'm sorry?'

'Tomorrow. Are you gonna come with us?'

Hope, caught on the hop, tried to think of a good excuse. Nothing immediately sprang to mind. 'Er ... I don't think ... I wasn't ...'

Lana came to her rescue smartly. 'Give the girl a break, Jackie. She's not here to work.'

'Just thought she might fancy a day out.'

'What she fancies is a bit of peace and quiet.'

'Maybe another time,' Hope said, smiling thinly. Had she been sussed already? Perhaps Jackie had guessed that this was one almighty charade. Even with the revamped hair and the skimpy pink vest, she probably didn't quite pass muster.

'In fact,' Lana continued, 'why don't you show her around, Ev? Take tomorrow off and give her the guided tour. You can introduce her to the joys of Kellston.'

Evelyn, who had hunched down in the corner of the sofa, instantly perked up. 'Oh, okay.' She turned towards Hope, smiling again. 'Would you like to? There's a few good shops round here, and there's the market too. Connie used to like it there. Mind you, that was mainly because—'

'For God's sake, Ev, she doesn't want to hear about Connie,' Jackie snapped.

Hope was surprised by the interjection, and the vehemence with which it was delivered.

Evelyn frowned and shrank back against the cushions. 'Aren't I even allowed to mention her name now?'

'You never stop mentioning it,' Jackie said. 'That's the problem. Every day it's Connie this and Connie that. It gets on my bloody nerves. She's gone, and at some point you're going to have to start accepting it.'

An awkward silence descended on the room. Hope looked over at Jackie, who was busily lighting another cigarette. Was it her imagination or were her hands shaking slightly? She wondered if Jackie's reaction was down to frustration at Evelyn's apparent inability to accept the situation, or if there was a more sinister reason why she didn't want Connie to be discussed.

Hope could feel Lana's eyes boring into her, willing her not to pursue the subject. In truth, the one person she *did* want to hear about was Connie Tomlin, but there was no reason to rush it. Thanks to Lana's intervention, she'd have all day tomorrow to pick Evelyn's brains.

'I was only—' Evelyn began, but any further discussion was interrupted by the ringing of the front doorbell.

'That'll be Pony,' Lana said, glancing at her watch. 'Let him in, will you, Jackie. My feet are killing me.'

Jackie made a huffing noise, her body tensing. For a second she looked as though she was about to object, to ask why *she* was the one who had to do it, but perhaps sensing that she'd already crossed the line once too often with Lana tonight, she obediently got up and trudged downstairs.

A couple of minutes later, she came back with a tall, skinny guy in his early thirties. Hope's immediate response was one of repulsion. He was abnormally pale, with a sly, furtive look about him. She watched as his eyes darted around the room.

'Hey, Pony,' Evelyn said, although not with any enthusiasm.

'Hi, Ev.' He nodded at Lana. 'Lana.'

Hope waited for him to say something to her, but he didn't. It was as if she wasn't there. His eyes seemed to scan over her face without his brain acknowledging her presence. Still, it gave her the opportunity to study him more closely. His skin, slightly clammy in appearance, was the colour of cold porridge, and he was sporting one of those odd faint moustaches on his upper lip. It was hard to tell whether it was some kind of fashion statement or if he just hadn't bothered to shave. He was wearing jeans, battered trainers and a grubby white T-shirt with dark sweat stains under the arms. His long greasy hair was tied back in a ponytail – hence the name, she presumed – and fastened with one of those thin red elastic bands that postmen tended to drop in the street. Hope knew that it wasn't right to judge by appearances, but had she been looking for a suspect for just about anything, Pony would have come at the top of her list.

'This is Hope,' Evelyn said. 'Hope, meet Pony.'

Hope, who'd been more than happy to be ignored, was suddenly the focus of his attention. His small, snake-like eyes stopped moving and she found herself subject to a leering gaze that seemed to slither over every part of her body. She squirmed as he peered intently at her breasts.

'I like your T-shirt,' he said.

Hope forced a smile. 'Thank you.'

'Pink. That's a good colour.'

Hope nodded.

Pony continued to stare at her. 'You're a Scorpio, right?'

'Pardon me?'

'Your birth sign,' he said.

Hope, who had never come across a man who was even the slightest bit interested in astrology, raised her brows. 'Pisces, actually.'

'Oh,' he said, clearly disappointed.

Lana hauled herself up from the armchair and ushered him out of the room. 'Come on, Pony. I need a word. Let's go into the kitchen.'

Obviously there were some transactions that Hope wasn't going to be privy to. She watched them leave, relieved to be free of Pony's attention. Turning to Evelyn she said softly, 'God, what on earth was all that star sign stuff about?'

Evelyn sat forward and grinned. 'Pony's got a thing about Scorpio women. Reckons they're the strongest sign of the Zodiac, that they've got weird powers or something. He asks every woman he meets what sign they are. Connie was a Scorpio. He was always trying to get into her pants.'

Hope remembered the birth certificate she'd found. Yes, of course, the tenth of November. She felt a thin shiver run through her.

Evelyn curled back into the corner of the sofa. Jackie sat down, picked up the remote and turned up the sound on the television.

It was about fifteen minutes before Lana and Pony completed their business and returned to the living room. Pony gave Hope

111

a quick glance, but his interest had obviously dwindled. Lana picked up Jackie's coat and held it out to her. 'Pony's going now. He'll be passing your place, so he can drop you off.'

Jackie didn't seem best pleased. Ignoring the coat, she stared up at Lana. 'You trying to get rid of me or what?'

'I just don't want you walking home on your own, love, not with that nutter on the prowl. It's not safe. And there's no point wasting your cash on cabs.'

'It's safe enough. He's only interested in the girls.'

'Yeah, well, if it's late and dark, he won't know whether—'

Jackie's voice was tight. 'You trying to say that I look like a prozzie?'

Lana raised her eyes to the ceiling. 'For God's sake, do you have to take offence at everything I bloody well say? What's the matter with you? All I'm trying to say is that the streets aren't exactly heaving at the moment. Lots of the girls are too scared to go out. If he's in the mood, and he sees a woman on her own, he might not be too fussy about whether she's doing business or not.'

'I'll take my chances.'

'Suit yourself,' Lana said wearily, placing the coat over the arm of Jackie's chair. 'Only don't come crying to me when the bastard bundles you into the back of his car, breaks half your bleedin' bones and uses you as his personal ashtray.'

Hope flinched at the warning, her eyes growing wide. Flint had mentioned the attacks, but hadn't gone into detail. Christ, what kind of a monster was out there? And what kind of a place had she come to?

Pony, who'd kept quiet until now, did a small restless shuffle with his feet, coughed and glanced at his watch. 'So are you coming, babe, or not? I've gotta make a move. My shift starts at nine.'

Jackie looked at him, and then at Lana. She gave one of her

112

sighs and slowly rose to her feet. 'Okay, if it makes you happy.'

'Thanks, love,' Lana said, giving her a gentle pat on the shoulder. 'And it only makes me happy because I won't have to spend the next half-hour worrying myself to death about you.' She looked over at the sofa, at Evelyn and Hope. 'And that goes for you two as well. I don't want anyone wandering around on their own after dark. Not even down to the shop, right?'

Evelyn murmured her assent. 'Sure.'

Hope gave an obedient nod.

Jackie put on her coat and picked up her bag. She didn't bother saying goodbye. A brief wave of her hand, directed at no one in particular, and she was off.

'See you tomorrow, then,' Lana said, following her out. 'I'll lock up behind you.'

Personally, Hope would have been as nervous getting into a car with Pony as she would have been walking the streets alone, but she presumed he must be safe enough. Lana wouldn't have encouraged Jackie to go with him otherwise. Once the three of them were out of earshot, she turned to Evelyn and said casually, 'So where does Pony work?'

'St Joseph's. It's the local hospital. He does the night shift in the, you know, incineration place.' She pulled a face, wrinkling her nose. 'I wouldn't fancy it. He gets rid of all the nasty stuff, what they cut out in operations and the like.'

Which explained a lot, Hope thought. Pony's extraordinary paleness was probably down to a basic lack of sunlight. He must be spending most of the day asleep. She could see how useful he would be to Lana; he could easily dispose of the stolen wallets, no questions asked. She found herself pondering on what else he could get rid of. How close had he been to Connie? Could he have—' But she quickly pulled herself up. This wasn't the time to start jumping to conclusions. Pony gave her the creeps,

113

but that didn't mean he'd had anything to do with Connie's disappearance.

Hope spent the rest of the evening watching TV. Or at least the other two were watching it. She was simply staring at the screen, at the images sliding across her field of vision. In her head she was trying to figure out what she'd ask Evelyn tomorrow, how she'd turn the conversation round to Connie and how she'd phrase the questions she needed to ask. By half past ten she was finding it a struggle to keep her eyes open. She yawned and put a hand over her mouth. It had been a long day, and it was tiring having to be on her guard all the time. Not that she'd had to make much of an effort over the last few hours. Since Jackie's departure, there'd been little in the way of conversation.

'I think I'll call it a night,' she said, getting to her feet.

'Sweet dreams,' Evelyn said. 'See you in the morning.'

'Night,' Lana said.

At the door, Hope stopped and turned around. 'Oh, does anyone need the bathroom? I thought I'd have a quick shower if that's okay.'

'Course it is,' Lana said. 'You don't need to ask. There's clean towels in the cupboard. Is there anything else you need?'

Hope shook her head. 'No, that's great. Thanks. Good night then.'

In the bathroom, she stood under the strong stream of water, sloughing off the dirt of the city. She'd only been in London since the afternoon, but already the dust had covered every inch of her, filming her skin, creeping between her toes and under her fingernails. And it wasn't just the superficial grime she was trying to wash away. It went deeper than that. Lying to other people, pretending to be someone she wasn't made her feel faintly dirty on the inside too.

Hope dried herself and went back to the bedroom. She pulled on a long, loose T-shirt and sat for a while on the edge of the bed, reviewing the wisdom of her being here. Could she really find out anything useful? Her investigative talents, if indeed she actually possessed any, had never been put to the test before. Her motives for agreeing to Flint's proposition were not entirely clear to her either. Nothing that had happened to Connie had been her fault, and yet she couldn't shake off the feeling that she bore some responsibility for it. It was as if everything in the world had to be balanced out – the security and happiness of her own childhood offset by the bitter harshness of her half-sister's. Some kind of universal counterweight perhaps. Not that her own life had been all sunshine and roses, far from it, but compared to Connie she knew she'd had it easy.

It was a further ten minutes before Hope crawled under the duvet and turned off the bedside lamp. There was a dull, heavy tiredness in her limbs, but her mind wouldn't stop whirring. Connie had lain in this bed too. What had she thought about, dreamed about? Had she been seeing someone, a boyfriend Lana hadn't been aware of? The last night she'd slept here, had she been happy, sad, afraid? Hope sniffed at the pillow, as if some remnant of Connie's scent might linger there, but there was only the faint smell of washing powder.

Not wanting to be in complete darkness, she had left the curtains partly open. A thin orangey glow from the streetlamp outside illuminated the pictures on the wall. Hope lay and stared at the Forest Bird. Its speckled breast was the last thing she was aware of before her eyes closed and she drifted into sleep.

Chapter Fifteen

DI Valerie Middleton strode down the centre of the corridor, the clatter of her heels sounding unnaturally loud in the night-time quietness of the hospital. Her mouth was tight with disappointment. Patti King, the fifth working girl to have been violently assaulted, hadn't been able to tell them anything new. The abduction had followed the same pattern as the rest: an attack from behind, a rag over her face – soaked in something like chloroform – and then removal to another location. There were no obvious clues as to where that place might have been. He must have bundled Patti into a car or a van, but like the four previous victims she could remember nothing more until she'd woken up, blindfolded and gagged, with her hands and feet tied together. And that was when the nightmare had really started . . .

Valerie shuddered as she recalled the broken, battered body of Patti King. Her face and neck had been slashed, one of her breasts almost sliced off, virtually every rib broken. Her body had been covered in cigarette burns. As with all the other girls, the bastard had come about as close to killing her as he could.

But he didn't want them dead, that much was clear. So what did he want? Living witnesses to his handiwork, perhaps.

Valerie cursed under her breath. 'Bloody shit!' As she glanced sideways, she caught her reflection in the glass window of one of the wards. Her hand rose to her head, automatically pushing back the wisps of blonde hair that were falling round her face. She'd left the flat in a hurry and hadn't had time to do anything but pull on her clothes and hastily tie her long hair back in a ponytail. Strictly speaking, she wasn't even on duty tonight, but she had left orders that if Patti King regained consciousness she was to be called immediately. It was always best to talk to the victims as soon as possible, to try and get their first recollections. The call had come just after eleven, when she was about to go to bed.

'So what are you thinking, guv?'

Valerie stopped walking, frowned and turned to her companion. DS Kieran Swann was looking up at her, craning his neck in that exaggerated, irritating way he had, as if he was staring at a giant. She wondered why it was that so many men, even those only marginally shorter than herself, seemed to view her height as a personal insult, some kind of deliberate slight on their own masculinity. It wasn't as if she was even particularly tall, only five foot eight in her stockinged feet, and she rarely wore heels of more than two or three inches.

'I'm thinking we should try again tomorrow. She may have remembered more by then.'

'You reckon?' Swann said, his tone making it clear that he didn't hold out much hope.

Valerie suspected he was right. If the statements of the previous victims were anything to go by, the chances of Patti King giving them an even remotely useful clue were slight. The monster was being too careful. The image of Patti, and her wide, frightened eyes, flashed into her mind again. 'To see the state of

117

her, you'd have thought it was a frenzied attack, wouldn't you, something mad and out of control. But it wasn't. It was slow and cold and calculated.'

Swann nodded. 'Just like the others. It's someone who likes to revel in it, someone who enjoys inflicting pain on women.'

'So we're looking for a man who hates women,' Valerie said. She gave a small, hollow laugh. 'That narrows it down.'

The assaults had begun in February, three in quick succession, the first in Hoxton, the second in Bethnal Green and the third in Kellston. Then there had been a gap of six months before they'd started up again. And now there had been another two attacks, four days apart, and both of them in Kellston. One had occurred around the back of the old car factory – an unpleasant, shadowy place where the girls often took their punters – and the other on a small road that ran off the infamous Albert Street. After their ordeals, lasting three or four hours, the two victims had been left in places public enough for them to be easily found.

'He's got to be local,' Swann said. 'He knows his way around too well, knows exactly where to find the girls, and where it's safe to dump them. And he must have a place to take them, somewhere he's not going to be interrupted.'

Valerie murmured her agreement. What all the victims had been sure of was that they'd been inside when they'd regained consciousness, and that they didn't think they'd travelled very far when the torture had finally been over. Although when you were in that amount of pain, she thought, the concept of time and distance didn't mean much. 'He could live anywhere in the East End, or close to it. Or he could have access to someone else's home. Or to an empty property.'

'He seems to have focused his attentions on Kellston.'

'Maybe it's just provided him with more opportunities recently. Since the attacks started, the girls have been more cautious. They're looking out for each other, taking down the numbers of cars, trying to avoid any unnecessary risks. So he has to drive around until he finds a girl on her own, somewhere dark and lonely where there aren't any witnesses. That area around Albert Street is a maze of little streets and alleyways. Lots of old abandoned buildings too. It's prime hunting ground for a bastard like him.'

Valerie started walking again, inwardly replaying her interview with Patti King. She quickly sifted through the information. What had she learned? Nothing. Absolutely sod all. The poor girl had no idea of where she'd been taken, or whether the man had been young or old. She hadn't seen his face, and his voice had never risen above a whisper. Despite the warmth of the hospital corridor, Valerie shivered. *The Whisperer* – that's what her colleagues were calling him at the station. He liked to taunt his victims with soft remonstrations of hellfire and damnation. And he never seemed angry – that was what all five of the girls had said – always quiet, even mildly apologetic, as if what he was doing was more a matter of duty than pleasure. She felt the hairs on the back of her neck stand on end. There was something horrifying, almost demonic, about a man who could calmly inflict such pain on his victims.

'And why the gap?' she said, thinking aloud. 'He attacks three girls and then suddenly stops. That's not usual. These things tend to escalate. So where's he been for the last six months – working away, in jail?'

'Family commitments? Broken leg? Visiting his sick mum across the other side of the country?'

'An attack of conscience?' she said cynically.

Swann shook his head. 'Why the fuck do they keep working when they *know* he's out there somewhere?'

It was a purely rhetorical question. Swann knew the answer just as she did: most of the girls were addicted to crack, to

119

heroin or crystal meth, and the craving for a fix was greater than any fear for their own safety. Valerie pushed her hands deep into the pockets of her jacket and breathed out a sigh of frustration.

They were heading towards the exit when PC Tom Aitken emerged from one of the side rooms. He was wearing the kind of expression that suggested his interview had been as about as rewarding as theirs.

Valerie smiled at him. 'Problem?'

'I sometimes wonder why we bother.' He jerked his thumb towards the room. 'Kid from the Mansfield. He was brought in a few hours ago when a neighbour found him crawling along the passageway. Someone's had a right go, but he won't say who. Claims he was jumped by a couple of blokes but didn't get a good look at either of them.'

Valerie peered over his shoulder, through the small glass window in the door. A young black man was lying on the bed. She didn't recognise him, although she probably wouldn't have recognised her own brother if he'd sustained the same kind of injuries. One of the boy's eyes was swollen and closed, and the lower left-hand part of his face, along with his chest, was swathed in bandages. He looked like an unfinished Egyptian mummy.

'You got a name?' she asked.

'Tallow. Benjamin Tallow.'

'You're kidding?' she said. Her response wasn't down to the fact that Benjie had got himself in trouble – yet again – but because she hadn't realised he was back in Kellston. He'd moved away more than two years ago and she hadn't heard anything of him since.

'You know him?'

Valerie wasn't surprised that Aitken had never come across the name before. The PC had only been at Cowan Road for ten months. 'Yes, we've nicked him a few times in the past:

120

shoplifting, joyriding, possession. He was probably doing a bit of dealing too, but we never caught him at it. He and his mother went to live up north. I didn't know he'd come back.' She peered through the window again. 'What's the damage?'

'A deep cut from the corner of his mouth to his jaw – it's going to leave one hell of a scar – a couple of broken ribs, and severe bruising and cuts to the upper part of his body. No internal injuries, but that was purely down to good luck.'

'Lovely,' Valerie said. 'I take it you don't believe his story?'

Aitken, a middle-aged copper with over twenty years' experience, gave a brisk shake of his head. 'No, whoever did this was right in front of him. He must have got a good look. And if someone did that to *my* face, I'd be sure to remember theirs.'

Valerie nodded. That Benjie Tallow wasn't prepared to talk hardly qualified as news. When it came to living on the Mansfield Estate, the only thing worse than being dead was being a grass. 'I'll be down here again tomorrow. Maybe I'll pop in and have a word.'

'Could be worth a go, guv. Perhaps you can jog his memory.'

'I'll see what I can do.'

They walked together to the main exit, where the two detectives said goodbye to their uniformed colleague. Aitken was returning to the station, Valerie and Swann to their respective homes. With nothing useful to report, she'd decided that her notes of the interview with Patti King could wait until morning.

'I don't like all this trouble on the Mansfield,' she said to Swann as they strolled across the car park. There was a chill in the air and she turned up the collar of her coat.

'There's always trouble,' he replied glibly.

'Not like this. It's been getting progressively worse over the past few weeks. Six known dealers hospitalised, and God knows how many others that may have been attacked but haven't wanted to report it. Something's going on – I mean something

121

worse than usual. Did you hear what happened to Jimmy Keyes? They found him lying by the gates with his right arm virtually hanging off. Claimed he'd been mugged. Jesus, if that's what muggers are doing these days . . .'

Swann lifted his stocky shoulders in a gesture that might have been indifference or simply resignation. 'You know what that place is like, guv. It's swimming in drugs, and every lowlife wants a piece of the action. It's bound to kick off from time to time.'

But Valerie couldn't be so dismissive about it. She was aware of the opinion among some of her associates that all-out warfare on the Mansfield wasn't such a bad thing. *Leave them to it. Let them kill each other. Who gives a damn if one more scummy dealer gets what's coming to him?* But she couldn't see it that way. There were plenty of decent, law-abiding residents on the estate. They had enough to put up with without being forced to live in a war zone too. And anyway, if you started putting people in boxes, dismissing them all as 'types', then you robbed them of any sense of humanity. Perhaps that made it easier for some coppers, but it didn't sit well with her.

She thought about Benjamin Tallow. He hadn't been a bad sort of kid, at least not when she'd last had any dealings with him. A bit on the cocky side, but nothing nasty or violent. And never any trouble when they'd hauled him in on one minor offence or another. He'd be eighteen or nineteen now. His mother had tried her best to keep him in line, but she'd been fighting a losing battle. What had her name been? Daphne, Delia? Something beginning with D. Valerie could see her face but couldn't bring the name to mind. It annoyed her that she couldn't remember.

Swann tilted his head, craning his neck in that artificial way to look up at her again. He had a faint smirk on his lips. 'You reckon it could be true, then? Are the commies about to take over?'

Valerie knew that he was referring to the rumours about a Russian gangster who was attempting to take control of the area. (Did anyone but Swann still use the term 'commies'?) Andrei Kozlov was the name being bandied around, a rich émigré who already owned a substantial number of properties, bars and clubs in the West End. 'What do *you* think?' she said.

'I think we should have nuked the bastards when we had the chance.' He laughed as he saw her glare at him. 'Only kidding, guv.'

'Glad you find it so amusing.' She was aware of sounding overly censorious, but she didn't have the energy, or even the will, to temper her tone. Her retort had little to do with what Kozlov might or might not be planning. She felt sorry for Benjie Tallow, for what had happened to him, but he wasn't at the top of her list of priorities. There was only one person at the forefront of her mind – a battered, tortured girl, a girl who'd been to hell and back – and she was no closer to finding out who'd attacked her. Frustration was gnawing at her bones.

Swann's only response to her sharpness was a slight shifting of his eyebrows, another of those gestures that she found so annoying. It was as if he was indicating that somehow *she* was the one who had the problem – a bad case of PMT, or man trouble perhaps – and that he was being gracious enough to overlook it.

Valerie felt the urge to snap at him again, to bring him down a peg or two, but she resisted the temptation. Whatever their differences, they still had to work together. She stopped beside her black BMW. 'We need to go through those files again, take a second look. If this guy's local, he has to have some kind of record.'

'No worries,' Swann said breezily. 'I'll get on to it first thing. Drive carefully, guv.'

Valerie got into her car and slammed shut the door. Swann's Vauxhall was parked about ten yards behind her, and she watched him for a moment in her rear-view mirror. He was a stocky, bull-necked man, with small pale eyes and a receding hairline. God, even the way he walked irritated her. Why did she dislike him so much? She suspected that it wasn't just that smirking, slightly condescending way he had of addressing her, or the fact that he viewed anyone with even marginally different views to his own as being in the wrong, but that he'd previously worked under Harry Lind. Deep down, she was worried about being compared and judged. Harry had been a great cop, but she had no desire to live in his shadow for the rest of her working life.

She waited until Swann had driven out of the hospital car park before turning on her engine. As she passed through the gates, she tried to dismiss Harry from her mind. She often found herself thinking about him, his face rushing into her head at the most inopportune of moments. It was almost two years now since they'd split, but they still met up regularly. It was as if a thread ran between them, an invisible bond they hadn't yet been able to cut. Her hands gripped the wheel. Was it because they'd once been good together, because they might yet have a future, or because neither of them could admit to failure?

Valerie's mouth tightened at the corners. She knew she had nothing to feel bad about – the blast that had destroyed Harry's career, and turned his world upside down, wasn't her fault – and yet a nagging guilt remained. Perhaps she hadn't tried hard enough to make the relationship work, had given up too easily. She still couldn't decide if it was circumstances that had torn them apart, or if they were fundamentally incompatible.

As she headed home, Valerie slowly relaxed. The traffic was light, and compared to daylight hours, it was a pleasure to drive through the streets. It was getting on for one by the time she pulled up outside Silverstone Heights, a gated complex of apartments just south of Kellston station. There were some people who thought such places were divisive, that they separated communities, but personally she didn't give a damn about their politically correct opinions. She liked the big, solid cast-iron gates, the numerous locks and alarms, and the sense of protection they provided her with. After a long, hard day battling against every known form of lowlife, the one thing she needed to be sure of was that she was secure in her own home.

She opened the window, inserted her card into the slot and watched as the gates slid smoothly open. She drove around to the car-parking area at the front of her four-storey block, pulled up and killed the engine. Most of the flats were in darkness, but the light from her living room shone out from the top floor. It was a disgraceful waste of electricity, but she hadn't relished the prospect of coming back to a dark and empty flat after her interview with Patti King.

As she recalled the fear on Patti's face, Valerie briefly squeezed shut her eyes before opening them again. She slapped her palms gently against the wheel. All she wanted was to do her job, and do it well. She had to wipe her mind clean of everything but the attacks on the girls. With that lunatic on the loose, she didn't need any distractions. Not Swann. Not Kozlov. And especially not Harry Lind.

She got out of the car and strolled the short distance to the communal front door. The light was on in the foyer and she could see inside to the clean tiled floor, the reproduction art deco walls and the healthy display of potted palms. She was in the process of tapping in the security code when the voice floated over the cool night air. It was a sound so soft, so hushed that it was barely audible.

'Val-er-ie.'

Startled, she turned and looked around. 'Who's there?' Her eyes quickly scanned the surrounding area, the car park, the paths that veered off to left and right and the patch of landscaped green adjacent to the building. She couldn't see anyone. Had she imagined it? Was her mind playing tricks? No, she knew exactly what she'd heard, and she could feel the presence of someone even if she couldn't see them.

For a while there was nothing, and then the voice came once more, soft but distinct. This time it had a more taunting edge. 'Val-er-ie.'

'Who's there?' she called out again. 'Who is it?' She whirled around trying to work out where the voice was coming from, but she couldn't pin it down. Aware that she was standing in the light from the foyer, providing a perfect silhouette and therefore a perfect target, she instinctively stepped into the shadows at the side. The adrenalin had started to pump and her heart was beating faster. She could feel the heavy thump in her chest, the rush of fear that could either impede or improve her reactions. She waited, holding her breath.

Nothing.

Her eyes peered intently into the darkness, whilst her left hand clutched at the phone in her pocket. Whoever was out there could be hunkered down between a couple of cars, or lurking behind one of the trees or bushes. She jumped as a light breeze rustled through the complex, lifting a stray sheet of newspaper and dragging it a few yards across the concrete.

She stood very still, undecided as to what to do next. Call for backup, or get inside as fast as she could? She strained her ears, listening out for any kind of movement. The seconds ticked by – ten, twenty, thirty. Nothing moved. Nothing happened.

She made up her mind.

Quickly, she stepped back to the door, punched in the code and slid into the foyer. She didn't bother with the lift, but took the stairs instead, bounding up them two at a time until she reached the fourth floor. She ran along the corridor, unlocked the door to her flat, slammed it shut behind her and pulled the bolts across. After dashing through the hall, she flicked off the light in the living room, opened the French windows and stepped out on to the balcony.

There was a good view from here, but the scene that lay beneath her was quiet, empty of all human life. Heaving from her rapid ascent of the stairs, she leaned her elbows on the balcony rail and waited for her breathing to slow. Her eyes sought out the shadows, the spaces between the cars, any place someone could hide, but there wasn't so much as a skulking cat. She heard a light cough come from the open window of one of the other flats, and then another, and then silence.

Had it been *him*? Although her stomach shifted at the thought, it was more through anger than fear. He must have known that she'd gone to visit Patti King tonight – and had waited for her to come home. Did he think he could scare her, intimidate her? Or was this just another part of his sick little game.

She tried to work out how he could have got inside the complex, but then it suddenly dawned on her that he might not have been inside at all. From where she was standing, she could see beyond the high perimeter wall, out over the street-lamp-dotted span of Kellston, but what she couldn't see was anyone who might be positioned directly behind the wall. He could have stood there until he'd seen her car pass through the gates, until he heard her car door close, and then . . .

But it was too late to catch him now. Even if her guess was right, he would have scarpered well before her feet had even touched the stairway. For a second she wondered again if she'd imagined it, if that low, sinister voice floating through the night air had only been a product of her imagination. No. She instantly dismissed the idea. The first time she could have misheard, mistaken some sound on the street for her own name, but not the second. Those three soft syllables continued to echo in her ears. *Val-er-ie.*

127

Her hands crept around the rail, her fingers gripping the cold metal. She recalled the board at the police station covered with pictures of the five disfigured women. Their brutal wounds laid bare for everyone to see. 'Fuck you,' she murmured. Then she screwed up her eyes and made a promise to herself: whoever he was, wherever he was, she was going to hunt him down. She was going to make the sick bastard pay for everything he'd done.

Chapter Sixteen

Hope turned her head on the pillow and peered towards the window. Through the gap in the curtains she could see a thin grey light starting to creep across the sky. Good, it was finally morning. She'd had a restless night, waking up every couple of hours, subconsciously alert to the sounds of a place that wasn't home, the unfamiliar creaks, the clicks and ticks and hums.

She heard the shower start to run and realised that the bathroom door opening or closing was probably what had woken her. She guessed it was Lana, getting ready for work. The early-morning rush would be a good time to catch commuters unawares, still drowsy from sleep, their heads full of unfinished dreams, their wits dulled by tiredness or too many drinks the night before. Hope reached out and turned on the lamp. She squinted at the face of the alarm clock: 6.30 a.m. Well, the woman might be a thief, but no one could accuse her of being a lazy one.

Huddling down under the duvet, she decided to stay in bed until after Lana had left. A truce may have been called, but Hope wasn't convinced that it would last. Anyway, she could do without another lecture on what she should or shouldn't say. No, she'd use this time usefully to think through her plans, to calmly figure out how she was going to get Evelyn to talk about Connie.

Despite her good intentions, Hope quickly drifted off to sleep again, and when she next awoke, the flat was silent and the clock said ten past eight. She got up, took another shower, and then applied her make-up, more than she would normally use but less than Lana had inflicted on her yesterday. She jumped a little as she saw the gold-coloured hair in the bathroom mirror; this new reflection would take a bit of getting used to.

Back in the bedroom, she slipped into her faded blue jeans, a white T-shirt and a pair of leather sandals. If they were going to be walking around, she had no intention of crucifying her feet in high heels. Outside, the sky was a bright clear blue, without a cloud in sight. It was going to be a beautiful day. She could only hope that it would be a productive one as well. Glancing at the Forest Bird on the wall, she gave him a nod. 'Wish me luck, then.'

When she entered the kitchen, she found Evelyn already seated at the large oak table. The younger woman was in her dressing gown, a flimsy cream-coloured silk wrap, and was sipping from a mug with her left hand whilst her right was tapping away at a laptop.

'Morning,' Hope said. 'Sorry, were you waiting for the bathroom?'

'No worries. Did you sleep well?'

'Like a log,' Hope lied politely.

Evelyn put down the mug, swept a wave of dark hair from her face and looked at her. 'You know, I can't ever sleep when I'm staying somewhere strange. I spend the whole night tossing and turning. It drives me mad. I keep waking up over and over, thinking that someone's creeping around the room, or hiding in the wardrobe, or standing by the bed with a knife just waiting to ...' As if it had suddenly occurred to her that these admissions might not aid any future nights' sleep, she let the sentence peter into nothing. Her mouth twisted into an uncertain smile.

Hope, not wanting her to feel awkward, gave her a friendly smile back. 'Yeah, I know what you mean. I usually find it difficult too. I guess I must have been tired out with the long train journey and all.' She turned and switched on the kettle, hoping that Evelyn wouldn't realise that it was only a little over two hours from Liverpool – hardly an epic trip. 'Do you want a refill?'

'I'm okay.' Evelyn pointed towards the counter by the sink. 'There's coffee in the perc, though. It's still hot. Help yourself. Or there's tea if you'd prefer. The bags are in the jar.'

'Thanks.' Hope switched off the kettle, then poured out a mug of coffee, inhaling the wonderful deep smell of the crushed beans. Lana certainly didn't stint on the minor luxuries of life.

'So,' she said, nodding towards the laptop. 'Anything interesting?'

'Only Facebook.'

'Ah, right,' Hope said, trying to inject the right level of enthusiasm into her voice. Although most of the population seemed to be on Facebook or Twitter these days, she'd deliberately avoided it. Perhaps she'd read Orwell's *Nineteen Eighty-Four* at an overly impressionable age, but the whole idea of laying bare her thoughts, feelings and opinions for all her acquaintances to read made her feel decidedly uncomfortable. It was, she considered, like inviting Big Brother into the privacy of your own home.

'Hey, shall I add you to my list of friends? That way we can keep in touch when you go.'

Hope shook her head. Admitting that she'd rather walk barefoot over red-hot coals than be on Facebook might not do much for the bonding process, so she rapidly scrabbled about for an excuse. 'Er . . . I'm not actually on it at the moment. I had some trouble so I closed it down. Just a bloke that was causing me grief.'

'Oh, poor you,' Evelyn said sympathetically. 'Was it an ex?'

The image of Alexander Cass instantly sprang into Hope's head. 'Yeah, and a really annoying one at that. You wouldn't believe what a pain he was.' That bit of the story was true at least. She took a sip of her coffee, wondering what he was doing now. Inflicting his charms, no doubt, on some other hapless female. As soon as the thought entered her head, her stomach twisted a little. She knew that she was better off without him, but the hurt remained.

'Men,' Evelyn sighed despairingly, as if she'd had her own share of troubles in that department. She yawned, stretched out her arms and got to her feet. 'Right, I'm off to grab a shower. If you want any breakfast, there's plenty of food in the fridge.'

'Thanks, but I can't handle more than toast and coffee in the morning.'

'Oh, me neither,' Evelyn said. She stopped by the door and looked back. 'Are you okay? Do you need anything else?'

'I'm fine. Go and have your shower.'

'I won't be long.'

'Take your time. There's no rush.'

After Evelyn had left, Hope stood by the window for a while, gazing down at the uninspiring view. The kitchen was at the rear of the flat, overlooking the bleak back gardens of Tanner Road – well, not so much gardens as expanses of cracked concrete and weeds. Most of them were being used as depositories for household junk: old chairs and sofas, broken TV sets, even the odd fridge or two. Whoever occupied the ground-floor flat had made a valiant attempt to impose some order on the wilderness of number forty-six, clearing a patch of ground near the house and filling it with pots of red and white geraniums.

Hope turned away. She glanced idly at the laptop sitting on the table, still logged on to Facebook, and suddenly had one of those light-bulb moments. If Connie had been a member too, she was bound to be on Evelyn's list of friends. And couldn't you access any of your friends' pages from your own? Hope felt a light flutter of excitement. If luck was on her side, she might be able to find out who Connie had been in contact with before she'd gone missing.

She went out into the passageway, checked that the bathroom door was closed and rushed back to the kitchen. If she was going to do this, she'd have to be quick. Fortunately, she had a basic idea of how it all worked. Alexander had shown her his busy page on more than one occasion – opportunities to prove to her how popular he was – and she was glad now that she'd paid attention.

She perused Evelyn's long list of friends until she found Connie's name and her photograph. She paused, transfixed for a moment by the sight of her half-sister's eyes gazing back at her, and then clicked on the thumbnail picture, held her breath and waited. A few seconds later she was connected to Connie's page.

'Yes!' she murmured triumphantly.

The last messages posted were from a few weeks back, mainly from girlfriends leaving messages like *Hi, haven't heard from you in ages* or *How are you doing, babe?* Casual friends, obviously, or they would have known that she was missing. Hope scrolled down to February, to the time that Connie had disappeared. Now the chat was of boyfriends, soaps, shoes and sex. In vain, she searched for anything that could be even remotely useful. Had Connie been seeing anyone? If she had, she'd been keeping quiet about it.

She clicked her tongue in frustration. The minutes were ticking by. It wouldn't be long before Evelyn returned, and the last thing she wanted was to get caught in the act. She frowned as she stared at the screen. Wasn't there something slightly voyeuristic about trawling through all this material, like a peeping Tom sneakily gazing though a bedroom window? But she smartly pushed the thought to the back of her mind. If she wanted the truth, she couldn't afford to be too fussy about the means she used to get it.

She skim-read through another score of messages, more of the same, before her eyes finally alighted on a line from someone called Sally Booth. *Hi Connie. Tried to call you earlier. Eddie wanted to know if you got the vo all right.* She looked at it, bemused, and was still trying to figure out what it meant when she heard the bathroom door open, closely followed by the soft flip-flop sound of Evelyn's slippers as she padded towards the kitchen.

'Damn,' Hope muttered, trying to navigate back to the original site. Her fingers, clumsy with panic, fumbled to find the right keys as the footsteps grew closer. She was sure that she was going to get caught. God, how would she explain what she was doing? Suddenly, more through good luck than good management, she was back on Evelyn's page. She shot up from the chair and went to stand again by the window.

Seconds later, Evelyn came through the door.

'Nice shower?' Hope asked stupidly, convinced that guilt must be written all over her face.

'Yes, thanks.' If Evelyn noticed how shifty she was looking, she didn't comment on it. Instead she picked up her mug, went over to the counter and refilled it from the percolator. 'I just need to get dressed. I'll only be five minutes.'

'That's okay. No rush.'

As soon as she'd gone, Hope breathed out a sigh of relief. She'd got away with it this time, but only by the skin of her teeth. She'd have to be more careful in future. Taking advantage of Evelyn's absence, she plucked her phone from her bag and called Flint.

'Hey,' he said, picking up after a couple of rings. 'How's it going?'

'Early days, but I did find something on Connie's Facebook page. It could be nothing, but it was posted in February, shortly before she disappeared.' She recited the message that Sally Booth had left. 'Did Connie ever mention her? Does it mean anything to you?'

There was a short pause. 'Eddie wanted to know if she'd got *what*?'

'The vo,' she said.

'Spell it for me.'

She did.

'Ah,' he said, as if he finally understood.

'Ah?'

'I'll make a few calls, get back to you later.'

And with that he was gone. Hope stared at the phone, irritated by the abrupt way he'd ended the conversation. Obviously the message had meant something to him, but it wasn't a something he'd been prepared to share. She considered ringing him back, had her finger poised on the redial button, but then decided against it. Evelyn would be back at any moment, and might overhear. She'd had one lucky break this morning – there was no point tempting providence.

Chapter Seventeen

It was getting on for eleven before Hope heard from Flint again. Her phone started to ring as she was standing in one of the tiny changing rooms of a designer clothes shop on the high street, pulling on a dress that she already knew she wasn't going to buy. At over a hundred quid, it was way too expensive for her budget.

'Can you talk?' he said.

Hope kept her voice to a virtual whisper. Although she could hear Evelyn chatting away to the sales girl, she was aware that the two of them were standing only feet away. 'If you're quick. Have you found out something?'

'Yeah,' he said. 'Eddie Booth was an old mate of Jeff's. I thought the name was familiar, but I had to check it out. Sally's his daughter. I managed to get hold of her, and apparently Connie *did* meet up with him in February.'

'And?'

'And that's about it,' he said. 'She's got no idea what they talked about, so if we want to find out, we're going to have to ask him ourselves.'

Hope felt a faint flurry of excitement. Perhaps all the sub-terfuge this morning had been worth it. 'Well, that's okay. We can do that, can't we?'

'There's only one small problem.'

'And that is?'

'He's in the nick.'

Hope felt her heart sink. 'Oh,' she said, disappointed. 'I guess that's the end of that, then.'

'What?'

'Well we can hardly—'

Her reply was interrupted by Evelyn shaking the curtain. 'Hope? Are you ready yet?'

'Almost,' she said. Then she murmured into the phone, 'Look, I've got to go.'

'What are you doing?'

'I'm on the high street with Evelyn. I'll call you back later.' She quickly zipped up the dress and stepped out through the curtains. She disliked these shops where there wasn't a full-length mirror in the changing room – designed, she was sure, so the sales assistant could rush over and lie about how amazing you looked. As it happened, it was Evelyn who smiled and clapped her hands together.

'Wow, you look wicked!'

Hope stared at her reflection in the mirror. Although she rarely wore dresses, she had to admit that this one was pretty special. She twisted to the left and the right, viewing it from all angles. The short black shift, simple in design but beautifully cut, seemed to have been made for her.

'You've got to buy it,' Evelyn said. 'You really have.'

The assistant, a brunette wearing too much shiny red lipstick, offered up an ingratiating smile and chipped in with her own compliment. 'Oh yes, it's a wonderful fit. And you won't find another one like it in a hurry. It's from our *exclusive* range.'

Hope tilted her head as if she was trying to make up her mind. She wasn't about to admit in front of the sales assistant that she couldn't afford it. 'I do like it, but . . . I'm not sure.'

'Have a think,' Evelyn said. 'We can always come back later.'

The brunette, sensing her commission beginning to slip away, made a final attempt to secure a sale. 'Well, I wouldn't think about it for too long. Garments like these do tend to move rather quickly.'

Hope, after a final glance in the mirror, retreated to the changing room and took off the dress. She wished now that she hadn't tried it on. Fingering the soft, light fabric, she wondered if she should go crazy and splash out with her credit card. Every girl needed a little black number – and this one was certainly special. But no, she had to watch the pennies, especially as she wasn't working at the moment. Before she could give in to temptation, she passed the dress through the curtain to Evelyn. 'Could you do me a favour and put this back on the rail.'

'You're not going to buy it, then?'

'When I win the lottery,' Hope sighed.

Evelyn nodded. 'Yeah, I know what you mean. Shame, though.'

Hope pulled on her jeans and T-shirt, one half of her already regretting that she'd let such a perfect dress slip through her fingers, the other half pleased that she'd shown some restraint. Funds were low and she couldn't afford to get into debt. Lloyd was always offering to tide her over, but she didn't want to take his money. He was doing more than enough by letting her live rent-free at the cottage. She wondered how the plans for the gallery were going, and made a mental note to call him that evening.

As she came out of the changing room, Hope was met by the sound of raised voices. A skinny blonde girl in thigh-high boots was raising a stink by the counter, her face pale and tight as she yelled at the assistant.

'You calling me a fuckin' tart?'

'I've told you before, you're not allowed in the shop. Now either you leave quietly or—'

'Or what? You gonna throw me out?'

Evelyn was waiting by the door, her arms folded across her chest. She was staring at the two women in the same mildly interested way she'd stared at the TV last night, as if the incident unfolding before her was simply another scene from one of the soaps.

'What's all that about?' Hope said.

'God knows.' Evelyn gave a tiny shrug of her shoulders. 'Are you ready, then? Let's head over to the market.'

Kellston market, held in a square about two hundred yards from the high street, was crowded with shoppers. It was noisy and alive, buzzing with activity. The brightly coloured stalls, selling just about everything from clothes and food, through CDs, DVDs and phones, to flowers, pans and bargain barbecues, were arranged in a haphazard fashion around the central war memorial. A few down-and-outs lounged on the shallow steps, blearily watching the world go by.

'Mind your bag,' Evelyn said, without any apparent hint of irony. 'This place is full of thieves.'

Hope caught snatches of hip-hop, rap and some old Tamla Motown as they strolled around in the sunshine. She breathed in the various smells that floated through the air: frying onions, hot chilli, curry, herbs and spices. It was a warm September day, the sky completely cloudless, and just for a while she almost forgot why she was there. Evelyn was chattering away, an easy and undemanding companion. Hope, trying to regain some of her focus, wondered when and how she should raise the subject of Connie.

It was as that very thought crossed her mind that she heard

the double bleep informing her that a message had landed in her phone. She slipped it from her pocket and checked the text. It was from Flint. *Can u talk? Where r u?* Stopping by a flower stall, she breathed in the scent of freesias as she sent a response. *NO. Text me. In the market.* She waited, expecting a response – something to do with Eddie Booth, perhaps – but none came. Hope must have been gazing rather earnestly at the phone, because Evelyn glanced over at her and said, 'Is that him?'

'Him?' Hope repeated, her heart missing a beat. Oh no, did Evelyn know about Flint? Had she somehow guessed that the two of them were in cahoots?

'The ex,' Evelyn said, grinning. 'You're staring at that phone as if you'd like to wring its neck.'

'Am I?' Hope said. She laughed with relief as she put the mobile back in her pocket. 'No, it was only, er . . . a friend, a mate of mine who lives in Camden. I was supposed to be meeting up with her on Friday night, but she's not sure if she can make it now.'

'Don't you hate it when people do that?' Evelyn took her arm and smiled sympathetically. 'Never mind. We're going to the pub on Friday. Why don't you come with us?'

'Thanks,' Hope said. 'I might just take you up on that.' She was guiltily aware, even as she spoke, that a part of her was thinking how she could turn the occasion to her advantage. People tended to talk more freely after a few drinks, and if she kept her ears open and asked the right questions, she might find out something useful.

It was a further ten minutes before her phone beeped again. On the pretext that she was looking for a present for an aunt, Hope was happily browsing through a pile of second-hand art books while Evelyn, a few stalls along, rummaged through a selection of cut-price T-shirts. She flipped the phone open and read the message. *Where in the market?* She frowned. What was

the matter with the man? Did he need to know her *every* movement? She'd already said that she'd call him later.

She was about to send a text back when she glanced up and
saw Flint standing by the monument steps. He was less than ten
feet away, looking left and right, his eyes scanning the crowd.
Her mouth fell open. Was he a complete idiot? Evelyn was close
by. What if she saw him, recognised him? She was considering
whether she ought to try and duck out of sight when his gaze
suddenly alighted on her, moved on, came back, faltered for a
moment and finally settled. His mouth broke into a smile. A
few seconds later he was standing beside her.

'Jesus, that's quite a transformation,' he said, staring at her
hair. 'I wasn't sure if it was you at first. It's very—'

'Never mind that,' she hissed. 'What the hell are you doing
here?' She glanced over his shoulder at Evelyn. 'Are you mad?
Do you want her to see you with me?'

'She won't notice, not if you don't draw attention to yourself.
Just keep looking down at the books.'

'What are you doing here?' she said again.

Flint picked up one of the hardbacks, a study of Matisse, and
started leafing through its glossy pages. 'I just wanted to make
sure you were okay.'

'I could have told you that on the phone.'

'It's not the same. People say anything they like on the phone.
You never know, unless you see their face, whether they're
telling the truth or not.'

Hope stared quizzically at him. She wasn't quite sure what he
was getting at. 'Well, you're seeing mine and I'm fine, okay. So
can you go now?'

'Well, there was something else I wanted to run by you.'

Hope looked nervously over his shoulder again. Evelyn was
still rooting through the T-shirts, a couple of chosen items
draped over her left arm. She didn't understand what Flint was

141

doing, it was such an unnecessary risk to take, but she sensed that she wouldn't get rid of him unless she heard him out. 'So tell me. But make it quick.'

Flint, indifferent to her urgency, carefully put the book down and picked up another. 'I've had a chat with Sally Booth. Eddie can see us on Friday, but she'll need to book the visit today. That's what the VO stood for by the way – visiting order. So what do you reckon? It could be our only chance to find out what he said to Connie.'

Hope wasn't overly enamoured of the idea. She'd never been inside a prison before and didn't see any reason to break the habit. 'Why can't Sally ask him?'

'Because she can't get down on a visit for a couple of weeks – she's a single mum with two small kids and the usual childcare problems.'

'What about the phone? He calls her, doesn't he? She could ask him then.'

'Right,' Flint said, a small frown appearing between his cool grey eyes. 'You want her to ask him about Jeff Tomlin over the phone? Eddie would be well pleased about that, especially as half the calls are recorded by the screws. I'm sure they'd be over-joyed to hear what he might have to say about an unsolved murder.'

'Oh,' Hope said, feeling faintly embarrassed by her own ignorance. 'Sorry, I didn't realise.'

'And anyway, she doesn't want to get involved in all this. She's prepared to organise the visit, but that's it.' He neatly slotted the book back into its row. 'So, are you up for it? Do I say yes or what?'

Hope couldn't think of a reasonable excuse for refusing. There wasn't much point in her being here if she wasn't pre-pared to follow up the few leads they had. 'I suppose,' she said reluctantly.

'Good. I'll get back to her, tell her we're on for Friday. I'll give you a bell later and let you know what time we need to meet.'

'Just send me a text.'

Flint raised an eyebrow.

'It's easier that way,' she said. 'It saves me the bother of having to explain who's calling. I don't want to have to lie all the time.'

'As you like.'

Hope could see Evelyn handing over money to the guy at the stall. Flint, however, showed no immediate sign of leaving. 'So was there anything else?' she said, eager to hurry him along.

'I should be the one who's asking you that. Have *you* found out anything else?'

'Give me a break. It's only been twenty-four hours. I'm working on it, but it's not going to help if Evelyn catches me talking to you.' In fact she had found out something – that Lana didn't trust him – but that was a piece of information she wasn't prepared to share.

Flint gave a low laugh. 'Okay, I get the message. I'll see you on Friday.'

'Yeah, see you then.'

She watched him stroll away, in that casual, languid style he had. He was like a cat, she thought, mysterious and unknowable, the kind of creature who only came to you when it wanted something.

A few seconds later Evelyn bounded up, waving a carrier bag and smiling broadly. 'Got some real bargains here,' she said.

'Great. Let's go and have some lunch and you can show me what you bought.'

As they made their way back towards the high street, weaving through the crowd, Hope was thinking about Flint. His sudden appearance had thrown her off balance. She was still feeling agitated, unable to figure out why he'd turned up at the market. But then, she considered, there was a lot about Flint she didn't understand. Perhaps on Friday she could take the opportunity to start changing that.

In the meantime, she had to concentrate on the job in hand. She was here for a reason, and that was to pick Evelyn's brains. She had to find out everything the girl knew about Connie.

Chapter Eighteen

Chris Street, who only fifteen minutes earlier had made the phone call to Mendez reluctantly agreeing to pay the inflated price for the merchandise, was in a less than happy mood. He shot up from his seat, glaring angrily at his brother.

'You did *what*? What's the fuckin' matter with you?'

Danny didn't bat an eyelid. Leaning against the filing cabinet, he pushed his hands into the pockets of his jeans and slowly shook his head. 'Just listen to me, right, before you go off on one. I turn up and that Benjie ain't got a scratch on him. The little scrote just passed it over, didn't he? Didn't even *try* and put up a fight. You want all the others to lie down too? Shit, if that's the way you want it, we won't have any gear left by the end of the week.'

'And the way you're going, we won't have anyone left to sell it. What's the point of putting our own dealers in hospital? You're doing Kozlov's dirty work for him.'

'No,' Terry said softly. 'Danny's got a point.'

Chris turned to look across the office. His father, comparatively sober for once, was sitting forward in the old swivel chair

145

with his elbows on the desk. 'You reckon?' Chris said. 'And what if Benjie talks to the filth? Danny boy here could be looking at a five-stretch, maybe even longer.'

'The kid won't talk,' Terry said. 'He's not that bleedin' stupid.'

But Chris wasn't so sure. Once people thought you were on the way down, that the net was closing in, they were all too eager to start blabbing to Old Bill. You only had to look at what had happened to the Krays to know that.

'Look,' Terry continued, 'if we let Kozlov walk all over us, we can kiss goodbye to this manor and the trade we do on it.'

'Too fuckin' true,' Danny said.

Chris sat down again, glancing warily from one to the other. Usually the two of them were at each other's throats, barely able to exchange a civil word, but a temporary truce appeared to have been established. How long it would last was anyone's guess, but it made a change from the constant bickering. 'So what do you suggest?'

'The obvious,' Terry said. 'First off we make sure our lads have got plenty of protection. Danny here can deal with that. Maybe we even sort out some nice little surprises for Kozlov's goons. And then we find a way to screw the bastard himself.'

'Oh yeah. And how do we do that exactly?'

Terry's thin lips stretched into a smile. 'Don't worry, son. I'm working on it.'

Chris gazed cynically at his father. He reckoned they'd be well buggered before the old man finished figuring that one out, but it wasn't a thought he was about to share. At least if Terry was preoccupied with Kozlov, he wouldn't be stressing about that bitch Kathleen – and that had to be a good thing.

Terry pushed back his chair and got to his feet. 'Get hold of Sol and Greysie,' he said to Danny, 'and get your arses over to the Mansfield. You know what to do.'

'Solomon's on Albert Street,' Chris said. 'The girls are stressing out about this psycho. Half of them won't go out while he's still on the loose.'

'Yeah, well, he can show his face again this evening. I reckon they can manage without him for a few hours.'

Danny made a rapid exit, eager to get on with whatever intimidation might be necessary, but Terry stopped for a moment by the door. He looked back at Chris. 'You think Kozlov might have something to do with all this crap with the girls?'

Chris raised his shoulders in a shrug. Perhaps his father's brains weren't quite as addled as he'd thought. 'It crossed my mind. I mean, it would be a way of keeping them off the streets, but on the other hand ... well, it's a lot of trouble to go to for a few lousy tarts. And it's not as though it's gonna hurt us that much; we do most of our business through the clubs.'

'I guess,' Terry said quietly. 'I wouldn't put it past him, though.' He stood there for a while, gazing blankly into space, before stepping out into the passageway and closing the door behind him.

As soon as Chris was alone again, he opened the drawer and took the letter out. Laying it flat on the desk, he stared down at the cold black print. Jenna had only been gone six weeks, but she'd already put the wheels in motion. He'd read the document three times that morning, but its content had barely sunk in. A divorce. She wanted a fuckin' divorce! And she'd got herself a fancy lawyer to help her screw him into the ground. He snarled at the double-barrelled name on the letterhead. She was probably screwing that pinstriped bastard too, albeit in a more pleasurable fashion.

Picking up the phone, Chris began to dial her number, but then slammed down the receiver. He wasn't prepared to give her the satisfaction. A part of him still wanted her back – they'd been good together, hadn't they? – but he wasn't going to beg. No point wasting his breath. Jenna's desertion, he suspected, had sod all to do with the atmosphere at home, and everything to do with the dwindling resources of the Streets. She'd seen the writing on the wall and decided to get out while there was still a few quid in the pot.

Well, she could go fuck herself! Chris crumpled the letter into a ball and chucked it across the room. It made him feel momentarily better. But seconds later, those niggling voices were whispering in his ear again. If his own wife believed that the Streets were finished, then what the hell was everyone else thinking? Unless they could find a way to stop Kozlov, everything they'd built up, everything they'd worked for, would be history by the end of the year.

Terry Street went through to the main area of Belles, and settled himself at a private table to the side of the stage. This was the place where he'd always done his best thinking, usually with a bottle of Scotch in front of him. He stared at the dancers. Nothing stirred in his groin, not even a flicker. He couldn't work out if that was because he was getting old, or simply because he'd seen it all before.

One of the waitresses, a tall, leggy blonde with oversized tits, scurried over to attend to him. She batted her false eyelashes and simpered. 'Can I get you anything, Mr Street?'

He was about to order a whisky but then changed his mind. If he was going to think through this problem with Kozlov, he had to stay off the hard stuff. 'Yeah, champagne – and get Anja to bring it.'

Her face took on a sulky expression, her mouth turning down at the corners. 'Anja?'

Shit, even the girls didn't have any respect these days. He gave her one of his stoniest looks. 'You got a problem with that?'

'No,' the blonde said.

'So what are you waiting for?'

She paused momentarily, as if trying to think of an answer, and then turned on her white stiletto heels and flounced off to the bar. Terry swore softly under his breath. *Stupid bitch!* He gazed around the room. Even for a lunchtime session, there were too many empty tables. Some of it was down to the current economic climate – those City boys weren't flashing the cash as much as they used to – but most of it was due to the competition. Kozlov had recently opened a new club within half a mile of Belles.

Terry studied the dark red walls, the chrome fixtures and fittings and the array of erotic pictures covering the walls. He stared at the dancers, at their curvy, glistening bodies, and started wondering if the whole place needed a major revamp: something new, something different, to bring the punters in. Perhaps he should pay a visit to Kozlov's joint and check it out.

He was still considering this idea when Anja arrived with the champagne and set the bucket down on the table. She was in her mid twenties, a slim brunette with the bluest eyes he'd ever seen.

'You like some company, Terry?' she said, in her sexy broken accent.

'No,' he said abruptly. And then, looking up at her, his expression quickly softened. 'Not right now, love. Maybe later, yeah? I'll pick you up about seven.'

'Sure,' she said, smiling. 'This would be good.'

Terry liked the way she said *sure*, as if it was a word she'd only recently learned and wanted to show off. Anja was from one of those East European places, Slovakia or Slovenia, something beginning with an S. He hadn't really been paying attention when she'd told him. For him, talking and fucking had never really gone together.

She touched him lightly on the shoulder. 'Later, then.'

He watched her as she walked away, his eyes grazing over her smooth brown thighs. He'd screwed plenty of women and thought nothing of it, but there was something different about Anja. They'd been sleeping together for a few weeks now, but she'd never asked him for anything. She was a good listener too, when he was in the mood for talking.

One thing that she'd told him that Terry did remember, perhaps because it was something he could relate to, was that she had a kid back home, a girl of seven. It set him thinking about his own daughter again, his beautiful Iris. She'd been the same age when Kathleen had taken her away. All that time he'd been forced to stay away from her. It still made him furious!

Terry sighed and automatically touched the thick, brutal scars on his throat. The past refused to let him go. He'd reached that stage in his life where there were more years behind him than in front, and the knowledge made him uneasy. He knocked back the champagne, emptying his glass before quickly refilling it again.

Solomon Vale rolled the black Jaguar E-type on to the Mansfield Estate and parked in front of Haslow House. He didn't have any worries about the car being vandalised. Even if the reputation of the Streets was on the skids, none of the kids were deliberately going to provoke the family. And especially not with Danny around. You only had to look at Danny the wrong way and he'd put a knife in your guts.

He watched as Terry Street's youngest got out of the car, opened the back door and let the dog out. Trojan thumped heavily to the ground, his head flicking from side to side, his brown eyes instantly alert. Solomon hung back for a moment, waiting until Danny had put the lead on. Past experience had taught him to be wary. The bull terrier, squat and solid, wasn't only vicious but unpredictable too. Once the bastard got its teeth into you, it would never let go.

Solomon liked working with the dog about as much as he liked working with Danny. The guy had a screw loose; he was a full-on crackhead, as loony as they came, and twice as dangerous. You could never tell when he was going to go off on one, and when he did, there was no stopping him. One day he'd go too far, and then . . . well, Solomon didn't want to be around to pick up the pieces.

Lizzie Street was the only one who'd been able to control the nutter, and now she was dead and buried. And the Firm was heading in the same direction. They were starting to be squeezed, rival gangs moving in from the west and the south. Hardly a day went by when some mob or other wasn't taking the piss. He'd thought all that would change once Terry got out of the slammer, but if anything it had only got worse. Now they had that piece of foreign shit edging in on them too.

How bloody wrong was that?

When Solomon had been a kid, he'd been in awe of Terry Street. The guy had been a legend. He'd owned the East End and everything in it. He'd strolled around in his fancy suits like some mega movie star, and everyone had worshipped him. But those glory days were over. Terry was all washed up. Sometimes prison did that to a man: dredged out the last bit of spirit and left an empty shell. If it hadn't been for Chris, who'd been good to him over the years, Solomon would have quit months ago.

Greysie pulled up beside the Jag in the dark green Range Rover and gave him a nod. There were six of them inside, all tooled up. Solomon reckoned it was too little too late – they should never have let things get so bad in the first place – but he was still up for a bit of action. At least it made a change from babysitting the whining tarts on Albert Street.

He got out of the car and glanced over at the three tall towers of the Mansfield Estate. Something in his stomach shifted. He'd grown up in one of the damp, stinking flats in Carlton House and wasn't about to forget it in a hurry. If there was one thing that gave him sleepless nights, it was thinking about living in this dump again. At the moment he'd got a nice little pad out Chigwell way, but if he wasn't careful, if he made the wrong choices, then . . .

Solomon tried to blank out this thought as he joined the others in front of the Range Rover. They all knew what they were there for. It was time to make a mark, time to reaffirm their authority over the Mansfield Estate.

A buzz of excitement was running through the group.

Danny looked at them and grinned. 'Okay. We all know what we're doing?'

There was a murmur of assent.

Danny's eyes were as bright and as cruel as his dog's. 'Good,' he said. 'Let's go get the fuckers!'

Chapter Nineteen

Hope picked for a while at her Caesar salad, and then put down her fork and took a sip from her glass of wine. The courtyard of the Speckled Hen was busy, but they'd managed to grab an empty table, shaded by a bright blue umbrella, in the far left-hand corner. She couldn't put it off any longer; it was time to start digging. Looking over at Evelyn, she smiled and said casually, 'So what, er, exactly happened to that other girl who used to live at Lana's? Connie, wasn't it?'

'Yeah. She went away.' Evelyn speared a tiny piece of lettuce and put it in her mouth.

Hope waited for her to continue, but that was the sum total of her response. 'Away?' she prompted gently.

Evelyn gave a small shrug of her slim bare shoulders. 'Mm.'

Hope hesitated, unsure as to how far to press her. Evelyn hadn't stopped chatting all morning, but now she seemed oddly reticent. Should she drop it and try again later? But she might not get another opportunity. 'Oh, you mean she moved out, went to live somewhere else.'

'No, she—' Evelyn stopped abruptly. Her face had become

the newspapers, but with the same tired arguments being bandied around: that the police should come down harder on the girls, inflict harsher punishments and get them off the streets; that they should be tougher on the punters who paid for their services; that a network of legal brothels should be set up where the girls would be safe and protected.

Valerie had no objection to the latter idea, but suspected that it wouldn't work. Most of the toms didn't view prostitution as a career choice – it was simply a means of making some quick money for their next fix or their next drink. They would rather take their chances on the street, go out when and where they wanted to, than have to comply with the rules and regulations of a legalised business.

She sighed, depressed by the line of thought. There would always be prostitution – it was a simple case of supply and demand. So long as men were prepared to buy, there would be women prepared to sell. And the bottom line was always cold hard cash. There was no simple solution and no easy way to change things. Too many of the girls, products of broken homes, broken lives, were caught up in that desperate never-ending cycle of the addict. Their need for a fix would usually outweigh any concerns for their personal safety.

Patti stirred and squinted through half-closed eyes. She peered at Valerie for a moment, as if unsure who she was, then, as it all came back to her again, she gave a low groan and turned her head away.

Valerie saw the cluster of cigarette burns on her neck and instinctively flinched. She knew her presence wasn't welcome, but she also knew that it was necessary. If they were going to catch the bastard, the sadist who was doing these things, she needed every bit of information she could gather. Patti might not want to talk, might not want to remember, but she had to try and make her.

So far Valerie had established that, like the other victims, she'd been held inside a building, that the flooring had been cool and smooth, like lino rather than carpet, and that while the torture had proceeded there'd been music playing. All the others had said that too, although no one had been able to recognise what it was. Something religious, a kind of chanting, was the best description she'd had to date. Had it been used to disguise other noises, sounds that might betray the location, or was it simply part of his ritual?

Leaning in, Valerie kept her voice low. 'Can you remember anything he said to you, Patti? Anything at all?'

A visible shudder ran through the girl. She slowly turned her face to look at Valerie again. 'That I was damned,' she murmured. 'That I'd made God angry. He kept saying he was sorry, telling me we ... we had to beg for God's forgiveness, that he was doing all this for me.' Her tongue slipped out to dampen her dry lips. 'He made me get down on my knees. Said I'd rot in hell. Said he'd cut my throat if I talked to anyone.' As if he might be lurking somewhere in the room, she lifted herself from the pillows and looked frantically around.

Valerie laid a hand gently on her arm. 'It's okay. You're okay. You're safe now.' Even as she uttered the words, she was aware of their emptiness. Patti, she was sure, would never feel safe again. 'Look, I know this isn't easy for you, but can you remember anything about his voice, his accent – was it local, northern, foreign? Was it old, young?'

'I couldn't ... he didn't ... didn't speak out loud. Not ever. He only ever whispered.'

She knew that none of the girls had seen the man's face – they'd all been blindfolded –so any kind of physical description was out of the question. 'What about smell? Was there anything distinctive? Aftershave, deodorant, sweat?'

Patti thought about this for a while. 'I dunno,' she said eventually. 'Maybe something. Like ... like disinfectant?'

165

Chapter Twenty-one

Valerie pushed through the double doors, walked smartly down a flight of stairs and into the hospital canteen. It was almost two o'clock and the lunchtime rush was over. Swann was sitting at an otherwise empty table in the centre of the room. He was eating a portion of what looked like shepherd's pie, relentlessly shovelling it into his mouth whilst simultaneously reading a copy of the *Sun*.

He glanced up as she approached, and nodded. 'Guv.'

Valerie pulled out a chair and sat down opposite him. She tried not to stare at the food, at the brown sludge that was congealing on the outer edges of the plate. Spending the last twenty-odd minutes gazing at Patti's injuries hadn't done much for her appetite. She felt a wave of nausea rise up from her stomach. After a few seconds it passed, leaving only a bad taste in her mouth. There was a half-full plastic cup of Coke on the table and she reached out for it. 'Do you mind?'

'Help yourself.'

Valerie took a few grateful swigs and waited for her stomach to settle. 'Thanks,' she said, putting the cup back down on the

Chapter Twenty-three

It was Friday, three days since Hope had come to London. She took one last look in the mirror. After spending the last half-hour trying on different outfits – just what did a girl wear for her first prison visit? – she had finally settled on beige linen trousers, a crisp white shirt and a pair of fancy high heels that she'd borrowed off Evelyn. The shoes were a tad tight but she reckoned she could manage for a few hours; it wasn't as if she'd be doing much walking. Around her neck was a heavy gold chain that was also on loan.

She had told Evelyn that she was meeting an old friend for lunch, but had come clean to Lana. They'd been alone in the kitchen, and Lana had slowly shaken her head, raising her eyes to the heavens as if the very idea was beyond ridiculous.

'So who exactly is this Eddie geezer?'

'Someone who used to know Jeff Tomlin. Connie went to see him. I think he may have told her something.'

'Connie went to see lots of people, love, and most of them were wasters. Blokes in jail . . . well, they get bored, frustrated. A pretty girl comes along, gives 'em some attention and they'll tell her whatever she wants to hear.'

'You think?'

'I *know*. Whatever this guy says, I wouldn't take it too seriously.'

Hope sighed at her reflection. Maybe Lana had a point, but the arrangements had been made. She glanced at her watch. It was ten to twelve. She was due to meet Flint on the corner of Tanner Road at midday.

By the time she got there, with five minutes to spare, Flint's Audi was already parked up outside the shop. He was flicking through an early copy of the *Evening Standard*, and put the paper down as she opened the door and got into the car.

'Oh, nice bling,' he said, and laughed.

Hope self-consciously fingered the chain around her neck. She'd been in two minds as to whether to accept when Evelyn had offered to lend it to her. It wasn't the type of thing she'd normally wear, but then prison wasn't the type of place she'd normally be going. 'Should I take it off? Do you think it's too much?'

'No,' he said, grinning. 'It's perfect. You'll fit right in.'

Hope gave him a look as she pulled on her seat belt. She knew that he was only winding her up, but there was something about him, about his whole persona, that made her feel oddly defensive. Sitting back, she folded her arms across her chest. 'Glad to see it amuses you so much.'

He grinned again, started up the engine and pulled away from the kerb. As they headed towards the high street, he turned briefly to look at her. 'Just relax, will you. You're only going on a visit. They're not going to keep you there.'

But Hope couldn't relax. She'd been out of her comfort zone for the past few days, and now it was about to get even worse. She had no idea what she'd say to Eddie Booth, and could only hope that Flint would do most of the talking. A part of her wanted to share her anxieties, but a greater part was too proud

182

to admit it. She wanted to know what it would be like to go into a prison, what the procedure was, but couldn't bring herself to ask. Instead she settled on a blander question.

'So where are we going, then?'

'HMP Maybourne,' he said. 'It's in Essex. Depending on the traffic, it shouldn't take more than an hour or so. You did bring some ID, didn't you?'

'I've got my driving licence.'

'Good.'

Hope shifted in her seat. There was one question that she simply had to ask. 'So this Eddie Booth, what's he inside for?'

'Does it matter?'

'It might, and anyway, I'm curious. It's no big secret, is it?'

Flint left a short pause before replying. 'Armed robbery, a bank job in Surrey. He's doing a twelve-stretch. Should be out in three or four years.'

'Ah,' she murmured. She had a sudden vision of men in balaclavas, wielding shotguns and screaming at people to lie down. Still, she supposed it was marginally better than him being a murderer or a rapist.

'But don't worry,' Flint said, 'they don't let him bring his gun out on visits.'

Hope smiled tightly. 'Jeff Tomlin certainly had some interesting friends.'

'Well, I was one of them, so I guess I can't argue with that. As it happens, I've never met Eddie myself, but I've heard he's okay. Your dad was the kind of guy who had an open mind. He always judged people on what they were rather than what they did.'

'You don't think those two things are connected, then?'

'Not necessarily. Your dad always said that—'

'And I don't think of him as my father,' Hope interrupted sharply, not wanting to know what Jeff Tomlin might or might

183

not have been in the habit of saying. He had been the type of bloke, she imagined, who was overly fond of justifying his own bad behaviour. 'Can you stop calling him that? Lloyd Randall was the man who made a home for us, who brought me up. Tomlin had nothing to do with it.'

Flint gave a small grunt, a noise that was probably meant to imply that Lloyd hadn't made much of a job of it.

Hope stared at him. 'What?'

'Nothing. I didn't say a word.' He was silent for a few seconds, then he added, 'Only, that wasn't the way Jeff wanted it to be. Fay kept him away from you. He tried. He really did. He wanted to be a proper father.'

Hope frowned and turned her face away. She didn't want to open that can of worms again. Her mother had said that Tomlin had callously abandoned them both, and of that single truth she was absolutely certain.

Flint tapped his fingers lightly against the wheel. 'I used to know a pimp called Randall, Bobby Randall. He was a nasty piece of work. Any relation, do you think?'

Hope didn't bother to reply.

Fifty minutes later, most of which had been spent in silence, Hope found herself gazing through the windscreen at the scenery unfolding before her. When she thought of Essex, it was usually of built-up areas like Ilford or Dagenham; she'd never really connected it to the countryside. But all around were fields, trees and open blue sky. They were driving, rather quickly, along a narrow, twisting lane with ditches on either side. Soon they passed through a village, a cluster of houses with a garage and a pub.

Hope hadn't noticed a station or even a bus stop in the last mile or so. 'I wonder how Connie got here.'

'I think I know the answer to that. Last February she asked if she could borrow the car, said she had to see someone out of town. I'm presuming this is where she came.'

Flint slowed the Audi as they came up behind a young woman on a horse. He swung carefully around the animal and its rider, and once there was a bit of distance between them, accelerated again. 'Not far now.'

Hope found herself pondering on how Connie must have felt as she approached the prison. Anxious, or excited? Perhaps a bit of both. 'Did you ever wonder if it was the right thing to do? Helping her, I mean.'

'You reckon I shouldn't have encouraged her?'

Hope looked at him, but he was wearing a pair of Ray-Bans and she couldn't see the expression in his eyes. 'I just . . . well, it all happened so long ago. There can't have been much chance of her discovering anything new. From what you said, even the police didn't get very far with the investigation.'

'Maybe not, but she had to try.' Flint paused. 'She was that type of person.'

Unlike herself, Hope thought. Wasn't that what he meant? Connie had been driven, determined, single-minded in her quest for the truth, whereas he reckoned *she* was only here out of some dull and stolid sense of responsibility. Except that wasn't true. At least, not any more. She couldn't claim to care that much about Jeff Tomlin's fate – it was shocking, but it didn't really touch her – but she *did* care about Connie's.

'What do you think she wanted to achieve?' Hope asked. 'Was it some kind of resolution, or was it revenge?'

'A bit of both, I suppose. Jeff's murder turned her life upside down. It destroyed Sadie, destroyed the whole family. She wanted to know why, to understand why it had happened. Perhaps that was the only way she'd ever be able to move on.'

Hope wondered how she'd have coped if the same thing had happened to her, but somehow it was hard to connect the terrible act of murder with the quiet, respectable streets of Albersea. 'Do you have any family?' she asked.

Flint kept his eyes firmly fixed on the road. 'No,' he said.

'No one at all?'

He hesitated. 'I had an older brother, Paul, but he was killed in a car crash when I was eighteen.'

'Oh, I'm sorry.'

Flint gave a slight shrug of his shoulders, but his face was tight and drawn. 'It was a long time ago.'

Hope waited, but he didn't go on. Feeling awkward at having raised the subject, she quickly changed tack. 'Evelyn mentioned something to me on Wednesday. Apparently Lana and Connie had a big fight the night before she disappeared.'

Flint gave her an interested glance. 'Really?'

Hope went on to repeat what she'd been told. 'I don't suppose it's that important. Lana's never tried to hide the fact that she wasn't happy about what Connie was doing. I think they had words on more than one occasion.'

'Yeah, but Lana never mentioned that particular row.'

'Jackie seems a bit on the jumpy side too. She certainly didn't want Evelyn talking to me about Connie.'

'You think she knows more than she's saying?'

Hope mulled it over for a few seconds. 'Hard to tell. She doesn't seem very happy about my being there, but I'm not sure if that's anything to do with Connie.'

Flint grinned. 'Just your endearing personality, huh?'

Hope pulled a face, although she was secretly glad that he'd gone into teasing mode again. 'At least I managed to find out something useful – and within twenty-four hours. How long have you been sniffing around?'

Temporarily distracted by the exchange, Flint missed the entrance to the jail, and had to brake sharply and reverse. 'Damn,' he murmured.

186

They were quiet as they wound the length of the twisting driveway. Hope was surprised by the building that appeared at the end of it. She'd been expecting the prison to be grim, even faintly Dickensian, but it was in fact a modern red-brick construction that, had it been stripped of its barbed wire, could have passed for a rather bland block of flats. There were a couple of car parks, a large one for the staff on the left, a smaller one for visitors on the right. Flint pulled the Audi into the latter and switched off the engine.

Hope undid her seat belt, feeling the butterflies start to flutter in her stomach. 'Do you really think Eddie Booth's going to tell us anything useful?'

Flint, keeping his hands on the wheel, slowly turned his head to look at her. 'Er ... about that "us". There's something I should have mentioned earlier. Eddie's not too keen on talking to me. In fact he isn't going to. Sally says the only person he'll speak to is you.'

Hope's jaw dropped open. She glared at him. 'What?'

'He doesn't see it as being any of my business.'

'But that's ridiculous.' She shook her head, feeling a wave of apprehension start to roll through her body. 'No. No way.'

Flint briefly lifted his hands from the wheel, and then dropped them again. 'I know it's not ideal, but—'

'But nothing,' she said. 'I'm not going in there on my own.'

'Connie did.'

She shot him a withering glance. 'Well, I'm not Connie.'

Flint raised his brows. 'Right. So I guess we've had a wasted journey.'

'And whose fault is that? If you'd been honest with me before we started off—'

'You'd have refused to come.'

'Exactly.'

'But now we're here,' he said, 'why waste the opportunity?

187

I'm sorry, I should have been straight with you, but I knew how you'd react. And this is the only lead we've got. It could be the best we'll ever get. It's only a prison, Hope. Nothing bad's going to happen to you. And if you do feel uncomfortable, you can get up and leave at any time.'

Hope wasn't just feeling anxious, but angry too. Flint had deliberately avoided telling her the truth, and she didn't like being manipulated. 'For God's sake,' she said. 'I'm only going to come out and repeat what he's said, so you may as well be there when he says it.'

Flint reached into the pocket of his shirt and took out a slip of yellow paper. 'I know, but I'm not on the visiting order, so that option isn't open to us.'

She stared at the piece of paper, at the single name written on it – her own.

'I'm only guessing here,' he said, 'but if Eddie's insisting on seeing you alone, then it's probably because he doesn't want to compromise himself. If he does have information about Jeff, there's a difference between telling you, his daughter, and telling a complete stranger. You're family and I'm not. What you choose to do with that information is down to you, and he can't be held responsible if you decide to pass it on. It may sound like a dubious distinction, but it's the way it works in his world.'

Hope didn't reply. She could, despite herself, see a bizarre kind of logic to the argument. It was a way of Eddie distancing himself. For a while she sat and stared through the windscreen at the officers coming and going from the main door of the prison. She knew it would be ludicrous to turn around and go home now.

She had to do it.

Snatching the VO from Flint's hand, she got out of the car, slamming the door hard behind her. She would have stormed off if she'd had any idea of where to go. Instead, she folded her arms and glared bleakly at the ground. She knew she was behaving irrationally – it was only a prison, not a lion's den – but a dark, tumultuous feeling was starting to brew inside her. Her reluctance to go through with this visit wasn't because she'd never been inside a jail before, wasn't even because Eddie Booth was a convicted armed robber, but because she sensed he would reveal something important – and she had no desire to be alone when she heard it.

Chapter Twenty-four

As Hope went through the indignities of the search procedure –
the metal detector, the patting down, the drugs dog sniffing
enthusiastically at her private parts – she tried her best to dis-
connect herself from what was going on. The whole process was
uncomfortable, not just because it was intrusive, but also
because it made her feel she must be guilty of *something*, even if
she didn't know exactly what it was.

Eventually she was cleared and allowed into the visiting
room. It was then that she hit her next problem. The inmates,
about twenty in total, were already seated at the tables, and she
had no idea which one of them was Eddie. She paused, making
a quick scan of their faces, eliminating the ones who already had
company, were too young, or were black or Asian. That left
three men, and of these, only one was still staring at her.

It had to be him.

Just her luck, she thought, smiling faintly as she made her
way across the room. Eddie Booth was in his late fifties, a great
bull of a man with massive shoulders and a neck the size of a
tree trunk. His head was completely bald, revealing the tattoo of

a lion above his right ear. As she got closer, she nervously took in his wide fleshy lips and pale suspicious eyes. She couldn't help but reflect that he was the kind of bloke you wouldn't want to meet down a brightly lit high street, never mind a dark alley.

'Mr Booth?' she said tentatively, when she finally reached him.

He nodded, getting to his feet. He wasn't that much taller than her, only three or four inches, but his body was as wide and as solid as a ten-ton truck.

'Hope Randall,' she said, putting out her hand. 'Thanks for seeing me.'

Eddie squeezed her fingers with rather more pressure than was strictly necessary. 'So you're Connie's sister.' His voice was deep, almost gruff, and the accent was pure London.

'That's right.'

He sat down again, gesturing for her to take a seat too.

Hope hesitated, unsure as to which to choose. There were four chairs arranged around a low circular table, and she was tempted to take the one directly opposite him – thereby putting the greatest possible distance between them – but decided that this would mean her having to talk a little louder than she wanted to. Instead, she sat down directly to his right, crossed her legs and tried to appear as if visiting an armed robber was a normal occurrence in her life, a situation she felt perfectly at ease with.

'So what are you after, love?' he said.

Hope, taken aback by his bluntness, took a quick breath. 'Well, Connie's gone missing, she's not been in touch with anyone for months, and we're . . . I'm worried about her.'

'Yeah, Sal mentioned it.'

'It was last February, not long after she came to see you.'

Eddie's eyes instantly narrowed to two thin slits. 'What are you saying?' he growled. 'You think I had summat to do with it?'

191

'No, no, of course not.' Oh great, she'd managed to antago-
nise him within the very first minute. 'It's not like that at all. I
didn't ... I wasn't ... I just hoped that you might be able to
help, you know, give me some clue as to what she was thinking.
I certainly didn't ... no, not in the slightest. I promise.'

While he was listening to this somewhat rambling explanation, Eddie had been staring fiercely at her face. 'You don't look
like her.'

'We're half-sisters,' Hope said, thinking that the change of
hair colour was more of a hindrance than a help at this particular moment. 'Same father, different mothers.'

'How do I know?' he said.

'I'm sorry?'

'How do I know that you're who you say you are?'

Hope, who hadn't even considered this situation arising,
gazed blankly back at him. 'Who else would I be?'

'You could be anyone, love. One of them reporters after a
juicy story. A nark. Old Bill, even. Yeah, one of them cold-case
coppers looking for a lead on an old murder.'

She frowned and shook her head. 'I'm not. And I had to show
ID when I booked in.' Unfortunately, her bag, with her driving
licence and bank cards, was now sitting in a prison locker.

'Anyone can get fake ID.' He jerked his chin towards the
prison officers standing by the door. 'Those muppets wouldn't
know the difference. And anyway, if you *are* a copper—'

'I'm not,' she insisted again.

Eddie's cold, intimidating eyes continued to bore into her.
Hope, feeling increasingly uneasy, shifted in her seat. What the
hell was she supposed to do now? Simultaneously alarmed and
exasperated, she threw up her hands. 'Look, I can't prove a neg-
ative, can I? I can't prove who I'm not, any more than I can
prove who I am. Why did you even agree to see me, if you
thought you were being set up?'

'Christ, no need to bite me 'ead off,' he said indignantly, as if he was the injured party in this whole affair. 'Got to ask, ain't I? Some geezer calls up my Sal out of the blue, says he's a mate of Connie Tomlin's and can her sister come and see me. Says it's important, says the girl's disappeared. Now I don't know this Flint bloke from Adam, so what am I supposed to think?'

It suddenly occurred to Hope that Eddie would have checked Flint out, made some calls – or got his daughter to make them – before agreeing to see her. And Flint must have got the thumbs-up from someone, or she wouldn't be here. So why the wind-up? She remembered what Lana had said that morning. Perhaps Eddie was just entertaining himself. Perhaps he knew nothing. And perhaps nothing was precisely what he'd told Connie.

'So where does that leave us?' she said. 'Do you want me to go?' In truth, she was hoping he'd say yes. She was afraid of Eddie Booth, didn't trust him, and it would give her the excuse she needed to get away.

But Eddie leaned forward, his big hands splayed out across his thighs. 'I didn't say that, love. Just need to watch me back, don't I? A man in my position can't be too careful.' A small smile – it was impossible to tell how genuine it was – hovered at the edges of his mouth. 'How come Connie came to see me on her own? Back then, I mean. Why didn't you come with her?'

Hope hesitated, reluctant to reveal her family history to a complete stranger, but decided there was no other choice but to be honest with him. Anyway, there was every chance he already knew the answer. 'Because I didn't even know she existed until recently. I didn't know about Jeff Tomlin's death either. I didn't ... I didn't have any contact with him while I was grow-ing up.'

Eddie continued to keep his gaze fixed firmly on her. 'So

you're Fay's daughter,' he said eventually. He made a sound that was halfway between a grunt and a laugh. 'That figures.'

It didn't take a genius to grasp that the remark wasn't meant as a compliment. Hope frowned back. She could have asked him what he meant, but decided not to go there. She probably wouldn't care for the answer. 'I didn't realise you knew her.'

'Yeah, I knew her all right.' He paused, the tip of his tongue snaking out to dampen his lips. 'The lovely Fay Weller. Let's face it, she ain't the kind of broad you forget in a hurry.'

It was a long time since Hope had heard her mother's maiden name – or, come to that, anyone refer to a woman as a broad. Eddie was clearly a man who held on to old habits. 'I suppose not,' she said. For better or worse, her mother had always aroused strong emotions in people. She'd been beautiful, bright and shining, but strong-willed and provocative too.

'So how's she doing these days?'

Hope opened her mouth, intending to tell him, but the words stuck in her throat. Even after six months, she still found it hard to say the words out loud. She had a sudden image of her mother, small and shrunken, lying in the hospital bed. By then the cancer had almost gained its victory, and those wide blue eyes, once so full of life, had been filled with a gruesome bewilderment. The vision, so stark and cold and final, continued to haunt her dreams.

'Managed to nab herself a rich husband, did she?'

Hope thought of Lloyd, but she didn't reply.

Another man, a more intuitive one, might have noticed her discomfort, but Eddie was hardly the sensitive sort. Oblivious to the emotions that were raging inside her, he carried on regardless. 'Christ, the last time I saw you, you couldn't even walk. Hoxton it were. The Corner Caff. Yeah, your old man brought you in. Pleased as fuckin' Punch he was, showing you off like you was the first baby to ever grace this bleedin' earth.'

He sniggered, amused by his own remark, then slapped his hands against his thighs. His face took on a lascivious look, his eyes shifting down to glance quite blatantly at her breasts. 'You've grown a bit since then, huh?'

But Hope knew that his memory was playing tricks. Jeff Tomlin had never set eyes on his first-born daughter. 'That wasn't me. It must have been Connie.'

He shook his head. 'Nah, it was definitely you, love. That was the same year my Sal was born. Aint gonna forget that, am I?'

Hope couldn't see any point in getting into an argument, so she simply smiled and let it pass. Now that Eddie seemed to have accepted her for who she was, she wanted to move on, to get this ordeal over with. The sooner she could get out of here, the better. 'So, about Connie's visit . . . '

'You got any cash on you?' he said.

Hope stared at him, the light suddenly dawning. So that was his game. Information in return for money. She should have guessed. Men like Eddie Booth didn't do anything for nothing. There was probably someone waiting outside, a collaborator ready to pick up the payment when she left the jail. 'I see,' she said coldly. 'How much do you want?'

Eddie shifted in his seat. His gaze slid swiftly towards the guards by the door, as if even from that distance they might have heard something. When he didn't immediately reply, Hope carried on. She was intimidated by him, but the outrage growing inside her was greater than her fear. 'I don't know what the going rate is for information about a murdered father. You'll have to help me out. How much did Connie pay you?'

Eddie glared at her for a moment. Then he moved forward and put his face very close to hers. She wanted to pull back, but was aware that he'd view it as a sign of weakness. She could smell his breath, a faint scent of spearmint along with the more distinctive whiff of tobacco. 'Yeah, cold hard cash,' he said. And then, very slowly, articulating each word with care, he added, 'For a cup of fuckin' tea.'

What? The blood rushed into Hope's cheeks. Mortified by her mistake, she lifted her hands to cover her face. Oh Jesus, what had she done now! She'd completely blown it. With a sinking heart, she recalled the prison officer at reception telling her that she'd have to leave her bag in a locker but could take up to ten quid in change for refreshments. She had six pound coins in her back pocket. 'Oh,' she eventually managed to stutter out. 'I'm so sorry. I thought—'

'You thought I was a bleedin' extortionist.'

Hope wished the ground would open up and swallow her. 'No ... yes ... I mean ... '

And then, amazingly, Eddie started to laugh. 'Shit,' he said. 'Do you really reckon ... God, are all you Tomlins completely fuckin' nuts?'

Hope, bemused by his reaction, dropped her hands and gave him a feeble smile. She'd been expecting him to get mad, to ask her to go, but instead he was behaving like it was the biggest joke he'd heard in ages.

Eddie shook his head, grinning widely. 'Look, love, my mouth feels like a camel's arse. Get us a brew – milk, three sugars, and then we'll have that chat about your dad.'

Hope, her face still a bright shade of scarlet, didn't need to be asked twice. Before he could change his mind, she quickly jumped to her feet and made her way towards the counter. Feeling almost crippled by shame and embarrassment, she joined the short queue and waited to be served. How could she have been so stupid? But the answer to that was easy. Despite Flint's positive reference, she'd been ready to think the worst of Eddie Booth before she'd even stepped through the prison door.

While she was standing in the queue, she sneaked a look around. Some couples leaned in eagerly towards each other;

196

others weren't quite so intimate. The hum of conversation filled the air, but there was a tension, too, like a string pulled tight and about to snap. A couple of prison officers strolled between the tables, keys jangling on their belts, their eyes forever watchful. There were no windows in the visiting room and the only light came from a couple of long fluorescent tubes. She was aware of a depressing heaviness descending on her, of the walls slowly closing in.

A couple of minutes later, Hope put the teas and a few bars of chocolate down on the table. She'd been practising her apology as she came back across the room. 'I'm really sorry about before. I shouldn't have, erm, jumped to conclusions.'

'Let's forget it, yeah. Unless you want to accuse me of somethin' else?'

'No, of course not,' Hope said swiftly. She sank down into her seat. 'Thank you.'

Eddie picked up the plastic cup by its rim and took a large slurp of tea. 'Okay, you want to know what I said to Connie. Well, the first thing I told her was this – I ain't got a clue who topped your old man.'

It was hardly a startling revelation, but as he appeared to be waiting for a response, Hope nodded. 'Okay.'

Eddie drank some more tea. 'You know what he was into, right?'

'He was an artist,' she said.

He looked at her.

'A forger,' she added.

'Yeah.'

Again there was a pause, as if Eddie was in two minds whether to proceed. Hope kept her mouth shut, not wanting to say anything that might discourage him from continuing. She'd made enough mistakes for one day. After a while he heaved out a sigh, and his large hands splayed out on his thighs again.

'Well, he was working with someone. The two of them were in business together. Don't ask me what the deal was, 'cause it ain't my place to say. I only told that sister of yours 'cause I reckoned he could tell her more about that time, about what was going down, than I could.'

Hope nodded again, eager to hear the name. A flutter of excitement had invaded her chest. This mystery man was, after all, the person Connie had chosen not to tell Flint about.

But Eddie hesitated once more. Perhaps, seeing the eager anticipation on her face, he was beginning to have second thoughts. 'What you have to understand,' he said, 'is that this fella had *nothin'* to do with what happened to yer dad. He wouldn't have hurt a hair on his head. I remember the day we heard the news, how Jeff had been shot and all, and he was well cut up about it.'

'I understand,' Hope said softly.

As if he wasn't entirely convinced, Eddie gave her an interrogatory look.

'Really,' she added quickly. She was literally on the edge of her seat, desperate to hear the name, sure that it was the lead they needed.

'And in case you're wondering, love, he wouldn't have hurt Connie either. No way.'

Hope took a sip of her tea. Her nerves were rattling as she put the cup down on the table. 'Yes, yes, I understand.'

'I dunno if she even got to see him. Terry's not too sociable these days. You'll have to ask him that.'

'Terry?'

'Terry Street,' he said, finally revealing the information she'd been waiting for. He was staring at her as if the name should mean something, but it didn't.

'Terry Street,' she repeated softly, making sure she remembered it. 'So how do I get in touch with him?'

Eddie gave her another of his dubious smiles. 'Shit, you've never heard of him, have you?'

'Should I?'

'You bloody would have if you'd grown up in the East End.'

'Well I didn't,' Hope said. Sensing an undercurrent of class warfare, she fought to keep the irritation from her voice. 'So if you could point me in the right direction, I'd be really grateful.'

Eddie puffed out his cheeks, expelling a small amount of breath. 'I suppose you could try Belles. It's a club he owns in Shoreditch. He used to run most of his businesses from there.'

'You haven't got a phone number for him, or a home address?'

'It doesn't work like that, hun. You've asked me for a name and I've given you one, and I've only done that because you're Jeff's daughter.'

Hope didn't press him. She'd got what she'd come for and would have to be satisfied with that.

Eddie leaned forward, lowering his voice. 'But I'll give you a piece of advice for nothing, girl – if you do get to see Terry, don't even hint at the idea that he had anything to do with Connie going missing. He won't be quite as forgiving as I was.'

Hope didn't need to be an East Ender to get what he meant. She felt a sudden tensing in her body, followed by a shiver of apprehension. 'Don't worry, I won't.'

Before she could say anything else, Eddie had hauled himself to his feet, signalling the end of the interview. Although there was still an hour left of visiting time left, she was clearly being dismissed.

'I hope you find her,' he said. 'She's a nice kid.'

Hope had lots more questions she wanted to ask – about Connie, about her mother, even about the man who'd been her biological father – but she wasn't going to get the opportunity.

She stood up and shook the oversized hand that was being offered to her. 'Me too. And thank you for your time.'

'I've got plenty of that, love.' Eddie gave her a thin smile. 'Mind how you go.'

As Hope walked towards the exit, she glanced back over her shoulder. Eddie Booth was watching her. She couldn't read the expression on his face. It might have been concern, but then again it might have been something quite different. She still wasn't sure how far she could trust him. Friend or foe? Had he given her the name of someone who might help – or someone who might kill? There was only way to find out, and the thought of it sent another brief shudder through her.

Chapter Twenty-five

Hope got into the Audi, closed the door and fastened her seat belt. It was only then that she met Flint's eyes. He was staring expectantly at her.

'Well?' he said.

She gave a small shake of her head. 'Let's get out of here first.'

Flint didn't argue. He started the engine, reversed out of the space and started back up the drive. 'Well?' he said again, once they'd cleared the gates and were back on the road. 'Any joy?'

Hope expelled a deep breath, relieved to have put some distance between her and the prison. The place had been suffocating, a lethal combination of iron bars, locks, watching eyes and too much testosterone. And Eddie Booth hadn't helped much either. But before she answered Flint's question, she had a moment's doubt, wondering again why Connie had chosen to keep the name from him. Then she abruptly remembered what had happened to her. Going it alone might have cost Connie her life.

'Terry Street,' she quickly blurted out. 'That's who Jeff was working with. Eddie says they had some kind of deal going, but swears that Terry didn't kill him. Anyway, that was the name he gave to Connie. He doesn't know if she ever went to see him.'

Flint's eyebrows shot up. 'Christ,' he murmured. 'I didn't see that coming. Your old man was mixing with the big boys.'

'How big?'

'About as big as they come. Back then, the Streets were virtually running the East End: drugs, girls, loan-sharking, extortion – you name it, they were doing it.'

'Murder?' she said.

Flint responded with a shrug.

Hope frowned at him. 'I'll take that as a yes. So Terry Street could have killed Jeff. And if he did, he wouldn't have been too happy to find Connie on his doorstep twelve years later. Perhaps he didn't like the questions she was asking. Perhaps he decided to shut her up for good. Perhaps—'

'Hang on,' Flint interrupted. 'Let's not get ahead of ourselves. If Terry and Jeff were working together, it must have been a lucrative deal. Terry wouldn't waste his time on anything less. And if your father was producing convincing fakes, and Terry had a rich client he was selling them on to, then why would Terry kill him?'

'I don't know. Deals can go wrong, thieves can fall out.'

'True enough,' Flint said. 'But it still doesn't make sense. Terry Street's not stupid. He wouldn't kill the goose that laid the golden egg. No more Jeff, no more paintings. Where's the logic in that? He might have given him a slap, but he wouldn't have put a bullet through his brain.' Flint drummed his fingers against the wheel. 'No, I just don't buy it.'

He was silent for a minute or two.

'What are you thinking?' Hope said.

'I don't know. Maybe the client realised he'd been sold a dud and didn't appreciate being taken for a mug. Or maybe the client was in on the whole forgery scam, just another link in a chain – Terry sells the paintings to him and he then sells them on to someone else. But if there was a painting this guy really wanted, something that was going to raise big bucks, and he didn't fancy sharing the profits—'

'He could have murdered Jeff and walked away with it.'

Flint nodded. 'Jeff was killed in his studio. What's your feeling about Eddie Booth? You reckon he was telling the truth?'

'Hard to tell,' Hope said. The image of Eddie jumped into her head, his great bull neck and intimidating glare. She decided not to mention the unfortunate misunderstanding they'd had. Even the recollection of it made her cheeks turn red. 'I don't suppose he'd have offered up the name if Terry really had been involved. I mean, why bother, unless he's got a grudge against him. He could just as easily have said that he didn't know anything, hadn't told Connie anything.' She frowned as she tried to unravel her ideas. 'On the other hand—'

'It could be a deliberate ploy to push us straight into the welcoming arms of Jeff's killer.'

And Connie's too, Hope thought, but didn't say it out loud. 'Exactly. It would be the easiest thing in the world, wouldn't it? If Eddie knows that Street's guilty, and wants to protect him, he could be trying to set us up. We follow up the lead, arrange a meet and present ourselves on a plate.'

'Possibly,' Flint said. 'A bit risky for Terry, though. There'd be no telling who else we'd mentioned his name to, and it would look kind of suspicious if the two of us mysteriously disappeared as well.'

Hope felt another of those chills run through her. Any sort of disappearance, mysterious or otherwise, hadn't been on her agenda when she'd agreed to come to London. In the back of her mind, she had still been hoping that Connie had simply taken off, decided to start again somewhere new, but the likelihood of that was receding by the minute. Connie had been asking difficult questions – and it was more than possible that someone had decided to shut her up for ever.

They passed through the village again, a sleepy place that seemed a hundred miles from the mean streets of Kellston. Hope glanced over at Flint. It wasn't the first time she'd asked, but sometimes the same question could get a different answer. 'Why do you think Connie didn't tell you about Terry Street?'

Flint barked out a laugh. 'Probably because she knew I'd warn her to stay well clear. Or make her promise that she'd take me with her if she was going to see him. And Connie didn't much care for being told what to do.'

'But why shouldn't she take you? Surely she would have realised it was the safest thing to do.'

'The safest, but not necessarily the most useful. It's the same scenario as with Eddie Booth – he'd talk to you, to someone directly involved, but not to a stranger. Perhaps she thought that Terry would only agree to tell her stuff if it was strictly between the two of them.'

'So not because she didn't trust you?'

Flint shot her a glance. 'Maybe that too. Do *you* trust me?'

Hope's hesitation told him everything, but she answered anyway. 'I hardly know you.'

'No,' he said. 'You don't.'

There was an awkward silence, or maybe it was only awkward for her. Flint didn't seem too bothered. Perhaps he was used to people not trusting him. Or perhaps he just didn't care. A few minutes passed. Hope stared out of the window, watching the road fly by, trying to get her thoughts in order. The only thing that was clear was that they had a lead and couldn't afford to let it go. 'So tell me about him, this Terry Street.'

'What do you want to know?'

'Everything.'

Flint paused, but only for a moment. 'Well, I've never had

the pleasure of meeting him in person, but I gather he's not the kind of guy you'd ever want to cross. He owns a few pubs in Kellston, some property, a lap-dancing joint in Shoreditch, but I reckon he makes most of his money from drugs and prostitution. In fact he probably runs most of the girls on Albert Street. He was big in his time, a real player if you know what I mean, but since he's come out of nick—'

'He's been in prison?'

'Yeah. He got out late last year, around Christmas, I think. Was done for murder about ten years ago.'

Hope drew a quick breath, her heart missing a beat. *Murder.* So the man Connie had gone to see – if she ever had gone to see him – had been a convicted killer.

'Anyway, rumour has it that he's lost his grip, and that other firms are muscling in on his territory. His wife ran everything while he was inside, and pretty effectively too. But Lizzie Street took a bullet just before Terry got out of jail.' He gave a small cynical laugh. 'God, that was quite a funeral, a real East End job – Victorian carriage, plumed horses, the whole caboodle. Half of London's gangland turned up, although whether they were there to commiserate or celebrate is another question altogether.'

'They didn't like her?' Hope said.

Flint grinned. 'From all accounts she was a prize bitch, but then you'd have to be to survive in that world. Scruples can't come too high on your agenda when you're dealing with the kind of people who'd stab you in the back soon as look at you.'

'So who killed her?'

'Take your pick,' Flint said. 'I'm sure plenty wanted to. Maybe even Terry himself, although being inside at the time, he had the perfect alibi. The cops have never arrested anyone for it. It's yet another of their unsolved murders.'

Like Jeff Tomlin, she thought. And maybe like Connie

too … but no, she didn't want to believe that. She couldn't afford to. If she was going to continue with the search, she had to hang on to every last shred of hope.

'There's a couple of sons too,' Flint continued, 'Chris and Danny, but apparently neither have their father's flair for the business. The younger one, Danny, is a real piece of work, the kind of human being for whom the word psycho was invented. There was even a rumour that—' He stopped suddenly, as if he'd already said more than he'd intended to.

'A rumour?' she said.

'It doesn't matter. It's only idle gossip.'

'Tell me,' she said. What she didn't know, she could only imagine, and that was the stuff that nightmares were made of.

'Forget it. Like I said, it's just gossip.'

Which only made Hope even more determined to pursue it. 'If you don't tell me, someone else will. I can always ask Lana.'

Flint muttered something that she didn't catch. As if he wished he'd never brought the subject up, he frowned, raised a hand and scratched at the five o'clock shadow on his chin. 'Well, apparently some woman made an accusation against him. She was pretty crazy herself, so God knows whether it was true or not.'

The first thought that sprang into Hope's mind was rape or some kind of sexual assault. 'Go on.'

Flint paused, as if searching for the right words. 'You remember me telling you that a bloke had got killed at that funeral parlour in Kellston? The one on the high street? It was around last Christmas.'

Hope gave a quick nod, sure that she knew where this particular story was going. *Like father, like son.* 'She reckoned Danny Street murdered him, right?'

'Hell, no. *She* was the one who killed him. She readily admitted to that. But the crazy cow did something else too. After she'd put a knife through his heart, she embalmed the poor sod, laid him out and prepared him for his funeral.'

Hope's eyes widened with horror. 'What?'

'Yeah, not a pleasant thought, is it. That's what I mean about her being cuckoo. The two of them worked at the parlour together. Alice Avery, she was called. I can't remember his name. He was the boss' son. God, imagine having something like that happen to your kid? She claimed they'd been having an affair, that he'd dumped her and . . . ' He gave a light shrug. 'What can I say? Some women just can't take no for an answer.'

Hope didn't respond to his flippancy. She was still feeling a sense of shock at the revelation, wondered why she hadn't heard about it before. It was the kind of gruesome tale that would have gone nationwide, the tabloids revelling in every detail. But then she suddenly realised what she'd been doing last Christmas – caring for her mother as she entered the final stages of her illness. During those months she'd rarely read the papers or even watched the news. For the second time that day, a wave of pain flowed over her. She slumped down in her seat and sighed. 'So what's it got to do with Danny Street?'

'She said the boyfriend owed him a lot of money, from gambling and drugs I think, and that Danny had beaten him up a week or so before.'

Hope lifted and dropped her shoulders again. Somehow, compared to what the woman had done, this didn't seem that extreme. 'And that's it?'

'Not quite.'

Hope could tell from his voice that there was worse, far worse, to come. She waited, not wanting to hear it but knowing she would have to.

Flint cleared his throat before he began. 'As the boyfriend didn't have the cash, Street asked for something else instead. He said he wanted to watch while she . . . er . . . while she embalmed the body of a young woman who'd died in an accident. Except it didn't stop there. According to Alice, he asked to be left alone with the corpse. It was fifteen minutes before she saw him again. You can draw your own conclusions.'

'Christ, why would she agree to that?'

'To save her boyfriend from getting his head kicked in again – or worse.'

'Jesus,' Hope murmured. Her hands twisted in her lap, her fingers quickly lacing and then unlacing again as she thought about this awful act. The last taboo. It made her feel sick and afraid, as if just by hearing about it she had inadvertently managed to brush shoulders with the Devil.

'The things people do for love,' Flint said.

Hope glanced at him. 'It may not be true. Wouldn't he have been arrested if . . . '

'No evidence,' Flint said flatly. 'And if there ever was, it all went up in smoke at the crematorium. The cops only had her word for it, and seeing as she's been sectioned, she's not what you'd call a reliable witness.'

Hope was beginning to wish she'd never asked. Sometimes ignorance *was* bliss. She swallowed hard, not relishing the prospect of following up the lead that Eddie Booth had given her. 'They sound like the family from hell.'

'That's one way of putting it.'

The sky had lost its blue since they'd set off from the jail. It was still warm, humid and sticky, but now a bundle of dark grey cloud hung ominously overhead. A few drops of rain spattered the windscreen. 'So where do we go from here?'

'The only place we can. We try and set up a meet with Terry.'

The knot in her stomach tightened. 'By "we", I take it you mean me. That's how it works, isn't it?'

'I wouldn't ask you to do that.'

Maybe not, she thought, but there was a difference between

asking and expecting. And if Terry Street refused to have Flint present, she'd have no choice but to see him on her own. The idea filled her with dread. Turning her face away, she gazed out through the side window. Her pulse had picked up its pace again, her heart beating hard in her chest. Every day that passed, every hour, every minute, she was being dragged ever deeper into a world she didn't understand – and didn't want to. But if she was going to find out what had happened to Connie, she had no choice but to carry on.

Chapter Twenty-six

He bares his teeth, snarling as he drives past the Mansfield Estate. It's barely five o'clock, but already the whores are out in force, parading around in their tight short skirts, showing the provocative curve of their tits to anyone who wants an eyeful. Scum, that's what they are. Harlots. He'd like to purge the world of every single one of them. There's a hard rain coming down, sweeping litter into the gutters, but it's not falling heavily enough to cleanse the pavement of this particular type of filth.

Peering through the sweep of the wipers, he thinks of the trash he's already managed to eliminate. It's a drop in the ocean, but a job well done all the same. No man, not even a desperate one, is ever going to want to touch their mutilated bodies again. Smiling, he remembers the look on their faces, their terror, their pathetic pleading. Each one of them was different but their words were all the same.

He glances down at the bible lying on the passenger seat beside him. 'For the lips of a strange woman drop as a honeycomb, and her mouth is smoother than oil,' he quotes out loud. 'But her end is bitter as wormwood, sharp as a two-edged sword. Her feet go down to death; her steps take hold on hell.'

An angry heat rolls through his body. He lowers the window a fraction, and feels the cool air blow against his face. God's air. The air that some aren't fit to breathe. That bitch Valerie Middleton will have got his message by now. She'll have understood the warning. His chest rises and falls with a frustrated rage. It's women like her who allow the whores to keep plying their trade, who do nothing to prevent it. If they are the outward face of evil, then she is the inner, secret force that enables it. She is the Devil's helpmate.

Valerie Middleton. Like a mantra, he repeats the name over and over. He already knows so much about her: where she lives, what she likes to wear, to eat, to drink, what car she drives, even her favoured way of doing her hair. He's been watching for a long time now. He knows the restaurants and pubs that she frequents, the gym she goes to, the friends she has. He knows about Harry Lind, the ex-cop private detective who used to be her lover. She's a tramp, like all the other tramps who walk the streets round here.

Detective Inspector Valerie Middleton. He hisses out her name one last time. He's seen her at the hospital, holding hands with the whores, muttering empty words of sympathy. Does she put herself in their shoes? Does she imagine what it must be like? Well, she won't need to imagine for too much longer. She's about to understand the true meaning of empathy.

He nods his head, his eyes gleaming with anticipation. For every piece of Devil's work, there's a price to be paid – and he's already started preparing the bill.

Chapter Twenty-seven

Hope was still thinking about her visit to Eddie Booth, about Terry Street, about all the horrors Flint had revealed to her, as she opened the front door to the house in Tanner Road and stepped into the communal hallway. Her entrance coincided with the appearance of an elderly man from the ground-floor flat. Small and frail-looking, his gaunt face was wrinkled like a walnut and topped by a thatch of pure white hair. A pair of pale wary eyes narrowed behind black-rimmed glasses, and she saw him hesitate as if in two minds as to whether to retreat back inside.

'Hi,' she said, smiling wide enough to try to allay any alarm she might have caused. 'I'm Hope. I'm staying with Lana for a while.'

Lana's name didn't seem to mean anything to him. Her smile didn't have much of an impact either. He stood very still, like a mouse cornered by a hungry cat, and stared fearfully back at her. A couple of seconds ticked by, and when he still didn't reply, Hope's awkwardness started to turn into dismay. His fear was almost tangible, something finely honed, as sharp as a blade.

Jesus, she thought, what on earth did he think she was going to do to him?

Unwilling to make a bad situation worse, Hope quickly headed for the stairs. Perhaps if she put some distance between them, he might relax a bit and not view her as a threat. It wasn't until she was halfway up that he eventually moved, pulling his own door closed with a soft but resounding click.

'It was nice to meet you,' she said, leaning over the banister, feeling unable to leave things on such a bad note. Causing distress to the elderly was hardly something to be proud of. 'Oh, and I like your geraniums.'

He turned and gazed up at her, all the time edging furtively along the hall as if she might be about to jump back down the stairs and physically assault him. His mouth opened a little and a thin, rattling breath slipped from between his lips. He didn't smile. He didn't speak. His only response was a barely perceptible nod of his head before he scuttled out of the door.

Hope frowned. Perhaps she needed to work on her social skills. It wasn't the first occasion today that she'd embarked on a conversation with the best of intentions and ended up making a pig's ear of it. She'd have to be more careful tonight. All the girls were going out for a drink, and if she was going to raise the subject of Connie, she was going to have to do it without putting her foot firmly in her mouth.

She was surprised to hear the sound of voices as she entered the flat. It was a quarter past five, and no one was usually home before the evening rush was over. For a second she paused, listening for who it was. One of the voices belonged to Lana, the other to a male she didn't recognise. And it was clear that an argument was in progress.

'I've already told you,' Lana was saying stridently. 'This is none of your damn business. Just keep out of it, okay. I know what I'm doing.'

'For Christ's sake, if you believe that, then you really are a fuckin' fool.'

'And since when did you become Mr bloody Mastermind?'

Hope was tempted to keep quiet, curious as to what it was all about, but then thought better of it. Her relationship with Lana was already on shaky ground – she was only here on sufferance – and Lana wouldn't be too pleased if she caught her eavesdropping.

'It's only me,' she called out breezily, as if she'd just that very moment opened the door.

There was a short, startled silence, and then a muttered exchange before Lana finally called back, 'We're in the kitchen, love. Come on through.'

Hope smelled the cigar, the distinctive scent of Cuban tobacco, before she saw the person who was smoking it. The tall, broad, middle-aged man was standing by the sink. He stared at her, his eyes a bland shade of grey, and flashed a smile that was perhaps more practised than sincere. A thin layer of salt-and-pepper hair was receding from his forehead, and the top of his cheeks, along with his slightly bulbous nose, was suffused with the scarlet tones of the drinker. He was dressed in a dark pinstripe suit with a waistcoat, white shirt and blue and cream striped tie. The triangular tip of a blue silk handkerchief poked out of his jacket pocket. The well-cut suit almost but not quite disguised the pronounced curve of his stomach.

'So how did it go?' Lana said, not bothering with any introductions.

Hope put her bag down on the table and shot a glance towards the man. This time, as he raised the cigar to his mouth, she noticed the heavy gold-link bracelet on his wrist and the gold signet ring on his little finger. The ring had a large black stone in it that might have been onyx.

Lana flapped a hand. 'Oh, don't mind Derek. He's a friend. He knows all about it.'

This was news to Hope, and not exactly welcome. She'd been under the impression that no one but herself, Lana and Flint were aware of the arrangement. Now it turned out that this stranger was privy to it too. 'I see,' she said tightly.

'No need to worry, love,' Derek said. He drew the flat line of his hand across his mouth. 'My lips are sealed. Your secret's safe with me.'

Hope, unlike some women, wasn't the kind who ever objected to terms like 'love' or 'darling' – she'd grown up in the North and was used to all kinds of innocuous endearments –but somehow, coming out of his mouth, there was a distinctly patronising quality about it.

'So what did this Eddie character have to say for himself?' Lana asked.

Hope would have told her the truth if Derek hadn't been there, but his presence made her uneasy. She had a split second to decide and came down on the side of caution. 'You were right. I shouldn't have bothered. It was a complete waste of time. Eddie Booth couldn't help. Connie went to see him, but he didn't tell her anything she didn't already know.'

It might only have been her imagination, but Hope thought she sensed a certain exhalation of breath, a relaxing of tension in the room. Lana pulled a face, her expression hard to decipher, but Derek's smile grew even wider.

'There you go, then,' he said. Leaning forward, he gave Hope a genial pat on the arm. 'Best to drop it, eh? There's nothing to be gained by all this palaver. You should get yourself off home, get on with your own life. I'm sure she's just met some bloke and taken off. It's not worth worrying about.'

'Perhaps,' Hope said.

Derek, hearing the doubt in her voice, looked from at Lana and then back at Hope again. 'No offence, love, I know she was your sister and all, but she wasn't the most reliable sort. In fact, to be perfectly honest, she was a selfish little cow who didn't give a toss about anyone but herself.'

Hope raised her brows. It was interesting, she thought, how people always prefaced their opinions with 'no offence' when they knew that was precisely what they were likely to cause. *A selfish little cow.* Hadn't Jackie said something similar? 'So you don't think it odd that she left without taking any of her things?'

'Probably meant to come back for them later, didn't she. The girl got an offer she couldn't refuse, and . . .' His heavy shoulders lifted in a shrug. 'Like I said, it's not worth worrying about.'

Hope gave him a thin smile. 'Well, let's hope you're right. Because if you're not—'

'Let's drop it, shall we,' Lana interrupted. 'We all want her to be okay. That's all that matters.' Taking hold of Derek's arm, she gently hustled him out of the kitchen. 'Come on, love, you're going to be late if you don't make a move.'

Hope watched him leave, scowling at his broad back. He left a trail of cigar smoke and a bad smell in his wake.

It was about five minutes before Lana returned. 'Sorry about that,' she said. 'He doesn't mean any harm. He's just being protective, trying to stop me from stressing out about it all.'

Hope wasn't entirely convinced by Lana's explanation, but pretended to accept it. 'That's okay. I understand. But was he right? About Connie, I mean. Was she really that bad?'

'Connie was no different to a lot of girls her age. She could be a pain in the arse one minute, an angel the next. And yeah, she could be trouble, she was always getting into one scrape or another, but at the end of the day she had a good heart. Derek didn't mean . . .' She gave a tiny shake of her head. 'He liked her really. I'm sure he didn't mean to upset you.'

'He didn't,' Hope said quickly. 'I'm just trying to get a clearer picture. It's hard when I never met her. Everyone's saying different things and I don't know who to believe.'

'Maybe you will get to meet her one day and then you can make your own mind up.' Lana fiddled with her hair for a moment, a distracted look on her face. 'So, no luck today, then? That Eddie couldn't tell you anything?'

Hope wondered if she should come clean now and mention Terry Street, but decided against it. Having already told a blatant lie in front of Derek, she knew it would make her appear untrustworthy. No, it was probably better to keep quiet, to wait until after she'd talked to the man. As she thought of this meeting with the local gangster, she felt her whole body tense. Eddie Booth, she imagined, was a kitten in comparison to Terry Street.

'You all right, love?' Lana said.

'Yeah,' Hope said, averting her eyes and getting to her feet. 'I'm fine. It's been a long day, that's all.' She went over and stood by the window. Gazing down on the garden, she was reminded of the earlier incident in the downstairs hallway. 'I bumped into your neighbour on the way in. You know, the old bloke who lives on the ground floor. I think I terrified the life out of him.'

'Oh, that's Mad Hughie.' Lana lifted a finger and made a whirring motion at the side of her head. 'Got a screw loose, if you know what I mean. He's ignored me for the past ten years, hasn't said a word. Acts like I'm bloody invisible. The only person he ever talked to was Connie.'

Hope was interested in this snippet of information. 'Really? How come?'

'I've no idea. Mind, Connie was the type who wouldn't take no for an answer. She probably *made* him speak to her. I told her to stay well clear. I said he might be an old geezer, but that didn't mean he was harmless.'

Hope looked back down on the garden again, at the bright

red and white geraniums glistening with rain. The only access to the area was from the ground-floor flat. She pressed her face against the cool pane of glass, stared hard at the untidy patch of ground to the rear and thought of how easily a body could be hidden there. If it had been buried in February, the weeds would have grown up by spring. Was it possible that . . . ? No, she was being crazy. The notion of an old man like Hughie being able to overpower a fit young woman and then dig a grave to put her body in was beyond ridiculous. But still she scanned the far reaches of the garden, searching for evidence of the ground being disturbed.

'What are you looking at?' Lana said.

Hope shook her head. 'Nothing.' She turned away from the window. If she wasn't careful, she'd start suspecting everyone. And her imagination was already running riot. There was enough to be concerned about – a meeting with Terry Street being at the very top of the list – without inventing new reasons to fear the worst.

Chapter Twenty-eight

After an hour-long briefing with Superintendent Saul Redding and other senior staff, Valerie Middleton returned to her office and slammed a pile of files down on her desk. She was feeling a mixture of anger and frustration. Although there had been no direct criticism of her handling of the investigation, she'd been aware of a subtle undercurrent of judgement: if progress was slow, then it had to be somebody's fault, and as she was in charge ...

'Damn it,' she murmured, wondering how the hell she was supposed to make any headway when the evil bastard never left evidence behind. And it wasn't as if her team weren't busting a gut – they were trawling through endless records, pulling in every likely suspect for questioning, harassing forensics for even the tiniest of clues, but a breakthrough still remained elusive.

Valerie swore softly under her breath again. The Whisperer, whoever he was, was running rings around them. And now, she was sure, he was making it personal. *He* was the one who had left the note on her windscreen. *He* was the one who had called out her name at Silverstone Heights. She searched her memory for someone who might bear a grudge, but the list, bearing in mind how many people she'd put away over the years, was a long one. And anyway, all her instincts told her that this wasn't some old con out for a spot of revenge. It was more complicated than that.

Looking up at the clock, she noticed it was ten past seven. She was due to meet Harry for a drink at half past. A copy of the local rag had been left in her in-tray, and as she pulled on her jacket, she paused to glance at the headlines. The paper, which usually devoted a generous number of column inches to how the police should be clearing the streets of prostitutes, was now castigating them for failing to do enough to protect the girls. There was a large piece about the Mansfield Estate too. A couple of days ago, while she was at the hospital, someone had hurled a Russian guy off a second-floor balcony. He'd survived, but only just. It was suggested by the journalist that the victim had been a loan shark and had 'gangland' connections.

Valerie folded the paper in two and stuffed it in her bag. She'd read the details later when she had more time. Quickly she ran a comb through her hair, applied a lick of lipstick and headed for the lift. Down in the foyer, just as she was leaving, she bumped into Kieran Swann, who was leaning against the front desk, his elbows on the counter, chatting to a pretty red-headed constable.

'You off then, guv?' he said.

Valerie nodded. 'See you on Sunday.'

'Meeting go okay?'

'Fine,' she replied calmly, careful to keep any hint of resentment from her voice or her face. 'Very positive.'

Swann grinned, as if he knew exactly how positive it had been. 'You want an escort back to the Heights?'

'No thanks. I'm going for a drink with a friend.' She didn't tell him she was meeting Harry Lind. Swann was a renowned

gossip, and she didn't want her business, no matter how innocent, being broadcast throughout the station.

'Jezebel,' he said.

Valerie glowered at him. His misogynist views, although ever
present, weren't usually quite so blatant. She glanced first
towards the constable, and then back at Swann. 'Pardon me?'

Swann's grin grew even wider. He paused for a second, relishing the moment. 'That quote,' he said, 'the one that was left
on your windscreen. I checked it out on the internet. It refers to
Jezebel. I thought you might like to know.'

Valerie took a fast breath, forcing a smile on to her lips. She
knew what he'd just done – attempted to show her up as an
over-touchy, humourless female – and privately gave thanks to
God that she hadn't reacted as vehemently as she might have.
'Really,' she said. 'How fascinating.' Then, without another
word, she turned her back, pushed through the doors and
stepped out into the cool evening air.

'Wanker,' she murmured, as she got into her car and yanked
her seat belt across. She'd spent the past hour having to endure
the barely disguised sniping of her senior colleagues, and
Swann's adolescent wind-up was the last thing she'd needed.
Her job was tough enough without having to deal with his
pathetic male ego.

Ten minutes later, Valerie pulled up at the Fox and killed the
engine. She had parked as close as she could to the entrance, but
still took the time to make a sweep of the surrounding area.
Maybe she was being paranoid, but better safe than sorry. She
had no intention of ending up like Patti King or one of those
other poor girls. Once she was certain that no one had followed
her into the car park, she got out, locked the door and walked
quickly towards the pub.

The inside of the Fox was busy and smelled of perfume,
wood polish and freshly poured beer. It was one of the better

pubs in Kellston, renowned for its real ales and trouble-free atmosphere. This evening, the place had that Friday-night sound about it, a delicious hum that you never got on any other day of the week. It was, she decided, a combination of relief, release and hope, and her own spirits rose as she gently elbowed her way through the crowd.

It was only after forging a path to the second, larger room that she eventually found Harry Lind. He was sitting at a table in the corner, sipping on a pint of Guinness and flicking through the evening paper. Although he was utterly familiar to her – the thin, almost gaunt face, the two deep vertical lines engraved between his brows, the dark hair greying at the temples – she still felt the very same flutter in her chest as she had on the first occasion they'd met. But that was just habit, she told herself, some sort of Pavlovian response that would have to be unlearned. They'd been apart for two years. They were only friends now, not partners.

As if sensing her presence, Harry suddenly looked up. His intense blue eyes met hers, lingering for a long moment before his mouth broke into a smile. 'Hey,' he said, getting to his feet and leaning forward to give her a peck on the cheek. 'How are you?'

'Ask me another,' she said, slipping off her jacket and hanging it over the back of the chair. She was relieved that he'd managed to grab a table before they'd all been taken. After spending most of last night and the early hours of the morning walking around the red-light district with a couple of colleagues, her feet were sore and aching. As she sat down, she slid them out of her shoes with a sigh of relief.

Harry indicated a glass of white wine on the table. 'I got you a drink.'

'Thanks. You're an angel.' She picked up the glass, took two large gulps and set it back down. 'Lord, I can't tell you how much I needed that.'

Harry looked at her again, raised his brows and laughed. 'Bad day, I take it.'

'You could say that.'

He closed the paper he'd been reading and tapped his fingers on the front cover.

'Anything to do with this?'

Valerie automatically reached for her glass again, but this time didn't pick it up. If she wasn't careful, she'd be over the limit before she realised – and she didn't fancy walking home with the Whisperer on the loose. 'That and the rest. I spent the last hour being grilled by Redding and company. They seem to think I can magic a result out of nowhere.'

'Don't worry about it. They're just doing what bosses always do – protecting their own backs.'

'Not to mention Swann,' she added. 'I'm sure he makes it his mission in life to try and wind me up. God, that man really gets on my nerves.'

Harry grinned. 'He's not so bad. He's loyal, if nothing else.'

Loyal to *you*, Valerie thought, but was careful not to say it out loud. 'He's got a funny way of showing it.'

'So no progress with the case?' he said, glancing down at the paper again. 'I take it Patti King didn't have anything new to offer.'

Valerie wasn't supposed to discuss her cases with anyone outside the force, and usually she stuck rigidly to this rule. It was only with Harry that she made an exception. She knew she could trust him implicitly, and was also aware of how much he missed the life of a cop. Being involved, even in a vicarious fashion, brought the light back into his eyes. She noticed how carefully he listened as she leaned forward and quietly related the facts to date. It was a relief, she found, to share the burden, to be able to openly express her doubts and worries without fear of being judged.

'You'll get him, Val. He'll make a mistake sooner or later.'

'It's the later I'm worried about,' she said. 'How many more girls is he going to attack before we get a decent lead? Redding's ordered extra patrol cars for Albert Street, but I'm sure that's going to do more harm than good. The girls don't like being watched by us, even if it is for their own protection. They think we'll drive the punters away, and they're absolutely right.'

'So they'll go somewhere else,' Harry said, understanding her concern. 'Somewhere business isn't going to be spoiled by the regular appearance of the boys in blue. Which means they'll probably split up, start working other streets, and won't be able to watch out for each other any more.'

'Exactly,' she said. 'Which makes it even more risky for them. And even easier for that bastard to get them on their own. I mean, that's his method, that's the way he operates. He never picks them up if anyone else is around. All of his victims were working solo. But try telling that to Redding. All he cares about is that he's *seen* to be doing something.'

'Like I said, he's just watching his back.'

'Yeah, but at whose expense? I spent half the night trying to get the girls to talk to me, to trust me, to share information they might have about any weird or violent punters they've come across, or heard about, in the last six months. And of course none of them were prepared to say anything in front of the others – you know what it's like – but I left a heap of cards. I was hoping a few of them might call when they'd had a chance to think about it.'

'Which they're hardly likely to do now, if most of their clients are being frightened away.'

'No,' she agreed.

Harry picked up his pint and took a drink. 'And?' he said.

'And?'

'Just call it a hunch, but I get the feeling you haven't told me everything.'

Valerie looked at him. Despite the time they'd spent apart, he still had that uncanny ability to read her like a book. She hadn't mentioned the note, or the sinister voice calling out her name. Should she tell him or not? She hesitated.

'Val?'

Knowing that he wouldn't stop probing until he heard the rest, Valerie reluctantly gave in. She told him first about the message that had been left on her windscreen, and then about the voice she'd heard at Silverstone Heights.

'Hell,' he said, the frown between his brows growing even deeper. 'Have you told Redding about this?'

'About the note,' she said. 'Forensics took a look, but the only prints on it were mine. Apparently, as Swann took delight in pointing out, the quote refers to Jezebel.'

'That figures. But if this guy's stalking you, then you have to be careful. I don't like it. You should have some protection. You should talk to Redding about—'

'There's no point,' she interrupted. 'It's not as though I can prove he was at the Heights. I'm not even sure he was. I start going on about hearing voices, about being stalked, and I'll give Redding the perfect excuse to take me off the case.' She emptied her glass of the last few drops of wine and sighed. 'For my own safety, of course,' she added cynically.

'So you're just going to let it go?'

'Well, it's not unusual, is it? The perp in these kinds of situations often connects with the officer in charge, or tries to. It's a power game. But the more he does it, the more likely he is to slip up, give something away or be noticed by someone.'

'I don't like it,' Harry said again, shaking his head. 'You could be putting yourself in danger. This guy's a psycho. You could be next on his list of victims.'

'So I'll be careful,' she said. 'There's no need to worry. I'm not going to go walking down any dark alleys on my own.'

He took a swig of his Guinness, and wiped the froth from his mouth with the back of his hand. 'Are you sure you want me on your patch?'

Valerie smiled. 'Why? Am I likely to regret it?' She hadn't reacted well the last time Harry had got himself involved in one of her cases, but that could happen wherever he was based. She touched the top sheet with the tip of her finger. 'You see this one? There's tons of space, much more than you've got now, and a flat on the floor above. Mac's got his own place, so you'd be able to have it. That's if you don't mind living over the office.'

'Yeah,' he said. 'It's definitely worth considering. I'll have a word with him and—'

A sudden burst of raucous laughter made them both turn to stare. A group of women were gathered around a nearby table that was already filling up with empty bottles. From the look of things, they were settling in for a long, boozy night.

'Isn't that Lana Franklin and her crew?' Harry said.

Valerie nodded. 'The very same. I'd check your pocket, make sure your wallet's still there.'

'Who's the blonde? The one on the left. I haven't seen her before.'

Valerie gazed at the slim, pretty girl with the long fair hair. Not a natural blonde, that was for sure – her brows were too dark – but men rarely noticed things like that. How old was she? About twenty-six, she estimated, ten years younger than herself. There was something slightly awkward about her, as if she didn't quite fit in. Glancing back at Harry, Valerie saw how closely he was looking at the girl. A tiny spark of jealousy ignited in her heart, but she was careful to keep her voice light. Who Harry fancied was no longer any of her business. 'Are you ogling, Mr Lind?'

'I don't ogle,' he said, his blue eyes flicking back to meet hers. 'I investigate.'

'Well, you're investigating very thoroughly.'

'That's the trademark of a good detective.'

Valerie forced a laugh. 'She must be the latest acquisition.' Somewhere in the back of her mind, she had a recollection of Lana reporting a girl missing. That had been months ago, and she'd heard nothing since. It had been one of those cases, she suspected, of thieves falling out.

'I've got an idea,' Harry said. He gestured towards the papers on the table. 'Why don't we go back to your place, have a coffee and take a look through these. If I can get together a short list, I can show them to Mac on Monday.'

Valerie hesitated. In her present frame of mind, being alone with Harry might be a temptation too far. He always knew exactly what to say, which buttons to push to make her feel better. She wasn't sure if she could trust herself. Since their separation, they'd ended up in bed on more than one occasion, and she didn't want to keep on going down that road.

'Or maybe you've seen enough paperwork for one week,' he said. 'How about if I just come back to the flat, check that's everything's okay and then go?'

'I don't need a bodyguard.'

'I know you don't, but do it for me, please? It'll put my mind at rest.'

'Okay,' she finally agreed. 'But just one coffee. I need to catch up on some of that sleep I missed last night.'

'Don't worry, I won't outstay my welcome.'

As they left the pub, Valerie's eyes lingered on the blonde girl, and she wondered how she'd react if Harry started a serious relationship with someone else. The thought filled her with unease. It was madness, she knew, because she and Harry could never get back together on any kind of permanent basis. Whatever those romantic novels might claim, love wasn't always enough.

Outside, she rapidly scanned the car park, alert to anyone

who might be lurking. Everything was quiet. Her gaze settled on her own car, relieved to find that the windscreen was empty. Although she wouldn't openly admit it, she was glad that Harry was there. She could take care of herself – she'd had plenty of practice – but occasionally it was nice to know that someone else was looking out for her too.

Chapter Twenty-nine

Hope smiled through her disappointment, raised her glass and took another sip of the weak vodka and tonic. It was getting on for closing time, last orders had just been called and her plan had come to nothing. Alcohol might have loosened people's tongues, but no useful revelations had slipped from their lips. No big secrets, no small ones, not even the sniff of a lead. Sharon, who she hadn't seen since Tuesday, had had nothing new to offer either.

'It's Evelyn I feel sorry for. The poor kid really misses her. She could text at least, let her know she's okay. It ain't too much to ask, is it.'

'Aren't you worried?' Hope had asked. 'I mean, it's odd her taking off and leaving all her stuff behind. You don't think . . .'

'Nah, Connie can take care of herself. She'll come back when she feels like it. Or when she runs out of dosh.'

It had been said with a breeziness that Hope found surprising, as if there wasn't anything to be alarmed about. But perhaps in this strange new world she'd entered, it wasn't that unusual for someone to drift in and out of other people's lives. To not be missed, Hope thought, was a terrible thing. And yet Connie *was* missed. Evelyn missed her. Lana missed her. She may have disappeared without a trace, but she hadn't been forgotten.

The chat with Sharon had kindled a brief group discussion, but no one had offered up any fresh insights into where Connie had gone or why, and after a while the conversation had moved on. Since then, Hope hadn't felt able to raise the subject again without arousing suspicion. Curiosity was one thing, persistent questioning quite another.

Hope glanced around the busy pub. The Fox was obviously a regular meeting place for Lana and her mates, providing an opportunity to catch up on the news and exchange gossip. Other girls, as well as the occasional bloke, had been coming and going all evening, some of them only staying for a few minutes, others for an hour or so. Much of the talk had been about the latest victim of the Whisperer. It was the first time Hope had heard the name, and it made the hairs stand up on the back of her neck.

The creepy guy, Pony, had shown up shortly after they'd arrived, adding to her feelings of fear and apprehension. She remembered the way he'd stared, his eyes quite blatantly roaming up and down her body again, as if he was mentally undressing her. She would have liked to have asked him about Connie, to gauge his reaction, but shied away from the prospect. He was the type of guy who would view even the most formal of approaches as a sign of sexual interest.

Although Hope had deliberately avoided meeting his gaze, she'd made a point of watching him. He'd contributed nothing, not a word, as the girls around the table related the latest tales of the Whisperer's brutality and torture. And yet he'd listened carefully, as if drinking in every lurid detail.

Thankfully, he hadn't stayed for long. After a while, he'd leaned across, murmured something in Jackie's ear and headed out of the pub. A minute later, Jackie had followed him. Hope had immediately noticed the difference when she'd come back. From sullen to smiling, from lethargic to hyper, Jackie had undergone an instant transformation. Hope guessed it wasn't down to the fresh air.

Hope sat back and sighed. She was tired, the day had been a wearing one, and she wanted her bed. She knew that she'd been pinning her hopes on this evening, desperate for a new lead. Without it she was left with no option but to go through with the meeting with Terry Street. A bitter dread, sour as bile, rose up from her stomach. What if she said the wrong thing again? Eddie Booth had laughed it off, but the infamous gangster might not be quite so forgiving.

Hope stood up, deciding to pay a final visit to the loo before they started on the walk back to the flat. The very thought of Terry Street made her bladder weak. She passed by the bar, where Evelyn was talking to a skinny blonde wearing a pair of thigh-high boots, a red miniskirt and a skimpy white vest. Hope recognised the distinctive boots before she placed the face. It was the girl who had caused the distraction at the clothes shop on Wednesday.

'Don't be daft,' Evelyn was saying. 'It ain't safe, Linzi. You know it ain't. Look what happened to Patti.'

Linzi shook her head. 'I gotta eat, babe. I gotta pay the bills. Don't worry. I can take care of myself.'

Hope guessed that the kind of bills she had to pay had little to do with rent or gas or electricity. Her gaze settled briefly on the girl, taking in the tangled fair hair, the dark circles under her eyes and the bright red slash of lipstick. Linzi wasn't very old, eighteen or nineteen maybe, but from what she was saying – and how she looked – it was clear that her habit outweighed her fear of the Whisperer.

Hope could barely begin to imagine what Linzi's life must be like, caught up in that perpetual cycle of selling herself for drugs, of using the drugs to blot out the misery of dealing with the punters, of having to go back on the streets as soon as her supply had run out. Perhaps not a cycle, she thought, so much as a spiral – and one that was bound to travel only in a downward direction.

She was still dwelling on the horror of it all as she pushed through the door and entered the corridor leading to the toilets. As she turned the corner, she saw Jackie standing outside the Ladies' with her back to her. Her heart sank. Jackie had been giving her the evil eye all night, but unless she retraced her steps, there was no way she could avoid her. She hesitated for a second before she realised that Jackie was talking on the phone and that whoever was on the other end of the line was getting an ear-bashing.

'Don't give me that. I need the fuckin' cash, man!'

Hope was instantly curious. As she quietly approached, her footsteps made silent by the carpet, she saw the fingers of Jackie's left hand clenching and unclenching, thumping rhythmically against her thigh. The girl's shoulders were tight and hunched, a hot rage emanating from every pore of her body.

'Nah, that ain't good enough. Two grand, that's what we agreed. Don't you dare piss me about!' Her voice took on an even nastier edge. 'Or do you want your little secret to come out? People are asking questions, man, and don't think I won't tell, because—'

Hope was only a few feet away when Jackie, sensing her presence, suddenly whirled around.

'I'll call you back,' she snarled into the phone, before flipping it shut. Her eyes narrowed and she glared at Hope. 'You fuckin' spying on me?'

'What?' Hope replied. 'I'm just going to the loo.' She went to walk past, but Jackie grabbed hold of her arm, her fingers digging into the flesh.

'Not so fast.'

Hope tried to pull away, but Jackie only tightened her grip. 'Let go of me.'

'Not until you tell me what the fuck you're playin' at.' She pushed her face into Hope's, breathing cider fumes all over her. 'Didn't anyone ever tell you to mind your own business?'

Hope stared back at her. To claim she wasn't intimidated would be a lie, but she knew better than to show it. Bullies thrived on other people's weaknesses. 'And didn't anyone ever tell you not to be so bloody paranoid. What's your problem, Jackie? You got a guilty conscience?'

Jackie, as if she'd been stung, gave a tiny jump and simultaneously released her hold. 'What the fuck do you mean by that?' Her tone was defiant, but her eyes told a different story. 'I dunno what you think you heard, but—'

'I didn't hear anything,' Hope lied.

Jackie continued to glare at her, trying to decide whether this might be true or not. 'You know what, love,' she hissed. 'You've outstayed your welcome. You're not wanted here. Why don't you just piss off back to wherever you came from.'

'I think that's up to Lana, not you.' And before Jackie could respond, Hope quickly pushed past her into the Ladies'. She locked the cubicle door and sat down on the loo, her heart racing after the encounter. Would Jackie follow her in? Hope was sure that she was more than capable of inflicting GBH on another woman, and she didn't fancy her chances if it got physical.

A minute passed, and then another. Hope gradually relaxed. And as she relaxed, she replayed the words she'd heard Jackie speaking. It had sounded like blackmail. She had definitely been threatening someone. But who was it? And what was the hold she had on them? Perhaps the night hadn't been such a failure after all. Jackie had secrets, and those secrets might have something to do with Connie.

Chapter Thirty

Chris Street woke with a jolt. It took him a moment to realise that the noise that had roused him was the sound of the phone ringing. As he reached towards the bedside table, he peered at the luminous green dial of the alarm clock. Ten past four. 'For fuck's sake,' he murmured. He'd been asleep for less than an hour.

'Yeah?' he said as he snatched up his mobile.

The voice on the other end was Solomon Vale's. He was talking quickly, and there was a lot of noise in the background.

'Slow down, slow down,' Chris said, struggling to absorb what he was being told. As Vale repeated the information, Chris pushed back the duvet and swung his legs over the side of the bed. 'Okay, give me ten minutes. I'm on my way.'

Swearing softly to himself, Chris pulled on jeans, sweater and a pair of trainers. He grabbed his car keys, picked up his phone again and hurried along the hallway. The door to Danny's bedroom was open, the room unoccupied. 'Dammit,' he muttered. Taking the stairs two at a time, he landed with a soft thud on the deep-pile carpet of the ground floor.

Next he tried his father's room, rapping hard on the door. No response. He pushed the door open. 'Dad? Dad, are you awake?' The room was in darkness, and he flicked on the light. The bed was empty. Great, no one home but himself. His father was probably shagging that Russian tart, and God alone knew what his brother was up to. Danny was always disappearing, refusing to say where he'd gone or what he'd done; he'd been at the club earlier, but had left well before closing time.

As he headed for the front door, Chris tried to call them both, but all he got was voicemail. He left two identical messages, without holding out much hope of either of them being picked up in the near future. He cursed again. As usual, he was the one left to deal with every bloody crisis.

Outside, the cold morning air nipped at his face. He gave a shiver, rubbing his hands together as he got into the Mercedes. Quickly he switched on the engine and the heat. Reversing out of the drive, he turned on to Walpole Close, took a right into Hatton Avenue, and put his foot down as soon as he hit the long, straight stretch of Kellston High Street.

It was another few minutes before he noticed the red tinge on the horizon. At first he thought it was the sun coming up, but then realised it was too early for dawn to be breaking. It was only as he slowed the car to turn on to Mansfield Road that he saw the smoke, great dark clouds billowing into the sky. And then, seconds later, the fire itself.

'Shit,' he said.

The Lincoln Pool Hall was a wide, low-slung one-storey building almost directly opposite the Mansfield Estate. It was alight from one end to the other, a raging inferno that was already out of control. Solomon had said there was a fire, but Chris hadn't been expecting anything quite as dramatic as this.

'Shit,' he muttered again. Pulling up, he turned off the engine and grabbed a pack of cigarettes from the glove compartment.

He'd been trying to give up, but this wasn't the time for self-denial. As he puffed hard on the fag, he stared dolefully through the windscreen. Four fire engines were doing their best to control the blaze, but to Chris's eyes, the powerful jets of water looked as ineffectual as a cat pissing on a bonfire.

With a sigh, he got out of the car. Instantly he felt a wave of heat, as if an oven door had suddenly been opened. Smuts of black soot drifted down and settled on his head and shoulders. He brushed them away as he began to walk towards the burning building. The Lincoln had been owned by the Streets for over twenty years, and was a good steady earner. This was the place where the local boys hustled, drank, did their drug deals and spent their cash. Or at least it had been. He heard the sound of shattering glass as yet another window blew out.

A small crowd, residents of the estate, had gathered to watch the spectacle. Most of them were wearing pyjamas or nightdresses under their coats. Chris pushed through them, irritated by their open-mouthed, gawping presence. *It's not some fuckin' floor show*, he felt like yelling, but decided not to waste his breath. Although aware that it was part of human nature to be fascinated by such things – you only had to watch the cars slowing down at the scene of an accident to know that – he didn't take kindly to this more personal disaster being the object of other people's ghoulish fascination.

Chris was looking around for Solomon when his eyes were drawn towards someone sitting on a low brick wall a few feet away. The man was hunched over and wrapped in a blanket. 'Christ,' muttered Chris, realising that it was Big Lenny Blyth, who'd had the dubious pleasure of managing the Lincoln for the past decade. In his dismay over the fire, he hadn't even thought about the flat that was attached to the premises – or the poor sod who might still be inside it.

He took a final drag of the cigarette, threw the fag end on the pavement and crushed it underfoot. Then he hurried over and laid a hand on the man's shoulder. 'You all right, mate?'

Big Lenny looked up at him and gave a nod. 'I'm okay, son.'

'You sure? Someone checked you out?'

'Yeah, yeah. I'll live. I'll tell you something, though, I ain't never been so glad to hear that bloody smoke alarm screeching in me ear.'

'I bet.' Chris made a mental note to check the batteries in his own alarms when he got home. 'Look, you'll need somewhere to stay. Give me ten minutes and I'll give you a lift back to our place. You can get cleaned up, have a drink and get some kip.'

'Ta, but my boy's on his way over. He'll be here soon. I can stay with him and his missus until I sort things out.'

'Okay, but let me know if there's anything you need.'

Big Lenny looked up at him again and grinned. 'Don't suppose you've got a bottle of Irish on you?'

'Sorry.'

'Well, I wouldn't mind a fag if you've got one going.'

Chris pulled the pack out of his back pocket, gave Lenny one and took another for himself. He lit them both and then gazed towards the firefighters swarming round the burning building. 'They any idea how it started yet?'

Big Lenny inhaled deeply, releasing the smoke in a long, thin stream. 'It weren't no bleedin' accident, that's for sure.'

Chris frowned. 'Is that what they've said?'

'Didn't need to, son. I could smell the petrol when I scarpered. The whole place stank of it.'

'Jesus Christ,' Chris said. Although he already suspected what the answer would be, he had to ask the question. 'You have any trouble tonight, anyone giving you grief?'

'Nah, no more than usual. There ain't been no strangers hanging about and I don't reckon it were one of the regulars.

Amount of time they spend here, be like burning their own home down.'

Chris knew he was right. This wasn't an attack on the Lincoln, but on the people who owned it. Ever since that Russki had been chucked off the balcony, and four of his dealer mates sent packing with their faces rearranged, some form of retribution had been on the cards. Kozlov wasn't the type to sit back and wait. For some people, revenge was best served cold, but that bastard preferred it hot and smoking.

Leaning down, he patted Lenny on the shoulder again. 'I'm glad you're okay, mate. And I meant what I said: anything you need, just give me a bell.'

Chris moved away, looking around for Vale. It didn't take long to find him. Standing head and shoulders above everyone else, Solomon was an easy spot. Chris noticed how the crowd, wary of the big man's height and bulk, kept a respectful distance. No one with any sense would consider invading his personal space.

Solomon turned, his dark face gleaming with sweat, as Chris appeared by his side. 'Boss.'

Chris nodded. 'Big Lennie reckons someone torched the place.'

Solomon gave a snort. 'Someone?'

Chris realised that Solomon's mind was working along the same lines as his own. Neither of them said the name out loud, but they both knew who was behind the fire. 'The old man's gonna do his nut.'

'You ain't kidding there,' Solomon murmured.

They fell into silence, gazing grimly at the inferno. The flames licked around the shattered windows, feeding greedily on the building. Chris could hardly bear to watch. This was worse than bad; it was a goddamn disaster. With the turnover from the other pubs and clubs in steady decline, half the girls refusing to work and their dealers being squeezed on a daily basis, cash flow was already at crisis level. Add in the payment they'd been forced to make to Mendez for the gear, and things were starting to look bleak. The loss of income from the Lincoln could be enough to tip them over the edge.

As Chris was making some fast mental calculations as to how long it might take to get the place up and running again – and that was only if the insurance agreed to pay out – there was a sudden splintering sound, a roar, an ominous groan, before the whole left-hand side of the building collapsed in on itself. There was a flash of light, an explosion of hot orange sparks. A collective sigh of awe rose up from the crowd.

'The filth are gonna want to talk to you,' Solomon said.

Chris glanced at him and nodded. The street was crawling with coppers trying to keep the spectators in line, encouraging them all to return to their beds. Fat chance of that while there was a free pyrotechnic display on offer. 'They can wait,' he said.

As he gazed back towards the fire, Chris felt a tightening in his chest. Andrei Kozlov had declared war, and the Streets would have to respond. But was this a battle they had any chance of winning? He had a bad feeling that it could be more than the pool hall that was going up in smoke.

Chapter Thirty-one

Danny Street was woken by a wide block of light coming through the gap in the curtains. The curtains were orange, a particularly bright and nasty shade. It was typical of the bitch to have not bothered closing them properly. He hissed through his teeth, angry at her carelessness. He had enough trouble sleeping without her making it worse.

Now he was awake, Danny knew he wouldn't be able to drop off again. The ice was calling to him, and he groped, eyes half closed, for the glass pipe and the torn package of crystals on the bedside table. As he sat up to sort his fix, he glanced across at the girl sprawled across the other side of the bed. She was naked, with one leg hanging over the edge, the foot almost touching the floor, as if she'd been meaning to get up but hadn't quite got round to it. There was an ugly glob of spittle nestling in the corner of her mouth, a soft trembling sound escaping from between her lips. The noise wasn't loud, but it still annoyed him. He didn't see why the stupid slut should sleep when he couldn't.

'Wake up,' he said, leaning over and shaking her hard. 'Yer snoring like a fuckin' pig.'

'What is it?' Bleary-eyed, she moved her head and stared up at him. 'What's wrong, babe?'

Danny scowled at her. 'How can anyone sleep with that bloody racket going on?' His temples were throbbing, a hammer beating on his brain, and his tongue felt thick and clammy. He'd been putting away the vodka last night, and now he was paying for it. But it would be all right, it would be okay once he got the pipe lit and had his first hit of the day.

She rolled out of bed and stood upright, her body swaying a little. 'I need the bog.'

As soon as she'd gone, Danny lit up, feeling the acceleration of his heartbeat, the dissipation of his aches and pains, the instant euphoria. That was better. He settled back against the pillows with a sigh. But even now he couldn't get any peace. He could hear a choking, coughing noise coming from the direction of the bathroom. He hoped the bitch wasn't throwing up. Or if she was that she'd make the effort to brush her teeth afterwards. He wasn't going to fuck anything that smelled like a sewer.

It was another few minutes before she returned. Now that his eyes could focus properly, Danny could see the discoloration around her neck, on the tops of her arms and her wrists. The brownish-yellow bruises were a reminder of how she wound him up, of how she made him do things he didn't always want to do.

'You gonna give me some of that?' she said.

There was something about her that put him in mind of Lizzie. That was why he kept coming back. The similarity was purely physical. The slag might look like his stepmother, but she hadn't got her smarts. An evil fuckin' genius, that was what Lizzie Street had been. He felt his cock stiffening as he imagined the way she must have looked when she'd come face to face with her killer: the fear in her eyes, the gradual realisation. He hoped the guy had taken his time before he'd squeezed the trigger, before he'd snuffed out her miserable existence for good. The day he'd heard she was dead had been the best bloody day of his life.

The girl crawled into bed and kneeled beside him.

'Danny?' she said, her blue eyes pleading. 'Come on, hun, don't be mean.'

Danny hesitated before eventually passing over the pipe. He was faintly resentful at having to waste any of the gear on her, but what the hell, there was plenty more where that came from. It was while she was making tiny sucking noises that he felt his rage start to grow again. Couldn't the slag do anything quietly? Even when they were screwing, she had to moan and groan like some overpaid whore. The tart didn't know how to keep her stupid gob shut. His gaze fixed on her bruises again. He didn't feel any regret. Some women deserved everything they got.

Perhaps sensing his antagonism, she stopped what she was doing and looked at him. 'What?' she said.

Danny glared back at her. She was too close to him. Why couldn't she keep her distance? He didn't need her tits in his face at this time of the morning. Gazing down at his groin, he saw that his erection had subsided as quickly as it had arrived. Snatching back the pipe, he shoved her roughly away, sending her flying across the bed.

'What's that for?' she said, her voice small and whiny. As she sat up again, she rubbed at the place on her shoulder where he'd pushed her. 'I ain't done nothin'.'

'You're breathing. That's enough.'

She must have heard the rumours about him and the girl at the funeral parlour, because her eyes immediately widened. Or maybe he was just being paranoid. The shit he smoked could do that to you. Either way, he didn't care. He was Danny Street. He could do what he liked, and no one could stop him.

'I don't want to listen to you, okay? Just shut the fuck up.'

She opened her mouth, but then, as his warning sank in, quickly closed it again. Perhaps the silly cow was finally learning. There was a silence. Danny, who'd been concentrating on the pipe, wasn't sure how long it had lasted. A minute? Ten? After he'd finished his smoke, he reached down, picked up his jacket from the floor and rooted through the pockets. He took out his phone and turned it back on. Four missed calls, two from his brother, one from Solomon, one from Welsh Kenny. And a voicemail message from Chris. He wasn't going to listen to it. Not now. His brother was always stressing out about some problem or another. Fuck him, fuck 'em all. Whatever they wanted, it could wait. He had unfinished business of his own to deal with.

Danny turned his face to look at the girl. She was hunched up in the corner of the bed, her arms wrapped tightly around her knees. 'Don't be like that, babe. Don't go all sulky on me. You know I don't like it.'

Her mouth was set in a pout, her full lips redder than they'd been before she'd gone to the bathroom. She must have put on some lippy while she was in there. 'You don't like me, more like.'

'Course I do,' he wheedled. 'You know I do. You and me, we understand each other.' He leaned towards her, pushing aside her long fair hair to plant a kiss on her bare shoulder. 'You're my girl. We belong together.'

'You're just saying that.'

But he could tell she was softening. That was the thing about tarts like her: for all their hard exteriors, for all their loud mouths and bluff, they still wanted to play Romeo and bloody Juliet. It didn't matter how badly he treated her, how much he knocked her about, she'd still come back for more. 'I'm saying it 'cause it's true.'

'You really mean that?'

Danny smiled at her. He liked to play these games, liked the feeling of control they gave him. He could blow hot and cold, treat her like a piece of shit, but she'd never leave him. Not like his mother had. Not like his older brother, Liam. Their deaths had ripped out his heart, and left a cold stone in its place. 'I'm mad about you, babe. You know I am.'

Unwinding, she shifted closer and leaned her head against his shoulder. 'Promise?'

He was feeling good now; not happy exactly, but as close to it as he could get. 'I promise.'

She slithered down the bed, her slim hips wriggling, and pulled him on top of her.

'Show me,' she whispered.

Danny didn't need asking twice. The ice had done its work. He was hard again now, his cock stiff and upright, the blood rushing through his veins. He was ready for it, eager, almost desperate. Grabbing both her arms, he pinned her down and stared into her face

'Danny,' she murmured.

But it wasn't quite right. *She* wasn't quite right. Closing his eyes, he tried to conjure up a different face, a very different time. As he forced her legs apart, he imagined another woman lying under him. Yes, that was better. As soon as he was inside her, as soon as he began to thrust, he clamped his hand against her mouth. She couldn't spoil it now. A groan rose to his lips. Yes, that was good, very good. This time he was going to do it exactly as he wanted. No noise from her. No sound. Not a single bloody breath . . .

Chapter Thirty-two

By Monday, it was evident that making any kind of contact with Terry Street was going to prove a problem. Hope sighed as she watched the rain streaming down the outside of the window. The season had slipped into autumn, the outside air was chill, and the gathering grey clouds were a perfect reflection of her mood. Connolly's, caught in that mid-morning lull between breakfast and lunch, was quiet. There were only four other customers in the café.

'So what now?' she said, looking back at Flint.

He gave a shrug. 'No one seems to have his number, or at least if they have, they're not prepared to pass it on. I've left messages all over the place, at all the clubs and pubs he runs, but he hasn't called back. I thought Belles was the best bet – that's where he always used to hang out – but they claimed he wasn't there.'

'You think they were lying?'

'Maybe.' He picked up a spoon and tapped it absently against the side of his cup. 'Terry doesn't seem too sociable these days. I even tried his house. It's in south Kellston and it's got the same level of protection as one of Her Majesty's jails. Gates, high walls, alarms, security. Perhaps it makes him feel at home. Anyway, I hadn't been there two minutes when some bruiser comes jogging down the drive and tells me to push off. Except he didn't put it quite as politely as that. I left a note saying I was a friend of Connie Tomlin's, that I needed to talk to him urgently, but that was Saturday morning and he still hasn't got back.'

'So he's avoiding you. That could mean he *does* know something about her.'

'Or the complete opposite. Let's face it, I've never met him before, so why should he bother to call? Especially if Connie never got to see him. Come to that, he may not even be in London at the moment.'

Hope put her elbows on the table and dropped her chin into her hands. This was all too frustrating. 'We can't wait around for ever. There must be some way of getting in touch. What about one of the sons?'

With a tiny clatter, Flint dropped the teaspoon back into the saucer. 'Yeah, but Danny's an out-and-out nut job. He'd rip your head off soon as look as you. We're better off staying away from him.'

Hope, recalling the rumours about Danny Street and the dead girl at the funeral parlour, wasn't about to argue. She immediately pushed to the back of her mind the thought of what the man might have done. It filled her with horror, and if she dwelled on it too long, fear would overwhelm her. 'And the other one?'

'I suppose we could try Chris, but if Terry's deliberately ignoring me, I don't see how—'

'Because anything's better than just sitting here doing nothing.'

Flint looked down at his watch. 'I guess we could head over to Belles, see if he shows up. It opens for the lunchtime session in an hour or so.'

Hope quickly got to her feet and pulled on her raincoat. 'Come on,' she urged. 'We may as well give it a try. What have we got to lose?'

'Hey, what's the rush? I've still got half a cup of tea here.'

But Hope was already heading for the door.

While they sat in the traffic on their way to Shoreditch, Hope related the events of Friday evening. She started with Lana's friend Derek. 'He seemed on edge when it came to Connie, a bit too eager to persuade me that she'd left under her own steam, and that there wasn't anything to worry about. I got the feeling he wasn't too keen on my staying at Tanner Road.' She frowned as she gazed through the windscreen at the slow-moving line of cars ahead. 'Do you know much about him?'

'A bit,' Flint said. 'His name's Derek Parr. He and Lana have been an item for a few years. He flogs cars, flash ones, and must be pretty good at it, judging by the motors on the forecourt. He's got a showroom in Kellston and a couple of others in the West End. He's married, of course, although I'm sure his wife doesn't understand him.'

'Married?'

He glanced over at her and grinned. 'You're not shocked, are you?'

Hope wasn't exactly shocked – infidelity was hardly headline news these days – but she was surprised. 'Somehow I didn't see Lana as the type who'd put up with being someone's bit on the side.'

'Perhaps it suits her.'

'Huh?'

Flint gave a shrug. 'This way she gets all the good stuff, and none of the bad: nice meals out, expensive gifts, the occasional weekend at a luxury hotel. No washing, no ironing, no running around after him or picking up his mess. When she doesn't see him, she's free to do what she likes, when she likes. Some women might view that as a result.'

'Some women,' Hope said drily. She couldn't see the point of a relationship that was based on deceit. Only having part of someone was worse than having nothing at all. Despite her disastrous relationship with Alexander, she still held on to the hope that one day she'd meet a man who'd want to spend the rest of his life with her.

'I suppose you're more the hearts-and-flowers type,' Flint said.

'Naive, you mean?'

'I bet you believe in soulmates, that there's one perfect person out there for you.'

Hope sensed that he was mocking her, and bristled. 'Not exactly. But a bit of commitment isn't too much to ask.'

'Sorry. Did I touch a nerve?'

'No,' she snapped back, thereby proving the very opposite of what she'd intended. Annoyed that he'd got under her skin, she turned the focus on to him. 'So what about you? Are you seeing anyone?'

Flint laughed. 'What do you think?'

'I think it's doubtful that anyone would put up with you.'

'You could be right.'

Hope shook her head, wondering what to make of him. She remembered Lana's warning about how Flint had his own agenda. It made it hard for her to trust him. 'I still don't know anything about you.'

'More than most,' he said. 'Anyway, you get what you see. I'm a simple kind of guy.'

But that, Hope knew, was about as far from the truth as it got. Flint was a mystery. He was the type of man who could say a lot and reveal very little. She was curious to know what made him tick, but the more she saw of him, the less she understood.

'Any more questions?' he said, his grin growing wider.

Hope thought about it for a moment. Then, not wanting to give him the satisfaction of running even larger rings around her, she decided it would be better to change the subject. 'Something else happened on Friday night.'

He listened carefully as she went on to tell him about her acrimonious encounter with Jackie Woods outside the Ladies'. 'I haven't seen her since then. She didn't come back to the flat with the rest of us, and didn't show up over the weekend either.'

'Sounds like she's putting the screws on someone. This whole thing with Terry Street could be a waste of time. Perhaps we should be looking closer to home.'

'But if Jackie knows something about Connie, about what's happened to her, wouldn't Lana have realised by now?'

'Maybe Jackie's not the only one with something to hide.'

Hope turned towards him, her voice faintly accusing. 'You've changed your tune. You said we could trust her. Lana, I mean.'

Flint gave another of his casual shrugs. 'Who knows.'

Hope felt a wave of frustration roll over her. So Lana didn't trust Flint, and Flint didn't trust Lana, and she was stuck in the middle, not knowing who – if anyone – was being straight. 'But you said—'

'Did you tell Lana about Terry Street?' Flint interrupted before she could finish.

She could tell where this was going, and felt instantly defensive. 'No, but that was . . . that was because Derek was there.'

'You could have told her after he'd gone.'

Hope knew he was right, but her reluctance to pass on the information had had more to do with how it might affect Lana's opinion of her rather than any natural distrust. 'Your point being?'

'That you've got your reservations too, and rightly so. Look, I'm sure Lana's not giving you the runaround, but that doesn't mean she's being completely honest either. The only real loyal-ties she's got are to herself and her crew.'

'Wasn't Connie part of her crew?'

'Yeah, and she's agreed to let you into her home, to give you free rein to find out what you can, but that's as far as it goes. Maybe she knows more than she's told us, maybe she doesn't. All I'm saying is that it won't do any harm to exercise some caution.'

What he was really saying, she thought, was that it wouldn't do any harm to keep her big mouth shut about anything they found out. She could gather that much, but what she wasn't so certain of was why. Did Flint know something she didn't? Did he have good reason to suspect Lana of being less than honest? Well, apart from the obvious. Lana's choice of career didn't exactly single her out as the most trustworthy person in the world, but then his record was hardly spotless either. 'I guess,' she murmured, a response she hoped was sufficient to convince him that she was on his side.

They were on Shoreditch High Street now, passing through the junction between Commercial Street and Great Eastern Street. Hope looked out at the crowded pavements, at all the people going about their business. She thought of her own studio back in Albersea, empty and silent. She thought of the sheets of glass with their deep gleaming colours. It was only when she was absorbed in work that she could escape from her problems, from her confusion and grief. At the moment, she had too much time on her hands, and her mind kept sliding back into the past, resurrecting old regrets and painful memo-ries. It was a relief to be out of the flat for a while, even if it did turn out to be a wild goose chase.

A minute later, Flint pulled the Audi up and parked on double yellow lines. 'That's it,' he said. 'That's Belles.'

The building, on the other side of the street, had an inter-esting art deco look to it. In its heyday it had probably been rather grand, but now the exterior was a shabby, fume-stained shade of grey, and the old stucco was peeling from the walls. There was a light coming from inside, but the large italic neon sign that ran across the front of the club had not yet been turned on.

Hope undid her seat belt and reached for the door.

'What are you doing?' Flint said.

'Going over to the club.'

'He's not here yet.'

Hope nodded towards the light. 'Someone's in there. It could be him.'

'It isn't,' he said. 'Check out the cars. Can you see a motor that looks like it belongs to any self-respecting gangster?'

Hope looked over to the side of the building, where there were parking spaces for four vehicles. Only two of them were filled. One was occupied by a battered white van, the other by a small silver-grey Honda. 'Maybe not,' she agreed.

Flint glanced at his watch. 'It's only twenty past eleven. They don't open the doors until twelve.'

'You seem very well informed about opening times.'

He raised his brows. 'Knowledge is power. Isn't that what they say?'

'No other reason, then?'

'I hope you're not suggesting what I think you are.'

'Why? Are sleazy lap-dancing joints full of half-naked women not your scene?'

Flint, aware that he was being probed, shook his head and smiled. 'Who said they were only *half* naked?'

Hope wrinkled her nose, and turned her attention back to the street. The rain had eased off since they'd left Kellston. Only a light shower was falling now, pocking the puddles on the pavement and dampening the shoulders of passers-by. Above the noise of the traffic, she heard the distinctive sound of whirring blades, and peered up at the grey, cloud-filled sky. The helicopter circled for a while and then took off. She dropped her gaze back to the street, and sighed. She wondered how long they'd have to wait. It could be hours. Maybe he wouldn't turn up at all. There was probably a manager who dealt with the mundane duties of opening and closing the club.

'I could have finished that cup of tea,' Flint said.

Hope didn't reply. She was quiet for a while, thinking about her meeting with Eddie Booth. Ever since she'd come out of that jail, something had been nagging away at her. She kept going over and over it in her head, and it still didn't make any sense.

'What's up?' he asked.

She twisted in her seat, uncrossing her legs and then crossing them again. 'Why should anything be up?'

'You don't have to talk to him,' Flint said, mistaking her fidgeting for anxiety at the prospect of approaching Chris Street. 'You can stay in the car.'

'It's not that.'

He turned towards hers, his cool grey eyes staring enquiringly. 'So what it is it?'

Hope hesitated, wanting to ask but afraid of getting an answer that might open up that proverbial can of worms. Some things were best left alone. But she couldn't leave it alone. The more she thought about it, the more it bugged her. 'I was just wondering how old Sally is? You know, Eddie Booth's daughter.'

The question took Flint by surprise. Whatever he'd been expecting her to say, it clearly wasn't that. She saw confusion flash across his face before he answered. 'I've no idea. Does it matter?'

She could have shrugged it off, said that it didn't, claimed that she'd only asked out of curiosity, but that would still leave her wondering. She took a deep breath before she spoke again.

'Eddie reckons I was born in the same year as Sally, and that when I was a baby, Jeff took me to some caff in Hoxton. Except my mother always said that Jeff left her before I was born, that he never even set eyes on me.'

'So you want to know if she was telling the truth.'

'Was she?'

'Well, I never met your mother. I've only heard Jeff's side of the story, so . . .'

'And I've only heard hers. So if I put them together, maybe I can start to figure out what really went on.'

'Or you'll just end up with two conflicting stories.'

Hope could see that was a probability, but she pressed on regardless. 'I'd still like to know what he told you.'

But Flint didn't seem eager to share the information. 'You sure you want to go there? Some things are best left in the past. It's not as though there's anything you can do about it now.'

'Look,' she said, 'I've spent most of my life thinking that Jeff Tomlin didn't give a damn, that he callously abandoned me and my mother. If that isn't the case, then I think I have the right to know.' She glanced back towards the club, noticing the heaps of sodden litter piled up near the door. Belles certainly wasn't the classiest of joints. Her voice had an irritated edge when she continued. 'Anyway, what else are we going to do while we're waiting?'

'All right,' he said, although not with much enthusiasm. 'Just don't forget that all I got was Jeff's point of view, and to say he was bitter about what happened would be the understatement of the year.'

Hope felt a flicker of apprehension. 'Go on.'

Flint looked away for a second, and then slowly turned to meet her eyes again. 'Jeff never stopped talking about Fay, especially after he'd had a few drinks. He was still crazy about her, even years after she'd left. When she'd got pregnant, he'd wanted them to get married, but she wasn't interested. I'm not saying she didn't care for him, but she'd gathered by then that he wasn't going to be the great success she might have imagined when they first got together. They separated for a while, and she went up north for the last few weeks of the pregnancy. After you were born, Jeff persuaded her to come back to London, but the relationship was soon on the rocks. About six months after having you, she took off again. According to Jeff, Fay liked the idea of being with an artist; she just didn't like the economic practicalities. It was all very well for him to be starving in a garret, but she wasn't prepared to share in the experience.'

Hope thought about the question Eddie Booth had asked: *Managed to nab herself a rich husband, did she?* 'You're saying she was mercenary.'

Flint gave a small shake of his head. '*I'm* not saying anything. I'm just telling you what Jeff told me. Anyway, I doubt if it was as straightforward as that. She had a baby to think about, and Jeff wasn't the most responsible of people. Don't get me wrong, he was a great guy, funny, talented, charming, but he had his faults like the rest of us. He could also be a bit . . . intense, if you know what I mean. If he wanted something, he wouldn't give up until he'd got it.'

'Except he didn't get my mother.'

'No, but it wasn't for the want of trying. And if she'd snapped her fingers, he'd have gone running back, even after he'd got hitched to Sadie.'

'He didn't love Sadie?'

'He settled for her. Poor Sadie was always second best, and she knew it. It's one of those classic tragedies, isn't it? Sadie loved him, he loved Fay, she . . . well, I presume she found someone else to love.'

'Lloyd,' Hope murmured. Although that wasn't until seven or eight years after her mother had left Jeff. Maybe there'd been someone else before Lloyd, someone she'd been too young to remember. She stared intently at the windscreen, her hands twisting in her lap, as she tried to process this new information. She'd been convinced that Jeff Tomlin had been the villain of the piece, but now she wasn't so sure. 'Why did she lie to me?'

'Why do people lie about anything? Maybe she thought a clean break would be for the best. Maybe she was trying to protect you.'

'From my own father?' Hope said incredulously. Tears of anger and bewilderment suddenly welled up in her eyes. 'It wasn't fair. I had a right to get to know him, for him to get to know me.'

Flint looked away, discomfited perhaps at having been the cause of her upset. 'Nothing's ever black and white. She must have had her reasons.'

But they were reasons Hope would never get the opportunity to ask her about. Her mother had taken her secrets to the grave. What kind of a father would Jeff Tomlin have been? Only one person knew the answer to that, and she was still missing. Hope thought of Connie, of the one remaining blood relative she had left on this earth, and felt a renewed determination to find her.

Chapter Thirty-three

The neon sign on the front of Belles flickered on at noon, and within ten minutes the first punters had arrived. They came by taxi, City boys mostly, tumbling out of cabs with wide grins on their faces. They laughed and joked, egging each other on. Hope watched them, her brows gathered in a tight frown.

'You don't approve,' Flint said.

'Why should I care?' she said. She was too preoccupied by what she'd been told about her father to be bothered about a bunch of lascivious males with more testosterone than they knew what to do with. 'But so much for the economic crisis.'

'They're just spreading what remains of the wealth,' he said.

'You reckon?'

'Or they could just be a pile of tossers.'

Hope couldn't argue with that.

It was another long half-hour before a dark green Mercedes drew up beside Flint's Audi, indicated, swung into the entrance to the club and parked beside the small grey Honda. A tall, broad-shouldered, dark-haired man got out. He was wearing a sharp suit, and a white shirt with the collar open at the neck.

'That's him,' Flint said. 'That's Chris Street.'

Hope quickly opened the door. 'I'll go. You wait here.'

'You sure?'

'Yes, I'm sure.' It was time, she decided, to stop relying on Flint and to take matters into her own hands. Dodging between the oncoming cars, she made a zigzag dash across the road and jogged up the path to the club. He was almost at the door before she managed to catch him.

'Excuse me,' she said. 'Mr Street?'

He turned to look at her, neither admitting nor denying his identity. His black hair was slicked back from a sharp-featured but not unattractive face.

Hope, trying to ingratiate herself, gave him a broad smile. 'Hi, I was wondering if I could have a quick word?'

'Isn't that what you're doing?'

Her smile hadn't had quite the effect she'd been hoping for. She could see the impatience in his eyes, and wished she'd worked out exactly what she was going to say while she was waiting in the car. 'I ... er ... I wanted to ask you about—'

'If you're after a job, you'll have to talk to the manager. He does all the hiring and firing.'

Hope, not entirely flattered at being mistaken for a wannabe lap dancer, shook her head forcefully. 'No, it's not that.' She saw him glance at his watch, and his obvious impatience made her even more nervous. 'No, it's ... it's about my sister, Connie Tomlin.'

'Never heard of her.'

She stared at him closely. There was nothing in his expression to say he wasn't telling the truth, but then he was probably the kind of man who lied as easily as he breathed. 'It's just that she's gone missing, you see.'

'Then it's the cop shop you're wanting, love. We don't deal in missing girls.'

'No, but I think she came to see your father. It was about seven months ago, and—'

'Well, you'd have to talk to him about that.'

He started to walk away, and before she could think, she laid her hand on his arm. 'Please, just five minutes of your time.'

Chris Street frowned down at her hand, his face tightening. 'Look, love, I can't help you, right? Now if you wouldn't mind, I've got work to do.' And with that, he abruptly shook her off, strode the remaining few feet to the club and disappeared through the door.

Hope's first instinct was to follow him, but one look at the pair of burly security guys, both glaring hard at her, told her the attempt would be futile. And even if she got inside, there was no saying that she'd have any more success.

With a heavy heart, and the knowledge that she'd thrown away a perfect opportunity, Hope walked back across the road and got into the car.

'No luck?' Flint said.

'Says he's never heard of her.' Hope leaned forward, put her head in her hands and groaned. 'Damn! I'm such a fool. I blew it completely. I shouldn't even have mentioned Connie's name. If I could have got him to talk to me inside the club, I'd have had time to explain properly.'

'Don't beat yourself up about it. We'll have to think of something else.'

She raised her face again. 'Like what, for instance?'

Flint gazed thoughtfully out of the window for a few seconds. 'I guess we're going to have to be more creative. Men like Chris Street aren't interested in the little people, not unless there's something in it for them.'

'Little people?' Hope said, lifting her brows.

'You know what I mean. People who don't move in their circle. We're irrelevant to them, invisible. We barely exist. He won't do you any favours unless there's something to be gained by it.'

'So what are you thinking?'

Flint's mouth crept up at the corners. 'Maybe,' he murmured softly. 'Maybe it would work.'

Hope could almost hear his brain ticking over. 'Tell me,' she urged. If there was any way of salvaging this situation, she wanted to know about it.

'What we need is a bargaining chip. We give him something he wants, and in return he arranges a meet for us with Terry Street.'

'Yeah, right,' she said, her hope rapidly dissolving into disappointment. 'And just what could we give him that he could possibly want?'

Flint got his phone out of his pocket and scrolled through the numbers until he reached the one he wanted. 'Hang on,' he said, raising the mobile to his ear. It was answered almost immediately. 'Hey, Duggie, it's Flint. How's tricks?' Hope couldn't hear the reply. 'Look, I've got a job for you. Usual rates. You up for it?' Another silence. 'No, it has to be now. Can you jump in a cab? We're in Shoreditch, parked across the road from Belles.' Silence. 'Yeah, yeah, that's good. Thanks, mate. See you soon.'

'Who's Duggie?' she said, when he'd ended the call.

'The best dip in London. Also known as the Artful Dodger. You'll like him; he's a sweet guy.'

'I'm sure,' she said doubtfully. Did Flint know all the thieves in London? 'But why have you asked him to come here?'

'Our bargaining chip,' he said, clearly delighted with himself. 'Duggie's about to relieve Mr Street of his wallet.'

Hope's eyes widened with alarm. 'Are you insane? You're going to get him to steal Chris Street's *wallet*?'

'Not steal it exactly, just borrow it for a while. Think how grateful he'll be when you return it to him.'

She shook her head in exasperation. This was madness. 'Saying what exactly?'

'That you came back to try and see him again, that you noticed it lying by the side of his car, and being the nice honest person you are, you decided to hand it over rather than nicking its contents and dumping it in the nearest bin.'

'And if he doesn't believe me?'

'Oh, he probably won't. But that's not important. You'll have got his attention, and that's what matters, isn't it?'

Hope half opened her mouth, intending to deliver some further objections, but none immediately sprang to mind. She bit down on her lower lip and thought about it some more. Although not exactly enamoured of the plan, it did have certain advantages. People were usually grateful for their property being returned, especially when that property was cash and credit cards. And if one good turn deserved another, she might just be able to persuade Chris Street to arrange that meet with Terry.

'So,' Flint said. 'Are you up for it?'

Hope hesitated. The only thing holding her back was cowardice. People with any sense didn't mess with the likes of Chris Street. But then again, what room was there for sense when a sister was missing and the only lead to her whereabouts was a man as elusive as a unicorn. If she threw away this chance, she might not get another. 'I suppose,' she said reluctantly.

'Try not to sound too enthusiastic.'

'You're not the one who'll have to go in there and tell him a pack of lies.'

'Hardly a pack,' Flint said. 'And I could do it if you don't want to.'

Hope was tempted to accept the offer, but she knew in her heart that it had to be her. If Flint returned the wallet and then started asking questions about Connie, it would be obvious to Chris Street that he'd been well and truly set up. However,

262

having been there earlier, *she* might just get away with it. 'No, it's okay. I'll do it.'

Flint shifted in his seat. 'You don't have to.'

'I know.'

'And you don't have to worry,' he said. 'You'll be fine.'

Which was all very well, except *he* wasn't going to be the one trying to strike a bargain with the Devil. Or the Devil's son, at least. What if something went wrong? What if Chris Street turned nasty; what if he realised what they'd done and . . . But no, she couldn't afford to think along those lines. She made an attempt to push all the negatives aside. She had to stay calm, not freak herself out. All she'd be doing was returning a wallet. There was nothing too difficult about that.

They were quiet for a while, neither of them saying anything.

Hope tapped her fingers restively on her thighs as they waited. She was fighting a losing battle against her fear, becoming increasingly concerned about what would happen once she was inside the club – if she ever actually managed to make it that far.

It was only ten minutes before another black cab pulled up outside Belles. This time the occupant, instead of heading inside, got out and crossed the road to the Audi. He was a young, slender guy, dressed in a regular suit and tie. Hope's first thought was that it was a stroke of luck that he'd been wearing a suit when Flint had called – she doubted he'd get into the club in jeans – but then she realised that, like Lana and the girls, he probably spent the early part of his mornings riding the tube. Dressed in the familiar uniform of the City boy, he'd look like any other commuter on his way to work.

Pulling open the door, Duggie climbed into the back seat. He brought with him a blast of damp air and the pungent aroma of cheap aftershave. 'Flint,' he said, leaning forward to slap him on the shoulder. 'Good to see you again, man.'

'You too. This is a pal of mine, Hope.'

Hope turned, forcing her lips into a smile. Nerves had made her mouth dry, and the 'hi' she came out with sounded small and croaky. Duggie gave her a friendly nod. He couldn't have been much older than twenty, and he had one of those butter-wouldn't-melt-in-his mouth faces, his skin clear and smooth, his eyes very blue. Which probably accounted for why he was so successful. No one would suspect him of anything more serious than having bad taste in shaving products.

'So who's the mark?' Duggie said.

Flint missed a beat before he spoke. 'Chris Street.'

Duggie instantly drew back, a thin whistle escaping from between his teeth. 'Aw, man! You want to get my bleedin' legs broken?'

'They won't get broken if he doesn't catch you at it. Of course, if you don't reckon you're good enough ...'

'I didn't say that.' There was a pregnant pause while Duggie considered it some more, clearly weighing up the risks against the value of his own reputation. 'But this is Chris Street we're talking about. If it all goes tits-up, I'm gonna be flat on my back sucking grapes for the next three months. And that's if I'm lucky. You hear about the last dip got caught on their premises? They busted his legs *and* his hands.'

'Then you shouldn't do it,' Hope said, her conscience getting the better of her. She wouldn't be able to live with herself if anything bad happened to him. 'Not if there's a chance of you getting caught.'

'That ain't gonna happen,' Duggie said, his chest puffing up even as he spoke. 'All I'm saying is this ain't your run-of-the-mill job. It comes with added risk. Not good for the blood pressure, right?'

'All you're saying,' Flint replied, 'is that you want more money.'

Duggie grinned. 'This is Chris Street's wallet, man. We're talking serious shit here.'

'Okay, how much do you want?'

'Double should do it.'

Flint laughed. 'I'm not Alan Sugar, kid. One fifty and that's my final offer.'

'One seventy-five.'

'What didn't you understand about final offer?'

'C'mon, I've got expenses. Got to pay to get in, ain't I? Then there's drinks to buy. I can't sit there without a drink.'

Flint thought about it some more. 'Okay, one sixty, but that's your lot. And don't go spending it all on the first nubile cutie who bats her eyelashes at you.'

Duggie grinned. He leaned forward again and put out his hand. 'Okay, man, you've got yourself a deal.'

Flint shook on it. 'Oh, and I want the wallet delivered with the contents still intact. Not a single penny missing.'

'As if,' Duggie said. 'Would I try to rip you off?'

Flint gave him a look that said more than words ever could.

'You sure you'll be okay in there?' Hope asked.

'Yeah, it'll be cool. They don't know me. I never usually work their joints.' He threw a faintly accusing glance at Flint. 'Ain't safe, is it? They don't like having their punters turned over, not by the likes of me, anyhow.'

'Don't worry,' Flint said. 'There won't be any comeback. He'll have his wallet returned ten minutes after you've lifted it.'

'What?' Duggie said, frowning. 'I don't get it. If you're just gonna hand it back, why do you want me to—'

'You don't need to get it. All you need to do is keep your side of the bargain.'

Duggie looked from Flint to Hope and back again. 'None of my business, right?'

'Got it in one.'

Duggie waited until another black cab drew up outside the club before uttering a breezy 'Here we go, folks,' and jumping out of the Audi. After crossing the road, he tagged along behind the four young blokes strolling up the path to Belles. He must have said something amusing to the two guys at the rear, because they both turned their heads towards him and laughed. One of the doormen waved them all inside without a second glance.

'Game on,' Flint murmured.

Hope stared hard at the door Duggie had just passed through. 'You think he'll be okay?'

'Course he will. The boy's a pro.'

But Hope's imagination was working overtime, and the images she was conjuring up did nothing for her peace of mind. Chris Street was a thug, a cold and brutal man. She'd looked into his eyes and hadn't liked what she'd seen. If Duggie made even the smallest of mistakes, there'd be no second chances. Street's retribution would be fast and savage – and that young dip's fingers would never pick pockets again.

Chapter Thirty-four

Almost an hour later, Duggie still hadn't come out of Belles. Hope alternated between gazing out of the window and looking at her watch. The minutes passed at a snail's pace, each one slower than the last. Flint, who seemed thoroughly relaxed, had put on the radio and was humming along to an old song by the Pretenders. 'Forever Young' floated over the airwaves, reminding Hope of Duggie's youth and making her feel increasingly guilty about what they'd asked him to do.

'Why's it taking so long?' she said.

'Don't worry, he'll be fine. These things take time. He has to choose his moment.'

'And what if he chooses the wrong one?'

'He won't.'

Hope was starting to wonder if the ends could ever justify the means. Since coming to London, her principles had entered a state of limbo. Living under Lana's roof, she'd quickly learned to put aside – or at least *pretend* to put aside – her sense of right and wrong. It had only been a week, but already the daily routine of the crew coming back to the flat and depositing their takings had become virtually normal to her. Her eyes had ceased to widen as they dropped the stolen cards into the bowls, or her inner morality to baulk at how they made their living. What they did was wrong, she knew it was, but she was prepared to accept it if it meant she might get a useful lead on Connie.

'What if Chris Street stays in his office?' she said. 'Duggie might not even get the chance to lift the wallet.'

'He'll come out at some point. He'll want to do the rounds, greet the regulars, that kind of thing. In the current economic climate, you have to try and hang on to your customers. Once he shows his face, it'll give Duggie the chance to get up close.'

And the chance to get caught, she thought. What if . . . But she pushed the thought aside again. If she kept dwelling on what *might* happen, she'd be a nervous wreck. 'Tell me something.'

'What?'

'Anything. Just something to stop me thinking. In fact, no, why don't you tell me some more about Jeff.'

'I thought you weren't interested.'

'I wasn't. But I am now. Is that a problem?'

'Course not,' he said, leaning forward to turn the radio down. 'Where do you want me to start?'

But Hope never got the opportunity to hear what he had to say. At that very moment, Duggie stepped out of Belles, glanced over his shoulder and swaggered across the road. It was clear from his grin that the mission had been successful. She gave a sigh of relief as he climbed into the back seat of the Audi.

'Just tell me I'm the business, man,' Duggie said, throwing a smart black leather wallet into Flint's lap.

'You're the business. I never doubted you for a minute.'

'Had to wait around,' Duggie said, placing his hands on the two seats in front and breathing beer fumes on to the side of Hope's face. 'He didn't show for a while.'

Flint opened the wallet and checked out the contents. Hope

could see about two hundred quid in twenties, as well as a lot of plastic.

'It's all there,' Duggie said indignantly, as if his honesty was being called into question. 'God's honour. I ain't even looked inside.'

Flint took a wad of notes from his own wallet, counted out the fee and passed the money over. 'Here. And thanks, I appreciate it.'

'My pleasure,' Duggie said. 'Only next time you've got business with the Streets, don't call *me*, right?'

'It's a promise.'

Duggie didn't hang about. As soon as he had the money, his hand was on the door. 'Okay, man. See you. Stay lucky.'

'You too.'

The car door slammed shut, and Hope turned to watch as Duggie strolled off down the road. His part of the job was done. Now it was down to her. She took a deep breath before turning back to Flint. 'I'd better get in there before he notices it's missing.'

'You might just want to . . .' Flint lifted his forefinger and indicated a spot just below his eye. 'You've got a bit of, er, stuff here.'

'Stuff?' Hope flipped down the mirror and stared at her reflection. Her mascara had run, leaving a black smudge under her lashes. Not the best look in the world. Getting a tissue from her bag, she dampened it and rubbed at the offending mark. Then she took a moment to examine the rest of her face. What she saw didn't do much for her confidence. Pale and drawn, she looked as scared as she felt. Quickly she put on some lipstick and ran a comb through her hair.

'You know, you don't have to—'

'I do,' she interrupted, before he could finish the sentence. 'How's that?' she asked, turning towards him. 'Better?'

'Fine.'

Fine didn't exactly swell her ego to bursting point, but it was clearly the best she was going to get. 'Okay, I'm ready.'

'Although you could . . .'

'What?'

His eyes flicked down to her chest. 'I don't know, maybe you could undo a button or two. That white shirt's kind of starchy.'

Hope's mouth dropped open and she glared back at him. 'I'm not going for a bloody interview.'

Flint grinned. 'Yeah, but no harm playing to your strengths. You're an attractive woman. Chris Street likes attractive women. Ergo—'

'Ergo nothing,' she growled.

'It was only a suggestion.'

'Well keep your rubbish suggestions to yourself.'

Before the last of her courage could desert her, Hope grabbed hold of the wallet, dropped it into her bag and jumped out of the car. She waited for a gap in the traffic and dashed across the road. *Men*, she hissed under her breath. And then, belatedly, she realised that he'd called her attractive. Did he really think that, or was he just buttering her up? You could never tell with Flint.

Looking over her shoulder, Hope saw him watching her. He gave her the thumbs-up. She nodded back. Then, as she headed for Belles, she got to wondering. Maybe he had a point. Maybe she shouldn't be so uptight about all this. If a bit of cleavage was going to help persuade Street to cooperate, it might not be that high a price to pay. She was aware that her moral compass was starting to waver again, that she was thinking of doing some-thing she would never normally do – but then these weren't normal times. She glanced down at her chest, trying to decide. She didn't have the biggest boobs in the world, but the bra she was wearing went some way towards compensating for nature's shortfalls.

There was a queue outside the door, but it was moving

quickly. She had to make up her mind, and fast. Well, she was only going to get one shot at this, so she'd better make it her best. Putting all thoughts of propriety aside, she furtively lifted a hand and undid two more buttons.

The queue shifted forward, and suddenly Hope was faced with one of the security guys who'd witnessed her earlier encounter with Street. He was a tall black guy with the kind of muscles that would make even the most recalcitrant of punters reluctant to pick an argument. And from the way he was look-ing at her, his brows shifting up an inch, she had no doubt at all that he remembered her.

'Yeah?'

'I'd like to see Mr Street, please. *Chris* Street.'

'You got an appointment?

'No, I don't have an appointment, but—'

'Mr Street don't see anyone without an appointment, love. That's the rules. Can't do nothin' about it. You give the club a ring, right, talk to the manager and maybe he'll fix something up.'

Having said his piece, he instantly dismissed her, waving in the men who were standing behind her.

'But I have to see him,' Hope insisted. 'It's important.'

The big guy gazed down on her. His patience, such as it was, was wearing thin. 'What don't you understand?' he said. 'I've already told you, you can't—'

'Mr Street will want to see me,' she said firmly. 'I've got something that belongs to him.'

'Oh yeah?'

Hope took the wallet out of her bag and held it up for him to see. 'This is Mr Street's. He dropped it earlier, and I'm sure he'd like it back.'

The big guy reached out a hand. 'I can give it to him.'

But Hope took a step back and shook her head. 'No thanks, I'd rather do it in person.'

271

'Like I said. Mr Street ain't available.'

'Well I wouldn't fancy being in your shoes when you tell him that you turned me away.'

She saw a flicker of worry pass across his face, and quickly took advantage of it. 'Why don't you give him a call. See what *he* says.'

The guy wavered for a moment, wondering perhaps whether he dared to try and snatch the wallet from her. Hope put it behind her back. If he made a move, she'd kick up a fuss, start yelling perhaps. It wouldn't do much for the reputation of the club, and it might even get Chris Street's attention.

But in the event, she didn't need to resort to such measures. The security man gave her an evil look and got out his mobile. 'Wait here,' he ordered, walking away. He stepped just inside the door and continued to glare at her as he spoke into the phone. She couldn't hear what he was saying, but doubted it was anything flattering.

A minute later, his expression still sour, he came back out. 'This way,' he said abruptly, with a jerk of his head.

Hope tried not to look too triumphant as she followed him inside.

Chapter Thirty-five

The foyer of Belles was painted a deep shade of red and covered with photographs of girls in various stages of undress. Hope lowered her eyes, focusing instead on the threadbare carpet. Through a pair of double doors she could hear the heavy thud of music, the sound of laughter and the clapping of hands. Her own palms were starting to sweat as she followed the man along a narrow corridor, and she surreptitiously wiped them on her trousers. Any minute now and she'd come face to face with Chris Street again. *Don't blow it this time,* she told herself. *Stay calm. Stay cool.* But that wasn't so easy with her heart hammering hard in her chest.

The man stopped and knocked on a door marked 'Manager'.

'Yeah,' a voice called from inside.

The black guy pushed open the door and stood aside. 'This is her, guv.'

'Thanks, Sol. You can go now.'

Hope stepped tentatively forward, and the door was closed behind her. She was standing in a large office with three separate desks. The walls in here were white, stained yellow near the ceiling, and all the furniture was black. The smell of stale cigarette smoke lingered in the air. Chris Street was sitting directly in front of her, leaning back in a swivel chair. He didn't bother to get to his feet. Instead he looked her up and down, and shook his head. 'You again,' he said.

'Hope Randall,' she said, introducing herself. She walked across the room and put the wallet on his desk. 'I wanted to return this personally. You dropped it outside the club.'

Street studied her for a while, then reached forward, opened the wallet and checked out its contents. His brows shifted up a fraction when he realised all the cash and cards were still there. 'Good of you. Thanks.'

'It's a pleasure.'

'I suppose you'll be wanting a reward.' He took a couple of twenties and pushed them across the desk. 'Is that enough?'

Hope didn't pick up the notes. 'There is something you can do for me, but it isn't that. I don't want your money. I just want five minutes of your time.'

As if his time was more precious than his cash, Street frowned.

'Please,' she said. 'I wouldn't ask if it wasn't important.'

He gave a weary shrug and gestured towards the chair beside her. 'You'd better grab a seat then. But make it snappy, I've got a lot on.'

'Thank you. I appreciate it.' Hope sat down, rapidly trying to gather her thoughts so she didn't come out with anything stupid. She didn't want to make the same mistakes she'd made with Eddie Booth. 'The thing is . . .' she began. Her lips were dry, and she ran her tongue across them. 'The thing is, I'm looking for my sister, Connie. She's been missing for a while now, and—'

'You want to know if she was working here? Is that it?'

'No, that's not it at all,' Hope said, the interruption not aiding her concentration. 'She wasn't. But I think she may have come here to see your father. It would have been some time in February.'

His dark eyes were suddenly wary. 'And why would she have done that?'

'Because she was trying to find out what happened to *our* father.' Hope, so tense she could barely breathe, made an effort to keep her voice steady. 'He was murdered twelve years ago. His name was Jeff Tomlin and he was a friend of your dad's.'

'And?'

Hope looked at him closely. Had she seen a flicker of recognition at the name? She wasn't sure. There had certainly been a change in his expression, but that could have been down to her mention of a murder. 'I think Connie might have asked him for help, for some information about the past. Perhaps he told her something, something important. Do you think that's possible?'

Street gave a shrug, but didn't reply.

'Only if he did, it might be a lead, you see, a clue to what she did next. Do you think he could have met up with her?'

'Could have. I don't keep tabs on the old man.'

'But he never mentioned it?'

'No.'

'Oh,' Hope said, disappointed. Digging into her bag, she retrieved her purse and took out the photograph of Connie that she'd found in the metal box. She passed it over to him. 'She's the one on the left. Do you ever remember seeing her?'

Street leaned forward, looked at the photo but then shook his head. 'No, I don't recognise her.'

'But that doesn't mean she wasn't here.'

'Doesn't mean she was, either.'

Hope, aware that she wasn't making a great deal of progress, decided to jump in with the million-dollar question. 'Well, could you arrange for me to see your father, so I can ask him for myself?'

'Be a waste of time,' he said.

Hope, frustrated, raised her hands into the air. She'd come too far – and Duggie had risked too much – to leave without a fight. 'But you can't know that. You've already said that you don't keep tabs on him. Doesn't that imply that you don't always know where he is or what he's doing?' Then, worried that she was sounding too aggressive, she hastily moderated her tone. 'Look, I'm not going to hassle him, I swear. I'm not going to cause any trouble. All I'm trying to do is find my missing sister.'

Chris Street sat back and put his hands behind his head. His poise was almost too casual. She noticed his gaze slide down towards her cleavage, before slowly lifting to her face again. There were a few seconds of silence before he spoke. 'Tell you what, how about we make a deal. I ask my dad if he'll see you, and in return you do something for me.'

Hope's response was cautious. 'I've already done you a favour. I've returned your wallet.'

'That doesn't count as a favour. It's every good citizen's duty to return lost property.'

'And what about missing sisters? Isn't it every good citizen's duty to help out with them too?'

Chris Street scratched his unshaven chin and grinned. 'Okay, how about this for a deal: you have dinner with me tonight, and I promise to ask my dad about Connie.'

The invitation came out of the blue, and left Hope temporarily speechless. Stunned, she stared back at him, not knowing what to say. It was then that she noticed the gold band on the third finger of his left hand. 'I don't think your wife would be too happy about that.'

Street barked out a humourless laugh. 'The delightful Jenna doesn't give a damn about what I do or don't do. We're separated. So how about it? What do you say – yes or no?'

Hope hesitated, but only for a second. If it meant she might get information about Connie, it would be madness to refuse. But she wasn't going to let him have it all his own way. 'How do I know you'll stick to your side of the bargain?'

'You have my word. Isn't that enough?'

Hope wasn't sure that it was, but she smiled back at him just the same. At the same time, she was rapidly juggling the pros and cons. The pros were simple – she might get a meet with Terry and be able to ask those all-important questions – but the cons involved spending the evening with a known gangster and fending off whatever lecherous advances might come after the food and wine. 'Okay,' she said finally, deciding that the advantages, on balance, had to outweigh the disadvantages. 'Do you like Italian?' When she'd been out with Evelyn, she'd noticed a restaurant on the high street that was displaying rave reviews in its window. 'There's a place in Kellston. Adriano's. Do you know it?'

'Yeah, it's not bad. Give me your address and I'll pick you up.'

But Hope didn't want him to know where she was living. Having the likes of Chris Street knocking on the door at Tanner Road wouldn't do her any favours with Lana. 'If it's all the same, I'd rather meet you there. Eight o'clock all right with you?'

'As you like,' he said. 'But you'd better let me have your phone number, just in case I get held up.'

Hope, reluctant to give out her number, tried to sound blasé. 'Is that likely?'

'Not likely,' he said, 'but possible. Things happen, and I wouldn't like to think of you waiting there all alone.'

Hope wasn't overly keen on the prospect either. She remembered an occasion when Alexander had failed to turn up and she'd been left sitting like a saddo in some swanky restaurant in Covent Garden. No, that was an experience she never wanted to go through again. 'Have you got something I can write it on?'

Street tore off a corner from one of the many sheets of paper littering his desk, and pushed it towards her.

Hope quickly scribbled down her number. 'You'd better give me yours too,' she said. 'Just in case something crops up.'

Instead of writing it down, he picked his phone up off the desk and dialled the number she'd given him. The mobile in her bag immediately started ringing. 'It's the right number, then,' he said.

'Why would I give you the wrong one?'

Street put the receiver down. Something close to bitterness invaded his voice. 'Why do women do anything?'

It was, she presumed, a rhetorical question, and so she didn't attempt to answer it. She got the impression from his tone that he and Jenna hadn't parted on the best of terms. She hoped she wasn't in for an evening of tedious recriminations. Being forced to share a meal with him was bad enough, but it would be even worse if he was going to spend the entire time talking about his problems with his ex. Having got what she'd come for, and not wanting to prolong the interview, she decided to make her escape. 'I'll let you get on, then.'

She had the door open and was almost out of the office when he said, 'Just one question before you go. How did you do that?'

'Do what?' she said, genuinely confused.

'The wallet,' he said. 'I couldn't have dropped it. I know I couldn't. It was in my inside pocket.'

Hope made her best stab at a mysterious smile. 'You figure it out. I'll see you tonight.'

Chapter Thirty-six

DI Valerie Middleton had already known that she wouldn't be welcome. That much had been made clear on the phone. Over seven months on, and the police still hadn't managed to arrest anyone. Gemma Leigh had long since lost faith in the justice system – if she'd ever had any to begin with. She was a small, thin, mousy-haired girl, but what defined her, of course, were the terrible scars on her face. Back in February, she'd had the misfortune to become the Whisperer's third victim.

Valerie had been going through her statement again, trying to jog her memory. 'Anything, even the smallest detail, could be important. Sometimes things come back.'

Gemma's grey eyes, one of them half-blind, gazed reproachfully back at her. 'I've told you everything I know. I can't remember nothin' else.'

'What about—'

'Why can't you leave me alone?' For what must have been the tenth time in an hour, Gemma jumped up from the armchair and went to stand by the window with her spindly arms wrapped around her chest. She'd been agitated ever since Valerie had arrived. Even when she was sitting down, she'd been unable to stay still, her hands constantly moving in her lap, one foot tapping relentlessly against the floor. There was a tiny tic on the side of her face, but it was impossible to tell if it was down to nerves or a permanent result of the assault.

Valerie let her be for a moment. The flat, on the fourteenth floor of Carlton House, was small, and sparsely furnished: an old caramel-coloured sofa, a blue armchair and a glass-topped coffee table with a crack running along the length of its surface. Someone had started to strip the old flowery paper from the walls, but given up before it was even half done. A closed door off to the right led to what must be the bedroom, and straight ahead was a galley-style kitchen. The whole place was shabby and depressing, the kind of space that spoke only of quiet desperation.

'Gemma,' she said softly, when a couple of minutes had passed. 'Have you thought any more about the counselling?'

Gemma gave a snort, and came back to sit in the armchair. 'What good's bloody counselling going to do?' She lifted a hand and jabbed at her disfigured face. 'It ain't going to sort this, is it? Even the fuckin' weirdos don't want to screw a tart who looks like summat out of *Halloween*.'

Valerie understood her bitterness, but could think of nothing to say to assuage it. She wondered how Gemma survived now she couldn't work the streets. Basic benefits, she supposed, but they wouldn't go far. And it wasn't as if anything was likely to change in the future. Her prospects had been bleak before the attack, but now they were a hundred times worse. This dismal flat, in this dismal concrete block, was as good as it was going to get.

'What's the matter?' Gemma said caustically. 'Embarrassed, are you? Got no comforting words to offer? You're all the same, you lot. You don't give a fuck about the likes of us.'

'That's not true. We *will* catch him, I promise. We'll make him pay for what he's done.'

'You think that'll change anything?' Gemma shook her head. Her hands had begun their restless dance again, her fingers scratching at her thighs. 'Even if you lock the bastard up for a thousand years, it ain't gonna give me my face back. So why don't you just get on with your investigating and leave me in peace.'

But peace, Valerie suspected, was a state of mind that would elude Gemma Leigh for ever. Her attacker hadn't just destroyed her face, but whatever hopes and dreams she might have harboured too. Sensing that it was time to go, Valerie stood up and dropped a card on to the coffee table, one of many that she'd left. It would probably go straight in the bin, but she had to keep on trying. 'Call me,' she said, 'if anything comes back to you. Or if . . . if you just want to talk.'

As if that prospect was about as remote as her waking up to find her former life restored, Gemma gave a disdainful nod. Then, eager to get rid of her unwanted guest, she hurried over to the door.

Valerie followed, still trying to think of something to say that would make a difference. Nothing original came to mind. 'Take care of yourself,' was the best she could come up with. And that was met with the same blank-faced stare as all her earlier attempts at creating a bond. Seconds later, she was standing in the corridor, listening to the sound of three solid bolts being pulled across. What she couldn't work out was whether Gemma was locking other people out, or locking herself in. Whatever the answer, one thing was clear – she had just walked out of a prison.

Valerie stood on the balcony for a while, gazing down on the ugly sprawl of the Mansfield Estate. The view was relentlessly depressing. The ground was strewn with litter, all the buildings decaying and covered in graffiti. It was a concrete jungle, and hopelessness seeped out of every pore. There but for the grace of God, she thought, grateful that she'd not been born into such an environment.

It was while she was standing there, pondering on the inequalities of life, that she spotted the two men walking towards the Carlton House car park. Even fourteen floors up, she could recognise them: Terry Street and his crazy son Danny. She sucked in a breath. What were they doing here? Trying to reassert their authority over the estate, perhaps. Rumour had it that the power of the Streets was under threat, and that other gangs were beginning to muscle in. A fire, started deliberately, had virtually destroyed the Lincoln Pool Hall on Saturday morning. Terry wouldn't be happy about that. He wouldn't be happy at all.

Valerie continued to watch as the two of them got into a Range Rover. She had nothing but contempt for Terry Street, but her real loathing was reserved for Danny. He was a violent sadist with an uncontrollable temper. She'd lost count of the number of times he'd been arrested but then managed to wriggle free of the charges; victims and witnesses alike were too afraid to give evidence against him. The only person who had spoken out was Alice Avery, but the statement of a mentally ill woman – a woman who had killed her own lover – would hardly have stood up in court.

The murder of Toby Grand had been one of the most disturbing cases she had ever worked. She could still recall Gerald Grand's chilling gasp of horror when they'd discovered his son's pale corpse laid out on the table. Toby's twenty-five-year-old face had been as angelic in death as it had once been in life. But his good looks had disguised a darker side to his character. He had used Alice Avery, pretending that he cared for her whilst simultaneously fleecing her of all her savings. Then, when she'd ceased to be of any further use, he had callously dumped her.

Most women, of course, did not turn to murder when they were used and abandoned, but Alice had not been most women. Fifteen years older than Toby, she'd been insecure, vulnerable, and mercilessly bullied by an overbearing mother. Pushed to the edge, she had reached her limit and eventually snapped. But her final act, bizarre as it seemed, had been one of love; after stabbing him to death, she had used all her skills as an embalmer to preserve his body in a perfect likeness of peace.

It was Valerie who had interviewed her in the small stuffy room at Cowan Road police station. Alice had talked freely, indeed even eagerly about everything that had happened, as if it were a relief to unburden herself. But Valerie had quickly realised that the case would never come to trial. It didn't take a psychiatrist to recognise that Alice Avery had killed Toby while the balance of her mind had been unhinged. The woman wasn't sane – and would maybe never be sane again.

Valerie still had her gaze fixed on the Range Rover as it pulled away. The murder and its aftermath had been both shocking and tragic, but it was what Alice had told her about Danny Street, his late-night visits to the funeral parlour, that had really made her skin crawl. On the last occasion, he had demanded to be left alone with the body of a recently embalmed young woman. There was no doubt as to what his intentions had been.

Valerie had believed what Alice had told her, but who else would take the word of a killer who was obviously deranged? With no corroborating evidence, it had been impossible to proceed. Although he'd been questioned, Danny Street, unsurprisingly, had denied everything. She could still remember the vile smirk on his face as he'd left the station with his lawyer.

Valerie sighed and made her way to the main stairwell, trying to decide whether to descend on foot or take the lift. The lift was quicker, but it smelled abysmal and was renowned for its habit of breaking down. The fourteen flights of steps, however, would be populated by a healthy supply of local yobs, dealers and muggers. She didn't fear for her safety – they all knew who she was – but she could do without the hassle.

In the event, her mind was made up for her. The lift pinged open and an elderly Asian-looking woman got out. She gave Valerie a wary glance before lowering her eyes and scuttling around the corner. Valerie stepped inside the open box. The lift still stank of urine, and she held her breath as it slowly descended. *Please don't break down,* she muttered as it lurched precariously from one floor to the next.

The long journey earthwards gave her plenty of time to think. She felt frustrated by what had happened with Gemma Leigh, annoyed at herself for failing to make any kind of connection. If the girl didn't trust her, she wouldn't talk even if she did remember something. But what could she have done differently? Gemma had settled into an acceptant despair: what was done was done, and the damage could never be repaired.

It was a relief when the lift finally stopped with a jolt on the ground floor. As Valerie stepped into the empty foyer, she reached for her phone. She wanted to talk to someone, and that someone was Harry. He was the only person who really understood. But no sooner had she pressed the button for his number than she cancelled it. What was she doing? She couldn't keep turning to him whenever things got tough.

Putting the phone back in her bag, she walked quickly towards her car. It was only as she got out her keys and bleeped open the door that she noticed the folded piece of paper stuck under the windscreen wipers. She knew instantly what it was, what it had to be. Her pulse began to race. So he'd been here. The Whisperer had been here.

She whirled around, rapidly scanning the surrounding area,

but already knew that he'd be long gone. Had he followed her here? He must have done. In the busy traffic of Kellston, it wouldn't have been hard to tail her. She was certain that no other car had followed her on to the estate, but he could have parked by the gates and waited for her to go inside.

She put on some gloves before touching the note. There had been two more missives since the one she'd received at the hospital, both full of hellfire and damnation, and both mailed to her at the police station from different London post offices. Neither of them had held any useful fingerprints, and it was doubtful that this one would either, but she wasn't prepared to take the chance.

She gingerly picked up the note by its edges, climbed into the car and locked the door behind her. Then, before she could think about it too much, she flipped the piece of paper open. It was typed in the same bold print, perfectly centred in the middle of the page, but this time the message was different.

What about the missing one? What about C?

Valerie stared at it for a long time. *The missing one.* What was he telling her? Her mouth went dry and she could feel her heart thumping in her chest. Oh God, was there another girl who'd been attacked, one they hadn't found? And did that mean he was still holding her, or did it mean that she was . . .

Throwing the note on to the passenger seat, Valerie started the car and pulled out of the space, but then abruptly braked again. She'd just remembered something. Hadn't the Streets been parked only a few yards away? She'd seen them leave but she hadn't seen them arrive. What if one of them had slipped the note under her wipers while she was talking to Gemma Leigh? Not Terry, she decided, none of this was his style – but what about Danny? He could easily be in the frame. He was certainly twisted enough.

While she was pondering on this possibility, she recalled Gemma's frequent trips to the window. From where she'd been standing, she'd have had a bird's-eye view of the whole area. It was a long shot, but it was worth a go. Getting out her phone, she scrolled down the menu and keyed in the number. It was answered after a single ring.

'Gemma? Hi, it's Valerie. I'm really sorry to bother you again but I need to ask you a question.' She paused, waiting for some kind of response; when none was forthcoming, she carried on regardless. 'While I was with you, you went to the window a few times. Did you see anyone hanging around the car park?'

'What do you mean?' Gemma said.

Valerie frowned, unsure as to how to make the question any clearer. 'Did you see anyone walking near the cars, or ... did you see any other car arrive?'

'No.'

'You're sure, no one at all?'

'Just said, didn't I?' And then, with a slightly more gleeful edge to her voice, Gemma added: 'Why? Has some arse had a go at your motor?'

'Something like that,' Valerie said. She couldn't mention the note, and she didn't want to. If Gemma got even a hint that the Whisperer had been this close to her, she'd be likely to freak. Valerie was sure, however, that the girl wasn't in any danger; her attacker had come to the Mansfield for an entirely different reason. 'I don't suppose you saw a Range Rover park here while I was with you?'

'No,' Gemma said again.

'Okay, it doesn't matter. Thanks anyway.'

Disappointed, Valerie said her goodbyes and hung up. There was no way of knowing whether Gemma was telling the truth or not. She glanced down at the piece of paper and banged her hands hard against the wheel, angry that the bastard had managed to slip away yet again. Her stomach churned as she thought about the contents of the note. They'd missed something, they must have. One of his victims hadn't been discovered, and the Whisperer didn't like his work to go unappreciated.

Valerie drove back to Cowan Road, cursing all the way. She flew through the doors of the police station, up the stairs and into the incident room. Kieran Swann was sitting in front of a computer, sipping from a plastic cup of coffee. He glanced up, his brows shifting a little, as she hurried towards him. She hurled the note down on the desk.

'Ah, shit,' he murmured.

'It was left while I was visiting Gemma.'

'So there's one we haven't found yet.'

'Check out all the girls with Christian names beginning with C reported missing over the past six months. No, in fact make that the past year.' Valerie's eyes were drawn automatically to the board containing the photographs of five brutally disfigured faces. Was it about to become six? 'And while you're at it,' she added, 'dig out everything we've got on Danny Street.'

Chapter Thirty-seven

Chris raised his head as his father stormed into the office with a smug-looking Danny in tow. He could see the tightness in the older man's shoulders, and felt his own body tense in response. Ever since he'd heard about the fire at the Lincoln, his father's rage had been steadily building. Now – with Danny fanning the flames, no doubt – he was only one step away from exploding.

'All right?' Chris asked. He knew they'd been on the Mansfield, giving some 'friendly' encouragement to the remaining dealers. The next consignment of coke would have to be shifted quickly if they were to keep from going under.

Terry gave a shrug. He went to the cabinet, poured himself a drink and knocked it back in one. After refilling his glass, he took it and the bottle over to the desk in the far corner of the room and sat down. His expression was tight; his dark eyes full of fury. He cracked his knuckles and stared hard at the door.

Danny leaned casually against the wall with his hands in his pockets. Chris knew he'd be off soon, doing whatever he did when he disappeared for hours on end. He didn't like to dwell on what those things might be. There was a difference between loving and liking, and it was a long time since he'd liked his brother.

'I had a visitor today,' Chris said, looking over at Terry.

Terry sipped his drink silently, his mind on other things.

'A girl called Hope Randall,' Chris continued. 'Said she was Jeff Tomlin's daughter. She's looking for her sister, Connie. Reckons she might have come to see you back in February.'

But still there was no interest. Not even a flicker.

'You remember Jeff Tomlin, don't you?'

Now, finally, his father returned his gaze. It was a cold, angry look. 'What you asking me that for? You think I'm fuckin' senile?'

'Okay, I'm only saying. Don't shoot the bloody messenger.' Chris was beginning to wish he'd never raised the subject. Still, at least the promise he'd made to Hope had been kept. He might have his faults, but no one could say he wasn't a man of his word. 'No need to have a go. I'll tell her she's got it wrong.'

And that would have been that, if Chris hadn't glanced at his brother. What he saw made him think again. Danny had that shifty look about him. Ever since they'd been kids, he'd always been able to tell when he was hiding something. 'What's the deal?' he said.

'What?' Danny said defensively, catching his eye for the briefest of moments before he looked away again.

'Don't give me that innocent shit. What do you know about Connie Tomlin?'

'Ah, for fuck's sake, it ain't nothing important.'

'Spill.'

Danny pulled a face, his mouth becoming sulky. 'Okay, she came here, right, trying to set up a meet with the old man. It was only a few months since he'd got out of nick, and I knew he wouldn't want some stupid bird messing with his head. Banging on, she was, about how her dad had been topped, and how she

289

reckoned the great Terry Street here might help her find out who'd done it.'

'And that was it? That was the only time you saw her?'

Danny lifted his shoulders a fraction. 'There may have been a few more. She was a looker, a right little piece, so I thought, why not?'

'How many more?'

'I dunno. It was ages back. Three, four?'

Chris was beginning to get the picture. 'So you strung her along, pretending you'd set up a meet?'

'Seemed a waste, nice piece of ass like that.'

'And then she went missing.' Chris glared at his younger brother, a bad feeling stirring inside him. He knew what Danny was capable of, especially when it came to women. 'Please tell me you had nothing to do with it.'

'Ah, for fuck's sake!' Danny almost shouted, pulling away from the wall. He started to pace around the office. 'Is that what this is about? Some lying bitch is trying to pin it on me, is she? What's her bloody game? What's she saying – that she's gonna go to the cops, stitch me up? Well I'm not having it! Give me the tart's number and—'

'Don't go off on one,' Chris said. 'No one's trying to pin anything on you.'

'Damn well sounds like it.'

'Then you're not listening properly.' Chris frowned. It was obvious that Danny had been on the gear again; his head was mashed, his paranoia rising by the minute. 'Hope Randall doesn't even know you saw Connie.' And it might be best left that way, he thought. 'How would she? She came here asking about Dad, not you. Your name wasn't even mentioned.'

Danny stopped pacing, took hold of the back of the chair Hope had sat in and stared hard at Chris. Eventually he sat down himself. He put his head in his hands and rubbed at his eyes. 'I never laid a finger on her, I swear. Last time we arranged to meet, she didn't show. Not a word. Not even a text.'

'Okay,' Chris said. 'I believe you.' In truth, he wasn't sure whether he did or not, but he preferred to keep him sweet until he'd found out all the facts. He could only hope that those facts wouldn't land them in the middle of a murder inquiry. As soon as the thought crossed his mind, he tried to suppress it. There was a limit to how much he could forgive, even when it came to his own flesh and blood.

Danny seemed to calm down a bit. He ran his fingers through his damp hair, and gave a grunt. 'Silly cow wasn't all there anyway.' He gestured with his head towards their father. 'Kept going on and on about this Russian painting. A Barra-something. I mean, shit, as if he'd be interested in some bloody painting.'

Suddenly Terry was all ears. 'What was that?'

Chris, surprised to find that his father was actually following the conversation, looked over at him.

'Some painting,' Danny repeated. 'She said you'd want to see it, that you'd help her if she brought it here. As if you'd give a toss about—'

But Terry had got to his feet and was looking even paler than when he'd first stepped into the office. 'What exactly did she say?'

'I dunno,' Danny said, smirking. 'I wasn't paying much attention. She had a rack on her, you know. I wasn't listening so much as—'

'I don't give a fuck about her tits. Tell me what she said.'

'How can I remember? It was months ago.'

Terry crossed the room and slammed his fist down on the desk. 'Then think, you stupid bastard!'

Danny flinched at the noise, confusion filling his eyes. For a moment he looked like a little boy being unfairly accused of something he hadn't done, but then his expression hardened.

No one talked to him like that, and especially not his washed-up, pathetic has-been of a father. Jumping up, he pushed his face into Terry's and snarled, 'What the fuck—'

'Hey!' Chris said, quickly getting up too. 'Let's just calm this down, right?' Rushing round the desk, he interposed his body between the two warring men. He had no idea what was going on, but as usual it was left to him to try and negotiate the peace. 'Dad? Why don't you sit down, yeah?' He turned to Danny. 'You too. This isn't solving anything.'

There was a moment when Chris thought neither of them was going to take a blind bit of notice – it wouldn't be the first time – but then Terry took a step back. He nodded at Chris, threw one last hostile glance at Danny and retreated to his chair. Picking up the bottle, he poured himself another drink.

Danny, still poised for a scrap, continued to glare at his father. He could feel the blood pumping through his veins. It was time the old man learned some respect. But eventually, realising that the moment had passed, he sat down too.

Chris let the dust settle for a minute, and then said, 'So what's so important about this painting?'

Terry barked out a laugh. 'Your stupid bloody brother here could have chucked away a million quid.'

'Now I know he's lost it,' Danny said.

'You know sod all!'

'I know that you're—'

Before it could all kick off again, Chris intervened smartly. 'What do you mean, a million quid?'

Terry gulped at the whisky. 'That's what the damn thing's worth – if it's what I think it is.'

'And what's that?'

Terry gazed down at the desk, muttering softly to himself, 'It must be. It has to be.' He looked at Danny. 'Did she say Baronova? Was that it?'

Danny shrugged, either unwilling or unable to give Terry the confirmation he needed.

'Who or what is Baronova?' Chris asked.

'Don't waste your time,' Danny said. 'He's talking shite. A million quid, my arse.'

Terry didn't rise to it. Instead he played with his glass, twisting it round and round in his hands. As if preoccupied by an inner monologue, his lips were moving but no sound came out. The seconds ticked by, but still he showed no sign of answering the question.

'Dad?' Chris eventually prompted.

Terry glanced over at him.

'Baronova?' Chris repeated.

'He was a Russian geezer, an artist. Didn't do much, only a handful of paintings, but they're worth a fortune. Two of them were nicked from a Dutch gallery in the sixties. They've been missing ever since.'

'Right,' Chris said, trying to put the pieces together. 'So you think this Connie Tomlin might have one of these paintings?'

'Did I say that?' Terry snapped.

In frustration, Chris raised his eyes to the ceiling. He waited, but his father didn't elaborate; he'd gone back to toying with his glass.

'See what I mean?' Danny said, still itching for a fight. 'He's bladdered, off his head. What are you wasting your time for? You'd get more sense from one of the tarts out there.'

Which was rich coming from him, Chris thought. God knows what cocktail of drugs was running through Danny's bloodstream. Wisely, he didn't express the sentiment aloud. If he was going to get to the bottom of all this, he needed a bit of calm in the room. A million quid could get them back in the game, and more – but he wasn't holding his breath. Although he hated to admit it, Danny, on this occasion, could well be right.

Suddenly Terry laughed. 'Bloody hell,' he said. 'That'd be a turn-up for the books. All this time and—'

'You want to share it with us?' Chris said, his patience starting to wear thin.

Terry continued to grin for a while, and then slowly nodded. 'Okay. What did Jeff Tomlin do? How did he make his living?'

Chris had recognised the name when Hope Randall had mentioned it, although he'd been careful not to betray the fact. Tomlin had been round the house a few times, had frequented the club too, although that was all years ago. A tallish man, he thought, but couldn't remember much more about him. 'He was an artist, wasn't he? A painter?'

'And a faker,' Terry said.

And then Chris finally saw the light. 'He faked the stolen paintings. Is that what you're saying?' He grinned back at his father, understanding how well a scam like that could work: whoever agreed to buy them would be the kind of private collector who wouldn't have any scruples about receiving stolen property, indeed the kind of collector who would pay over the odds to own something that had once hung in a prestigious gallery. Of course the paintings would never be able to be on show, but for some people it was the hidden pleasures that were the most satisfying.

'Got it in one. They were the best pieces of work Jeff had ever done – bloody genius – and they would have been worth a bomb if they hadn't been nicked. Some bastard didn't just put a bullet through his head, they cleaned out his studio as well.'

'So they knew about the fakes?'

'Why else?' Terry said. 'Tomlin was an unknown artist with a shabby studio in Soho. No one would guess he'd got anything worth robbing.' He shook his head. 'Fuck knows how they found out about them. I was gonna put the word out, get a few rumours flying around in the right places, but Jeff was hit before I'd even got started. That's what I don't understand. We kept well quiet about it.'

So quiet, Chris thought, that even he and Danny had been unaware of the deal. They'd heard that Tomlin had been topped, of course, but they'd had no idea about the rest. Why was that? Another example, perhaps, of the lack of trust Terry Street had in his sons. He quickly pushed the thought aside; there were more pressing matters to attend to. 'Okay, but if they *were* nicked, how come Connie Tomlin had one of them?'

'Good question,' Terry said, glancing over at Danny. 'And if wonder boy here spent more time thinking with his brain rather than his dick, we might know the answer.'

'Or maybe she was just taking the piss,' Danny said defensively. 'No one saw the picture, did they? Could have been a scam. Maybe that's why she didn't come back. The tart got cold feet when she realised who she was dealing with.'

'You saw her,' Terry said. 'More than once. You must remember something else.'

'It was you she wanted to talk to, not me.'

Terry's eyes bored into him, two bright stripes of red appearing along his cheekbones. 'But you decided to keep quiet about it, to choose who I should or shouldn't see. If you hadn't—'

'Jesus,' Danny said. 'You were never sober enough to string a sentence together, let alone have a bleedin' conversation.'

Chris jumped in before it all began to escalate again. 'Maybe the pictures weren't at the studio,' he suggested. 'Could Tomlin have moved them, put them somewhere else? Or put *one* of them somewhere else?'

Terry continued to glare at Danny for a few seconds, then bent his head and sighed into his glass. 'So where has it been for the past twelve years?'

'He was married, wasn't he? What about the missus?'

'Nah,' Terry said. 'If it had been at the flat, Sadie would have said. I mean, she'd have been desperate to get shot of it, and quick. She wouldn't have wanted it anywhere near the kid.'

'And now the kid's disappeared,' Chris said. 'And her sister's come looking for her.' He glanced towards Danny again, but his brother refused to meet his gaze.

'Or at least that's what she says.' Terry swallowed the last of his drink, stared hard at the bottle, but resisted the urge for a refill. 'Maybe she and Connie are in this together. Shit, there's only one way to sort this. I take it she left a number? Get on the blower and give her a ring, tell her to get over here now.'

'No need,' Chris said. 'I thought she might be trouble, so I arranged to see her this evening. I didn't want her making a fuss at the club.'

'Good. So where's the meet?'

Chris put his hands down on the desk and slowly spread his fingers. 'Er, I was thinking it might be better if I saw her on my own.' He could see that Terry was about to object, so he got in fast with his reasons. 'We've already met, so she might be more relaxed if it's just the two of us. I can arrange a formal meet for tomorrow. By then we'll have a better idea of what she's really after.'

'Yeah, right,' Danny said, smirking again. 'And we can all guess what it is *you're* after. If Jenna finds out, she's gonna cut your bloody cock off.'

Chris still hadn't got round to telling them that Jenna was history. So far as they were concerned, she'd gone to take care of her sick mother in Spain. And that was the way he preferred it; he could do without his brother's snide remarks or his father's useless advice. 'It could give us the edge. If she thinks she can trust me, she's more likely to open up. I'll find out where she's coming from, and *you'll* have time to figure out what to do about it.'

Terry frowned while he thought it through, but eventually he came out with the answer Chris had been hoping for. 'Okay, but don't fuck it up. And make sure you get her over to the house tomorrow. If she has got that painting, we need to make a deal before she goes somewhere else.'

Chris nodded. 'No problem.' He leaned back, putting his hands behind his head. He could have made the call to Hope. Why hadn't he? He couldn't work out if it was because he wanted to prove himself to his father, or because he wanted time alone with her. Perhaps it was a bit of both. His father's opinion still mattered, despite his pretence that it didn't. And he'd always liked girls with a bit of fire in them. Hope Randall was a challenge – and he was more than willing to take her on.

Chapter Thirty-eight

Flint parked on the corner of Tanner Road and switched the engine off. Turning to look at Hope, he shifted up his brows. 'I'm still trying to figure out why you said yes.'

She'd been wondering much the same thing for the last twenty minutes. 'I don't know. Because it seemed like a good idea at the time? I figured that if he *did* know something about Connie, he might be more inclined to talk over dinner.'

'You don't have to go. You could always cancel.'

She was tempted – sharing pasta with a known gangster was hardly her idea of a great night out – but in her heart she knew she had to go through with it. 'No, if I do that, he's just going to get the hump, and then we'll never find out if she went to see Terry. At least this way he might actually ask his father.'

'You want me to book a table?'

'Won't he do that?'

'I meant for myself. I could come along, make sure every-thing's okay.'

'God, no,' she said. 'Please don't do that. I won't know where to look. You'll make me feel too self-conscious. Don't worry. I'll be fine on my own. It's a public place, it'll be safe enough. And I can get a cab home after.'

'If you're sure. But you've got my number. Just give me a ring if you want to get out of there in a hurry. I can come and pick you up.'

Hope tried not to think too hard about the reasons why she might want to leave in a hurry. They all made her feel slightly sick. 'Course,' she said, as brightly as she could muster. 'Thanks.'

She was about to go – she had a date to get prepared for – when a mink-coloured Jaguar purred past them and pulled up outside Lana's place. The car idled at the kerb for a while, the driver staring up at the windows of the house. Then he pulled out his phone to make a call,

'Is that Derek Parr?' Hope said. It looked like it might be, but she could only see the back of his head.

'Yeah, he must have come to pick up Lana.'

'Bit early for her to be home.' Hope glanced at the clock on the dashboard. 'It's only ten past two.'

'Well, all work and no play . . . '

But a minute later, the front door opened and it was Jackie who came jogging down the steps. She went round the car to the driver's side and bent her head to the window. Parr passed her a large brown envelope, which she snatched from his hand and quickly opened. She rifled through the contents and scowled. Although neither Hope nor Flint was close enough to hear what she was saying, the displeasure on her face could have been spotted a mile away.

'Now why would Derek Parr be giving Jackie cash?' Flint said.

'You can't be sure that's what it is.'

'I'd bet my life on it.'

Hope watched as Jackie became more animated, waving her arms around. 'Maybe the money's for Lana.'

'Then he'd give it to Lana. And even if he did trust Jackie with it, which is doubtful, it wouldn't be any of her business if it was short.'

Hope slid down in her seat in case Jackie happened to glance along the road. She didn't fancy round two if she was caught 'spying' again. 'What's she doing now?'

'Giving Derek more verbal. Bearing in mind what you over-heard at the Fox, I reckon we're looking at a classic case of blackmail.'

'You think Derek could have . . . ' Somehow Hope couldn't bring herself to use the word *killed*. She recalled standing in the kitchen, Parr's hand reaching out to touch her arm, and felt a shiver of revulsion. 'Could he have had something to do with Connie going missing?'

'If he did, then Jackie's playing a dangerous game.'

'But why would he want to harm Connie?'

'Maybe he didn't,' Flint said. 'This could be about something completely different.'

'Except both of them are pretty eager to avoid talking about her. That's kind of odd, isn't it?'

Flint didn't answer directly. Instead he said, 'Okay, she's gone back inside. It's safe to get up now.'

Hope, shifting into an upright position, was just in time to see the Jaguar disappearing round the corner. 'I'd better give it a few minutes before I go in. I don't want her to suspect that I saw her with Derek.'

'Yeah, probably a smart move. If she knows you're on to her, she won't be too happy. And the delightful Jackie isn't the type to hide her feelings.'

Hope didn't need reminding of it. 'Oh, thanks for that.'

'Sorry,' he said. 'All I meant was that it pays to keep your cards close to your chest.' He paused, glancing down at her breasts. 'Talking of which, it may be sensible to do a little rearranging before you walk down the street. Not that I'm complaining, but you wouldn't want the local punters to get the wrong idea.'

Mortified, Hope stared down at her cleavage. In her haste to get away from Belles, she'd forgotten all about what she'd blatantly put on show. 'Oh God, why didn't you tell me?'

'I just did.'

'I meant earlier.'

Flint grinned. 'I can see why he asked you out to dinner. Poor guy never stood a chance when faced with your . . . er, womanly wiles.'

'Very funny,' she said, her fingers fumbling with the buttons. 'Although if I remember rightly, it was *your* suggestion.'

'And here was me thinking that you never listened to a word I said.'

Five minutes later, Hope got out of the car and made her way to number forty-six. The sky was grey, filled with clouds, and the rain began to spatter on the pavement as she walked up the steps. As she reached the top, she turned and looked back over her shoulder, just as she had done at Belles. But there was no sign of the Audi. Flint had already gone.

The hallway was cold, and she hurried up the two flights of stairs. At the door to the flat, she hesitated for a moment, preparing for her next encounter with Jackie. Just act normal, she told herself, although she wasn't entirely sure what normal was these days.

She found Jackie in the kitchen, hunched over a mug of coffee with a face like thunder. 'Hi there,' she said in as friendly a manner as she could muster. 'You're back early.'

But Jackie wasn't in the mood for pleasantries. 'What's it to you?' she snapped. 'Keeping a time sheet?'

Hope fought hard to keep her smile in place. 'Just saying.'

301

'Well don't.' Jackie grabbed her mug and handbag and stomped off to the living room.

'Nice to see you too,' Hope murmured as she flicked on the kettle. She'd been hoping to sneak a peek inside Jackie's bag, to find out for sure what was in that envelope, but the chances of her getting the opportunity seemed remote. Instead she made herself a drink and retreated to her bedroom. She'd use the time alone to prepare for tonight.

Flicking through the contents of the wardrobe, it soon became apparent that she didn't have anything suitable to wear. Plenty of shirts, sweaters, trousers, but nothing that screamed style or sophistication. Not that she was trying to impress, of course she wasn't, but she wanted to look decent. He was the type of man who probably liked his women to make an effort when he was paying for their dinner.

Suddenly Hope's eyes alighted on the little black dress. No, she couldn't. She wouldn't dare. The darn thing was stolen, and it would be just her luck to find herself seated at the very next table to the red-lipped salesgirl who'd tried to persuade her to buy it. But then again, what were the chances of that?

Lifting the dress from the rail, she took it over to the mirror and held it up in front of her. It *was* beautiful. She touched the soft fabric, fighting what she already knew was a losing battle with her scruples. In order to make herself feel less guilty about the decision, she made a promise to raid her credit card and send the cash anonymously to the shop. That way, she figured, the dress was only temporarily stolen. It was hardly a distinction that would stand up in court, but it was the best she could do in the circumstances.

It was almost seven o'clock when there was a light tap on the bedroom door. Hope had showered, washed and dried her hair, and was now sitting at the dressing table battling with her nerves while she put on her make-up.

'Come in.'

Evelyn put her head round the door and smiled. 'Ooh,' she said, her eyes widening. 'Where are you off to? Have you got a date? You have, haven't you?' She bounced into the room and sat down on the bed. 'I thought you might have been avoiding Jackie. She's just gone. She's in a right strop for some reason.'

'Tell me about it,' Hope said. She wanted to ask if Jackie had left anything behind for Lana, but couldn't think of a diplomatic way of doing it. Anyway, Flint was probably right. Jackie was in all likelihood putting the squeeze on Derek Parr, although what she had on him was still a mystery.

Evelyn pulled her knees up and wrapped her arms around them. 'So who's the lucky guy? Where did you meet him? What's his name? Where are you going? I want to know all about it. I bet he's gorgeous, isn't he.'

Hope laughed. 'Hey, slow down! It's nothing special. Just dinner with someone I bumped into the other day.'

'What's his name?'

'Chris,' Hope said, deliberately omitting his surname and hoping that Evelyn wouldn't ask for it. 'He's, er ... a kind of friend of a friend. It's only a meal. It's not really a date.'

Evelyn glanced at the little black dress hanging on the hook on the back of the door. 'Yeah, yeah, I believe you. You wouldn't be wearing *that* if it wasn't a date.'

'Well, I thought I'd better give it an airing after all the trouble you went to. Oh, and thanks again for ... for getting it for me.'

'No probs,' Evelyn said. 'Tell me some more about this guy.'

'There's nothing much to tell.'

'What does he do? What does he look like? Come on, don't hold out on me. I want to know *everything*.'

'Well, he's tall, dark-haired, brown eyes.' Hope racked her brains for some career other than gangster, but her mind had gone blank. 'I'm not sure what he does these days. We haven't had a chance for a proper catch-up yet.'

'And where's he taking you?'

'We're meeting up West,' Hope said, not wanting to mention Adriano's. She had a sudden horrifying vision of Lana and Evelyn peering through the window of the restaurant and seeing her there with Chris Street. 'I've got a cab ordered for eight.'

'Better get a shift on, then.'

Hope got to her feet, took off her dressing gown and picked the dress off the peg. As she slipped it over her head, she deliberately changed the subject. 'So what sort of a day have you had?'

'Piss poor, to be honest. I may as well have stayed home.'

'Have you ever thought about . . . I don't know, doing something different?'

Evelyn looked faintly astonished. 'Christ, what else *could* I do? I've not got qualifications or nothing. I didn't even finish school. Anyhow, Lana's been good to me. It wouldn't be fair to quit on her, would it?'

'I suppose not,' Hope said, although she couldn't help wondering if Lana had the better part of the deal, financially at least. She smoothed down the dress and glanced over at Evelyn again. 'What do you think?'

'You look great. You'll knock him dead.'

Hope turned to the mirror and examined her reflection. Not too shoddy, she decided, for an artist who spent most of her time in T-shirts and jeans. She turned to the left and the right, examining the dress from all angles. Yes, it worked; it was simple but effective. Now all she had to do was apply the same technique to Chris Street. If everything went according to plan, she might finally get that meeting with Terry.

Chapter Thirty-nine

The cab drew up outside Adriano's, and Hope paid the driver and got out. It was almost seven minutes past eight, late enough to be fashionable without being rude. She stood quite still for a moment, taking long, deep breaths while she tried to cloak herself in the identity of another Hope Randall, a girl who was quick-witted and shrewd and more than capable of dealing with the likes of Chris Street. 'You can do this,' she murmured. Then, before what remained of her courage could desert her, she swung through the glass doors and stepped into the restaurant.

It was busy inside, and pleasantly warm. A hum of conversation filled the wood-panelled room, along with the sound of knives scraping against plates. A host of waiters, all dressed in black and white, flitted effortlessly between the tables. One of them came over and offered to take her coat. Her eyes quickly scanned the diners, until she saw Street sitting near the back. Good, he was already here.

As she made her way towards him, he looked up, made a fast up-and-down survey of her body, returned to her face and smiled. She smiled back, trying to keep it natural, to stop the wariness from reaching her lips. She had to concentrate too on balancing on the high heels she'd borrowed from Evelyn. One wrong move and she could end up in someone else's pasta.

When she got to the table, Chris appeared to experience a moment of indecision, as if not quite sure whether to stand up or not. In the event, he settled on a compromise, lifting himself partly out of his chair while making a vague gesture towards the seat opposite him.

'Glad you could make it,' he said.

As she sat down, Hope noticed that he'd shaved since the afternoon, and was wearing a different, although equally elegant, suit. This one was pale grey, and the shirt was white enough to be brand new. She nodded. 'You too.'

He picked up an open bottle of wine, half of it already gone. He'd either been here for a while, or he'd had a thirst on him when he arrived. 'Would you like a glass of red, or would you rather have something else?'

'Red's fine,' she said.

As he poured out the wine, she noted that the gold wedding ring had disappeared from his finger. Had he been telling the truth about the separation from his wife, or was he just a chancer, hoping to get lucky? But this isn't a date, she reminded herself. She had to think of it as more like a recce, an exploration into foreign territory to map out the terrain and get a feel for the enemy.

'So,' he said, 'shall we get the business side of things over and done with?'

Hope picked up her glass and took a ladylike sip. What she really wanted were two or three very large gulps to steady her nerves, but she needed to be careful, to not drink too much in case her tongue got careless. 'If you like,' she agreed casually.

'Okay, well I talked to my father and he's agreed to a meeting. Tomorrow, if that's all right with you.'

Hope was taken by surprise. She'd been half expecting him to fob her off, to string her some line about how his dad was away on business, or he hadn't had the chance to talk to him yet. 'Yes, that's good,' she said. She could feel her heart starting to beat faster. Maybe, just maybe, she was about to make a break-through. 'So he did see Connie, then?'

'She came to the club – but he'll discuss all that with you tomorrow. Shall we say midday? You can come to the house. I'll give you the address.' He took a pen from his inside pocket and began to write on the back of a business card.

Hope's feelings of excitement were immediately replaced by suspicion. Anything could happen behind closed doors. It wasn't sensible or safe to be alone with *any* members of this family. 'No, not at the house. I'd rather meet somewhere else.'

Chris Street frowned, stopped writing and looked up at her. 'Somewhere else?'

'Yes,' she said firmly.

'So where?'

Good question, she thought. Where could she suggest? The flat was obviously out of bounds. The Fox was the next place to come to mind, but she quickly dismissed it too. Some of Lana's friends might be there, and although it was unlikely that they'd remember her from Friday, it wasn't impossible – the East End grapevine was too efficient for her to take the chance. If Lana heard that she was mixing with the Streets, she'd have a fit; Hope's suitcase would be packed and sitting on the doorstep before she'd had time to draw breath. Then she recalled the pub she'd been to with Evelyn. 'There's a place round the corner, the Speckled Hen. How about that?'

Chris shook his head. 'Too busy,' he said.

'What's wrong with busy?'

'What's right with it? You never know who might be ear-wigging.'

'There are tables outside,' she said.

Chris glanced towards the window, where the rain was falling heavily against the glass. 'And if it's still pouring down? You want us to bring our umbrellas?'

Hope could see his point. Being soaked to the skin was hardly conducive to a friendly chat about a missing sister. Then she remembered somewhere else. 'Well, what about that wine bar on the high street. Wilder's?' She'd never been in it herself but had passed it a few times. It was the kind of place, she imagined, that wouldn't be too packed on a Tuesday afternoon.

Chris Street frowned again. 'Is that some kind of joke?'

From the way his body stiffened, Hope was instantly aware that she'd done what she was best at and put her foot right in it. 'What do you mean?'

He continued to stare at her for a while before his expression softened. 'Are you telling me you really don't know?'

Hope didn't need to feign her ignorance. 'Know what?'

'It's belongs to my stepbrother, Guy Wilder,' he said. 'My dad would rather cut his throat than step foot inside that bar.'

'Oh,' she said, wishing that she'd done a little more research into the Street family history before opening her big mouth. Families, as she was well aware, could be more than complicated. She was about to apologise when she remembered that she wasn't *that* Hope Randall tonight. The new version of Hope, the one stylishly packaged in a stolen black dress, would never apologise for anything. 'Well, where do you suggest then?'

'How about the Hope and Anchor,' he said. 'Seems fitting, bearing in mind the name and all.'

'And where's that?'

'Down by the station. Would that be public enough for you?'

Hope, unable to think of anywhere suitable herself, could see no other choice than to agree. She gave a light shrug of her shoulders. 'I suppose it'll do.'

A waiter arrived, dropped off the menus and disappeared again. She gave hers a cursory glance before looking back at Street. 'There's one other thing, though. I want to bring someone with me. His name's Michael Flint. He's a friend of Connie's; he's been helping me search for her.'

She waited for the protest, for the shake of the head that would tell her it was impossible. But he didn't seem the slightest bit fazed by the suggestion.

'If you like.'

'Right,' she said, amazed but relieved. 'Midday, then. We'll see you there.'

'Good. Now would you like to order, before we both die of starvation.'

An hour and a half later, Hope had worked her way through a starter of scallops, a main course of sea bass and several more glasses of wine than she'd intended to drink. It was probably a crime to forgo the pasta in a good Italian restaurant, but she hadn't been able to resist the fish. Chris had gone for the carpaccio, followed by a char-grilled steak. He was the type of man, she imagined, who *always* ordered steak.

But she was, surprisingly, having a better time than she'd expected. Chris Street might be a lot of things, but he certainly wasn't boring. The two of them had been doing a guileful dance round each other all night, both trying to gain as much information as they could whilst giving away as little as possible.

'You still haven't told me what you do,' he said.

'Haven't I?'

'You know what my game is.'

'I doubt it,' she said. 'Not all of it at least.'

'Clubs, pubs, entertainment, that kind of thing.' He smiled, showing his very white teeth.

'Come on, play fair. Don't hold out on me.'

Hope lifted her glass and took another sip of wine. 'I work for myself. I run my own business.'

'Doing what?'

She smiled back at him. 'Whatever it takes.'

'A woman after my own heart.'

The light in the room was dim, and the candles flickered on the table. Chris Street had a dramatic sort of face, all light and shadow, with high, sharp cheekbones, dark brows and deep-set eyes. As Hope gazed into those eyes, she had to remind herself, yet again, that she was here for a reason – and that reason wasn't to provide an evaluation of his level of attractiveness.

There were a few seconds of silence before he said, 'Do you get on then, you and your sister?'

Hope was deliberately evasive. She wasn't sure how much he knew, but thought it best to keep the facts to a minimum. 'We didn't actually grow up together. We had the same father but different mothers.'

'Your father was Jeff Tomlin,' he said.

Hope nodded. And then, wondering if he could provide her with some more information, she quickly added, 'Did you know him?'

'No, not really. He was my dad's friend – well, his and Lizzie's. He used to come to Belles, and to the house occasionally, but I don't remember much about him.' Chris left a short pause before asking in an overly casual way, 'He was an artist, wasn't he?'

Hope, although slightly on the wrong side of sober, hadn't drunk enough to be unaware that the man in front of her was fishing. 'You already know the answer to that.'

A waiter appeared and cleared their plates. He glanced from one to the other. 'Anything else, sir, madam? A dessert?'

'Just coffee, thanks,' Hope said.

'The same for me,' Street said. He waited until the waiter had left before continuing. 'Yes, your old man was quite a talented guy by all accounts.'

'It has been said.'

'So, just out of interest, are we talking one or two?'

'I'm sorry?'

Chris Street put his elbows on the table, leaned a little closer and lowered his voice. 'I'm thinking maybe two. Two daughters, two paintings. It has a kind of balance to it.'

Hope furnished him with a thin smile. She didn't have a clue what he was talking about, and had the feeling that she wasn't going to like it when she did. 'You're guessing,' she replied, trying to play it cool while she thought of what to say next.

He laughed. 'Okay. You don't want to discuss it now. I understand. You'd rather leave it until tomorrow, huh?'

'Well, I was under the impression that we'd concluded the business side of affairs at the start of the evening.'

'You're right,' he said. 'But I just wanted to let you know that my father will pay a good price for it . . . or *them.*'

Hope was finally beginning to understand that Terry Street's motives in agreeing to see her had little to do with Connie and a lot to do with something else entirely. Her brain frantically battled to put the pieces together. Two paintings? Her father's paintings? The fakes he used to produce? But Flint had told her that the studio had been cleaned out on the night Jeff Tomlin was murdered. So why would Terry Street think she had a painting in her possession? There was only one logical answer – Connie must have told him that *she* still had one. And it must have been an important piece or he wouldn't be so interested. Hope came to the obvious conclusion that if Terry found out that she was coming to the meet empty-handed, he was highly unlikely to tell her what he knew about Connie. It was a risky game, but she had no choice but to let Chris think that she had what his father wanted. Quickly, she flashed him a smile. 'Well, his idea of a good price could be very different to mine.'

He grinned back at her. 'It's all a matter of negotiation.'

The coffees arrived and Hope was grateful for the distraction. Worried that any further probing might expose her as the fraud she was, she tried to change the subject. 'So, at least you don't have any sisters to worry about. You've just got one brother, right?'

Chris Street lifted his brows. 'Actually, I do have a sister, a half-sister like you.'

It was news to Hope. Flint had mentioned the infamous younger brother Danny, but hadn't said a word about any other siblings. 'Oh, I didn't realise.'

'No, well I only found out about her last year.'

Hope could relate to that. 'What's her name?'

'Iris. But don't ask me anything else about her, because that's about the sum of my knowledge. I only met her on a couple of occasions, around the time of my stepmother's funeral. She took off as soon as she realised who her real father was. Having Terry Street for a dad was clearly too much to take.'

'And you're not curious about her?'

He shrugged. 'Why should I be?'

Hope gazed at him over the rim of her coffee cup. She'd felt much the same when Flint had told her about Connie, but things had changed a lot since then. 'Why *shouldn't* you be?'

He looked away from her, his eyes settling briefly on the table before meeting her gaze again. 'It's a long story. I won't bore you with it now. Maybe next time.'

So he was planning on a *next* time? Hope wondered how she was going to get out of that one. Chris Street may have been good company for the evening, but she had no intention of repeating the experience. However, she couldn't afford to let that slip with an important meeting looming on the horizon. 'I'll look forward to it,' she said.

It was getting on for eleven by the time they left the restaurant. Outside, the air was chill and the rain was still coming down. Hope took her umbrella from her bag and put it up, while Chris stepped between the parked cars and looked for a cab to hail. It was while he was peering into the distance that a large, flashy black motor drew up across the other side of the road. The first thing Hope thought, in an absent kind of fashion, was that they'd left it a little late to get a meal; Adriano's had stopped serving a while ago. But then the tinted window on the passenger side slid silently down and a hand appeared. And in that hand was a gun. And that gun was pointing straight at Chris Street.

Hope stood rooted to the spot. This couldn't be real, it couldn't be happening. She opened her mouth but no sound came out. The blood was pumping through her veins, an icy fear sweeping her body. But still her legs refused to work. Her eyes were fixed on the gun, and nothing else existed. One tiny squeeze of the trigger, and . . .

What happened next was a blur, a sequence of events that she was only vaguely aware of. Chris leapt back, grabbed hold of her and pulled her down behind one of the parked cars. The umbrella clattered to the ground.

'Don't move,' he ordered.

Crouched on the pavement, her head pressed against his chest, she could hear the thumping of his heart and feel his quick warm breath on the back of her neck. They must have only been there a few seconds, but it felt like an eternity. She was waiting for the sound of the car door being opened, of heavy footsteps pounding towards them. They were slightly to the side of the restaurant, out of sight of the waiters and the few remaining diners. She closed her eyes and prayed.

And then a chilling laugh came from across the road. 'Next time, son, you won't be so lucky.'

There was a short pause before the driver put his foot down and accelerated away. The squeal of brakes echoed in the night air, and then there was silence.

Slowly Chris Street got to his feet, pulling her up with him. Hope clung to his arm, her legs feeling like jelly.

'You okay?' he said.

She managed a nod.

'Come on,' he said. 'Let's get you home.'

Eventually she found her voice. It was small and trembling, but she just about managed to get the words out. 'What are you t-talking about? Aren't you going to ... to call the police?'

'What could the cops do about it? They're well gone now.'

'Christ, someone just tried to kill you.'

'No, I don't think so. More of a warning than an actual murder attempt.'

Hope stared at him, unable to believe he was being so blasé about it. But then she saw the expression in his eyes and knew that it was all a front. For just a moment he had come face to face with his own mortality, and it had shaken him up as much as it had her. 'Do you know who it was?'

'I can take a pretty good guess,' he said, although he didn't share the information with her. 'You sure you wouldn't rather come to the house tomorrow?'

Hope gazed back along the street, in the direction the car had taken. She wondered which was more dangerous, being behind closed doors with Terry Street, or in a public place where anyone could see them. She decided, on balance, that she'd rather take her chances at the Hope and Anchor. 'No, let's stick with the original arrangement.'

'Okay. Whatever's good for you.'

A cab came along with its light on, and Chris smartly raised his hand. As they tumbled into the back seat, Hope finally breathed freely again. She leaned forward and gave the cabbie her address, her desire to get home overriding any reservations about letting Chris Street know where she was staying. As she sat back, she found her shoulder pressed up against his, but she didn't move away. Just for a while, she needed to feel the reassuring pressure. She recalled the way he'd pulled her down behind the car, making sure that she was safe. He deserved some credit for that. She could think of plenty of men, Alexander included, whose first thought would have been to save their own skin.

'I'm sorry,' he said. 'It's not exactly been the perfect end to the evening, has it?'

Hope glanced at him, managed a smile and then turned her face away to look out of the window. Could he feel her trembling? The fear was still with her, the panic only just beginning to subside. Not for the first time, she wondered what the hell she was doing. She was out of her depth, involved in a game where there was no rule book, no set of instructions. One wrong move and it would all be over.

Chapter Forty

Hope had experienced a restless night, waking repeatedly to a heavy thump of dread in her chest. Every time she'd dozed off, her dreams had been invaded by a hand stretching out of a car window, a hand that was holding a gun pointed in her direction. A faceless voice called to her over and over again: *Next time. Next time.* Eventually, too haunted by the nightmares, she'd got up and made herself a cup of tea. Sitting alone in the kitchen, she had watched the second hand move slowly round the clock on the wall. Four o'clock in the morning, she'd decided, was the loneliest time on the planet.

It was almost dawn before she finally dropped off properly, and now she was being woken again by a light knocking sound. She opened her eyes to see Lana's head peeking round the door. 'Hope? You'd better get up. It's eight thirty. The cops are coming round in half an hour.'

'What?' Hope groaned. As she rose groggily from the depths of sleep, her first thought was of the night before. She presumed that Chris Street must have decided to report the threat. Which would mean that the police would want a statement from her.

316

Which in turn would mean that everyone else in the flat would find out who she'd had dinner with last night.

Lana came into the room and carefully closed the door behind her. She came over and stood by the bed. 'They want to talk about Connie,' she said softly.

Hope was suddenly wide awake. She threw back the duvet, sat up and swung her feet to the floor. 'Have they found her? Do they know where she is?'

'Sorry, love, I don't think so. They just want to ask us some more questions.'

'Oh,' Hope said. Her shoulders slumped in disappointment.

'Just be careful what you say in front of the others. Everyone's here, including Jackie and Sharon. If you look too interested, they're going to get suspicious.'

'Don't worry. I'll keep quiet.'

Lana pulled one of her faces. 'Make sure you do. The girls will have a fit if they find out I've been lying to them.'

Hope nodded. 'I'll get dressed. I'll be out in a minute.'

As soon as Lana had gone, Hope put on her dressing gown and crossed the hall to the bathroom. She had a quick shower, brushed her teeth and briefly met her reflection in the mirror. Not the prettiest of sights. Too much wine and a lack of sleep had combined to make her skin look dull and grey. There were dark shadows under her eyes, and her hair was a tangled mess. She'd better slap on some make-up before she met the law. And then she remembered, like a heavy stone dropping in her stomach, that this wasn't the only meeting she had today. She and Flint were due to see Terry Street at midday.

While she was pulling on her jeans, she tried not to think about what might happen later. She hadn't exactly lied to Chris, but she hadn't been entirely honest either. Giving the impression that she was in possession of that painting might not have been such a smart idea after all. And Flint still didn't know anything about it. She'd sent him a short text when she'd got back last night, informing him that she was home safely and arranging to meet in Connolly's at eleven. An hour should be sufficient to get him up to speed and for them to decide what they were going to do next.

As she combed her hair, Hope pondered on when the police had rung. It must have been after she'd gone out yesterday, or very early this morning, otherwise Lana and the crew would already have left for work. And if nothing had changed, what did they want? She felt another shifting in her guts. Perhaps Lana was wrong and they *did* have some news about Connie.

What if it was bad?

She quickly pushed that thought away, but it came bouncing back twice as hard. What if Connie was . . . But no, she couldn't afford to dwell on it. If she did, she'd start to panic, start to fall apart. There was no point letting her imagination run riot. She'd find out the truth soon enough.

With shaking hands, Hope smoothed foundation into her face, adding eye shadow, eye liner and mascara, and finally a lick of lip gloss. She sighed at the mirror. Well, she wouldn't win any beauty pageants, but she wouldn't frighten the horses either. Anyway, it was the best she could do in the time available.

She headed for the kitchen, desperate for a hot strong coffee to shake her brain properly awake. Evelyn was already there, standing by the sink, aimlessly moving mugs and spoons about while she waited for the kettle to boil. She turned as Hope came in, her eyes full of fear.

'Lana told you?' she said.

Hope gave a nod. 'Try not to worry.' If what she saw on the TV was to be believed, the police didn't tend to ring ahead when they had seriously bad news to impart. Didn't they simply turn up on the doorstep? 'I'm sure it's just routine.'

'But it's been ages. The filth weren't interested before, so why now?'

Hope tried to think of something reassuring to say. 'I don't know. Maybe it's some kind of follow-up.'

Evelyn thought about that for a moment, but didn't look convinced. Then she forced a tiny smile and said, 'Sorry, I haven't even asked about your date last night. How did it go?'

'Oh, it was okay. Nothing special. Come on, let's get that coffee made. I'll tell you about it later.'

Detective Inspector Valerie Middleton arrived on the dot of nine. She was a tall, elegant woman in her thirties, an ice-cool blonde with shrewd eyes and a very direct gaze. It was the type of gaze, Hope suspected, that didn't miss much. She'd have to be careful, more than careful, not to betray her innermost emotions.

Jackie, Sharon and Evelyn had occupied the leather sofa. As there were only two other places to sit, Hope perched on the arm of the sofa, next to Evelyn. Lana directed the inspector towards one of the armchairs before making the introductions. She worked her way through the crew before finally reaching the cuckoo in the nest. 'And this is Hope Randall. She's staying with us for a while. She didn't know Connie.'

The inspector stared rather intently at Hope.

Hope deliberately held her gaze, wondering if that made her seem more or less guilty of harbouring secrets. She'd read somewhere that it wasn't true about people avoiding your eyes when they were lying, and that in fact it was more common for people who were telling the truth to look away. All of which made her feel faintly confused. 'Maybe you'd rather talk in private. I can always—'

'No, don't go,' Evelyn said, quickly grabbing hold of her hand. 'You can't. It's all right if she stays, isn't it?'

319

The inspector gave a light shrug. 'Whatever you want. It's no problem for me.'

'Good,' Evelyn said, squeezing Hope's fingers even harder. Her face was tight and drawn, her palm damp with anxiety.

'So what's this all about?' Lana said.

Inspector Middleton took a notebook out of her bag and flicked through the pages. When she found the place she wanted, she paused, took a few seconds to read what was written there and then looked up at Lana. 'Connie went missing in February. Friday the eleventh, right?'

Lana nodded impatiently. 'Yes.'

'And you've not heard anything from her since?'

'Of course we bloody haven't,' Lana snapped. 'I already told the guy who phoned last night. Don't you people ever talk to each other?'

The inspector gave her a glance but didn't appear to take offence. 'Perhaps if you could talk me through that day. Connie left at what time in the morning?'

'About six thirty,' Evelyn said. 'I was going to walk down to the station with her, but she didn't wait. By the time I was out of the shower, she'd gone. I think she wanted to get out of the flat before—' Evelyn stopped suddenly, bit down on her lip and gazed intently at her feet.

The inspector waited. 'Before?'

'What she means,' Lana said, 'is before *I* got up. We'd had a bit of a row the night before. It wasn't over anything important. I was just nagging her about always leaving her stuff lying around. I was tired of picking up after her. She probably shot off early in case I had another go.'

'And she was on her way to work?'

There was an uneasy silence in the room.

'She was looking for a job,' Sharon said. 'I think she was planning on going up West and checking out the agencies.'

'I see,' the inspector said, her tone suggesting that she didn't believe a word of it. 'Kind of early for that, wasn't it?'

Sharon smiled sweetly back at her. 'Perhaps she wanted to get some breakfast first.'

The inspector referred to her notes again. 'It says here that Connie's father was Jeff Tomlin. He was an artist, yes? Murdered twelve years ago?' She lifted her head, her gaze travelling from one woman to the next until she'd covered everyone in the room.

'What's that got to do with anything?' Jackie said.

'I'm just making sure that all our details are correct.'

Lana suddenly sat forward, her eyes flashing. 'Fuck your bloody details. What are you really doing here? You lot don't make house calls unless there's a damn good reason for it. Have you found a body? Is that it?'

Hope drew in a sharp breath, and at the same time felt Evelyn flinch beside her.

'Calm down,' Sharon said. 'That's not what she's saying.' Her eyes darted back towards the inspector. 'Are you?'

'No, of course not. But it does state here . . .' she glanced briefly down at the notes again, 'that Connie had been making enquiries about the death of her father. Is that true?'

'Yeah, well,' Lana said. 'You lot were so bloody useless, someone had to do it.'

'Had she been talking to anyone in particular?'

'I've no idea,' Lana said. 'She was trying to get in touch with some of her dad's old mates. That's all I know.'

Inspector Middleton smiled thinly. 'So she didn't give any names?' She looked round again. 'Not to any of you?'

'No,' Lana said firmly, speaking for them all.

Hope had the impression that she'd seen the inspector somewhere before. She had one of those distinctive faces. She racked her brains but still couldn't place her. Maybe it would come back to her later.

'I don't see what this has got to do with Connie disappearing,' Jackie said. 'I mean, she's probably not even missing. Not really.'

The inspector raised her pale brows. 'What do you mean?'

'I dunno. She could have just taken off, gone to stay somewhere else.'

Evelyn glared hard at Jackie. 'She wouldn't have stayed away for this long. She'd know we'd be worried sick.'

Jackie made a huffing noise in the back of her throat, as if to suggest that there was no accounting for what Connie was capable of. 'Maybe that's what she wanted.'

'That's so nasty. How can you—'

Lana interrupted before the exchange could turn into a row. 'It's been over seven months,' she said, addressing the inspector, 'and we haven't heard a word from you in all that time. So why all the interest now? I still don't understand what you're doing here.'

'Just updating our records,' the inspector replied smoothly. Then before Lana could probe any deeper, she quickly continued, 'So no one heard from Connie during the day? No one got a phone call or a text?'

Apart from Hope, everyone shook their heads.

'And what time were you expecting her back?'

'No particular time,' Evelyn said. 'Lana and me, we were the first ones home. That was about . . . about half seven, quarter to eight, I think. It was later than usual. We stopped off at the Chinese and got a takeaway. It was busy, so we had to wait a while.'

'And I didn't come round until later,' Jackie said. 'About nine or thereabouts.'

The inspector glanced at Sharon.

'I wasn't here at all,' Sharon said. 'Not that night. I had to pick the kids up from my mum. Friday's her bingo night.'

The inspector made a point of staring hard at her notes again. 'But it says here that you didn't report Connie missing for several more days.' She lifted her head, a question mark furrowed on her brow. 'Why was that?'

'I explained all this at the station,' Lana said. 'I thought she'd got the hump over the disagreement we'd had and gone to stay at a mate's for a while. She'd done it before, so we weren't that worried.'

'But then she didn't turn up for Lana's birthday,' Evelyn continued. 'That was on the Tuesday. And she wouldn't have missed that, not over some daft row.'

Inspector Middleton gave a brief nod. 'So we've no way of knowing whether she came back at any time during the day. Perhaps she came home and went out again?'

'How the hell could we know that,' Lana said, 'if we weren't here ourselves?'

'You said earlier that she was untidy, that you were tired of picking up after her. Maybe she made a cup of tea and didn't bother washing up the mug. Maybe she left the milk out of the fridge. Maybe she took a shower and left the towels on the floor. Maybe ... well, all I'm asking is if, thinking back, there was anything out of place when you got home.'

'It was months ago,' Lana said crossly. 'And I can't remember where every damn mug is when I go out in the morning.'

'I didn't notice anything,' Evelyn added. 'I'm not saying that I definitely would have, but if it had been something obvious ...'

Inspector Middleton snapped shut her notebook and placed it in her bag. 'Okay. Well, thank you all for talking to me again. I appreciate your time. If you do recall any of the names of the people Connie was trying to trace, perhaps you could let me know. Anything could be helpful at this stage.'

'This stage?' Lana repeated. 'What's that supposed to mean?'

'The stage where we really haven't got very many leads. Although we will, of course, continue to make enquiries.'

'So that's it, is it? That's the sum total of everything you've got to tell us?'

The inspector rose to her feet. 'I'm afraid so.'

A thin hiss escaped from Lana's lips. She crossed her legs, uncrossed them, then crossed them again, a series of quick, brisk movements, as if she was trying to stop herself from leaping out of the chair and grabbing the inspector by the throat.

Inspector Middleton looked down on her, her face expressionless. 'Please don't bother getting up. I'll see myself out.'

There was a studied silence until the front door clicked shut. Lana threw Jackie a look. Jackie, immediately understanding what she wanted, shot out of her chair and went into the hallway. She returned immediately. 'Yeah, no worries. She's gone.'

Lana raised a hand to her mouth, chewing on her knuckles. 'That bitch knows more than she's saying.'

'You're not wrong there,' Sharon said.

Evelyn's fingers tightened again around Hope's. Her voice was small and shaky. 'W-what do you mean?'

'What she means—' Jackie began stridently. But Lana shot her a warning glance and she instantly shut up.

'Nothing, love,' Lana said, forcing out a laugh. 'Don't listen to me. I get the feeling she might be trying to cause trouble for us, that's all. She's the type. I've seen it before. Female cops always feel the need to prove themselves. She probably just wanted the chance to have a good look round, see if she could spot anything dodgy here.'

'Yeah,' Sharon said. 'Don't worry, Ev. I'm sure Connie's fine.'

Hope gave Evelyn's hand a squeeze. 'Lana's right. If they'd found out anything for definite, they'd have had to tell you.' But even as the words came out of her mouth, she was aware of how disingenuous they sounded. Lana was right. The inspector *did* know more than she was saying. The woman was on to something, and that something was unlikely to be even faintly related to good news.

Chapter Forty-one

Detective Inspector Valerie Middleton turned as she got out of her car and gazed back through the gates of the police station. She had an odd pricking sensation at the back of her neck, an eerie feeling that she was being watched. Standing very still, she watched as one, two, three cars went by, and then a couple of pedestrians. No one paid her any attention, not even a glance in her direction.

After thirty seconds had passed, she shook her head, walked across the forecourt and went into the foyer. Could she trust her instincts, or was she getting paranoid? Recently she'd been paying more attention when she was out and about, but if the Whisperer was on her tail, he was doing a damn good job of it.

Valerie jabbed in the security number, passed through the glass doors and went up the stairs. On the third-floor landing she stopped again to look out of the window. From here she had a clear view of Cowan Road, but again there was no suspicious activity, no cars parked illegally, no one loitering with intent. A sigh slipped from her lips. Perhaps this bad feeling she had was simply a result of her earlier interview with Lana Franklin's crew.

That had not been a comfortable experience. Lana was too smart to be fobbed off with talk of routine or follow-ups; the sudden interest in Connie Tomlin had set all her alarm bells ringing.

Valerie frowned as she strode along the corridor and into the incident room. Kieran Swann was already back, sitting at his desk with a pile of files in front of him. He glanced up as she took off her coat and sat down.

'So how was it in the den of thieves?' he said, grinning.

She didn't return his smile. 'No one's heard from Connie Tomlin. Seven months on and still not a word. She's what, twenty-two? In this world of mobile phones, of social networking sites, just how likely is that?'

'Not very,' Swann agreed.

'How's it going with you?'

'Carole Ann Barker,' he said. 'Forty-three years old, went missing from her home in Hackney about three months ago. Worked at a call centre near Waterloo. Didn't turn up one morning and never been heard of since.'

'So not the Whisperer's usual type,' Valerie said. 'Unless she was doing a spot of moonlighting in the evenings. Any evidence of that?'

Swann shook his head. 'But she does have a history of mental problems. And it's not the first time she's gone AWOL. On the last occasion, she was missing for around six months; she was sleeping rough apparently.'

'And the others?'

'Catherine Bryson and Clare Holt are both safely back home. Their families just didn't bother to inform us.'

'Which leaves Connie Tomlin as the one most likely.' Valerie felt her heart sink. 'That girl's disappearance was reported ages ago, and no one took a blind bit of notice.'

'That's because it sounded like a falling-out, nothing more.

Franklin said they had a row, didn't she?' Swann had a good root through the papers on his desk before eventually finding the sheet he was looking for. 'Yeah, here we are. They'd had an argument on the Thursday night. Connie left early in the morning and didn't come back on the Friday night. Lana Franklin couldn't have been that worried if she didn't report her missing until the following week.'

'She probably wasn't,' Valerie said. 'Not at first. She just thought Connie was off sulking somewhere. What about the bank records? Have you checked them?'

'Yeah, not a single deposit or withdrawal after the eleventh of February, but to be honest, not a whole lot of action before then either. She wasn't what you'd call a regular saver. She only had a couple of hundred in her account.'

'So it doesn't really prove anything either way. Connie Tomlin was a dip. She wouldn't have found it too difficult to get her hands on some easy cash, not with her skills. She probably lived off what she managed to lift and didn't bother with the bank.'

'But she still doesn't fit the profile,' Swann said. 'All the other victims have been toms. Why would our Whisperer suddenly change tack? Why choose her?'

Valerie sat back and thought about it. 'I don't know. Maybe it was a mistake. She lives near Albert Street, doesn't she? She's young. She's pretty. She probably wears the kind of clothes the bastard doesn't approve of. Maybe she did come back later that night. Maybe she was just in the wrong place at the wrong time.'

Swann put his elbows on the desk, his brows settling into a frown. 'So where the hell is she now? This isn't the Whisperer's usual MO. He takes the girls, he tortures them, he dumps them somewhere they'll be found. So why the change? Everything about this is wrong. It doesn't add up. It doesn't make any sense.' He lifted a hand and ran his fingers through his slightly greasy hair. 'Are we even sure the last note was from him?'

Valerie considered the possibility. 'Well, if it wasn't, it must have come from someone in the know. Same design, same size and type of paper, same positioning of the message on the page. Left on my windscreen like the one at the hospital. So if it didn't come from him, the only other source must be an accomplice, a partner, or someone closer to home.'

'Oh, come on,' Swann said. 'You can't be suggesting—'

'I'm not suggesting anything. But you know how leaky this place can be at times. Someone might have let slip about the notes.'

'So what you're saying is that we could be looking at some bleeding nutter just trying to wind us up?'

'It's possible.'

Swann stared hard at her. 'But not probable?'

Valerie held his gaze for a moment before glancing away. She looked briefly around the room, at the desks, the banks of computers, the familiar faces, before her eyes met his again. 'No, I still think it was from him. Call it gut instinct. And I think he's pissed off that we're only crediting him with five victims instead of six.'

'So what next?'

'We're going back to Lana Franklin's place this evening, see if we can talk to the occupants of the two other flats in that house. No one was around this morning; perhaps we'll have better luck later. I've tried a few of the other neighbours, but most of them are students passing through. A couple of people recognised her photograph, but they couldn't remember when they last saw her.'

'Yeah, well I'm not sure who *I* could remember seeing seven months ago.'

Valerie acknowledged the comment with a small nod. 'I also

talked to the guy who runs the corner shop, Jamal Dhanuka. He recognised her too, but was equally vague about when he last saw her. Said he had a feeling it was around the time one of the local girls was attacked, but wasn't sure which one. He said Connie came in there fairly frequently, although he didn't know her name.'

'The girl could have been Gemma Leigh,' Swann said. 'That would fit with the dates.'

'Yeah, it would. Still doesn't explain why Connie hasn't been found, though.'

'You think Franklin's crew are being straight with you?'

'Couldn't swear to it,' Valerie said. 'One of the girls, Evelyn, was pretty upset. And I don't think she was faking it. But Jackie Woods didn't seem that bothered, reckoned Connie had just moved out and moved on.'

'Could have been a domestic,' Swann said. 'Big row that got out of hand, someone picked up a knife and next thing you know ...'

'And then what? They haul her body down two flights of stairs and bury her in the garden?'

'Wouldn't be the first time.'

'Then why bother to report her missing?'

Swann gave a shrug. 'In case someone else did, I suppose. She must have other friends. Perhaps they were trying to cover their backs.'

'And the note?'

'Maybe it's not Connie Tomlin he's referring to. We only have the names of the ones who've been reported missing. There must be others who've simply slipped under the radar.'

Valerie lifted her hands in a gesture of frustration before dropping them back on to the desk. Her thoughts veered off in a fresh direction. 'There's a new girl staying at Lana's place. Hope Randall.'

'A replacement for Connie, I suppose.'

'I'm not so sure.' Valerie recalled seeing the fair-haired woman in the Fox, remembered too the way Harry had looked at her. 'There's something odd about the set-up. I can't quite put my finger on it. Can you do a PNC check on her?'

'You mean now?' Swann said.

Valerie stared at him. 'Sorry, are you too busy?'

Swann's brows did that irritating shift upwards, as if her curtness had its roots in something other than the fatuous nature of his question. After a short pause, he leaned forward, tapped a few keys on the computer and waited. 'Nothing on Hope Randall. No arrests, no convictions, no cautions. She's clean.'

'Maybe Hope Randall isn't her real name.'

'Perhaps you could ask her tonight.'

'Perhaps I'll do just that.' She pointed towards the heap of files on his desk. 'Is one of those the file on Danny Street?'

'Three of them, actually. Danny boy likes to keep himself busy.'

'Pass them over, then.'

Swann did as he was told. 'You really think Street could be the Whisperer?'

'Why not?' she said. 'Whoever's doing this is one sick bastard, and Danny Street fits the bill exactly.'

Chapter Forty-two

He walks quickly, with his head down, muttering softly to himself. No one takes any notice. No one cares. He's just another man in a sea of lost souls. He doesn't need to look up to be aware of where he's going. He knows these streets like the back of his hand, could negotiate them blindfold. He knows where the filthy, hollow-cheeked harlots ply their trade, and every dim, dirty alleyway they lead their victims to. 'You want business, mister? You want a good time?' Nothing is hidden from him. He sees it all, and sucks it deep into his lungs like fetid air.

He's not far from Albert Street, but he won't turn down there. No point in drawing attention to himself. And anyway, most of the whores are working other patches now. The presence of the police has been driving the customers away. Like cancer spreading through a body, the bitches have drifted further north and west and east, fouling and polluting the new pavements they patrol.

'Harlots,' he mutters. 'Abominations of the earth.'

And then he gets to thinking about the law again. His eyes narrow into two thin slits. Soon, it will be soon. The clock is ticking for Detective Inspector Valerie Middleton. She knows he's out here, waiting for her. She feels his presence in the hairs that stand up on the back of her neck. She thinks of him before she goes to sleep at night, and when she wakes up in the morning. He's counting down the hours until she's finally his. It's her confession he wants most of all, her admission of guilt, her acceptance of responsibility. Yes, this has all been her fault. The blame lies squarely on her shoulders.

He feels a mixture of emotions, but mainly anticipation, fear and regret. Fear that something will prevent him from carrying out the vital final stage, regret that his work will soon be over. But no, God won't forsake him in his hour of need. A shield of burning love will guard and protect him.

He has it all planned out, exactly what he'll do. She thinks she's smart, but she's not as smart as him. A low laugh slips from between his lips. When his mission is complete, the world will be a better place; it will be free of the woman who has caused him so much pain.

Bye bye, Valerie. Sleep tight.

Chapter Forty-three

Flint was tucking into an all-day breakfast of sausage, bacon, egg, mushrooms, fried bread and beans, while Hope drank her coffee and gazed out of the window. 'Some of us were up at the crack of dawn,' he said, as if her silence was a criticism of his eating habits.

She turned to look at him, knotting her brows. 'What?'

'I said ... Oh, it doesn't matter. So do you think this gun was for real, then?'

Hope glanced around in case anyone else had heard. 'Keep your voice down, can't you? It looked real enough to me.'

'Could have been Kozlov, or more likely one of his goons. I don't suppose he does his own dirty work.'

'Kozlov?'

Flint speared a piece of bacon with his fork and lifted it up, but didn't put it in his mouth. 'Andrei Kozlov, a Russsian émigré with links to the mafia – the Russian mafia, that is. Got his finger in a lot of pies: property, drugs, prostitution. Most of his business is conducted up West, but he's been sniffing round the East End recently. He's the type of guy who can spot an opportunity when it comes his way – and if the Streets go under, he'll be ready and waiting to plug the gap in the market.'

'Are they likely to go under?'

'I've heard Kozlov's been undercutting them, getting his dealers to flog the gear at half the usual price. No one's going to buy off the Streets if they can get it cheaper somewhere else. Of course once the competition's out of the way, Kozlov will put the prices up again.'

'Are you going to eat that,' Hope said, looking at his fork, 'or just wave it around?'

Flint popped the bacon into his mouth and chewed. 'What's bugging you? Don't tell me: you've got a stinking hangover, right?'

'No,' she hissed back. 'What I've got is a meet with a notorious gangster in less than half an hour, and still no idea what I'm going to say to him. He thinks I've got a painting that I haven't got, and I doubt he'll be too pleased when he finds out the truth.'

'Yeah,' Flint agreed. 'Might be best to keep quiet about that.'

'And if he asks me straight out?'

'Then you lie. We *both* lie. Let's find out exactly what this painting is before we close any doors behind us.'

Hope gave a frustrated shake of her head. 'And that's your brilliant plan, is it?'

'Got a better one?'

Hope hadn't. But she still didn't like it. It had been one thing playing Chris Street along last night – especially under the influence of a few glasses of wine – but it was quite another to blatantly lie to his father in the bright light of day. Terry Street was not the type of man, she was sure, who'd take kindly to being messed about. Still, she should have thought of that before she opened her mouth. It was too late to backtrack now. They'd have to front it out and hope for the best.

Flint mopped up his beans with the last quarter of fried bread. 'So the law didn't have anything new to add about Connie.'

Hope had told him about the visit from the police when she'd first arrived, but they'd quickly got distracted by the events of last night. 'No, nothing new. It was a woman, Detective Inspector Valerie Middleton. Do you know her?'

Flint grinned. 'Despite my record, I'm not familiar with *all* the cops in London.'

'I didn't mean ...' Hope flapped a hand impatiently. 'Whatever. But I think *something's* going on. More than just a routine follow-up, that is. Lana reckoned Middleton was holding out, and I'm inclined to agree with her.'

'Well, maybe with this maniac on the loose, they're just covering their backs.'

'You don't think—'

'No,' Flint said hurriedly. 'If anything had happened to her, we'd have heard. Or at least Lana would have heard.' He pushed his plate away and picked up the mug of tea. 'So what were your impressions of the charming Mr Street, then?'

'Before or after he had a gun pointed at him?'

'Was there a difference?'

Hope had been trying not to think too much about the taxi ride home, or about the warm pressure of Chris Street's shoulder against her own. It hadn't meant anything. It hadn't been more than a moment of comfort. 'It did colour the evening somewhat,' she replied, as dismissively as she could.

'A chip off the old block, I should imagine,' he said.

'He has his good points.'

'Really?' Flint's face tightened a little. 'I spent the whole evening worrying about you. Perhaps I shouldn't have bothered.'

Hope heard the hard edge in his voice and frowned. It was the first time he'd expressed any real concern for her safety. She'd grown so used to his flippancy that she almost took it for granted now. 'I wasn't—'

'Forget it,' he said sharply. He gave her a look that she couldn't quite decipher, before drinking the rest of his tea and looking at his watch. 'We'd better make a move. Are you ready?'

'As I'll ever be.'

'You'll be okay,' he said. 'You'll be fine. Let's just play it cool and see what happens.'

Hope smiled thinly back. It was what *could* happen that was making the hairs on her arms stand on end.

The Hope and Anchor was located only fifty yards away from the Fox, but it was a very different kind of pub. The interior was shabby, the brown lino floor scuffed and stained and pitted with cigarette burns, the ancient flock wallpaper worn away in lines where the backs of chairs had continuously rubbed against it. There were only a few customers inside, all elderly men hunched over their pints. A scarred wooden counter arced around the right-hand side, and it was against this counter that Chris Street was leaning. He was wearing yet another of his elegant suits, this one a dark shade of blue.

He smiled as Hope approached, his gaze holding hers. 'Hope. It's good to see you again. You've recovered from last night?'

'Which part do you mean exactly?' she replied, doing her best to stay in the character of that other Hope Randall, the one who took things in her stride, the one who didn't think twice about the occasional gun being pointed at her dinner companion. She searched his face for any signs of anxiety *he* might be feeling about it, but could see nothing. He was perfectly calm and composed. Maybe in his line of business such threats were a regular occurrence.

'Well, I hope it wasn't *all* bad.'

'This is Michael Flint,' she said, avoiding a direct answer. 'Flint, this is Chris Street.'

They shook hands, cautiously eyeing each other like two territorial tomcats.

'Would you like a drink?' Chris said.

Hope refused. 'No thanks.'

'Not for me,' Flint said.

'Or a coffee?' Chris said solicitously to Hope. He touched her lightly on the arm.

She was reminded of the taxi ride again, and felt a light blush invade her cheeks. She was also aware of Flint glaring hard at the other man's hand. 'I'm fine, thank you. Shall we just get on with it?'

Chris nodded and led them to the back of the pub, where there was an old-fashioned snug. A scribbled note sellotaped to the door read: *Closed for Private Function*. Terry Street was sitting at one of the three small round tables positioned by an empty fireplace. He rose to his feet as they entered the room. Hope could feel her heart starting to beat faster as she gazed at the man they'd come to see. He was shorter than his son, less broad across the shoulders, but there was still a sinewy strength about his body. He looked to be in his early sixties, and had a gaunt, hollowed-out face, with iron-grey hair slicked back from his temples. His eyes were deep set, dark and searching.

'So you're Connie's sister,' he said. His voice had a peculiar rasp to it, a sound that bordered on the sinister.

Terry Street's shirt was open at the neck, and Hope tried not to stare at the vicious scars on his throat. 'Yes. Hope Randall.' She glanced towards Flint. 'And this is Michael Flint, a friend of mine.'

Terry didn't move to shake hands with either of them. He didn't offer them a seat either. Instead he turned his head and addressed his son. 'Get Anja in here, would you?' Then he looked at Hope and Flint again. 'You'll understand that in the circumstances I need to take precautions.'

Hope didn't understand what he meant. 'Precautions?'

'In my line of work, you can never be too careful.'

Chris Street came back with a slim brunette with very blue eyes. She gave Hope a faintly hostile look before walking over to her and starting to run her hands down her arms.

'What are you doing?' Hope said, jumping back. 'What—'

'Don't worry,' Flint said calmly. 'Mr Street here is just making sure that we don't have any concealed weapons on us. Or microphones.' He spread his own arms to let Chris pat him down. 'As he says, you can never be too careful.'

'Nothing on him,' Chris said to Terry.

Hope, with little choice, reluctantly stepped forward again. The girl's mouth, a perfect Cupid's bow, curled a little at the corners as her hands made a fast but thorough search of Hope's body. It was a reminder to Hope of the procedure she'd had to go through at the jail when she'd gone to see Eddie Booth. And that in turn reminded her to be *very* careful about what she said today.

Anja stepped back and nodded. 'She clean too, Terry.'

'Good. You can get back to the club now. Solomon will give you a lift.'

The girl left without another word.

Terry gestured towards where he'd been sitting. 'Okay, let's get down to business.'

The four of them pulled out chairs and gathered round the table. Hope was glad that the younger brother, Danny, wasn't there. She was thankful for any small mercies at the moment.

'Right,' Terry said, placing his elbows firmly on the table and leaning forward to gaze directly at Hope. There was aggression in his eyes, a hardness that made her quail. 'I take it you have the Baronovas? Or at least one of them?'

Hope swallowed hard. *Baronovas?* What was he talking about? It was the name of an artist, she presumed, but not one, despite all her college courses, that she'd ever heard of. 'I need to know what you said to Connie first.'

'All in good time. Once we've agreed on a price, and once the paintings have been handed over, then and only then will I tell you where Connie Tomlin went.'

Hope's heart began to race even faster. 'So you do know where she is?'

Terry's face grew sly. 'I know where she *went*. That doesn't mean she's still there now.'

'We've only got the one painting,' Flint said. 'If Connie offered to sell you the other, why didn't you buy it there and then?'

'We had an agreement,' Terry said. 'She wanted to check that my information about her father was correct before we sealed the deal.'

'And what was that information?' Hope asked.

Terry tilted his head to one side, a sigh escaping from his lips. 'Bring me the painting and I'll tell you. What shall we say? Fifty grand?'

Hope stared back at him, staggered by the figure.

But Flint shifted in his seat and gave a cynical laugh. 'Come on, Mr Street. Please don't insult us. It's worth twenty times that and you know it.'

Hope shot a glance at him, her eyes wide and confused. Was he just guessing, or did he really know the value?

Terry gave a shrug. 'In an open market, perhaps, but not when it has to be sold ... quietly. You can't take this painting to auction, or to any ordinary art dealer. And of course you can't afford to have it examined too closely.' He looked at Hope. 'Not that your father wasn't expert at what he did, love, but techniques have moved on, and forgeries are easier to detect than they used to be. No, you have to find someone who isn't going

340

to look *too* closely at the picture – it'll pass all the superficial tests, I'm sure of that – and who wants to believe that it's genuine. That's half the battle, you see. But you have to be aware of who these interested parties might be, and how to approach them. Otherwise you could well find yourself in a long conversation with the law.'

'True enough,' Flint said. 'We're not disputing that. But fifty thousand, that's way off the mark.'

Hope wondered if he was overdoing it. Haggling over the price of a painting they didn't actually possess seemed a step too far.

Terrry leaned back, folding his arms across his chest. 'Yeah, but then there's the other fifty grand that Jeff borrowed all those years ago.' His gaze slid over to Hope again. 'Your old man had a bit of trouble with the loan sharks, love. He was overly fond of the gee-gees. What I'd call a hopeful gambler rather than a smart one.'

'That still only makes a hundred,' Flint said.

Terry's shoulders lifted again. 'But I have all the expenses – and all the risk. Once you've sold it to me, you're free and clear, but I've still got to find a buyer.'

Hope sat quietly, a wave of disappointment flooding over her. It was obvious that Terry wasn't going to divulge anything about Connie without first seeing the picture. And as they didn't have the picture, this was all leading nowhere. She had to keep on trying, though. 'Please tell me something about Connie. Tell me she's safe, at least.'

But Terry was unyielding. 'A deal's a deal. What shall we say? Two days? Three?'

'Three,' Flint said, standing up. 'There are arrangements to be made.'

'Very well.' Terry flapped a hand, dismissing them. 'We'll meet here again on Friday. Same place, same time.'

Chris Street hadn't opened his mouth during the conversation, but as Hope and Flint started to walk away, he said, 'Just out of interest, Hope, how did you get hold of the painting? Jeff Tomlin's studio was cleaned out after he was killed; as I understand it, they took everything that was there.'

Hope held his gaze, her disappointment starting to slide into anger. 'I'll tell you that when you tell me where Connie is.'

He smiled at her, but she didn't smile back.

Flint opened the door, and then looked back over his shoulder at Terry. 'Oh, and Mr Street, no tails please. And don't even think about a spot of breaking and entering. The painting's in a safe place, not at my flat or Hope's. If there's even the hint of an attempt, the deal's off for good.'

'I give you my word,' Terry said.

Hope doubted that his word was worth much. She hesitated, in two minds as to whether she should make one final plea about Connie's whereabouts, but Flint took her elbow and propelled her out of the snug. 'Leave it,' he whispered in her ear. 'Time to go.'

She didn't argue with him.

They had parked the car at the Fox, and during the two minutes it took to walk back there, the only words spoken came from Flint. 'Jesus,' he murmured, as they crossed the road, 'that Street's a piece of work. I wouldn't like to meet him when he's in a bad mood.' Hope was too despondent to reply. What she was thinking, however, was that Terry Street would be in exactly that frame of mind when he discovered they'd been stringing him along.

As she climbed into the passenger seat of the Audi, Flint went to open the boot. He came back seconds later with a laptop computer, flipped open the lid and booted it up.

'What are you doing?' she said.

'Checking out Baronova. We may as well know what we're supposed to have.' He made a clicking sound with his tongue as he pressed down the keys. 'Yeah, here we go. Fyodor Baronova, born 1900 in Moscow, died of TB in 1926. Part of the Russian avant-garde movement. He didn't produce much, only half a dozen paintings. I guess that's what makes them so valuable.'

'Or eight,' Hope said wryly, 'if you count the extra two Jeff Tomlin created.'

Flint continued to read. 'Jesus, the last one that went up for sale sold for over a million at Christie's.'

'Are you serious?'

'Hang on a moment, there's something else.' Flint's mouth slowly widened into a grin. 'Ah, shit, I get it now. That's smart, that's very smart.'

'Get what? What do you mean?'

Flint shook his head, his eyes sparkling. 'There weren't any new paintings. Two Baronovas were nicked from a Dutch gallery in 1964 and never recovered. What Jeff must have done was reproduce the ones that were taken. That way, when he and Terry Street sold them on, the buyer would believe he was purchasing stolen property and wouldn't be able to risk having them expertly analysed in case they were recognised. The buyer would probably arrange for a few basic tests by some dodgy "art expert", but Jeff's work would pass those with flying colours.'

Hope could see that it was a clever idea, especially with the likes of Terry Street being involved. With his criminal background, the prospective buyer wouldn't have a problem with believing the fakes were the genuine article. The only risk involved was that the original paintings might one day be found.

Flint tilted the screen so she could see it. 'Want to take a peek?'

Hope gazed down at the paintings her father had, apparently, so expertly copied. Immediately she felt a shiver run through her. The two pictures, which were obviously a pair, depicted a series of images, one containing a man, the other a fair-haired woman, both staring into mirrors at various stages of their lives. They were painted mainly in shades of blue, and the expressions on their faces ranged from blankness through horror to despair. They had an eerie, disturbing quality that made her want to look away, and yet at the same time drew her ever further in.

'Yeah,' Flint said, as if reading her mind. 'They are kind of weird, aren't they. It's like gazing into someone's soul. You can't imagine anyone actually *wanting* to look at them every day.'

He moved the screen back and continued to scroll through the site. Suddenly he let out a laugh. 'Here, listen to this. It's a quote from a journalist called Akinsha: *If you burned all the fakes of Russian avant-garde now hanging in galleries and private collections around the world, the West would obtain a valuable new source of energy.*'

'Very amusing,' Hope said, the images of the man and the woman still drifting uncomfortably in her head. 'But how does any of this help us, or Connie? We don't have the picture and we have no idea where it is.'

Flint gave her a sideways glance. 'Well, I've been thinking about that. Maybe Connie doesn't need our help. Maybe she changed her mind about Street and found another buyer.'

Hope frowned at him. 'Do you really think that?'

'I don't know,' he said, 'but it would explain a lot. If she'd made an agreement to sell the painting to him, she wouldn't want to hang about if she'd reneged on the deal, and she wouldn't want to be traced either. Which would account for why she hasn't been in touch with anyone, not even Lana or Evelyn.'

'But why leave all her things behind? If she knew what she was going to do, she'd have had time to pack, to get organised.'

'Not if Terry got wind of what was going on. She could have come home that Friday to find Street or one of his goons waiting outside the house. She could have realised she'd been sussed, turned tail and done a runner. If she'd already got the cash, she could have headed for the nearest airport.'

Hope thought about it. There was a certain logic to his reasoning, but she still didn't want to believe that her half-sister could be lazing on a sunny, palm-fringed beach while she was risking her skin consorting with the likes of Terry Street. 'Except Connie's main interest, surely, was what had happened to Jeff. Wasn't the painting just a means to an end, a way of getting Terry to help her?'

'At the beginning, perhaps,' Flint said, 'before she found out what it was actually worth. She would have known the painting was a fake, but maybe it was only when she approached Street that she realised the full value of it. A hundred grand, even fifty, would be a lot of cash to someone like Connie.'

'A lot of cash to most people,' Hope replied drily. 'But it still doesn't mean that she sold it to someone else, took the money and ran.'

'No,' he agreed, 'of course it doesn't.'

They were silent for a while, both gazing out across the bleak concrete space of the car park. Hope's spirits, low enough already, were rapidly plunging to even greater depths. The more she thought about it, the more she could see that Flint might have a point. Connie had spotted an opportunity and grabbed it. And who could blame her? Her life had been a hard one, a world away from her own, and chances to escape didn't come around too often.

'You okay?' Flint said.

Hope didn't feel okay. Not even close. She was beginning to realise that she would probably never find out the truth about what had happened to Jeff Tomlin. A week ago she wouldn't have cared, but a lot had changed since then. She was about to share this sentiment with Flint when her phone started ringing. She took it out of her bag and checked the caller. 'It's Lloyd,' she said. 'I'd better take it.'

Hope wasn't sure why she got out of the car. It was something to do with not wanting to lie to her stepfather in front of Flint. Somehow it was easier to do it out of earshot. She painted a smile on her face as she paced round the Audi in the thin, drizzly rain. But the smile soon faded as she listened to the voice at the other end.

'Everything all right?' Flint said, as she climbed back in.

Hope shook her head. 'No, not so good. He says it's just a dose of flu, but it sounds like more than that. After my mother died, he—' She stopped, her hands wrestling briefly in her lap. 'I mean, he went to pieces. I thought things were starting to improve, but now I'm not so sure. I don't like him being on his own. It's not been that long, you see, and—'

'So you'd better go home,' Flint said. There's nothing you can do here anyway. If Connie did take off, then at least we know that she's safe.'

'But what about Terry Street? We're supposed to see him again in three days.'

'There's no point. Not if we don't have the painting. I think he's as much in the dark as we are about Connie. He's just trying to play us.'

Hope's frown grew more pronounced. 'He's not going to be happy when we don't turn up.'

'Yeah, well, what's he going to do about it?'

Hope looked into his cool grey eyes and gave a tiny shake of her head. 'That's what I'm worried about. He's not the type to let things rest.'

Chapter Forty-four

By one o'clock the next day, Hope's train was pulling into Albersea. Unsure as to whether she would return to London or not – Connie seemed to have disappeared into thin air – she had packed all her belongings and said her goodbyes to Lana and Evelyn. Lana, she could tell, was relieved to see her go. Evelyn, who was losing yet another friend, had hugged her close and made her promise to stay in touch.

Hope dragged her suitcase to the taxi rank, wondering if this was the end of it all. No resolution as regarded the murder of her father. No resolution as regarded Connie. So many loose ends and no way of tying them together. Her frustration was deep and dark, a black seam of disappointment that ran through the very heart of her. With a sigh, she got into the back of a waiting cab and gave him the address.

As the driver made his way through Albersea, she looked out of the window at the neat familiar streets with their neat familiar houses. Nothing had changed. Of course it hadn't. She'd only been away for a week. It felt longer than that, as though she'd been on a prolonged journey and had come back a different person. If she'd felt alienated from these surroundings before, she felt it even more keenly now. But there was Lloyd to consider – and he had to be her priority.

Before leaving Tanner Road, Hope had made a search of Connie's room in case the painting was hidden there somewhere. She'd taken the two framed prints down from the wall and examined them closely, but there was no evidence that they'd been tampered with in any way. She'd looked on the underside of drawers and at the back of the wardrobe, checked under the mattress, and even peered closely at the edges of the carpet in case it had been pulled up and a gap created under the floorboards. But even while she'd been going through the process, she'd known that it was pointless. If Connie was gone, then in all likelihood the painting was too.

The cab drew up outside the cottage. Absently, Hope paid the driver and got out. As she walked up the path, she was mentally replaying yesterday's meeting with Terry Street. Something was nagging at her. Why had Flint been so sure of how valuable the painting was before he'd even looked up Baronova on the web? Had he already known about it? Maybe Connie had confided in him, revealed her secret, even promised him a share of the profits if he helped track down Jeff Tomlin's killer. She remembered Lana's warning about how Flint had his own motives. And the man was just as much a mystery to her now as when he'd first arrived on her doorstep.

She put the key in the lock, turned it and pushed open the door. Even though her absence had been a short one, the inside of the cottage had a slightly musty smell. She kicked the heap of junk mail aside with her foot, and after dumping her case in the bedroom went through to the living room and opened all the windows. A chill wind, laden with ozone, caught the curtains and made them billow out. She breathed in the salt air, hauling it deep into her lungs.

She started thinking about Flint again. Perhaps she was looking at it all from the wrong angle. Wasn't it also true that Flint was smart enough to realise that Street wouldn't be involved in the deal unless it was a lucrative one, and to hazard a guess that the gangster would offer them a fraction of what the painting was worth? So maybe he *had* been straight with her. Maybe everything he'd told her was true.

Good guy or bad guy? For a while she played with the two conflicting notions, but came to no definite conclusion. Except that she wanted him to be the good guy. No, more than that, she *needed* him to be. But that was only because she couldn't bear the idea of having been deceived and manipulated. It didn't have anything to do with those cool grey eyes, with the way he teased her, or the look of his mouth as it widened into that slow, seductive smile.

Hope pulled herself up sharply. What on earth was she thinking? There was nothing like that between her and Flint. She was just confused, her emotions in turmoil. And maybe she was missing a man in her life. Yes, that must be it. Even Chris Street had seemed surprisingly attractive after a few glasses of wine.

Quickly she closed her mind to any further soul-searching. It was irrelevant. There was every chance she'd never see Flint again. With a shrug of her shoulders, she tried to clear all thoughts of him and of the past from her mind. It was Lloyd she had to concentrate on now, and she couldn't do that if her head was full of ghosts.

Half an hour later, Hope was on her way to Lloyd's flat. She turned up the collar of her coat and walked briskly, keeping her head down against the cold wind blowing off the Irish Sea. At the corner of his street, she went into the supermarket and picked up a carton of chicken soup and four soft bread rolls. It might not be the comforting chicken broth that her grandmother would have made, but it would have to do. To her basket she added eggs, a loaf, a few microwaveable ready meals, a packet of paracetamol, and three fresh lemons to squeeze into his whisky.

Walking adjacent to the park, she saw that it was empty today, the office workers preferring to eat their lunches indoors, the mothers opting to keep their toddlers in the warm. She stared at the empty swings, the roundabout and the slide with a faint feeling of nostalgia; she could remember coming here as a child, could still recall that tingle of excitement. She wondered wryly why it was that going round and round in circles was so thrilling when you were an infant, and yet so frustrating when you were grown up.

She paused at the entrance to Parkview, taking a few seconds to gather her thoughts before pressing the buzzer to Lloyd's flat. As she climbed the flight of stairs, she tried to put the last week behind her, to focus entirely on the present.

Lloyd was waiting for her, the door open. There was a moment of mutual shock as the two of them came face to face again. Hope was distressed by the greyness of his skin, by his thin cracked lips and red-rimmed eyes. He reeled back, trying to disguise *his* surprise with a laugh.

'Your hair,' he said. 'God, I almost didn't recognise you.'

Hope, who'd forgotten all about the new image Lana had foisted on her, raised her hand self-consciously to her head. 'Oh, yes. I just fancied a change. You don't like it?'

'No, no, I didn't mean that.' He ushered her inside. 'It's just . . . different, that's all. It'll take some getting used to.'

Good different or bad different? she might have asked, but decided not to put him on the spot. In the living room, she studied him more closely. 'You're all skin and bone. Have you eaten anything at all over the past few days?'

'A little.'

'Yeah, I bet.' She made her way to the kitchen. 'I've brought some soup. You can manage that, can't you?'

Ten minutes later, they were sitting by the window with two steaming bowls of chicken soup in front of them. A heavy shower of rain was battering the glass and obscuring the view of the park. Lloyd toyed with his soup but didn't eat much. Hope watched him carefully, trying to judge his mood. Was it just the flu that had brought him down, or was he being crushed by another bout of dark depression.

'Will you stop doing that,' he said after a while.

'Doing what?'

Lloyd smiled. 'I haven't got much of an appetite, that's all. I'll be all right when I've shaken off this bug.' He tore off a tiny piece of bread, dipped it in the soup and slowly chewed it. 'You didn't need to come back on my account, you know.'

'I didn't,' she lied.

'So did you have a good time in London?'

'Yes, not bad. It was nice to ... er ... catch up with everyone.' She tried to think of something else to say about her recent trip, but nothing came to mind. Not wanting to tell him more lies, she smartly changed the subject. 'How's it going with the gallery?'

'Good,' he said. 'All the stock from Liverpool was delivered yesterday. I'm going over there this afternoon to start on the inventory, make sure everything's turned up safely.'

'You're doing what?' Hope said incredulously. 'You can't do that, Lloyd. You're ill. You need to get some rest.'

'We're supposed to be opening next week. I'm behind schedule as it is.'

'So let me do it,' Hope said. 'Give me the keys and the list. I can check it out. Any problems and I'll let you know.'

Lloyd hesitated.

'Come on,' she said. 'Just how much are you going to get

done in your state anyway? Stay here and put your feet up. I'll make you a hot toddy before I go.'

'Are you sure? I could always come with you and—'

'I can cope,' she said firmly. 'You need to concentrate on getting better, or there won't be any grand opening next week. I'll give you a call later, let you know how it's going.'

And with that, it was decided.

Hope made her way along King Street, battling to keep her umbrella up while the wind whipped at its edges, continually threatening to turn it inside out. Lloyd had chosen a good location for the gallery, right in the middle of the main street, and next door to a good restaurant. There would be plenty of passing trade, even in the winter months.

Stopping by the door, she noticed that the new sign had already been installed. *Fay's* was inscribed in gold across a dark green background. Hope gazed up at it, both touched and saddened by this homage to her mother. Before the tears that were pricking her eyes could begin to flow freely, she got out the keys and hurried inside.

She disabled the alarm with the code Lloyd had provided, and then locked the main door behind her. With so much valuable stock on the premises, she couldn't be too careful. Before starting work, she took a quick tour round the empty gallery. There were three interconnecting display rooms, a toilet and a tiny kitchen, all recently whitewashed and still smelling of paint. New wooden flooring had also been laid. The heels of her boots made a sharp tapping sound against the oak as she strolled from one area to another, visualising how it would look when the paintings had been hung.

Yes, she thought, her mother would have been pleased with it.

The door that led down to the basement was in the last of the three rooms. Hope unlocked it, found the light switch and descended the flight of steps. She could immediately see why Lloyd had wanted to make a start: the paintings and photographs, all with protective covers, had been stacked against the walls, and there must have been over a hundred of them. It would take her a while to work through the inventory and make sure that everything was here.

Two hours later, Hope was still ploughing through the list. At the beginning, she had found herself frequently stopping to examine the canvases, tilting her head appreciatively or otherwise, but now she was simply checking off the numbers on the back and making sure they tallied with the description she had.

Seeing so many examples of other people's creativity reminded her that she'd been neglecting her own work recently. This evening, after she'd been to see Lloyd, she'd start on a new glass panel. A pattern of tulips or sunflowers, perhaps. Or maybe even irises – yes, tall, slender blue-violet irises. She frowned. Why had she thought of that? Chris Street and his half-sister, of course. Which instantly got her thinking about Connie again.

Her mind began to whir. What had happened to her? What was she doing now? Had they missed something important, a clue that had been staring them in the face? And how much did Terry Street really know? Burdened by the weight of so many unanswered questions, her shoulders slumped. She recalled how they'd never got to the bottom of that business with Jackie – but then she could be blackmailing Derek Parr over anything: another mistress, perhaps, or some piece of dodgy dealing she'd found out about.

Hope shook her head, trying to concentrate on the task in hand. She moved towards the corner of the room, where three paintings were stacked against each other. They were a little apart from the others and were wrapped in older, different-coloured covers. She pulled the cover of the first one aside and looked for a number on the back. Nothing. The second and the third were the same. That was odd.

Removing the covers completely, she stood the paintings side by side and stepped back to examine them properly. All three were variations on the same theme, depicting a red-light district at night – Soho, perhaps – with its strip joints, prostitutes, pimps, punters and dealers. The women leaned in doorways, displaying their wares. The men passed by, some eyeing them blatantly, others in a more furtive style. They were skilfully painted, evocative and throbbing with life, but there was an underlying darkness to them too. As she looked more closely, Hope saw the pain in a young girl's face, the cruelty in the features of the man who was watching her. She observed a tall, thin, crow-like priest standing to one side, a bible crushed against his breast. The more she stared, the more she saw, until she felt the need to look away. There was too much hidden agony in the paintings, too much despair.

It was only as her gaze slid back that she felt her heart miss a beat. There was no proper signature, but in the bottom left-hand corner were the initials *JT* and the date 1998. Could these be her father's paintings? Not the fakes he'd made his living from, but the real thing. Though if they were, she couldn't understand what they were they doing in the basement of Lloyd's new gallery. It wasn't as though they could have belonged to her mother; by 1998, Jeff Tomlin and Fay had been separated for years.

Hope scanned down the inventory again, but could find no mention of the pictures. However, now that her curiosity had been roused, she couldn't let it rest. Picking up the phone, she dialled Lloyd's number. He answered after a couple of rings.

'Hi,' she said. 'It's only me. Everything's going fine, except I've come across three paintings that I haven't got listed. Scenes of Soho, by the looks of it. Do they mean anything to you?'

There was an over-long pause at the other end of the line. When Lloyd finally spoke, his voice sounded odd. 'I've no idea. It must be some kind of mistake.'

'Mistake?' she repeated.

'Yes,' he said. 'Don't worry about it. Just put them to one side and I'll sort it out.'

But Hope needed to know if they really were her father's. 'Er, they have the initials JT on them. I was wondering if—'

'I just told you,' he exploded sharply. 'Weren't you listening to a bloody word I said? They're not part of the collection. There must have been a mix-up with the delivery.' He drew in an audible breath, and released it as a sigh. 'Sorry, Hope, I didn't mean to snap. I'm just tired, that's all. I've not been sleeping much recently.'

'That's okay,' she said, bewildered by his response. Lloyd, even in his deepest depressions, wasn't ever the type to go biting heads off. 'Look, shall I get us something to eat for supper tonight? I'm just about to finish up here.'

'Thanks, that's really sweet of you, but I think I'm going to have a bath and get an early night. I'm sure you could do with a rest too. Why don't we catch up tomorrow lunchtime?'

'Okay. I'll hang on to the keys and do the rest in the morning.'

'You're an angel,' he said. 'How would I manage without you?'

'See you tomorrow, then.'

'Bye, Hope.'

She put the phone back in her bag, her hands trembling a little. Lloyd's unexpected outburst had shaken her up. She couldn't work out if it had been directly connected to the paintings, or simply a symptom of his illness. Perhaps she'd caught him at a bad time. She may even have woken him up. But neither of these explanations seemed entirely adequate. Her gaze flicked back towards the canvases, towards the scenes of lust and lechery, of greed and yearning. A cold knot was beginning to form in her stomach. She had an ominous feeling that she had just opened a whole new can of worms.

Chapter Forty-five

Benjamin Tallow jumped at the sound of the doorbell. Huddling down into the sofa, he pulled the blanket more tightly around him. It was late, and he wasn't expecting anyone. Experience had taught him to be cautious; the last time he'd answered the door to an uninvited guest, he'd lived to regret it.

There was another ring, and another, and then the sound of the letter box opening. 'Come on, man. I know you're there. It's only me. Jimmy B.'

Still Benjamin hesitated. Jimmy was sound, a small-time dealer like himself, but he wasn't in the mood for company. Then again, maybe he'd have some weed on him, and a smoke could be just what he needed at the moment.

'Come on. Let me in. I'm freezin' me nuts off out here.'

'Okay, okay,' Benjamin shouted back. Slowly he got up, every muscle in his body protesting. He'd only been out of hospital for a day, and even with the pills they'd given him, his body still felt like it was on fire. Every movement of his head caused a white-hot pain to scream down the side of his face. Grimacing, he lifted a hand to lightly touch the dressing; even that small pressure caused him to flinch.

Plodding into the hall, he put the light on and carefully pulled back the bolts. He opened the door and nodded at Jimmy. 'Hey,' he said.

Jimmy B was shuffling on the spot, his skinny arms crossed over his chest, his hands clamped under his armpits in a vain attempt to keep warm. His gaze shifted quickly sideways, before sliding back to focus on a point slightly south of Benjamin's eyes. 'Sorry, man,' he muttered. 'Had no choice, did I?'

Benjamin had only a fraction of a second to try and make sense of this apology before a figure stepped out of the darkness and straight into his line of view. As if he'd been thumped in the stomach, he felt the air fly out of his lungs, and his legs begin to buckle. Jesus Christ! It was Terry Street, Terry bloody Street! His first instinct was to slam the door shut, but the older man was too fast for him. His heavily booted foot was across the threshold before Benjamin's brain had even passed the order to his hands.

'Now, son,' he said, in that weird rasping voice of his, 'no need for any unfriendliness. I just want a little chat. Why don't we go inside, where it's more private.'

But private was the one thing Benjamin didn't want. The last time he'd had a private chat with a member of the Street family, half his face had been sliced off. Had Terry come to finish the job? Gripped by fear, by panic, he felt a shifting in his bowels. What could he do? What could he say? He thought about begging, but his throat had seized up. His mouth opened and closed like a drowning fish, each movement tugging painfully on his stitches. He looked pleadingly towards Jimmy B, but Jimmy was staring determinedly at the ground.

'You can fuck off now,' Street said to Jimmy. 'I'll settle up with you later.'

Jimmy nodded, and quickly slunk off down the passageway.

Terry turned back to Benjamin, his thin lips widening into the semblance of a smile. 'Just the two of us, then, son. Aren't you going to invite me in?' But even as he spoke, he was already pushing past.

Benjamin stood paralysed, his left hand still tightly glued to the side of the door. If his legs had been capable, he'd have tried sprinting to freedom, but his knees were shaking too much for him even to attempt it. So it was happening again, history repeating itself, and there was nothing he could do about it. A slow wave of resignation rolled over him. He was too tired and battered to fight against the inevitable.

'Well don't just stand there,' Street said, glancing over his shoulder. 'Get the fuckin' kettle on. I'm gasping for a brew.'

Benjamin stared at him, bewildered. What kind of man asked for a cup of tea before he beat the shit out of you?

'Ah,' Terry said dismissively. 'You're not still stressing over that bit of trouble with Danny, are you?'

'I'm s-sorry, Mr Street,' Benjamin finally managed to stammer out. 'It won't never happen again. I swear. They had a gun, see, they made me hand it over. I didn't mean for—'

'Forget it,' Terry said smoothly. 'What's done is done, right? Time to move on.' He strode on down the hall. 'Kitchen's through here, is it?'

Benjamin followed, wondering if this was some kind of sick game. If Terry hadn't come about the lost gear, then what was he doing here? Perhaps he was just trying to lull him into a false sense of security before lashing out like his son. You could never tell with men like Street. They had their own set of rules, their own way of righting wrongs.

Terry Street pulled out a chair and sat down at the table. 'You make the tea, son, and then we'll talk. I've got a nice little proposition for you.'

Benjamin's hands were trembling as he switched on the

359

kettle and washed out a couple of mugs in the sink. He opened the fridge, took out an unopened pint of milk and grappled with the carton. A teaspoon went spinning to the floor. His fingers wouldn't work properly, wouldn't grip, and every action took twice as long as it should have. And all the time he was aware of Street's cold, dark eyes drilling a hole in his back.

Eventually Benjamin got the brew made and carried the two mugs over to the table. He laid one carefully in front of Street, taking extra care not to spill any of it. Then he sat down in the chair opposite.

Terry Street gave him a nod. 'Now you see, Benjie ... you don't mind me calling you Benjie, do you?' He carried on without waiting for a response. 'I've got a bit of a problem, and I'm thinking you could help me out. I need someone I can trust, someone who won't let me down. You made a mistake, yeah, there's no arguing with that, but I'm prepared to overlook it. That's if you'll do something for me in return.'

Benjamin, had he been a braver man, might have claimed that a brutal beating had pretty well evened out the score, but in truth he was scared witless and prepared to agree to just about anything.

Street gave him a hard look, a searching look, as if undecided as to whether to proceed. He took a sip of his tea and put the mug back on the table. 'You sure you're up for this?'

Benjamin leaned forward, an earnest look on his face. 'You can trust me, Mr Street. I swear on my life.'

A few seconds ticked by, but finally Terry Street seemed to make up his mind. 'You know the club Diamond Lil's?'

'In Shoreditch, yeah?'

'That's the one. I want you to go there on Saturday night and ask for a man called Kozlov. *Mr* Kozlov to you. Say that you need to speak him about Terry Street. If he's not there, then you wait. As long as it takes, right?'

Benjamin nodded. 'As long as it takes,' he repeated dutifully.

'Now you got to play this smart, son, 'cause Kozlov ain't no fuckin' fool. When you do get to see him, you say you've got some information he might be interested in buying, that you know about a big deal I've got going down. If you play it right, acting like you've got a grudge against me on account of your recent troubles and all, he shouldn't have too much trouble believing you.'

Benjamin's hand fluttered anxiously up to his jaw before settling back down on the table again.

'You tell him you've heard about a painting I'm going to buy, an old Russian painting that's worth a lot of money. Now this painting's well iffy, right? It was one of a pair nicked from a gallery in Holland in the 1960s. You tell him I'm going to get it on the cheap because the man who originally bought it has recently died, and his widow's got the jitters about stolen property littering up the house. You tell him I'm in talks with the dealer who's selling it for her. You tell him I've already got another buyer lined up and I'm going to make a whole lot of profit. You tell him you're not happy about that on account of what my son did to your face.'

Benjamin concentrated hard, trying to absorb it all. 'What if he asks me other stuff, like ... I dunno, what the name of the painter is? Or the dealer?'

The thin-lipped smile appeared on Terry's face again. 'You see, that's why I chose you, Benjie, because you got brains.' As if to prove his point, he gave a couple of quick taps to his forehead. 'Sure he's going to ask you stuff. And when he does, you're going to say that you can't remember the name of the artist, something beginning with B perhaps, but that you'll give him the name of the dealer if he makes it worth your while. Ask him for a grand.' He laughed, an odd, hoarse-sounding noise. 'A grand. Not bad for stitching me up, yeah? You could have a nice little holiday with that, somewhere sunny, somewhere with a few tasty girls to keep you company.'

'But I don't get it,' Benjamin said, confused. 'Why do you—'

'You don't need to get it, Benjie. You just need to repeat what I've told you. And when you see the colour of his money, you give him this.' He reached into his pocket, took out a business card and slid it across the table.

Benjamin picked up the card and looked at it. *Tom Montgomery*, it said, and underneath, in smaller print, the words *The Montgomery Gallery*, along with an address in Mayfair.

'You think you can manage that, Benjie?'

'Yes, sir. Yes, Mr Street.' His head was bobbing up and down now like one of those nodding dogs. 'But . . . but can we just go over it again?'

Terry Street's thick-knuckled hand snaked across the table and coiled tightly around Benjamin's wrist. 'Sure we can. We'll go over and over it until you're fuckin' word perfect. You don't want to let me down, son. I don't like to be disappointed.'

Chapter Forty-six

Hope woke to the sound of silence. For a while she lay on her back, staring up at the ceiling. Something was missing. What was it? And then she realised: no doors opening and closing, no water rushing through the pipes, no kettle boiling, no footsteps or hushed voices. She'd got used to the endless comings and goings of Lana's chaotic household, and now the silence felt unnatural.

Pushing back the covers, she sat up, swung her legs over the side of the bed and planted her feet on the carpet. It was a chilly morning, and she shivered as she stood upright and reached for her dressing gown. A quick shower, a bit of breakfast, and then she'd head off to the gallery. With luck, she'd have the job done by lunchtime. Thinking of the gallery reminded her of Lloyd's aggressive response to her query about the paintings. Did she dare raise the subject again? Well, she was going to have to if she wanted to get to the bottom of it all.

Forty minutes later, Hope was back at Fay's. She made her way down to the basement, took off her coat and picked up the inventory. With only a quarter of the stock left to check, the job shouldn't be a long one. But first, she decided, she'd take another look at those paintings. Perhaps she'd missed something. Perhaps, somewhere on the old protective covers, there was a clue as to the identity of the artist.

But as her gaze swung across the room, her mouth dropped open. Where the three canvases had been stacked, now there was only empty space. What? She stared hard at the gap, as if by sheer force of will she could fill it up again. Her pulse began to race. Oh God, had there been a break-in, had she forgotten to lock the door, had someone got in and ... But no, the door had definitely been locked when she'd arrived a few minutes ago, the alarm still set. And nothing else had been disturbed. There was only one other possible explanation – Lloyd had come here last night and removed the paintings.

There would be another set of keys, of course there would, but what could be so important about those canvases that they had to be instantly spirited away? Despite being ill, something must have compelled him to leave his nice warm flat and drive over to King Street. Hope shook her head, unable to make any sense of it. She thought about calling him, but was still wary after yesterday. No, she'd leave it until they met up at lunchtime. That way she could ask him to his face.

Distracted as she was, she began work on the inventory again, slowly circling the room as she ticked off the items on the list. Last night she'd intended to do some sketches for her own new panel, but hadn't got any further than picking up a pad and pencil. Her mind had kept wandering, just as it was now. She had sat for a long time, gazing into space, before giving up and going to bed.

She still couldn't get her head round who Jeff Tomlin had really been. A fraudster, yes, there was no doubt about that, but perhaps not the heartless man her mother had made him out to be. If Flint was to be believed, he hadn't actually chosen to abandon either of them. She realised with a pang that she envied Connie the years she had shared with Jeff. Lloyd had been a good surrogate, always kind and loving, but nothing could change the fact that he wasn't her real father.

There was more she could have asked Flint about Jeff, and now she wished that she had: like whether he had ever mentioned her, for instance, or what made him laugh, or what he liked to do when he wasn't knocking out his clever forgeries or gambling on the horses. She thought again about the Soho paintings, and mentally tried to recreate the images she'd seen. Were they a reflection of his own inner turmoil, or of something more objective? Jeff Tomlin, she suspected, had been a complicated man – but a man, for all his faults, that she would have liked the opportunity to get to know.

She was still pondering on all this when her phone started ringing. She looked at her watch. It was five past ten. The little blue screen of the mobile told her that the caller's number was unrecognised.

'Hello,' she said.

There was a short pause before a rasping voice came down the line. 'I take it we're still on schedule for tomorrow?'

Hope almost dropped the phone. How the hell had Terry Street got hold of her number? But then she remembered: she'd given it to Chris when she'd gone to see him at Belles. 'Er, I'm not sure if—'

'No excuses, love. We've got a deal, remember? Bring the painting to me tomorrow, midday like we arranged. That's if you want to see your pal Flint again.'

Hope felt her whole body go cold. Pressing the phone to her ear, she spluttered, 'W-what? What do you mean?'

'Let's just call it a form of insurance. Don't worry, he'll be fine so long as you stick to your side of the bargain.' Street gave a coarse laugh. 'I'd put him on the line, only he's kind of tied up at the moment.'

Hope, struck dumb, stared stupidly at the floor. What should she say? If she told him that she didn't have the painting, would *never* have the painting, it could spell the end for Flint. She couldn't endanger his life like that. The only way forward was to play for time.

'You know what you've got to do,' Street said. 'And don't even think about going to the law. You so much as dial 999 and I'll hear about it. You understand?'

'Y-yes, I understand. I'll be there.'

'Tomorrow, then, and don't be late.'

He hung up abruptly, and Hope listened to the silence he left behind before slowly lowering the phone from her ear and placing it on the table. Panic was rioting inside her, one thought tumbling manically on top of another. How could they have been so stupid as to lie to Terry Street? What would he do to Flint when she didn't produce the painting? Twenty-four hours, that was all she had. She began pacing the basement, up and down, up and down, raking her fingers through her hair. Oh God, oh God! Surely she had to take the chance and go to the police? It might be Flint's only hope. But then again, she could be signing his death warrant.

She stopped suddenly as another idea occurred to her. What if she tried talking to Chris Street? He was the only member of that family who seemed even faintly reasonable. She could call him up, explain what had happened, try and get him to use his influence. Hurrying back to the table, she snatched up her mobile and scrolled through the menu. But just as she was about to press the button, she had second thoughts. No, this wasn't something she could do over the phone. She had to go back to London and see him face to face. It was Flint's only chance. She had to speak to Chris in person, beg if she had to, so long as she could make him understand that nothing his father did to Flint would make that damn picture reappear.

Grabbing her coat, Hope rushed up the stairs and through the gallery. Quickly, she set the alarm before closing the door and locking it behind her. Then she set off at a jog for Lloyd's flat. It was still raining, and she was halfway down the street before she realised that she'd left her brolly behind. Well, she wasn't going back for it now. She'd just have to get wet. After everything that had happened in the last five minutes, a soaking was the least of her worries.

Lloyd frowned as he opened the door to his flat. 'You're drenched,' he said, staring at her bedraggled figure. And then, seeing the expression on her face, he added, 'Are you all right, Hope? What's wrong?'

As she stepped inside, there was nothing Hope would have liked more than to confide in him, to tell him about the whole sorry mess she'd managed to get herself into. It was all there on the tip of her tongue, but she managed to bite back the words. The story was too long, too complicated to go into now. And she was certain that Lloyd would insist on ringing the cops.

'Yes, yes, I'm fine. I've just had a bit of bad news, that's all. A friend of mine, she's been . . . been in an accident. It's quite serious. She's in hospital. I'm going to have to go back to London.'

'Of course you must,' he said. 'That's terrible.'

'I'm sorry, I mean about the gallery and everything, but I'll come back as soon as I can.'

'Don't worry about that. Stay as long as you need to. Have you got time for a coffee before you go?'

Hope glanced at her watch. Almost ten thirty. 'No, I'd better get on. I need to go back to the cottage and throw some things in a bag.'

'Look, you're soaking wet. You'll get pneumonia if you go out again like that. Stay for a coffee, and I'll call a cab to take you home.'

Hope hesitated, then said, 'Okay.' Ten minutes wouldn't make much difference, and a cab would save her the walk home.

Lloyd got her a towel from the bathroom and then disappeared into the kitchen. 'Oh, about those three paintings,' he called out to her. 'I was right. It was a mistake. They were supposed to be delivered to another gallery. I felt like some fresh air last night, so I took a stroll down to Fay's.'

Hope didn't really believe the story, but she had too much else on her mind to pursue it. The questions she had would have to wait until her mind was clearer, her thoughts less preoccupied by what Flint must be going through. Please God, she prayed, don't let anything bad happen to him.

She went over to the window, looked down on the park, but soon turned away. She was too anxious, too restless to stand still. Resuming the pacing she'd started in the gallery, she rubbed the towel through her hair as she strode from one side of the room to the other. It was on her second turn that she noticed the maroon passport lying on the dresser. Was Lloyd planning a trip? She hoped so. A holiday would do him good once Fay's was up and running.

Stopping, she laid the damp towel around her shoulders and picked up the passport. She flicked it open, wondering if his photograph was as bad as hers. As she smiled at the mug shot, her gaze slid over to the name: *Robert Lloyd Randall.* She'd never known that his first name was Robert. Still, she supposed it wasn't that unusual – lots of people probably chose to use their middle names instead.

'What are you doing with that?'

Hope jumped. It was the voice she had heard on the phone yesterday, hard-edged and icy. She turned to look at him. His eyes were blazing, his face tight and angry like a stranger's. For

368

the very first time in her life, she was actually afraid of her step-father.

Lloyd put the two mugs of coffee down on the table, took a step forward and snatched the passport out of her hand. 'Do you always go rooting through other people's things?'

'I wasn't rooting,' she said defensively, feeling the blood rise into her cheeks. 'It was just lying there and...'

He opened the top drawer of the dresser, threw the passport in and slammed the drawer shut again. 'Jesus Christ,' he growled, 'is there nothing private in this world?'

Hope gazed up at him, wide-eyed and confused. This wasn't the Lloyd she knew, the man who was normally so kind and considerate. 'I'm sorry.'

For a long moment, he continued to glare at her. But then, as if he suddenly realised what he was doing, a stricken look came over him. Briefly he covered his face with his hands, a low groan leaking out from between his fingers. 'No, I'm the one who should be sorry. Forgive me. I shouldn't have ... I don't know what I was thinking. I've been ... I don't know ... Things have been getting on top of me recently.'

'It's all right, I understand,' she said, although she wasn't sure that she did. Even in the months immediately after her mother's death, he had never behaved this strangely. 'But I think I'll skip the coffee. I really need to get home and pack.'

'What about the taxi?'

'There's a rank down the road. I'll pick one up there.'

'I'm so sorry,' he said again. 'I should never have—'

'Forget it. It doesn't matter.' She felt awkward now rather than afraid. That was twice in two days that he'd turned on her, and she couldn't understand why. Despite her discomfort, she forced herself to lean forward and kiss him on the cheek. 'Take care of yourself. I'll be back soon.'

As she hurried back down the stairs and out into the rain,

369

Hope had a cold, sick sensation in the pit of her stomach. The ground beneath her seemed to be constantly shifting. She had the feeling that everything was starting to fall apart, and there was nothing she could do about it.

Chapter Forty-seven

Hope caught the train from Liverpool and was in Euston by two o'clock. From there she took a cab to Kellston, a stop-start journey that felt interminably slow. Sitting in the back seat, willing the cars in front to move, she racked her brains trying to come up with a convincing argument to present to Chris Street. But however much she played around with the facts, they didn't sound any better. The bottom line was that she didn't have the painting, nor did she have a clue to its whereabouts. No matter how this truth was packaged, the Streets wouldn't be impressed.

That sick, panicky feeling began to take hold of her again, tugging at her insides. Perhaps she *should* go to the police, tell them everything. What about the woman who'd come round to the flat. Inspector Middleton, wasn't that her name? Surely she could be trusted. But no sooner had the thought occurred to her than Terry Street's threat echoed ominously in her head. Men like Street had informants everywhere, and the police force wouldn't be an exception.

Hope gazed out of the window, seeing nothing more than a

long line of cars, a blur of faces. Her hands were clenched in anxiety, and she could feel her fingernails digging into the soft skin of her palms. Too afraid to dwell on what she had to do next, her thoughts skittered off in another direction. What was going on with Lloyd? She replayed the incident with the passport, and saw again the hot fury in his eyes. Instinctively, she drew back, pressing her spine into the seat. What she couldn't understand was why he should react so badly to her sneaking a look at his photograph. And then, out of nowhere, a memory jolted through her like a small electric shock. It was something Flint had said on their way to the jail: *I used to know a pimp called Bobby Randall.*

Hope's mouth fell open, and her pulse quickened. Perhaps it hadn't been the photo that was bothering Lloyd, but the name. Was that what he'd been so angry about? Was it possible that . . . But immediately she pulled herself up. What was wrong with her? This was her stepfather she was talking about, the kind, generous, funny man who had shown her nothing but affection for the last twenty years. Well, apart from the two recent incidents, but that had been completely out of character. He was no more a pimp than she was a prostitute. And how many Robert Randalls were there in the country? Probably thousands. It was a sign of her own disturbed state that she could even think of such a thing.

But as the taxi trundled on, the cabbie thankfully keeping silent, Hope found herself unable to shake Flint's words from her thoughts. Yes, of course Robert Randall was a common enough name, but how many of them could there be who'd known her father? Wasn't that a coincidence too far? But as quickly as the idea arrived, she slapped it away. Flint hadn't actually said that her father had known Bobby Randall, only that *he'd* known him. There was a difference. Except . . . well, it might still put them in the same social circle. And if Jeff Tomlin had created those atmospheric Soho pictures, then he was more than likely to have been acquainted with the people he was painting.

Closing her eyes, Hope tried to put a stop to the warring voices in her head. Perhaps *she* was the one going crazy, not Lloyd. She attempted to think of something else, something less disturbing, but instead her mind perversely jumped to Terry Street and what he was likely to do to Flint when he found out that the fake Baronova was lost for ever.

After what felt like a lifetime, the cab finally turned into Tanner Road and drew up outside number forty-six. It was a good thing she'd held on to the keys, as at this time of day, no one was likely to be home. Flying up the stairs to the flat, she opened the door and hurried inside. 'Hello?' she called out tentatively, but as she'd expected, there was no reply.

Hope went to her old room, hurled her coat on the bed and made a decision. Before going to see Chris Street, she'd have one more thorough look for the painting. It might be hopeless, it probably was, but at least she'd have covered all the angles before throwing in the towel and falling on his mercy.

Before starting the search, she backtracked to the hall and put the chain on the door in case anyone came back unexpectedly. With luck, if Lana's crew stuck to their usual schedule, she'd have a good few hours to check every possible hiding place. Where to begin? She'd already looked through Connie's room, the bathroom seemed unlikely – too damp to hide a painting – and so she went to the living room instead.

Standing in the centre of the room, she did a three-hundred-and-sixty degree turn, trying to spot any possible hiding place. Under the sofa? Under the chairs? But these were likely to be pushed around when the hoovering was done. She tried them anyway, only to find a thin layer of dust, a fivepence piece and a dried-up piece of mushroom. After dumping the coin and what was probably the remnant of somebody's pizza in the ashtray, she pushed her hands down between the leather cushions, but only came up with more fluff. Where else? Her eyes alighted on the fireplace, and she got down on her hands and knees to peer up the chimney. It had been blocked off, and anyway she was pretty sure the painting wouldn't fit. Scrambling back to her feet, the only other place that occurred to her was behind the large plasma TV, but that was screwed firmly to the wall. Surely Connie wouldn't have dismantled it? No, it would have been too heavy, and too much trouble to go to if she needed to get hold of the painting in a hurry.

Next, Hope tried the kitchen, starting with the space under the sink. But there was only the usual array of cleaning products, a box of candles, two glass vases and a hammer. She pulled a chair over, stood on it and checked the top of the cupboards. Nothing but dust. She tried the sides of the fridge and the washing machine, but the gaps weren't wide enough to insert a canvas.

Returning to Connie's room, Hope heaved out a sigh. She was rapidly running out of ideas. There were always the two other bedrooms, but surely Connie wouldn't have hidden it in either one. There'd have been too much chance of it being discovered by accident. Her gaze panned around the room again. Maybe she'd missed something. Had she really checked it thoroughly? This was, after all, the most likely hiding place.

She began another, more thorough search, pulling out all the drawers from the dresser, checking the undersides of them again and then peering inside the empty shell. Nothing. She left the drawers lying on the floor while she investigated the wardrobe, dragging it partly away from the wall in order to check the back of it. More nothing. The chair was too flimsy for her to stand on, so she went back to the kitchen and brought back one of the sturdier wooden ones. She climbed up, peered on to the top of the wardrobe but found only a couple of old metal hangers.

Determined not to give up, she whipped the duvet and sheet off the bed. She made a through search of the mattress, looking for any place where it might have been cut open, the painting inserted inside and then stitched up again. She'd seen that once in a movie. But yet again she was disappointed. 'Connie,' she murmured. 'Where did you put it? Where did you put it?' Even as she asked the question, she guessed it was irrelevant. Even if the picture had once been hidden here, it had probably long since been removed.

Hope slumped down on the bed, leaned forward and put her head in her hands. This was useless, a complete waste of time. Then, as she slowly lifted her face again, her gaze fell on the Paul Klee print, *Forest Bird*, and an idea suddenly snapped into place. Forest Bird. Fyodor Baronova. Same initials. Just another of those coincidences, or something more? Even though she'd already checked it before leaving for Albersea, she wondered if she'd made a mistake. She'd thought the print was too light to be hiding anything behind it, but maybe the canvas wasn't as heavy as she imagined.

Leaping to her feet, she snatched the picture off the wall, sat back down, ripped the brown tape off the back and began dismantling the frame. With her breath coming in short, fast bursts, she shook the sheet of glass out on to the bare mattress and flipped over the piece of hardboard. She was sure she was right. She had to be. But her excitement died as quickly as it had arrived. There was only one picture inside, and that was of the speckled Forest Bird. Hope let out a groan. She could have wept with frustration.

It was at that very moment that a small voice, tentative and bewildered, came from behind her. 'W-what are you doing?'

Hope looked up sharply to see Evelyn standing at the entrance to the room. Oh God. How long had she been there? And how had she got in without Hope hearing? It took her a second to realise that she must have been in the flat all the time. Her bedroom door had been closed, and Hope hadn't thought to take a look inside.

Evelyn's dark eyes were wide with confusion as she surveyed the chaos in the room, the upturned drawers, the duvet thrown on to the floor, the picture that had been ripped apart. 'Hope?'

Hope could instantly see what was going through her head: that she'd returned while they were all out at work in order to turn the place over. She jumped up, horrified. 'No, no, it's not like that, I swear. Please, you have to let me explain.'

Chapter Forty-eight

Evelyn sat on the bed, her mouth partly open, while Hope, barely pausing for breath, raced through the events that had led to the current situation. It was a disjointed and somewhat garbled account, starting from when Flint first arrived on her doorstep and finishing with his recent abduction by Terry Street.

At the end of it all, as if the first revelation had only just sunk in, Evelyn said, 'You're Connie's sister?'

'Yes. Well, half-sister. We had the same father, Jeff Tomlin, but I never met him. And I never even knew that Connie existed.'

'Why didn't you tell me?'

Hope could see the disappointment in her face, her dismay at having been deceived. She reached out, intending to touch her on her arm, but Evelyn shrank back. Hope quickly returned the hand to her lap. 'It wasn't that I didn't trust you. I wanted to tell you, honestly I did. But if I'd said anything, you'd have had to keep the secret too. We figured that people wouldn't talk, not openly at least, if they found out who I really was. Do you see?'

'I wouldn't have told anyone,' Evelyn said sadly. 'I could have helped.'

'I know that now. I'm sorry.'

'So all that stuff Lana was spouting about you getting in trouble up north, having to lay low for a while, that was just a pack of lies.' Evelyn's frown grew deeper as the extent of the deception began to sink in.

'I'm sorry,' Hope said again. 'And please don't blame Lana. It wasn't her fault. She was trying to do what was best for Connie.'

'And that story about your mother? Was that all rubbish too?'

Hope shook her head. 'No, that bit was true. She did have cancer. She died six months ago.'

Evelyn's face softened a little, but not enough to suggest she was anywhere close to forgiving her. She sat and stared, as if Hope was a stranger she was meeting for the very first time.

Hope, unable to bear the intensity of her gaze, looked down at the floor. 'God, you must hate me. I would if I was in your shoes. And it's all been such a bloody waste, all the lies, all the skulking around.' Tears rose to her eyes and she wiped them away with the back of her hand. 'And now Terry Street's got hold of Flint and won't let him go until I give him the painting. But I haven't got the damn thing and I don't know where it is, so what am I supposed to do? Jesus, it's all such a nightmare.'

'Do you think he might have Connie, too?'

Startled by the question, Hope glanced up. 'No, I don't think so. No, I'm sure he doesn't. He claims he knows where she went, but he's probably lying.'

Evelyn was quiet for a moment, then, without another word, she got up and walked out of the room.

Hope couldn't blame her. Since her arrival at the flat, Evelyn had shown her nothing but kindness, and she'd thrown it all back in her face. Why hadn't she had more trust in her? The more lies you told, the more complicated it got, until the web was so sticky there was no escaping from it. Hope gazed around the room despairingly. What next? Well, there was only one thing left to do: she'd better bite the bullet, get over to Belles and break the bad news to Chris Street.

Wearily, she got to her feet.

'Hope?'

Hope turned to see Evelyn standing by the door again. She was carrying a large tartan suitcase, which she dropped on to the bed. 'You'll be needing this.'

'It's okay,' Hope said. 'I brought a bag with me. And don't worry, I'll be gone as soon as I've tidied up here.'

'Look inside.'

'Pardon?'

'Just look inside.'

Hope leaned down and unzipped the case. It was empty apart from a hard, flat oblong object, about fourteen inches by ten, covered with bubble wrap. She glanced up at Evelyn, and Evelyn nodded. As Hope began to strip the wrapping off, her heart started beating faster. It couldn't be. It couldn't. But then, suddenly, it was revealed – a picture just like the one she'd seen on the internet, the fair-haired Russian woman gazing into mirrors, the series of odd, disturbing reflections in deep shades of blue. The fake Baronova. 'W-what . . . ' she stammered in astonishment. 'I don't understand. How did you . . . '

Evelyn managed her first smile since seeing Hope again. 'I took it after Connie went missing. You were right about where she hid it; it used to be behind that bird picture. She showed it to me once, said that it was valuable, but I didn't really believe her. She used to say stuff sometimes, you know . . . ' And then, as if Hope might suspect her of theft, she quickly added, 'But that wasn't why I took it. I thought Lana might rent out the room to someone else and get rid of the pictures. I wanted to keep it for Connie, for when she came back. But I'm sure she'd want you to have it. She liked Flint. She wouldn't have wanted him to get hurt.'

Hope felt like she was about to burst into tears. Her fingers lightly touched the painting, tracing the edges of the mirrors. 'Do you mean it? Can I really take this and give it to Terry Street?'

Evelyn gave another tiny nod, her voice barely audible. 'I don't think Connie's coming home, is she?'

And Hope suddenly realised what finding the painting meant – that Connie hadn't sold it to someone else and taken off. So Flint's theory was out of the window, and Connie's disappearance was as much a mystery as it had always been. A shiver ran through her as she thought of the alternatives. 'I don't know. I hope she is. God, I really hope she is.' Then, aware of the importance of what Evelyn had done, she stepped forward and wrapped her arms around her. 'Thank you so much for this.'

This time Evelyn didn't shrink from her, but returned the hug, burying her face in Hope's shoulder. The two of them stayed like that for a while, their friendship renewed, the past forgiven. It was Hope who eventually pulled away with a sigh. 'I'm supposed to hand the picture over tomorrow, but I can't see any point in waiting. I think I'll go to Belles and do it now.'

'No,' Evelyn said. 'Don't do that.'

'Why not?'

'Get Terry Street to come here. That way he can bring Flint with him and you can see that he's safe before you hand the picture over. The painting in exchange for Flint, yeah?'

Hope could see that this idea was much more sensible than her walking into the club with a fake Baronova under her arm. 'You're right,' she said. 'But what if Lana comes back? She won't be too happy if she finds Terry Street here.'

Evelyn looked at her watch. 'You've got a good few hours yet.

Go on, give him a ring. The sooner you do it, the sooner this will all be finished.'

Hope got her phone out of her bag and found Chris Street's number. She preferred to talk to him than to Terry. With Evelyn standing by her shoulder, she took a deep breath and pressed the button. It rang five times before he eventually picked up.

'Hope,' he said smoothly. 'How nice to hear from you again.'

Hope scowled at the sound of his voice. 'I've got what you want. Bring Flint here in half an hour and I'll give it to you.'

'Half an hour? I'm not sure if—'

'That's the deal,' she said. 'Take it or leave it. Forty-six Tanner Road. Ring the top bell.'

'Hold on a minute.' Chris Street put his hand over the phone while he talked to whoever else was in the room. Then he came back on the line. 'Okay, we'll be there.'

'Good,' Hope said, and immediately hung up. Her hands were trembling as she put the phone back in her bag. 'It's done.'

Evelyn gave her arm a squeeze. 'Come on. While we're waiting, we can get this lot tidied up.'

As they put everything back in place, Evelyn told Hope what she knew of the history of the painting. 'About nine months after Connie's dad died, there was a fire at the flat they were living in and she and her mum had to get out quickly. They both took what they could, but there wasn't much time. The first thing her mother grabbed was the painting. Connie thought it was just because it had belonged to her dad, that it had sentimental value, but she found out later that it was worth a lot of money.'

Hope recalled the metal box containing Connie's meagre possessions, the burnt photograph, the birthday cards, the man's gold wedding ring. She thought of how Connie must have felt as everything else went up in flames. 'Did she know the painting was a fake?'

'Yeah, but she said it didn't matter, that she knew someone who'd buy it off her anyway.' Evelyn carefully slotted the drawers back in place, and then glanced over her shoulder. 'But it wasn't the cash she was after. She wanted to know who'd killed her father. She *needed* to know who'd broken up her home. It was all that mattered to her.' Suddenly, as if it had all got too much, Evelyn slumped down on the bed and started crying. 'It's awful, everything's too awful.'

Hope rushed over and tried to comfort her. 'I know,' she said, 'but we can't give up yet. She may still be out there somewhere.'

'It's not that,' Evelyn said between sobs. 'Well, it is that, but it's the other thing too.'

The other thing? And then it occurred to Hope that she hadn't even asked why Evelyn was home at this time of day. 'What is it? What's wrong?'

'You haven't heard,' Evelyn said.

'Heard what? Tell me what's the matter.'

Evelyn got a tissue from her sleeve and snuffled into it. 'It's Linzi ... Do you remember Linzi? She was the girl at the shop on the high street, you know, the one with the long boots? That day I took the black dress.'

Hope nodded, a bad feeling starting to stir in her chest. 'Yes, I remember her.'

Evelyn broke down again, her voice sounding small and strangled. 'He ... he got her. The Whisperer got her. It was last night. They found her in the morning. I went to the hospital, but ... but they wouldn't let me see her. She's still unconscious, Hope. I think she's going to die.'

Chapter Forty-nine

Detective Inspector Valerie Middleton stared bleakly down at the gruesome photographs, evidence of the Whisperer's latest handiwork. Her eyes roamed over the multiple cigarette burns to the girl's face and neck, as well as the vicious slashes to her breasts, thighs and arms. Valerie had got the call at eleven thirty last night, just as she'd been about to go to bed, and she hadn't been home since. Now she was running purely on caffeine, rage and adrenalin. The bastard had struck again, and this time it looked like the girl might die.

The latest victim was Linzi Marshall, another local prostitute, and the pattern was a familiar one. She'd been abducted at some point after eight o'clock, brutally tortured, and then casually dumped in front of the burnt-out remains of the Lincoln Pool Hall. The SOCO team had gone over the ground with a fine-tooth comb, but as usual there'd been nothing. Forensics was still working on her clothes, but if past experience was anything to go by, there'd be little joy there either.

'Any news from the hospital?' Valerie asked, for what must have been the tenth time.

Swann shook his head. 'Go home, guv. Get a few hours' shut-eye. I'll give you a bell if anything changes.'

Valerie was reluctant to leave, but until Linzi Marshall regained consciousness – if she ever did – they had nothing new to go on. Perhaps Swann was right and she should try and get some sleep while she still had the opportunity. 'Okay, maybe I will. But make sure you call if—'

'I'll call,' he said. 'I promise.'

As Valerie drove through Kellston, the light was starting to fade. She'd intended to go straight back to Silverstone Heights, but on impulse she swung a left at Station Road and carried on up to Albert Street. This was where Linzi Marshall had last been seen. But, with the patrol cars still making their regular rounds, and too many of the punters being scared away, she'd taken off for somewhere quieter at around eight o'clock.

Albert Street, unsurprisingly, was virtually deserted. All the toms had heard the news and most weren't prepared to take the risk. Only a few of the toughest girls, or maybe the most desperate, stood huddled together under a lamppost, smoking cigarettes and waiting for business. Valerie drove past them, took a right turn and then another, and came out in Tanner Road.

The missing Connie Tomlin was still bothering her. Although she and Swann had talked to the couple who occupied the first floor – who could tell them nothing – they still hadn't managed to speak with the ground-floor tenant, eighty-one-year-old Hughie Fowler. She was sure he'd been in when they'd called, but he hadn't answered the door. It was one of those loose ends that niggled away at her. If Connie was the Whisperer's missing C, then any clue as to what had happened to her that day in February could be absolutely crucial.

As she drove past number forty-six, Valerie noticed that the lights were on in Fowler's flat. Sleep, she decided, could wait.

Pulling up sharply, she managed to squeeze the car into one of the few available spaces, before hurrying back to climb the steps and ring on the doorbell. Again there was no response. Moving back, she was just in time to see a twitch of the curtains. So, old Hughie was either the antisocial type, or he was deliberately avoiding her. Valerie wasn't in the mood for being ignored. Rapping sharply on the window pane, she pressed her badge to the glass and said loudly: 'It's the police, Mr Fowler. I'd like to talk to you.'

There was a short delay before the light went on in the hall, and another, slightly longer one while he fumbled with the lock. Eventually the door opened and the old man's rheumy eyes gazed up at her. 'What do you want?' he said.

'Detective Inspector Valerie Middleton.' She put her badge close to his face. 'I'd like to talk to you about a missing girl called Connie Tomlin. Do you mind if I come in?'

The Mercedes rolled into Tanner Road thirty-five minutes after Hope had made the call. She'd been prowling around the room, going backwards and forwards to the window, but had still managed to miss the exact moment of its arrival. When the doorbell rang, she gave a jump and rushed over to look outside again. The car was already parked opposite the house, with its interior lights on. She could make out the driver, the big black guy she'd met at Belles, and then, with a rush of relief, she realised that Flint was sitting in the back. Good. So they *were* sticking to their side of the bargain.

Evelyn, who'd been huddled in the corner of the sofa, stood up. 'Do you want me to stay, or—'

'No, you'd better not. You've got enough on your plate without getting involved in all this.'

'Okay, I'll wait in the bedroom.' Evelyn lifted her hands, her fingers crossed. 'Good luck.'

'Thanks.'

The bell went again, and Hope hurried along the hall, out of the door and down the stairs. She opened the main front door to find both Chris and Terry Street standing on the other side. Chris, who was carrying a briefcase, gave her a friendly smile. 'Good to see you again,' he said, as if this was a purely social visit. His father, however, remained grim-faced, acknowledging her with only the barest of nods.

Hope looked between them towards the car. 'What about Flint?'

'When I've seen the painting,' Terry said. He gave her the kind of glare that suggested any argument would be futile.

She hesitated, but then stood aside to let them in. 'Second floor.'

As they climbed up the stairs, Chris glanced over his shoulder. 'So, you've been okay, then?'

Hope's brows rose a little. She was amazed by his nonchalant attitude. He and his father had abducted Flint, threatened to kill him, and now he was enquiring after her well-being. 'Fine,' she replied tightly. 'You had any more guns pointed at you?'

Terry made a disapproving grunting noise, but Chris only laughed before he replied, 'Well, at least that's one night you won't forget in a hurry.'

Inside the flat, Hope led them into the living room. The painting was lying on the table, and she saw Terry's eyes instantly light up. He went over, placed his fists either side of the fake Baronova, and stared long and hard at it. A hiss of breath escaped from between his lips.

'Is that it?' Chris said, gazing down at the blue canvas with a frown. She could tell from his expression that he was wondering what all the fuss had been about.

Terry's thin lips finally stretched into a smile. 'That's it.' He looked over at Hope. 'Your daddy was one clever bastard.'

One *dead* clever bastard, Hope could have reminded him, but her main concern now was securing Flint's release. 'So what about your part of the deal? You'll let Flint go?'

Terry gave a jerk of his head to his son, and Chris went over to the window. He must have given a signal to the driver, because a few seconds later, Hope heard the car door slam. She went over to look, and saw Flint standing by the Mercedes. The light was dim and it was hard to tell what state he was in. The driver said something, and Flint leaned back against the car, folding his arms across his chest.

'We'll let him in on our way out,' Terry said.

Hope turned away from the window. 'What about the rest?' He'd also promised her information on Connie.

'Give her the case,' Terry said to Chris.

Chris put the briefcase on the table beside the painting, and flipped open the lid. Hope's eyes grew wide as she saw what was inside – it was full of neatly stacked banknotes.

'Fifty K,' Terry said. 'Like we agreed.'

Although Hope remembered the offer he'd made at the Hope and Anchor, she hadn't actually expected him to pay out. Having presumed that the new deal was a straight swap, the painting in exchange for the safe return of Flint, she was temporarily speechless. Slowly, it dawned on her that she was in the process of selling a fake painting to one of the most infamous gangsters in London. As a cold sliver of panic started to worm its way down her spine, she wanted to tell him to stuff the money, before she recalled that it wasn't actually hers to refuse. The painting belonged to Connie, and if she was still alive, it was up to her to decide what to do with the payment.

'You want to count it?' Chris said, grinning as he piled the notes up on the table.

Hope shook her head. She glanced back at Terry. 'But what about Connie?'

He gave a shrug of his shoulders. 'What about her? You've got the cash, you've got your boyfriend back, what more do you want?'

Ignoring the boyfriend comment, Hope continued to press him. 'But you said you'd tell me where she went. *Please,* that was part of the deal.'

Terry Street picked up the painting by its edges, placed it carefully in the empty briefcase and snapped shut the lid. Only then did he raise his eyes to look at her again. 'Never believe everything you're told, darlin'.'

Hope clenched her hands in frustration, but what could she do? Pleadingly, she gazed towards Chris. 'Do you know anything, anything at all?'

To his credit, he had the grace to at least look apologetic. 'Sorry. But hey, I wouldn't worry too much. I'm sure she's okay.'

Terry picked up the briefcase and swung it down by his side. 'Right, let's go.'

Hope's first thought was to try and prevent him from leaving, but in her heart she knew it was pointless. Terry Street had got what he wanted, at the price he wanted, and that was the end of it. No matter how much she begged, he couldn't tell her what he didn't know. Frustrated and disappointed, she followed them back through the hall.

Chris waited until his father had started walking down the stairs before turning to her and saying softly, 'In case you're wondering, none of this was my idea. I told him you could be trusted, that you'd deliver the picture without . . . well, without having to force the issue.'

Hope stared back at him, thinking just how wrong he was. If they hadn't taken Flint, she wouldn't have come back to London, wouldn't have turned Connie's room upside down and wouldn't have had to explain everything to Evelyn. And without Evelyn's intervention, the tidy exchange that had just taken place would never have happened.

Possibly Chris mistook her silence for some semblance of understanding, because he produced that white-toothed smile of his again. 'Call me. If you ever fancy a drink.'

It was on the tip of her tongue to say *When hell freezes over*, but with Flint still waiting outside, it was a satisfaction she thought it wiser to forgo. 'Goodbye, then,' she said, dismissing him as politely as she could.

'Bye, Hope. Take care of yourself.'

She waited, watching until he turned the corner of the stair-well and disappeared from view. Eventually she heard the distinctive click of the front door opening, followed by a murmur of voices before the door was closed again. And then there was silence. She held her breath, suddenly afraid that the Streets had reneged on the deal and decided not to free Flint after all. Where was he? What was going on? It felt like an eternity before she recognised the sound of footsteps coming quickly up the stairs.

As Flint finally came into view, Hope's first reaction was one of shock. His face was badly bruised, his left eye almost closed, and there was dried blood in his hair and down the front of his shirt. He came to a halt as he reached the landing, smiling wryly as he saw her expression.

'Don't worry,' he said. 'It's not as bad as it looks.'

For a moment, Hope stood and stared, and then, pushing aside her normal reserve, she took a step forward and wrapped her arms tightly around him. 'Thank God you're safe.'

Chapter Fifty

While Evelyn went to and fro producing sandwiches, coffee, brandy and even a bottle of antiseptic, Hope related the events that had eventually led to the discovery of the painting. Flint, perched on the edge of the sofa, listened intently. She was talking too much, she realised, as she rattled through the story, but after that impulsive embrace she was now feeling awkward and confused and was doing her best to try and disguise it. It had only been relief, she told herself, nothing more. Flint was an ally, perhaps even a friend, and no one wanted to see their friends get hurt. And yet none of that quite accounted for the fiery blush that was still raging on her cheeks.

'The painting was under the bed?' Flint said, clearly astonished and amused in equal measures.

Evelyn dropped a wad of cotton wool in front of him. 'I wasn't trying to hide it, was I? I was just keeping it safe until Connie came back.'

At the mention of Connie's name, a brief silence descended on the room. They were all suddenly aware of her absence, and of what that absence could mean.

'Well, I'm very grateful,' Flint said. 'I get the impression that Mr Street is a man who likes to get his own way. And as we didn't have a clue where the picture was . . .'

'That's okay,' Evelyn said. She stood over him for a moment, staring hard at the bruises. 'Does it hurt? Was it terrible?'

They were questions that had been on the tip of Hope's tongue too, but which she hadn't quite managed to articulate. In fact she was still finding it hard to even look at him directly.

Flint's hand rose briefly to his face. 'No, it doesn't hurt. I'm fine. Really I am.'

'I'm glad.' With tears in her eyes, Evelyn abruptly turned away and walked over to the window.

As if he might have inadvertently offended her, Flint raised his brows and glanced at Hope. This time she forced herself to meet his gaze. 'Evelyn's friend Linzi was attacked last night,' she said softly. 'She's in hospital. She's in a bad way.'

'Christ, I'm sorry,' he said. 'Are you all right, Ev?'

Evelyn gave a light shrug of her shoulders, as if to imply that bad news was all she expected to hear these days. She folded her arms across her chest and gazed up into the darkening sky before slowly lowering her gaze to the street. Suddenly her whole body stiffened. 'Hell,' she said, whirling around. 'It's Lana, Lana and Jackie.'

Hope shot up from the chair. 'What? It's not even five o'clock.' But even as she said it, she was aware of why they would have come home early. With Evelyn so upset, Lana wouldn't have wanted to leave her alone for too long.

'And there's someone with them,' Evelyn said. 'I think it's that copper from the other night.'

Hope hurried over to the window. Evelyn was right. Lana and Jackie were standing by the gate, talking to the tall, blonde inspector. She felt a cold wash of dread sweep through her. What were the police doing here? It was less than fifteen minutes since

Flint had been returned. Had they been watching the house, waiting until the deal was completed before they stepped in to make their arrests? Perhaps Terry and Danny Street were already in custody, and now it was her turn. 'Oh God,' she groaned.

Flint got to his feet too, and came to stand behind them, taking care to keep out of view of anyone who might glance up at the flat. 'What's going on?'

'They're still talking,' Evelyn said. Then her voice rose an octave. 'No, no, they're coming in. They're coming up the path.'

Hope, momentarily paralysed by fear, was kicked back into action by a burst of adrenalin. Looking round, she saw the cash piled up on the table and hastily began picking it up and piling it into Flint's arms. 'Help me get rid of this,' she yelped.

In a frenzy of activity, Flint and Hope quickly ferried the notes through to Connie's room and threw them on the bed, while Evelyn cleared the coffee table of plates, bottles, mugs and cotton wool. Even as they all dashed around, Hope could feel her fear growing. A simple search of the flat was all it would take to establish her guilt. Her final act was to shut the bedroom door on Flint and tell him to keep quiet.

After her conversation with Hughie Fowler, Valerie had needed to talk to Lana Franklin and her crew. She could have walked straight up to the flat and knocked on the door, but as it was still relatively early, and she could do without a wasted journey up two flights of stairs, she'd decided to try the bell first. It was as she was coming out of the front door that she'd spotted Lana and Jackie Woods approaching along the street, and had walked down the path to meet them at the gate.

Both women had looked about as pleased to see her as they would the grim reaper. She'd watched them exchange glances, and Jackie had muttered something, but Lana had shaken her head. Had Valerie asked to search their bags, she was certain she'd have discovered all kinds of ill-gotten gains, but that wasn't the purpose of the visit.

After explaining why she was there, the climb up the stairs was made without another word being exchanged. On the second floor, Lana got her keys out and unlocked the door, but only managed to open it an inch. The chain was on. Frowning, she put her mouth to the gap. 'Evelyn? Ev, are you there? It's only me.'

There was an odd scurrying sound from inside before the dark-haired girl, Evelyn, finally came to the door and released the chain. She looked pale and flustered, as if she'd been caught doing something she shouldn't. 'Sorry, I was just . . . er . . . '

Lana walked inside and patted her gently on the arm. 'It's all right, love. I understand. You were just feeling a bit nervous, yeah, with everything that's happened?'

Evelyn nodded, her mouth attempting but not quite achieving a smile. Then her anxious eyes alighted on Valerie.

'Oh,' Lana said, 'the inspector wants another *quick* chat with us.' She stressed the word as if to emphasise to Valerie that she was not expecting her to stay for long. 'It's about Connie, but don't worry, hun, it's only a few more questions about the day she went missing.'

'It's about Connie?' Evelyn repeated.

Valerie gave her an enquiring look. For some reason the girl seemed faintly relieved, as if she'd been expecting to hear something else. Still, this lot were probably up to their necks in so many dodgy dealings that any visit from the law was going to be unwelcome.

In the living room, Valerie took the same armchair she'd occupied on her previous visit. Hope Randall was already there, sitting on the sofa and flicking through a magazine. She had a rather shifty look about her too. And Lana, she noticed, seemed surprised to see her.

'Hope! I didn't realise—'

'I called her,' Evelyn said quickly. 'I called her this morning about Linzi. She came straight back.'

Lana raised her eyebrows but didn't say anything more.

Valerie waited until everyone had sat down. Lana took the other armchair, while Evelyn and Jackie sat beside Hope on the sofa. The only person missing was the Blunt girl, but Valerie was happy to proceed without her; from what Hughie had told her, she was pretty sure that Sharon hadn't been here on the night in question.

'Right,' she said, without any further preamble. 'I'd like to talk to you all again about the day Connie Tomlin went missing.'

Jackie didn't even try to disguise her annoyance. She lit a cigarette, threw the match in the ashtray and virtually spat out her response. 'Oh, for fuck's sake, this is ridiculous. We've already been through it all once. What's the matter with you? Haven't you got anything better to do? You should be out looking for the sick bastard who attacked Linzi Marshall last night.'

Evelyn made a faint whimpering sound and put her hand over her mouth.

'I can assure you that we're following up every possible lead on that case,' Valerie said, omitting to mention that this could be one of them. 'But I would appreciate your help with some . . . some discrepancies regarding the events of the evening of the eleventh.'

'Discrepancies?' Lana said. 'What do you mean? What are you talking about?'

Valerie let her gaze roam over each and every one of them before she spoke again. 'It appears that Connie *did* come back that night, at around seven o'clock.' She paused before dropping the bombshell. 'And that someone else also returned to the flat fifteen minutes before her.'

Hope Randall suddenly leaned forward. She stared hard at Valerie, her eyes bright with interest. 'What?'

'Who told you that?' Jackie pulled hard on her cigarette and exhaled a thin stream of smoke. 'It's crap. None of us saw her that night.'

'Oh yes,' Valerie continued. 'Someone did. In fact two people did. One of them lives downstairs. Your neighbour Hughie Fowler.'

Jackie barked out a laugh. 'That senile old git? Jesus, he probably sees Napoleon every second Thursday.'

Valerie smiled thinly back at her. 'Really? As it happens, he appeared quite lucid to me. And he specifically recalled the date, because it was his son's birthday the next day. He claims he was sitting by the window looking out for Connie, as she occasionally did some shopping for him at the weekends. He wanted her to buy a bottle of whisky for his son.'

'Go on,' Hope urged. 'What else did he say?'

Valerie wondered why the girl was so eager to know. So far as she was aware, Hope Randall hadn't even met Connie. Just avid curiosity, or something more? 'He went out into the hall to have a word, but couldn't get much sense out of her. She was unsteady on her feet, apparently, slurring her words and smelling of drink. He asked her about the whisky and she said she'd call round the next morning, but she never turned up.'

'He's saying she was drunk?' Evelyn said.

'Maybe she was upset about the row,' Valerie suggested. 'Or maybe she'd been out celebrating. Didn't one of you mention that she was job-hunting that day?'

No one said anything. Valerie, who knew the value of silence, waited for someone to fill the gap. A few seconds ticked by before Hope Randall chipped in again.

'You said someone else was here.'

'Yes,' Valerie replied. She made another slow scan of the

assembled faces before her gaze eventually settled on Jackie Woods. 'Mr Fowler said he saw you come in before Connie.'

'Me?' Jackie spluttered out. 'That's complete crap! I didn't come over until nine o'clock.'

'Not according to Mr Fowler. He claims you arrived before she did.'

'Well he's talking bollocks! The stupid sod doesn't know his arse from his elbow. I wasn't here.' She looked over at Lana. 'I *wasn't.*' Her angry gaze flew back to Valerie. 'If he's so sure he saw me that evening, why hasn't he said anything until now?'

'Because nobody asked him,' Valerie said. 'And about a week later, when he asked *you* where Connie was, you told him that she'd moved out.'

'So what?' Jackie said defensively. 'That's what we all thought.'

'Not all of us,' Evelyn said softly.

Jackie swung her head round and glared hard at Evelyn. 'So you think I had something to do with her going missing? Is that what you're saying?'

Evelyn drew back. 'I wasn't—'

'Wasn't what? Calling me a liar? Jesus, some kind of a mate you are.'

Lana quickly intervened before it could go any further. 'Look, Inspector, if Jackie says she wasn't here, then she wasn't. I think Mr Fowler must be mistaken. He probably just got his dates mixed up. I mean, he is an old man. Maybe he was thinking of the week before.'

'That wouldn't have been the eve of his son's birthday,' Valerie said. 'And did Connie come back drunk the week before?'

But Lana, protective of her crew, stood her ground. 'He must have got it wrong.'

Valerie pursed her lips. 'Well someone certainly has.' She was certain that Jackie Woods was lying – the girl looked guilty as hell – but there was little she could do to prove it. It was Hughie Fowler's word against hers, and even though Valerie knew who she believed, it didn't get her much closer to what had really happened that February night. The only way forward was to put more pressure on Jackie. She was on the verge of doing this, already formulating the questions in her head, when her phone began to ring. Drawing it out of her bag, she saw that it was her sergeant.

'Excuse me,' she said, quickly getting to her feet. 'I need to take this.' She went through to the hall, closing the living room door behind her. 'Swann,' she said, the phone pressed close to her ear. 'You've got some news.'

'Yeah,' he said. 'I've got that all right.'

Valerie felt her heart miss a beat. 'Tell me.'

'I just heard from forensics. They found a tiny amount of sperm on Linzi Marshall's clothing, and guess what?'

'We've got a match for it? Christ, tell me we've got a match.'

'Got it in one,' Swann said. 'And it's our good friend Danny Street.'

'Yes!' Valerie said triumphantly, slapping her palm hard against the wall. 'Get your ass down to Belles. I'll meet you there. Let's pull the bastard in.'

Chapter Fifty-one

Hope saw the flush of excitement on Valerie Middleton's face as she flew back into the living and grabbed her bag off the chair.

'I'm sorry,' the inspector said. 'I have to go. It's urgent.' As she headed back towards the door, she paused, turned on her heel and gave them all a final stare. 'Maybe you could have a good long think about what we discussed. I'll be back in touch shortly.' And then directly to Lana: 'Don't worry, I'll see myself out.'

After she'd gone, a heavy silence fell over the room. Glances were furtively exchanged between the four remaining women. Hope, relieved that the visit had not been connected to the painting, but frustrated by the sudden termination of the inspector's enquiries, stared hard at Jackie.

Jackie glared back at her. 'What the fuck are you looking at?'

But Hope wasn't intimidated. After Terry Street, Jackie barely registered on the Richter scale of threatening behaviour. And she wasn't going to let it go. It was time the truth came out. 'You were here, weren't you? You saw Connie. Why don't you admit it?'

Jackie leapt up, her mouth in a thin, tight line. Standing over Hope, she reached out her hand and shoved the glowing end of her cigarette dangerously close to her eyes. 'Say that again, bitch, and I'll fucking bury you!'

'Stop it!' Lana ordered.

'No,' Jackie said. 'Why should I? What's any of this got to do with her anyway? Why's she poking her nose into other people's business?'

Hope had had enough. Slapping Jackie's hand out of the way, she jumped up too and stood face to face with her. 'If you've got nothing to hide, why don't you explain why you've been black-mailing Derek Parr?'

The accusation clearly rocked Jackie. She took a step back, but quickly tried to laugh it off. 'Did you hear that, Lana? Did you hear what she said? She's a fucking loon. She's off her head.'

But Hope wasn't going to stop now. Turning to Lana, she said, 'It's true. I heard her on the phone, and I saw her on Monday. She was taking money off him.'

Lana looked bemused, her eyes quickly darting between the two of them.

Hope didn't want to hurt Lana, but there was no way back now. 'Call him,' she said. 'Give him a call and ask him why he's been handing over cash to her ladyship here.'

'Jackie?' Lana said. 'What the hell's going on?'

'It's bollocks!' But Jackie's face had gone white, and she suddenly looked scared. 'She's lying. She's making it up.'

'Just like Hughie Fowler's making it up?' Hope said. She looked over at Lana again. 'Don't you want to know the truth? Go on, ring Derek. Let's hear what he has to say about it all.'

Lana hesitated, but eventually picked up her phone off the coffee table.

'What are you doing?' Jackie snarled. 'Don't listen to her. The bitch is just trying to stitch me up!'

Hope kept her response quiet and calm. 'Well, if you've got nothing to hide, you don't need to worry, do you?'

Lana turned the small silver mobile over in her hands before eventually pressing a button and lifting the phone to her ear. Jackie huffed out a breath, and then the room fell silent while everyone waited. There was a short delay before the call was answered. 'Derek,' Lana said stonily. 'I need to talk to you.' Short pause. 'No, it can't bloody wait. It's important. You need to get over to the flat right now. Ten minutes, yeah?' And with that she hung up. She dropped the phone back on to the table and raised her gaze to Jackie. 'If you've got anything to tell me, you'd better do it right now.'

For a moment, Jackie looked as though she was about to start protesting again. But then she leaned down, stabbed the cigarette out in the ashtray and slowly straightened up. With her hands on her hips, she stared defiantly at Lana. 'It had nothing to do with me. It wasn't my fault. It was your fucking boyfriend who went for her.'

As Evelyn let out a gasp, Hope felt her own heart miss a beat. Oh God, it was happening, the truth about Connie was finally coming out.

Lana leapt out of the chair, grabbed Jackie by the arms and started to shake her. 'What do you mean? What the fuck are you saying?'

'Let go,' Jackie demanded, struggling to free herself. 'Get your bloody hands off me or I won't say another word.'

Lana's chest was heaving, her breath coming in short, fast pants. But eventually, although she continued to glare hard into Jackie's eyes, she released her grip. 'So start talking!'

Jackie glared back at her, rubbing resentfully at her arms. 'Yeah, okay, so I was here that night, but I never laid a finger on her. It had nothing to do with me.' She gave a scornful laugh. 'No, it was *your* fuckhead boyfriend who waited for her down the road, claimed he wanted to talk about a surprise party for your birthday, and then walked her down the alley and put his hands around her throat.'

'But why?' Hope said, not understanding.

'You'll have to ask him that. Maybe he just gets a kick out of beating up women.'

Lana slumped back down into the chair, shaking her head vehemently. 'No, it isn't true. He isn't like that. He isn't.'

Evelyn lifted her knees and wrapped her arms around them. She peered up at Jackie, her eyes big and round. 'Derek *killed* Connie?' she said hoarsely.

Jackie raised her own eyes to the ceiling. 'Of course he bloody didn't! She came back here, didn't she, and told me what'd happened. And she wasn't pissed, she was just in shock. She'd bought a bottle of wine that got smashed when Derek went for her. That's what the old git downstairs must have smelled.'

'So if she came back,' Hope persisted, 'then what happened? I mean, what happened *next?*'

Jackie pushed her hands into her pockets. 'Went out again, didn't she. She'd just finished telling me what Derek had done when she noticed that her locket was missing, a silver one she always wore. It must have come off when he attacked her. She went back out to look for it.'

'That was a present from her dad,' Evelyn whispered. 'It meant everything to her.'

'And you let her go out again on her own?' Hope said, astounded. 'You let her walk out of here when she was in that state? Why didn't you go with her?'

Jackie gave a shrug. 'She was okay. And anyway, I was waiting for someone.'

'Who?' Lana said.

'It doesn't matter who.'

'Pony, wasn't it?' Lana said accusingly. 'Bringing round your latest fix, right? Because that bloody crap you shove up your nose is more important to you than anything or anyone else.'

Jackie didn't deny it, but she didn't take it lying down either. 'Don't go preaching to me, love. It wasn't my boyfriend who scared her shitless. Maybe you should start looking at your own lousy choices before you start criticising mine.'

Lana made a low growling sound in the back of her throat, but didn't answer back.

'For God's sake,' Hope said, 'you must have wondered what had happened to her. To Connie, I mean. Weren't you worried when she didn't come back?'

Jackie gave another of her dismissive shrugs. 'I thought she'd taken off, gone to stay with friends for a while. I reckoned that while she was out looking for the locket she'd had time to think about stuff.' She gave Lana a sly glance. 'Maybe she figured you were in on it too, that you knew what Derek was planning on doing all along.'

'She could *never* have thought that,' Lana said, but there was a sudden hint of doubt in her voice.

'That's why I didn't tell,' Jackie continued. 'I thought I'd better keep my mouth shut until everything blew over. I didn't fancy being next on Derek's list. And then as the weeks went by and Connie didn't get in touch, I knew she'd left for good. Well, who could blame the poor bitch? She was probably terrified that he'd come back and finish the job.'

Hope wondered how much of this, if any, Flint was listening to. 'And so that's when you decided to blackmail Derek Parr?'

There was a twitch at the corner of Jackie's mouth. 'Why not? I didn't see why he should get away with it. I told him I'd go to the cops, tell them he'd assaulted Connie and that maybe he'd even finished the job when she went out to search for the locket. I knew he wouldn't want the law crawling all over him and his business.'

Evelyn hugged her knees even closer, her face full of anguish. 'You didn't give a damn about Connie. All you were interested in was the money.'

Jackie gave a sneer. 'And you think Connie ever gave a toss about you? Once she was out of here, she never looked back. Just how many times has she been in touch with you, exactly?'

Evelyn's face crumpled, and she started to cry again, great hot tears rolling down her cheeks.

Hope glowered at Jackie. 'Leave her alone,' she said, before shifting up the sofa and putting her arm around Evelyn. 'At least she cared about Connie, which is clearly more than you ever did.'

The exchange was interrupted by the sound of the front doorbell. Lana stood up and hurried out of the room. A couple of minutes later she was back with Derek Parr in tow. They could hear him complaining as he came through the hall. 'What's all this about, Lana? I was supposed to be home by now. You know what she's like when—' He stopped mid-sentence as he walked into the living room and saw the row of cold, expectant faces staring back at him. 'What's going on?'

'They know,' Jackie said. 'They know what you did to Connie.'

The shock on Derek's face was clear for everyone to see. Instantly, his hand rose to his neck and he fiddled with the knot of his tie. 'What?'

'So it's true, then,' Lana said, her eyes full of dismay.

Derek nervously cleared his throat. 'Connie? I didn't do anything to Connie. Why would I—'

'Oh, for fuck's sake,' Lana said. 'Skip the bullshit. Jackie's already told us. If you didn't do anything, then why were you paying her? You *were* paying her, weren't you? You were giving her cash to keep her filthy little mouth shut.'

For a moment Derek seemed in two minds as to whether he

should deny it, but finally he had the sense to realise it was pointless. 'It was nothing. I don't know what that cow has told you,' he said, glancing at Jackie, 'but I barely touched the girl. It was a warning, that's all.'

Lana spread her hands out in front of her, a mixture of confusion and disgust in her voice. 'A warning? A warning about what?'

'She was stirring up trouble. She swore to you that she'd stay away from the Streets. She promised, didn't she? But she was a bloody liar. I saw her with Danny Street at Belles, all over him like a rash. I know what she was doing, raking up that shit about her father again. And once Terry Street found out what her game was, it wouldn't just be *her* mouth he'd want to close. He'd be worried that you knew all about it too.' His hand rose briefly to his tie again. 'I just wanted to make her see that she was putting you in danger.'

Lana was quiet for a moment, and then she shook her head. 'No, that wasn't the reason. You didn't do it to protect me. It was your own arse you were covering. You thought Terry Street had killed Jeff Tomlin, and that Connie was going to find a way of proving it. If she did, that would have meant Terry going down again. And that would have been it for the Streets, wouldn't it? With Lizzie in her grave, this time there'd be no one to keep things running smoothly. That firm would be on its knees in a month.' She choked out a cynical laugh. 'And your bloody business too, seeing as you launder half their dodgy money through your books.'

Hope could tell from Derek's expression that Lana had got it spot on. 'The stupid bitch was going to ruin it for everyone,' he spat out resentfully. 'So I gave her a slap. So what? She needed telling. She bloody well deserved it!'

There was a shocked silence before the door to the living room suddenly flew open, banging hard against the wall and making everybody jump. Like a charging bull, Flint came storming in with blind fury in his eyes. Before Derek Parr could even begin to comprehend what was happening, Flint had landed a right-hander to his jaw, a punch that sent the older man flying backwards on to the floor. And then Flint was on top of him, hitting him over and over again and screaming into his face, 'You bastard! You fucking bastard!'

Hope, terrified that Flint was about to commit murder, launched herself on to his back and tried to grab hold of his arm. 'That's enough. Stop it!' When she had no success, she turned and yelled at Lana, 'Help me!' It took the combined strength of both of them to eventually drag him off.

Groaning, Flint stayed hunched on the floor with his head in his hands. His shoulders were heaving, his whole body still shaking with rage.

'He's not worth it,' Hope said, crouching down beside him. As he raised his face, she could see the tears in his eyes, and it was then, with a jolt, that she realised that his feelings for Connie had been stronger and deeper than she'd ever understood. It was love she saw in those grey eyes, love and pain and grief and loss. God, he had actually *loved* her. He had been *in love* with Connie.

Chapter Fifty-two

It was a quarter past eight, the morning air chill and damp, as Hope walked briskly along the high street. Despite the cold, she was glad of the chance to escape from the strained atmosphere in the flat. Evelyn, still traumatised by what had happened to Linzi Marshall, was now struggling to come to terms with the revelations about Connie. And Lana was still raging over Derek's part in it all. Not to mention Jackie's.

Hope pushed open the door to Connolly's, and scoured the busy café. The breakfast trade was in full swing and it took her a while to search the sea of faces, but finally she saw Flint squashed into a corner by the window. He must have been there for a while, because there was a used plate in front of him with the remnants of what had probably been bacon and eggs.

'You okay?' she said, squeezing into the seat opposite. She hadn't spoken to him since he'd stormed out of the flat yesterday. He hadn't answered his phone, and the only response she'd got, after trying half a dozen times, was a brief text at midnight asking her to meet him here in the morning.

Flint glanced up, giving her a rueful smile.

Seeing his bruised face, Hope wondered at her capacity for asking stupid questions. Of course he wasn't okay. He'd been abducted by the Streets, beaten up, and then heard the shocking news that the woman he loved had been attacked by Derek Parr. 'Sorry,' she said. 'You don't have to answer that.'

'No, *I'm* sorry. I shouldn't have just taken off.'

But Hope understood why he had. The temptation to finish what he'd started with Derek Parr must have been overwhelming. 'If it's any consolation, Lana kicked the bastard out as soon as he managed to get on his feet again. She chucked Jackie out too.'

'Poor Lana,' he said. 'Her crew's getting smaller by the day. She must be wishing she'd never set eyes on either of us.'

'It would've all come out eventually. It was bound to, especially with the police sniffing around.'

The waitress came over, cleared the table and asked if they wanted anything else. Hope ordered a cappuccino, and Flint asked for another tea. After she'd gone, Hope said, 'So what do we do about Derek? Do you think we should report him?'

Flint shrugged his shoulders. 'What's the point? It'll only be our word against his. And it all happened months ago. Without any real evidence, without Connie, there isn't a hope of the cops pursuing it.'

Hope suspected he was right. 'So do you think she *did* take off because of what he did? I mean, what Jackie said makes a kind of sense. Connie could have decided that it wasn't safe to go back to the flat, especially if she wasn't sure whether Lana was involved or not.'

'Lord, what do I know?' Flint raked his fingers through his hair and frowned. 'It only seems like five minutes since I was saying that she'd probably flogged the painting, taken the money and run. And how wrong was I about that?'

'Not just you,' Hope said, understanding how guilty he felt.

407

'That's how it looked. We weren't to know what Derek had done.' As he gazed bleakly out of the window, she took a moment to study him more closely. He'd had a wash and a shave since yesterday, and was dressed now in faded blue jeans and a plain black sweater. But nothing could erase the pain from his face. 'I never realised,' she said tentatively. 'How ... how close you were to Connie.' She blushed as she spoke the words, knowing that she was probably revealing more of her own feelings than she wanted to.

Flint turned his head back to look at her, his grey eyes narrowing a little. 'It wasn't like that.'

But Hope knew what she had seen. His feelings, however, were his business and she would have to learn to suppress her own. It was her sister he cared about, not her. If she had ever thought that some kind of relationship might be growing between them, she realised now that it had all been in her imagination.

The waitress arrived with their hot drinks, and as soon as she'd gone, Hope changed the subject. 'Something odd happened when I was at home. In Albersea, I mean.'

Flint listened as she told him about the paintings that had disappeared from Lloyd's new gallery. 'The thing is,' she said, 'they were painted in the same year as Jeff Tomlin died, so if they were his, what was Lloyd doing with them? By that time Jeff and my mum had been separated for years.'

Flint didn't seem to think there was much of a mystery. 'Have you thought of the obvious answer? Maybe he bought them. Jeff might not have been the most successful artist in the world, but he did sell some of his work from time to time.'

Hope nodded. 'It's possible, but then why would Lloyd deny that they were his? And would *you* buy three paintings off your wife's ex?'

'It would depend on how much I liked them – the paintings, that is, rather than the ex. He could have bought them as a straightforward business investment, hoping they might increase in value.'

'Well why didn't he just say that? Why pretend it was all a stupid delivery mistake?'

'Unless it was,' Flint said. 'Have you thought about that? Maybe they're not Jeff's paintings at all.'

'So why the big drama? Why the visit to the gallery to get rid of them before I went back the next day?'

Flint gave a shrug. 'It's not that long since your mother died. He's still grieving. People do odd things when they're grieving.'

Hope hesitated before sharing the final piece of information. She was starting to wonder if she was losing the plot, creating mysteries where none existed and generally being about as disloyal to Lloyd as she could be. But that business with the passport was still bugging her. 'Didn't you say once that you knew a pimp called Bobby Randall?'

Flint stared at her, bemused. 'Where did that come from?'

'I'll explain in a sec,' she said. 'But do you know if he's still around? I mean, when was the last time you saw him?'

'I've got no idea. Why do you—'

'Well, was it last month, last year, five years ago? Come on, you must be able to remember.'

Flint took a sip of his tea while he thought about it. 'I dunno. Years ago, I guess. But what the hell has Bobby Randall to do with anything?'

She told him about Lloyd's passport, about the fact that his name was really Robert Randall. 'I know it sounds ridiculous. Oh God, it probably *is* ridiculous, but he snatched it out of my hand and went ape. That's not normal, is it?'

'The man's probably just got a thing about his passport photo. I doubt if he's the only one.'

'No, it was more than that. I'm sure it was.'

For the first time that morning, Flint's mouth broke into a

smile. 'Christ, I've heard of conspiracy theories, but don't you think this is stretching it a bit? Bobby Randall was a nasty, vicious pimp who beat up on his girls, pushed hard drugs and generally went out of his way to make other people's lives a living hell. Does that sound like your stepfather?'

'No, of course not.' Still, she couldn't quite let it go. 'But what did he look like? How old was he? Please, I know you think I'm nuts, but just humour me.'

'Ordinary, I guess. White, medium height, late forties, brown hair.'

'What colour were his eyes?'

Flint raised his brows. 'Jeez, I haven't got a clue. I didn't spend much time looking into them.'

Hope frowned, still without the definitive answers she craved. 'Did Jeff know him?'

'Sure he did. Everyone in Soho knew Bobby Randall, and everyone hated his guts.' He glanced down, twisting the cup of tea around in his hands before slowly lifting his eyes to meet hers again. 'Come on, Hope. You can't really think it's the same person. It's impossible.'

She knew he was right, but she also knew that she'd seen something in Lloyd's face that day that she'd never seen before, something hard and cold and angry. But there had also been something else, and she thought it might have been fear.

'You should go home,' Flint said. 'There's nothing more you can do here.'

'And you? What are you going to do?'

'Keep on searching, I guess.'

Hope stared down at her untouched cappuccino. 'It feels bad, just giving up on her.'

'You've done everything you can. I'll stay in touch, let you know if I hear anything.'

Hope nodded, gave a sigh and gazed out of the window.

Across the road, and diagonally to the right, she could see a constant stream of people going in and out of Starbucks. As she watched, her mind on other things, she saw a tall, blonde woman come out carrying a brown paper bag. 'That's Valerie Middleton,' she said. 'The inspector who came round to talk about Connie.'

Flint twisted his head and followed her line of sight. He'd only caught a glimpse of her yesterday from the window of Lana's flat. For the rest of the time he'd been hidden in the bedroom. 'The one in the black coat?'

'Yeah, that's her.' On impulse, Hope pushed back her chair and stood up. 'I'm going to talk to her. She knows something, I'm sure she does. Why else would she keep coming round?'

Flint looked at her and shook his head. 'She's a cop, Hope. She's not going to tell you anything.'

'You finish your tea. I'll be back in a minute.' With that, she rushed out of the café before Valerie Middleton could disappear from view. It might be a waste of time, it probably was, but she wasn't prepared to give up on Connie just yet.

Chapter Fifty-three

By the time Hope had managed to dodge between the cars and get across the road, Valerie Middleton had a good thirty yards on her. She broke into a jog, glad that she was wearing her trainers for once, rather than the high heels she'd been forcing her feet into recently. Weaving in and out of the crowds of commuters, she eventually caught up. The inspector was talking on the phone, and so Hope hovered behind her, waiting until she'd finished.

'Yes, I'm on my way. His brief's coming in again at nine.' Pause. 'Yes, it's that creep Bradshaw.' Pause. 'Okay, okay. I've just grabbed a coffee. I'll be there soon.'

'Excuse me,' Hope said, as soon as the inspector had finished.

Valerie Middleton stopped walking and turned to look at her. Her eyes took a moment to register who it was. 'Oh,' she said. 'Hello.'

'I was wondering if I could have a word. It's about Connie Tomlin. I'm her sister, you see, and—'

'You're Connie's sister?' Inspector Middleton's brows lifted in surprise. 'I wasn't aware that she had one. Why didn't you say? Lana told me that she didn't have any family.'

'It's a long story. I won't go into it now. But I need to know what's going on. You were right about Connie coming back to the flat that night, but she went out again. That's when she disappeared. And the police haven't been the slightest bit interested until now, so there must be something going on. What do you know? What is it you're not telling us?'

The inspector stared at her for a moment, and then looked purposefully down at her watch. 'I can't really talk at the moment. Why don't you come down to the station later and we can have a chat then. About midday? Would that be good for you?'

'You think something bad has happened to her, don't you?'

'I didn't say that. All I meant was—' But whatever the inspector meant was interrupted by her phone going off again. 'Excuse me,' she said, reaching into her pocket. 'Valerie Middleton.' She listened to someone for about twenty seconds, and then said, 'Right now?' She glanced at her watch again. 'Well, if you think it's that important. Yes, I suppose I could. I'm not far away. All right, I'll see you in a minute.' After hanging up, she said to Hope, 'I'm sorry, but I really have to go.'

Disappointed, Hope watched her stride off down the road. She was about to turn around and go back to the café when frustration got the better of her. Why should she have to wait? If the inspector had some information, why couldn't she reveal it now? On impulse, Hope hurried after her. Being polite was all very well, but occasionally it paid to be pushy. She was hoping that this would be one of those times.

Hope caught up with Valerie Middleton again just as she was stepping through the door of the closed-down funeral parlour of Tobias Grand & Sons. Hope hesitated, but then, too impatient to hang about outside, quickly followed her in. 'Just five minutes,' she pleaded. 'Surely you can spare me that.'

The inspector, who was advancing towards a desk on the far

side of the room, looked less than pleased at her reappearance. 'Look, I've already said I'll talk to you later.' But before she could voice any further protests, a door to the side of the reception area opened and a tall, slightly stooped middle-aged man dressed in a black suit and tie came out. He had a long, lugubrious face like a bloodhound, and his head was almost bald. His gloomy expression was only marginally relieved by an overly solicitous smile.

'Mr Grand,' Valerie said. 'Gerald. How are you?'

The smile on Gerald Grand's fleshy lips slowly faded. 'Ah, I didn't realise you were bringing someone with you.'

'She's just going,' Valerie Middleton said firmly. She gave Hope a cool, hard look. 'Aren't you?'

Hope gave a nod. She knew when she wasn't wanted, but she wasn't going to give up that easily. 'Okay, I'll go. But I'm going to wait outside. I *have* to talk to you.'

Gerald Grand, with the clear intention of showing her out, walked over to the door. Hope, aware that it was time to make as dignified an exit as she could, waited for him to open it. But he didn't. Instead, bizarrely, he turned the key that was in the lock and slipped it into his pocket. Hope watched him go through this process with more puzzlement than anything else. Why on earth was he. . . ?

But as he turned around, she saw what was in his hand. There was a gun pointing straight at her.

Her first response wasn't shock. It was more a dull confusion. What? This had to be a joke, some sort of game. You couldn't be hit by lightning twice. It hadn't been that long since she'd been hunkered down outside Adriano's with some other lunatic pointing a gun in her direction.

'Move,' he ordered, gesturing towards the inspector. 'Get over there. Stand beside her.'

Hope quickly did as she was told.

'Gerald?' Valerie Middleton said, sounding bewildered. 'What are you doing? Why are you—'

'Phones,' he said curtly. 'Put them on the floor and slide them over to me.'

Valerie lowered her voice and spoke to him softly. 'Gerald, whatever the problem is, this isn't the way to solve it. Come on, you know me. We're friends, aren't we? It doesn't have to be like this. Just put the gun down and we can talk.'

But Gerald Grand obviously wasn't in the mood for talking. 'Phones,' he ordered again, waving the gun at them. 'Now!'

Reality was beginning to catch up with Hope. She could feel the dull thud of her heart in her chest. Careful not to make any sudden movements, she got her mobile out of her bag and leaned down.

'No, you first,' Grand said, glaring at Valerie Middleton.

'This is madness,' the inspector said. 'I'm due at the station any minute now. When I don't arrive, they're going to come looking for me.'

'Yes, they might be expecting you,' he agreed. 'But they don't have a clue as to where you actually are.'

'I called them. I told them I was coming here.'

'Oh please, Inspector. Don't insult my intelligence. I was watching you from the upstairs window. You didn't make any calls after I spoke to you.'

Hope, with a sinking feeling, realised that this was true. And Flint wouldn't know where she was either. How long before he started to get concerned? Not for a while yet, she thought.

'Now, are you going to give me your phone, or would you rather I blew the little lady's brains out.' He moved the gun so it was pointing directly at Hope's head. 'Be quick about it. I'm not used to handling these things. It would be a shame if it . . . accidentally went off.'

This time Valerie obeyed the instruction. She took the phone from her pocket and slid it gently across the floor.

'And now the other one,' Grand said.

Valerie took Hope's phone from her hand, briefly meeting her gaze as she did so. She gave a small nod that was probably supposed to be reassuring, but all Hope could see in her eyes was fear.

Keeping the gun on Hope, Grand bent down, picked up the two phones and turned them both off. 'There,' he said, dropping them on to the coffee table. 'That's better. Now we won't be disturbed.'

Hope glanced around the reception area. There was an old sofa to her left, its arms worn thin through years of use, and to its side a large potted palm that was dying from neglect. On the wall was a display of sepia photographs, scenes from Kellston and Bethnal Green and Shoreditch showing how they used to look. The whole room smelled of dust and decay and abandonment. She recalled what Flint had told her about a murder being committed here, and gave a shudder.

'Now,' Grand continued, 'put your hands behind your heads and walk out, walk out *slowly*, to the back.' He tilted his own head towards a corridor that led out of the reception area. 'Let her go first,' he said to Valerie. 'You follow on.'

The inspector raised her hands but didn't immediately move. 'What's this all about, Gerald? I don't understand. Surely you could explain that at least.'

Gerald Grand glared back at her. His voice was icy cold. 'It's about justice, my dear. It's about the justice that's owing to my son. You let that bitch get away with murder, and now you're going to pay for it.'

Valerie shook her head. 'Alice Avery didn't get away with anything. She's locked up, Gerald, she's in a mental institution. There's every chance that she'll never be released.'

416

Gerald Grand gave a snort. 'I know about those places. That's not punishment, nothing like. You let her plead insanity and get away with it. She seduced my son and then she murdered him in cold blood. And now she's laughing at me. She's laughing at what she did to my boy. Someone's got to pay for that, Inspector. It's only right.'

'This isn't going to bring Toby back,' Valerie said. 'I understand how upset you are, but—'

'Start walking,' Gerald said, addressing himself to Hope. 'Keep going until you get to the door at the end.'

As Hope set off down the corridor, her stomach churning, she was trying to remember everything else Flint had told her about the murder. The woman had been crazy, that was what he'd said. She hadn't just killed the man, she'd embalmed him too. Hope could see how that would be enough to send any father over the edge.

Valerie started talking again. 'Why don't you let her go, Gerald. She hasn't done anything. It's me you want. This has nothing to do with her.'

Hope glanced over her shoulder, just in time to see that sinister smile creep on to Grand's lips again. His tongue slid lightly across his upper lip. 'It's a little late for that, don't you think?'

'She won't say anything. Will you, Hope?'

But Hope, who quickly turned to face forward again, never got an opportunity to reply.

'Oh *please*, Inspector, let's not get into the realms of the ridiculous. Better surely to accept the vagaries of fate.'

So that was what she was, Hope thought, a vagary of fate. Why the hell had she ever followed the inspector? She could be back in Connolly's, warm and safe, with the rest of her life to look forward to. It wasn't a brave thought, not even a very honourable one bearing in mind the fact that Valerie Middleton would still have come here, but it was hard to be courageous with a gun pointed at you.

Hope had only a vague perception of her surroundings as she walked steadily on. She was faintly aware of a couple of rooms off to her right, both with their doors closed. Lowering her gaze for a moment, she noticed how the centre of the beige carpet had been worn away down the middle, and found herself wondering in a slightly hysterical way how many grieving people had passed along here before her.

She stopped when she reached the open door at the end of the corridor, and stared at the flight of stone steps that led to the basement. Once they were down there, nobody would be able to hear them. It would be like descending into an abyss.

'Keep going,' Gerald Grand ordered.

Hope hesitated, but what choice did she have? A part of her was hoping that the inspector would do something dramatic: turn abruptly, take him by surprise, knock the gun out of his hand, perhaps. But another fast glance over her shoulder showed her how ludicrous this idea was. Gerald Grand was keeping his distance. Not so far that he couldn't fail to miss if he pulled the trigger, but far enough to prevent any impromptu attempts at escape.

'Move!' he urged impatiently.

Reluctantly, Hope started walking down the steps. Her legs were beginning to shake and she had to force herself to put one foot in front of the other. She had almost reached the bottom when she heard the door at the top slam, and then the ominous click of a key turning in the lock. This time she didn't look back.

Passing through another door, she found herself in a white-walled room. It was cool and bright and sterile. To the right, another, smaller room ran off it. Directly in front of her was a counter with a pair of sinks, and an array of jars and bottles and hoses and tubes. There was a metal trolley to her left, but the dominating feature was the stainless-steel table in the centre. Two dreadful thoughts occurred to Hope simultaneously: that this was the funeral parlour's embalming room, and that it was in this very place that Gerald Grand's son must have been laid to rest by Alice Avery.

'Over there,' Grand said, gesturing with the gun again. 'By the sink, both of you.'

The two women silently made their way across the room. When they reached the sink, Valerie turned and said, 'Where did you get the gun, Gerald?'

Hope was momentarily perplexed. There were more important questions, she reckoned, than where the damn pistol had come from.

'My father's,' he said. 'A souvenir from the war. It's a Luger. Had you noticed? Good German craftsmanship. And yes, in case you're wondering, it *is* loaded.'

'I thought it was. A Luger, I mean. Was your father Tobias Grand, or was that your grandad? I've never been quite sure.'

Hope suddenly realised that she was attempting to make some kind of connection with the man, to keep him talking, to distract him from whatever his intentions were. And those intentions, she feared, did not involve then walking out of here alive.

But Gerald Grand wasn't going to be drawn. Instead he said, 'I hear you've got Danny Street in custody.'

Hope started at the name, immediately wondering if his arrest had anything to do with the fake painting.

Valerie Middleton frowned. 'Who told you that?'

'Oh, you know what Kellston's like. Nothing's a secret for very long.' He sighed, his face assuming a somewhat pained expression. 'Such a waste of time,' he said, shaking his head.

Valerie gave a light shrug in response.

419

'You're a trifle slow on the uptake today, Inspector.'

'Am I?' she said.

Gerald Grand smiled again. And then, in a low taunting voice, he began to chant her name: 'Val-er-ie, Val-er-ie.'

Hope, standing shoulder to shoulder with the Inspector, felt her flinch. She glanced at her, not understanding what was going on, but what she couldn't fail to comprehend was the look of horror that had suddenly appeared on Valerie Middleton's face. Hope's gaze moved swiftly back to Gerald Grand, and then down to the metal trolley he was standing beside. Her eyes alighted on the pack of cigarettes, the lighter, the coils of rope and finally the scalpel with its shiny blade and silver handle. She remembered the girls in the pub, and the stories they had told. Hope's chest heaved with fright, and her pulse began to race. Oh, Jesus Christ – she was face to face with the Whisperer.

Chapter Fifty-four

Flint checked his watch. It was over twenty minutes since Hope had gone chasing after the inspector. He was surprised she wasn't back yet, but not especially worried. She must have persuaded Valerie Middleton to stop and talk to her. He picked up his phone and called again. Her mobile was still turned off. That wasn't entirely unexpected either. She wouldn't want any interruptions if she was talking about Connie.

Flint waited another five minutes and then wandered out into the high street. Perhaps they'd gone to have a coffee somewhere. He crossed over and went to peer through the window of Starbucks. They weren't in there. Keeping his eyes peeled, he carried on up the street, trying to remember if there was another café nearby. Maybe they'd gone to the police station; Cowan Road wasn't that far away. Yes, that was probably it. He'd head in that direction and meet her on her way back.

But by the time he arrived outside the building, there was still no sign of Hope. He hung around outside for a while, pacing up and down the pavement and staring up at the windows. And then the concern began to kick in. It wasn't like

Hope to just leave him sitting in Connolly's without even a text to tell him what was happening. For five or ten minutes perhaps, but not for half an hour. She was too polite for that. Ah hell, had she done something stupid, harassed the inspector perhaps, and managed to get herself arrested? It didn't sound like the Hope Randall he'd got to know, but then that Hope seemed to be changing every day. The girl he'd met in Albersea wouldn't have had the front to tell a bare-faced lie to Terry Street either.

Should he go in and ask?

Flint hesitated. He had an aversion to cop shops. Over the years, he'd spent more time in them than he cared to remember. But what was the alternative, other than freezing to death out here? Too impatient to wait any longer, he took a deep breath and walked up to the door.

Sergeant Kieran Swann looked up at the clock again. Where the hell was the inspector? On her way, she'd said, and that was a bloody half-hour ago. And why wasn't she answering her phone? Danny Street's lawyer, Bradshaw, was starting to lose patience. The interview was already late starting, and Swann couldn't put it off for much longer. If she didn't get here soon, he'd have to arrange for someone else to take her place.

His phone rang and he answered it. There was an important call for DI Middleton. Did he know where she was? No, he didn't know. It was Gemma Leigh. Would he talk to her? Okay, put her through.

A small voice came down the line. 'Hello?'

'This is Detective Sergeant Swann.'

'I need to speak to Inspector Middleton.'

Swann raised his eyes to the ceiling. Although sympathetic to the Whisperer's victims, he had enough on his plate at the moment without what was bound to be another enquiry as to how the investigation was going. Possibly she'd even heard that

422

someone had been arrested. The police couldn't do anything in Kellston without half the population knowing about it five minutes later. 'She's not here, I'm afraid. Can I help?'

Gemma hesitated. 'Will she be in soon?'

Swann wished he knew the answer to that one. 'Probably. I don't know exactly when. You want me to give her a message?'

'I suppose,' she said. She paused again.

'Or you could just call back. Would you rather do that?'

Gemma thought about it. 'I'm not sure.'

Swann glanced up at the clock again. 'It's up to you.'

Finally she made a decision. 'Could you ... could you tell her that I did see someone in the car park when she came to see me on Monday. It was just after she arrived. I was looking out of the window and ... well, I didn't think it was important, but—'

'You want to tell me who it was?' Swann was suddenly interested. If she'd seen Danny Street hanging around Valerie's car, it would be one more nail in his coffin, a link between him and the messages left on her windscreen. He waited while Gemma embarked on another of her elongated pauses. 'Gemma?' he said.

Finally she gave him the name.

Swann pulled a face. He thanked her and hung up, disappointed. Almost immediately, his phone went again. It was Rachel at the front desk. There was a man called Flint in the lobby. Could he come and talk to him? It was about Inspector Middleton.

'Okay, I'll be right there.'

Swann stood up, but then on impulse sat right back down again. Typing in the name Gemma Leigh had just given him, he ran a quick PNC check. As the information came up on his screen, his mouth fell open. 'Fuck,' he murmured.

*

423

Hope was down on the floor, leaning against the wall with her knees bent and her legs tied at the ankles. Her hands were behind her back, also fastened with rope, and a black silk scarf had been placed around her mouth. There was a sharp, pungent smell of disinfectant in the room, and that, along with the scarf pressing hard into the corners of her lips, made her want to gag. While she concentrated on her breathing – she mustn't be sick or she could choke – she carefully moved her hands, surreptitiously wriggling her fingers in the hope that she could eventually get free.

Grand had forced Valerie to tie her up. Had he checked more carefully, he would have realised that the knots around her wrists weren't as tight as they could have been, but he was eager to get on with the highlight of the show and probably didn't view Hope as much of a threat. She was a vagary of fate, an inconvenience that would have to be dealt with later, but for now all his concentration was focused on Valerie Middleton.

The inspector had been made to strip and then lie down on the table. She had her hands cuffed behind her and her ankles bound. Ropes had also been wrapped around her chest and hips and thighs. Unable to move, she was completely at his mercy. Hope couldn't see her face and was glad that she couldn't. She could see *his*, though, and what she saw made her blood run cold. His eyes, full of loathing, gazed down on his victim with sadistic pleasure.

'Danny Street,' he said contemptuously. 'How could you ever have thought that brainless lowlife was responsible? A serious error of judgement, Inspector, but I'm hardly surprised.'

Valerie Middleton's voice was thin and strained, high-pitched with fear. 'All those girls, Gerald. Why did you hurt them?'

'Whores, each and every one. And you let them walk the streets. I had to save them, my dear, just like I'm going to save you.'

Abruptly he turned away, and started to walk towards Hope. The gun was in his right hand, and for one horrifying moment she thought she'd been wrong about him dealing with her later. Maybe he was going to do it now. Maybe he was going to put that Luger up against her head and shoot her stone dead. Her heart hammered in her chest as he drew closer and closer. Were these the last few seconds of her life? Was this it? She held her breath, silently praying to a God who appeared to have deserted her.

But Gerald Grand didn't even glance in her direction. As if she'd become invisible, he ignored her completely. Instead he reached out towards something on the counter above her. There was a soft click, and then the sound of religious chanting, monks perhaps, began to drift through the air. Grand walked back across the room and put the gun down on the trolley. Head tilted, he stood and listened to the music.

Valerie started to talk again, trying to delay the inevitable, to hang on to every last minute she could. 'You can get help. I can help you. You don't need to do this.'

Gerald Grand loomed over her, smiling. 'Give me any plague, but the plague of the heart: and any wickedness, but the wickedness of a woman.'

'Is that from the Bible? Doesn't the Bible also talk about for-giveness? Do you think Toby would have wanted this?'

'Toby wasn't given the chance to say what he wanted. That bitch Avery made sure of that.'

'She was sick, Gerald. She was ill. The woman didn't know what she was doing.'

Grand's face was pale, and the dome of his forehead glistened with sweat. He gave a dismissive wave of his hand, as if he'd heard enough, then he reached out for the pack of cigarettes on the trolley. Slowly, very slowly, as if every action had to be savoured, he slid off the wrapping, flipped open the lid, removed the piece of silver paper, then drew out a cigarette and put it in his mouth.

'*Please*,' Valerie pleaded.

Hope's teeth bit down on the gag, her hands automatically clenching into two tight fists. She knew what was coming next. She wished she could close her eyes or look away, but she seemed unable to. As if transfixed, she felt compelled to keep on watching.

Gerald Grand gazed down on his victim's naked body as he lit the cigarette. He inhaled deeply, exhaling the smoke in two long streams from his nose. He waited. His voice when he spoke was quiet and controlled. 'Of the woman came the beginning of sin, and through her we all die.'

'No,' Valerie begged. 'Please don't—'

But already Grand's hand was descending, carefully choosing its spot, propelling the burning end of the cigarette into the soft flesh of her shoulder.

Valerie's cry of pain echoed through the basement.

Hope leaned forward, struggling against the gag, against the ties that were holding her. She watched as Grand inflicted two more burns, two more jabs in quick succession. Valerie's screams cut through her like a knife. She wanted to put her hands over her ears, to block out the cries. Frantically she twisted her wrists, trying to break free. It was as if she had entered another world, a Dantean vision of hell. She was watching the Devil at work, and there was nothing she could do about it.

Then suddenly there was silence. No, not silence exactly; the music was still playing, but the screaming had stopped. And then, gradually, a soft moaning sound began to drift across the room.

Gerald Grand stood back, looking down on Valerie with a changed expression. The contempt had left his eyes, to be replaced by something darker. Possessed by religious ecstasy, he had moved on to another plane. 'You must ask for God's forgiveness, Valerie. You must open your heart to him, tell him how you've sinned.'

'I d-do,' she stuttered out. 'I have. I'm sorry.'

'Valerie, my dear, those are just empty words. You have to *mean* it.'

Her voice was sounding frantic now. 'What do you want me to say? Tell me what you want.'

Grand started to circle around her, putting the cigarette close to her neck, her breasts, her stomach, letting her feel the heat before slowly withdrawing it again. 'You're not trying, Valerie. God doesn't like it when we don't try.'

Suddenly Hope thought she heard something. She drew in her breath. There had been a noise from above, she was sure there had. A creaking sound. Footsteps? She strained her ears, trying to hear over the sound of the music. But now there was nothing. Tears of frustration filled her eyes. It was just her imagination playing tricks.

'Maybe this will help concentrate your mind,' Grand said to Valerie.

Hope watched him transfer the cigarette to his left hand, then pick up the scalpel and hold it up in his right. The blade caught the light and glinted. Her stomach lurched. Terror flooded her veins like a river bursting its banks. No, she couldn't bear to be a witness to this. Desperately, she tried to free herself, fighting against the knots whilst trying to keep the rest of her body still. And suddenly she could feel first one hand, and then the other ripping free. The rope slid silently to the ground.

'Last chance,' Grand said, as the thin, cruel blade descended towards Valerie's chest.

Hope had no time to think. Looking frantically around, she noticed a large glass bottle of fluid sitting under the sink to her right. Stretching over, she grabbed hold of its neck and flung it as hard as she could towards Gerald Grand's head.

She was close, but not close enough. The bottle missed by inches, hitting the wall instead, smashing into a thousand pieces and showering him with glass and liquid. Oh Christ, no! Her one opportunity and she'd blown it. In despair, she sank her head into her hands.

But taken by surprise, Grand dropped the cigarette he was holding. There was a weird whooshing sound, and a blue flame ran along the floor, up his ankles, up his legs, his groin, his chest, until engulfed in fire, he began to scream, twisting round and round in circles, his arms flailing like some gruesome whirling dervish.

Hope, her ankles still bound, began to crawl across the melting lino, trying to reach Valerie before the fire did. The stench of burning flesh filled the room, and Grand's screams grew ever louder. But even above this terrible sound, she could hear something else – a hard, steady hammering on the basement door. Seconds later, the door caved in and there was a heavy pounding of footsteps on the old stone steps.

Then everything became a blur, a rush of faces, of movement, of shouts and orders, all mixed in with Gerald Grand's persistent shrieks of pain. Time passed, although she wasn't sure how long. The next thing she knew, Flint was bending down, pulling her back into a sitting position, his hands on her shoulders, his eyes gazing into her face. 'Hope, look at me, look at me. Are you hurt? Are you all right?'

It took a while for her eyes to focus. Was this for real? Was it actually over? Tears of relief began to pour down her cheeks, but she couldn't actually speak. A nod was the best she could manage. Gazing over his shoulder, she saw that two uniformed officers had dragged Gerald Grand to the ground and doused the flames with a fire blanket. Now the only sound he was making was a long, persistent groan. Valerie Middleton was off the table, her nakedness covered by a man's black overcoat. The room, awash with fire extinguisher foam, had gradually passed from chaos into order, but something was still wrong. It took Hope a moment to realise what it was. As Flint untied the ropes around her ankles, she leaned into him and murmured, 'Turn it off.'

He shook his head, not understanding.

'The music,' she pleaded.

Instantly, he jumped to his feet and slammed his hand down on the CD player. Suddenly everything went quiet. Even Gerald Grand was silent. It was then that Hope heard a sound she hadn't noticed before. It was coming from the room that led off from the one they were in. It was the low, eerie hum of refrigeration. And she wasn't the only one who heard it.

The balding, middle-aged officer who had given Valerie his overcoat began to walk in the direction of the noise. The inspector, despite what she'd just been through, followed close behind. Her face, hauntingly pale, was grim but determined. Flint watched them both, his eyes fixed on their backs. Hope looked at him and saw a shadow pass across his face. And then he too fell into line.

Like a sleepwalker, Hope got to her feet and followed them. The adjoining room contained a bank of stainless-steel units, and she watched from the entrance as the man began to pull out a series of long metal drawers, opening and closing them one after another. She couldn't see much – the three people in front of her impeded her view – but her heart was beating hard and fast, her soul pleading that they wouldn't find what they were looking for.

And then came the sound she'd been dreading. The sudden intake of breath, the horrified gasp. Maybe there'd been more than one, but it was Flint's that she heard, that she recognised. His legs must have buckled, because he took a small stumbling step back, and it was then, like a curtain drawing open, that she glimpsed her sister for the very first time.

429

Hope lurched forward from the door. Flint tried to stop her approach, but she pushed him gently aside and gazed with desolation on the body. Connie, her long brown hair tumbling around her shoulders, had been laid out in a white nightgown edged with lace. Her eyes were closed, her arms crossed and lying on her chest. Around her neck was a tiny heart-shaped silver locket.

She no longer looked like the girl in the photograph, the girl with the smiling mouth and the easy laugh. All the life had been drained out of her. Her skin was pale and waxy, her lips too pink against the ivory of her face. Hope knew instantly that she had been embalmed, just as Gerald Grand's son had been embalmed by Alice Avery.

Reaching out, she tentatively touched her sister's hand. The flesh was icy cold. 'Connie,' she murmured. And then her head began to spin, and everything went dark.

Chapter Fifty-five

It had been two days since Hope had looked into the eyes of the Whisperer, borne witness to what could only be described as evil, and finally endured the horror of gazing down on the dead body of her sister. Now, back in her living room at Albersea, she was wondering how she would ever come to terms with it all. Although there had always been the possibility that Connie would not be found alive, nothing had prepared her for the aching void, for the grief that was tearing at her guts.

She had intended to get the train home from London – Connie's funeral wouldn't take place until next week – but Flint had insisted on driving her. She wasn't sure whether that was because he didn't want to be alone, or because he didn't want her to be alone. Neither of them had spoken much on the journey. He had put the radio on, but she couldn't remember a single song that had been played.

She gazed bleakly across the table. Flint was toying with his omelette, occasionally putting a small piece in his mouth but for the most part just moving it around the plate. Neither of them was actually hungry; she had only made the meal for something to do, something to distract her for a while. She gave up the pretence of eating, put down her fork and sighed.

'You got anything to drink?' Flint said suddenly.

'There's some wine in the fridge.'

'Nothing stronger?'

Hope was about to say no when she remembered the bottle of Jack Daniel's that Lana had thrust into her hands as she was leaving Tanner Road. *Here, love, take this. You may need it later.* She got to her feet, rummaged in the bag that was still lying where she'd dropped it on the sofa and held up the bottle. 'Will this do?'

'I'll grab some glasses,' Flint said, heading for the kitchen.

Hope sat down again and glanced at her watch. It was ten past seven in the evening, dark outside and wet. Her eyes felt sore and gritty, and every muscle in her body ached. She hadn't been able to sleep much for the past couple of nights, too afraid of the nightmares returning to allow herself to drift off properly. It was probably a bad idea to drink, especially on an empty stomach, but she was way beyond rational thought. Exhaustion was slowly draining her of everything but the desire for oblivion.

Flint came back, broke the seal on the bottle with one fast twist and sloshed out two generous measures. Sitting down, he raised his glass to his lips and knocked half the whiskey back in one. Then he raised his grey eyes to Hope. 'She wouldn't have felt any pain,' he said. 'The cops reckon it must have happened quickly. That kind of exposure to chloroform wouldn't usually kill anyone – Grand normally used just enough to knock the girls out – but apparently Connie had a strong allergic reaction, followed by a heart attack. Cardiac arrest, that's what they said.'

He frowned and took another drink. Now that he'd started talking, he didn't seem able to stop. 'Grand must have seen her when she went back to look for the locket. Lots of toms use that alley; he must have presumed she was one too. Or maybe he just didn't care. She was probably dead before he even got her back to the funeral parlour. So she was spared that at least. She didn't have to go through what those other girls—' He stopped, and quickly shook his head as if trying to free his mind of the horrifying images that had suddenly climbed inside. 'She wouldn't have suffered. That's something, isn't it?'

Hope took a gulp of her drink, the neat alcohol having an instant impact on her. She felt it flood through her veins like liquid fire. A spark of anger made her careless with her tongue. 'How do they know she didn't suffer? The police always say that kind of thing.' But as soon as she'd uttered the words, she wished she could take them back. She saw his eyes fill with pain, and realised too late that what he'd been looking for was some sort of reassurance, an agreement that this version of events might actually be true. 'I'm sorry,' she said, bowing her head. 'I didn't mean that. They're probably right. I'm sure they are.'

Flint gave a small shrug of his shoulders. 'I should never have come here. I don't mean today, I mean *ever*. If you'd never known about her, you wouldn't have had to go through all this.'

This time Hope was quicker on the uptake. The last thing he needed was to feel guilty about her on top of everything else. 'Don't say that. Don't even *think* that. I'm glad you came. I always will be. If it hadn't been for you, I wouldn't have known that I'd got a sister. I wouldn't have known that Connie existed.'

'That might have been better.'

'No,' she insisted. 'It wouldn't.' She wanted to say more, to try and bridge the gulf between them, but her mind had gone blank. Flint's grief seemed too deep and impenetrable for her to even begin to break the surface.

For a while they sat in silence, the only sound the steady pounding of the rain against the window. Hope thought she should get up and pull the curtains across, but somehow she couldn't find the energy to do it. Eventually she said, 'I wish he was dead. Gerald Grand, I mean. How comes he gets to live after what he did to Connie, after what he did to *all* those girls?'

Flint played with the glass, turning it around in his fingers. 'If he does survive, he'll spend the rest of his years in jail. And with the kind of burns he's got, they're going to be pretty painful ones. Every time he looks in the mirror, he'll get a reminder of what he did. Maybe that's an even worse punishment.'

Before she could respond, Hope's phone started to ring. She went over to the sofa and picked it up. It was Lloyd.

'I was passing,' he said, 'and I saw the lights were on. Thought I'd better check that you weren't being burgled.'

'No, it's only me. I just got back. I was going to give you a call later.' She had no idea if Lloyd had heard about the Whisperer on the news, or seen it in the papers. If he had, then the name Connie Tomlin might have rung a bell with him. The police hadn't released Hope's name to the press, so as yet he didn't have a clue about her part in it all.

'Can I come in?' he said. 'I'm parked outside.'

Hope had wanted some time to get her thoughts together before embarking on what was going to be a long and complicated story, but as he was already here, she could hardly say no. 'Sure. I'll see you in a minute.' She put the phone down and looked at Flint. 'That was Lloyd. He's outside.'

Flint stood up. 'You want some privacy? I could take a walk and come back later.'

Hope shook her head. 'No, of course not. Stay. It's fine. I want you to. Anyway, it's pouring down out there.'

The doorbell chimed, and Hope went to answer it. When she came back into the living room with Lloyd behind her, Flint was still standing up. He made a movement as if to put out his hand, and then stopped dead. She heard his sharp intake of breath, and then his murmured 'Jesus Christ.'

Hope looked first at Flint, his eyes wide and disbelieving, and then at her stepfather. The blood had drained from Lloyd's face, and his mouth was contorted in a rictus of shock. There was one of those harsh, brittle silences, before Flint recovered himself enough to say, 'Well, well, long time no see.'

Hope's heart began to pump as she realised that the two of them knew each other. Oh God, so she'd been right about that passport: Lloyd *had* been trying to hide the name from her. 'Will someone tell me what's going on?'

But Lloyd kept his gaze firmly focused on Flint. After a few seconds, the shock left his face, to be replaced by something more like resignation. 'I've often wondered who it might be. You wait and you wait, sometimes you even forget, but not for long. Deep down, you always know that it's going to happen one day.'

Hope felt panic creeping over her. All her worst suspicions, the ones she'd hated herself for, the ones she'd tried to bury, came bubbling to the surface. No, she couldn't deal with this, not after everything else she'd been through. But there was no escaping it either. 'Tell me,' she murmured again.

Flint looked hard at Lloyd. 'Shall I do the honours, or will you?'

Lloyd gave a thin smile. 'I wouldn't want to deprive you of the pleasure.'

'Hope,' Flint said tightly, 'let me introduce you to ...' He hesitated, as if he realised the impact of the bombshell he was about to drop.

But Hope already knew what he was going to say. *Bobby Randall.* Pimp, loan shark, lowlife – maybe something even worse. Why else had Lloyd tried to hide those pictures? They had probably been stolen from her father's studio the night he was killed. She wanted to put her hands over her ears, to refuse to listen. She wanted to run from the room, but her legs were like lead. For a few seconds she fell into denial, refusing to believe, but then reality kicked in. Whatever the truth was, she had to hear it. Glancing at Flint, she nodded, as if to give him permission to say the name.

Flint looked down at the ground before raising his grey eyes again. Still he didn't seem quite able to speak. Finally, after taking a quick breath, he managed to spill out the words. 'This is Jeff Tomlin,' he said softly. 'Your father.'

Hope's mouth dropped open. Shock ran through her, as devastating as a tremor from an earthquake. 'What? It can't . . . it can't . . . I don't . . . ' Her legs suddenly buckled, and she stumbled back on to the sofa. She leaned forward again, briefly covering her face with her hands. Then, looking up, she stared at Lloyd. 'But my father's dead. He was murdered. Jeff Tomlin was murdered. What does he mean? What's he talking about?'

She wanted him to laugh, to say it was ridiculous, but he didn't even try and deny it. As if a mask had slipped from his face, he suddenly looked quite different, like a man she'd never known, a complete and utter stranger. 'I'm sorry,' he said. 'Sorry that you had to find out like this.'

Flint went to the table and picked up his drink. He took a couple of swallows before saying, 'I think your daughter deserves an explanation.'

Lloyd took a moment, his brows crunching into a frown. He glanced at Hope, gave two fast blinks, and began pacing around the room. 'What can I say? I loved your mother and I wanted her back, wanted you *both* back, even after we'd been apart for eight years. I couldn't live without her. Do you understand?' He didn't wait for an answer, but swiftly carried on. 'Fay wouldn't even consider us getting back together unless I could prove I could support her. So I lied. I went to see her in Albersea, told her that I'd got hold of some money and was going to buy a small art gallery in Liverpool. That was when I started doing the forgeries. Do you know about them?'

Hope couldn't speak. Instead, she gave a small mute nod.

'Well, with the cash I got from those, and with everything else I could beg, steal or borrow, I managed to maintain the pretence, at least for a few years, that everything was going well. The truth of course was that I was getting deeper and deeper into debt.'

'And that's when you decided to do your disappearing trick.' Flint said.

Lloyd gave him a thin smile. 'I always knew that one day Jeff Tomlin would have to cease to exist. It was the only way I could be free, and be with Fay on a permanent basis. Bobby Randall was a loan shark who used to come to the studio in Soho and sit for me occasionally. It amused him to have me paint him. He was usually stoned or pissed, and once when he'd passed out I took a look in his wallet. That was when I got the idea for stealing his identity, only using his middle name instead of his first. He was off the radar so far as the authorities were concerned, never paid a penny in tax, didn't even have a bank account – he paid for everything in cash – so it seemed like the ideal solution.'

'And what did you tell Fay?'

'That I'd been in trouble in London, serious trouble, and that I'd be dead if anyone ever found me. That's why I had to use a different identity. She agreed to go along with the deception.' He paused again, glancing at Hope. 'Actually, I think she found it quite exciting. It would mean you never knowing who I really was, but that was the price we had to pay.'

Hope stared up at him, speechless.

Flint spoke again. His voice was cold, hard-edged. 'And what about the price Sadie had to pay? You never told her about Fay, did you? Running two households must have been expensive.

437

What did you do? Split the time between the two families, saying you had to work away?'

Hope, who'd dropped her head, quickly jerked it up again. 'What?' She suddenly remembered that when she was younger, Lloyd *had* spent a lot of time away from home, often for a week or so at a time. Buying trips, he'd called them, claiming he was going to Paris or Rome or Milan.

'You could have left her,' Flint said, 'got a divorce before you married again. But then the lovely Fay might not have been quite so keen to have you back if she found out you were already married to somebody else. Hardly a case of undying love, was it? Or maybe there was another reason why you were so keen to hold on to Sadie. You knew that one day you were going to need her to help with that disappearing trick of yours.'

Lloyd pushed his glasses up his nose, his frown growing deeper. 'That wasn't the reason, not at the beginning. I was just ... I don't know. I didn't want to hurt Sadie or Connie. I did care about them, I swear I did. But as time went by, I was getting more and more in debt. I owed Randall over twenty grand, other loan sharks more than thirty, and a gangster called Terry Street had leant me fifty as an advance against a pair of Russian paintings I was copying.'

'The Baranovas,' Flint said.

Lloyd stopped pacing for a second. 'My, we have been busy, haven't we?'

Flint's upper lip curled. 'So there was only one way out, and that was to create the biggest forgery of all – your own death. And for that, you needed someone to identify the body. Jesus, you don't do things by half measures, do you?'

As one revelation followed another, Hope's head began to reel. She felt like it was slowly filling with a dense, impenetrable fog. And then with a terrible shiver that ran from the top of her spine to the bottom, the fog separated just enough for her to realise that no one had spoken yet about the most horrifying act of all.

'You killed him,' she whispered. 'You murdered Bobby Randall.'

Lloyd gave another of his shrugs. 'He was a vicious bastard, the lowest of the low. You think any of his girls missed him? I bet they never even reported him missing. I did the world a favour, freeing it of that scumbag.'

Hope thought she was going to be sick. 'Did my mother know? Did she know what you'd done?'

Lloyd shook his head.

Flint interjected again. 'But poor Sadie did. She covered for you, identified the body as yours. Oh, and she played the grieving widow to perfection; she certainly had me fooled. But of course she didn't have a clue that you weren't just going to dump your old life, but her and Connie too. What did you tell her, that you'd lie low for a while, go abroad perhaps, and get in touch with her again when everything had calmed down?'

Lloyd didn't dispute any of it. 'I'm not proud of what I did. But I loved Fay.' He looked at Hope again. 'The two of you were everything to me. And when she came back into my life – you were what, about eight then? – I couldn't bear the thought of losing either of you again.'

'But you had the Baranovas,' Flint said. 'They'd be worth a fortune – maybe even a million if you could actually convince the buyer they were real.'

'Except Street was going to take half the profit, and by the time all my other debts had been paid off . . . sure, I'd have had money for a while, but it wouldn't have lasted long. And then I'd be back to square one. Anyway, I couldn't carry on with the double life I was leading. I couldn't cope with it any more.'

'So you went behind Street's back, cut him out of the deal and flogged the paintings yourself.'

Lloyd gave a brisk shake of his head. 'No, not both of them. I left one for Sadie, along with the phone number of a man she could take it to. He was a dealer with Russian contacts. I told her that if she didn't hear from me after six months, something must have gone wrong, and she was to sell the painting to him. The money would be enough to take care of her and Connie.'

'Blood money,' Flint hissed. '*Guilt* money. And of course you didn't call, you never got in touch with her again. And she couldn't go to the police and report you missing because you were supposed to be dead, and she'd already identified the body.' His face was tight and angry. 'Oh, and by the way, she never did sell that painting. She kept on waiting for you to come back. She kept on waiting for two long years until she finally managed to kill herself.'

Lloyd pursed his lips, but didn't respond.

'Connie's dead too,' Flint said brutally. 'Did you know?'

'I'm sorry to hear that.'

Suddenly Hope snapped. 'Sorry?' she screamed at him, jumping up from the sofa. 'Is that all you've got to say? Your own daughter's dead, my *sister's* dead, and that's the best you can do?' She could see no remorse on his face, no real sorrow. Her father's heart was made of stone.

Lloyd took a step back, raising his hands as if to fend off a more physical attack. He frowned at Hope, and then shot a glance at Flint. 'Ah, is that what he told you? I get it now. Well, I'm afraid I'm not the only one who's been economical with the truth. Connie wasn't actually my daughter.'

Hope shook her head. She wanted to hit him, to beat her fists against his chest, and it took every ounce of restraint to keep herself from doing it. Was he incapable of opening his mouth without a lie coming out? 'I've seen the birth certificate. Your name's on it.'

'Four years after your mother left me, I got back with Sadie.

She was pregnant with another man's child, but she wanted us to be a *real* family, for me to raise Connie as my own. I went along with it. I felt I owed her that. But I could never love Connie the way I loved you. She wasn't my own flesh and blood.'

Hope's head had started to spin again. 'So who was her real father?'

Lloyd glanced towards Flint. 'Why don't you ask him?'

Flint, she noticed, was looking decidedly uncomfortable. She stared at him, and her heart missed a beat. *No, it couldn't be.*

Flint must have seen the expression on her face, because he quickly blurted out, 'It wasn't me. Sadie had an affair with my brother, Paul. It didn't last long, and he died in a car accident before he even knew he was going to be a father.'

Hope's eyes widened. 'You're Connie's uncle?'

'Yes, but she never knew. To her I was just a friend of her parents. Sadie wanted to play happy families, and who was I to stand in her way? I thought it was for the best. Paul was dead, and Jeff was willing to raise her as his own.'

'Of course you agreed,' Lloyd said snidely. 'It saved you the bother of having to take any responsibility for her yourself. It suited you just fine.'

Flint kept his gaze fixed firmly on Hope. 'There's probably some truth in that. We're talking over twenty years ago. I was eighteen, selfish and immature. My brother was dead, and the only other person I cared about was myself.' He lifted the glass to his mouth, draining the whiskey before he spoke again. 'Then, when Connie was about ten, and six months after Jeff was apparently murdered, I ended up in jail. I got a five-stretch for fraud, and by the time I came out, I didn't even know where Connie was. I should have looked for her, tried to track her down, but I told myself she was better off without me. In the end, she was the one who found me.'

441

'You lied!' Hope felt like a fly captured in a web by two fat spiders spinning their silken threads faster and faster around her. 'You said she was my sister.'

'Yes, I lied. But would you have helped me otherwise? I needed someone else to care, someone to help me look for Connie.'

Hope felt his deceit like a knife slicing through her ribs. How stupid she'd been. How gullible. God, she'd even managed to convince herself that she and Connie had a family resemblance. She had seen what she'd wanted to see, and so had Lana. Yes, even smart, savvy Lana had believed that part of his story.

Suddenly, it was all too much. She couldn't take any more. Her world was falling apart, and there was nothing she could do about it. She had to get out, out of this room, this house, away from these two men who were slowly crushing the life out of her. Turning, she hurried into the hall, grabbed her coat, flung open the door and stepped into the rain.

She began to jog down the road, pulling on her coat as she went. Then, desperate to put as much distance as she could between herself and the cottage, she broke into a run, her legs shaky but determined, her arms swinging wildly beside her. Sloshing through the puddles, she ran faster and faster, gulping in the cool night air until her chest was heaving and she thought her lungs would burst. On and on. Where was she going? She didn't care. The rain poured down her face, mingling with her tears. Away was the only word in her head. As far away as she could get.

As the beach came into view, she slowed down to a walk, too exhausted to keep on running. She wasn't surprised to find herself here. This was the place where it had all started, where Flint had told her about her murdered father, where her first sisterly feelings for Connie had begun to stir.

But all that had been a lie.

There was no one else on the beach. The weather was too wretched for even the most hardy dog walkers to venture out. The tide was in, the black water licking at the sand. Lights from the promenade caught the surface of the water and made it glisten. As the wind tugged at her hair, Hope walked towards the pier and the sparse shelter of its burnt-out remains.

Once she was underneath the rusted iron girders, she knew that she couldn't be seen from the street behind. She stood very still, listening to the waves, to the sound of the rain falling on the water. She thought of the moment when Lloyd had put the gun to Bobby Randall's head. What had he felt as his finger tightened on that trigger? What had he been thinking? He'd made a pact with the Devil, and it was all unravelling. She understood now why he'd reacted so strangely when she'd found those paintings. He must have taken them from the studio on the night he'd committed that terrible act.

Bowing her head, she tried to pray, but no words came to her lips. Everything she'd thought was real was just an illusion. She didn't know who she was any more. Her whole life, her whole existence, had been built on lies and deceit. And now a wrecking ball had swung through her world, shattering it into a thousand tiny pieces, leaving only rubble in its wake. Everything was broken.

As she looked up again, Hope felt the black sea beckoning to her. Her gaze lingered on its smooth, glistening surface. One step at a time. That was all it would take. First her feet, then her ankles, her stomach, her chest . . . until eventually . . . oblivion. The water would close over her, take away the pain, cleanse her finally of all this horror. It was that easy. Slowly she began to walk forward, until the waves slid across her shoes. The water was icy cold, but still she walked on. As the sea lapped around her knees, she drew in her breath.

It was then that she heard a voice softly calling from behind her: 'Hope.'

She didn't look round. It was nothing. She had just imagined it. Go on, she urged herself. Get this over with. Get it finished.

The voice came again, louder this time. 'Hope, please come back.'

She turned. There was a girl standing on the sand, a girl dressed in white, with long brown hair flowing down around her shoulders. Her smile, although Hope had only ever seen it in a photograph, seemed completely familiar.

'Connie,' Hope whispered. For a second her heart seemed to stop. But this wasn't real. She knew it couldn't be. It was her mind playing tricks.

Still the girl stood there, her hand extended, reaching out to her.

Hope squeezed shut her eyes, the tears spilling down her cheeks. She thought of all Connie had been through, all she'd had to endure in her short life. As a child, her home had been broken too, but somehow she'd found the courage to carry on. In the end Connie had been robbed of her future, had it cruelly snatched from her, whereas Hope was voluntarily throwing hers away.

She blinked open her eyes again, but the vision was gone. She looked to the left, to the right; no one was there. She was all alone. An ache rolled through her body, as deep and raw as if Connie had been freshly lost. She looked once towards the horizon, where the sea softly merged into the darkness of the sky, and then towards the land.

And she knew what she had to do.

Slowly she made her way back to the shore. Shivering with cold, and with water dripping from her clothes, she gazed along the length of the empty beach. From somewhere far away she heard the rippling sound of laughter, a reminder that the world kept turning, that there could be joy as well as pain. There were always choices. She could only hope that this time, with a little help, she'd made the right one.

Epilogue

Hope stood in the piazza and gazed up with pleasure at the pan-elled dome of the Basilica di Santa Maria del Fiore. The warm May sunshine fell softly against her face, reminding her of how good it felt to be alive. She couldn't claim to be happy exactly – that particular emotion would probably elude her for a while – but she had managed to achieve a state of relative contentment.

It was eight months now since she'd come to Florence, and she'd never once regretted the decision. Soon she would step inside the cathedral and begin the afternoon's work with the rest of the team. The restoration of the stained-glass windows was slow and painstaking, but for her it was a labour of love. While she was concentrating on the glass, on the leading, on the vibrant colours and intricate designs, she could forget about everything else. She worked hard, ate, slept, took Italian night classes twice a week and occasionally went out with the new friends she'd made. Yes, she was getting by. She was finally start-ing to heal.

But the past, she knew, would never leave her. Lloyd – she still couldn't bring herself to call him Jeff, or even think of him as her real father – had disappeared a few days after the awful truth had come out. His car had been found abandoned at the beach, along with a suicide note. It had been addressed to her, and had said quite simply: *I'm so sorry. Please forgive me.* She had told the police that he'd been depressed after the death of her mother.

Before making his exit, Lloyd had transferred everything he owned into her name. She had sold it all, the flat, the cottage, the gallery and its contents, but she hadn't kept the money. How could she? It was money made from murder, from lies and deceit. To have spent even a penny of it would have made her feel like she was profiting from evil. The fifty thousand she'd received from Terry Street for the fake painting, she had given to Evelyn – perhaps the nearest person to a sister Connie had ever had.

As for Flint, she hadn't seen him since Connie's funeral. They had stood on different sides of the church, and afterwards she'd left before he could speak to her. She still thought of him sometimes, she couldn't help herself, but she understood now that her feelings had never been reciprocated. He had simply used her to get what he wanted.

That desolate evening, her last one in Kellston, she had taken a walk down the high street. Her final act of the day had been to slide an envelope under the door of the dress shop. And then, all debts discharged, she had been free to leave.

Detective Inspector Valerie Middleton put down the file she was reading, and gazed out of the window. A thin May sun cast its rays across the forecourt. The slim golden bands made the concrete shimmer, and she smiled at the sight, thinking that summer would soon be here. It was a summer that not so long ago she thought she'd never live to see.

Valerie still had flashbacks to that terrible day eight months

446

ago, but they were gradually receding. The scars on her arm would never disappear, but she was learning to live with them. And compared to Gerald Grand's other victims, she knew she'd got off lightly. She had three people to thank for that: Gemma Leigh, Hope Randall and her old adversary Kieran Swann. If Gemma hadn't made that call, if Hope hadn't thrown that bottle, if Swann hadn't run the PNC check on Gerald Grand and discovered he'd received a six-month ban in February for careless driving ... But what ifs could drive you crazy. Grand lived in Chigwell, and his case had been heard in the local magistrates' court. With no reason to suspect him, they hadn't thought to run a check before. If they had, they'd have discovered that the van he'd used had been off the road during the gap between the attacks.

Valerie picked up the file again and stared hard at the name on the front: Danny Street. That vicious piece of lowlife still remained at liberty, which couldn't help but make her seethe. Linzi Marshall had eventually regained consciousness and confirmed his story that she'd had oral sex with him on the evening of her attack, but by then they had known the true identity of the Whisperer anyway. Valerie had made a mistake about that, she'd got it wrong, but one day Street would make a mistake too, and then she'd have him. 'Give it time,' she murmured.

She glanced out of the window again, and her thoughts drifted off in another direction. A couple of months after Connie Tomlin's funeral, an unsigned letter had arrived at Cowan Road, along with a bank draft for a substantial amount of cash. The anonymous donor had asked that it be divided between the victims of the Whisperer. She often wondered who had sent the money, but suspected she would never find out. It wouldn't change what Gerald Grand had done, but it might give those girls a chance to get back on their feet.

Valerie was returned to the present by the appearance of

447

Kieran Swann swaggering across the forecourt with his hands in his pockets. It was funny how that walk didn't irritate her any more. Their relationship had improved vastly since he'd come charging into the basement of Tobias Grand & Sons. Perhaps it had taken a show of vulnerability on her part to bridge the gap between them. There was one thing, however, that she had still not quite recovered from: Kieran Swann had seen her naked, and that, she was afraid, was an experience she might never get over.

Chris Street leaned back in his smart swivel chair, put his feet up on the desk and placed his hands behind his head. Life was good. Eight months ago, the family had been on the brink of bankruptcy, and now here they were about to reopen a newly refurbished Belles. With the Lincoln Pool Hall rebuilt, and their stronghold on the Mansfield Estate re-established, the Streets were back in business. He had to admit that he'd been wrong about the old man. Terry Street still had it, although it had taken a crisis to shake him out of the black depression that had gripped him for so long.

Chris grinned as he thought about Andrei Kozlov. The Russian bastard had fallen hook, line and sinker for Benjie's story, hot-footing it round to Tom Montgomery's gallery in Mayfair, and offering almost nine hundred grand for the picture. As soon as the 'Baranova' had been handed over, Tom had made an anony-mous phone call to the Arts & Antiques Unit of the Met. They'd picked up Kozlov along with the painting. The experts were still fighting over whether it was genuine or not. Kozlov's fancy lawyers would probably keep him out of jail, but he'd never see his money again. And while he was tied up fighting the law, he didn't have the time or the cash to waste on screwing over the Streets. Tom Montgomery, better known as Billie the Con, had disappeared within the hour, taking his 'gallery' with him.

Chris Street wasn't usually one for regrets, but today he found himself wondering what had happened to Hope Randall. He'd tried to call her, but her phone had been disconnected. It was a shame that hadn't worked out. Occasionally someone came into your life and there was a spark, a fizz of electricity. But her heart, he suspected, had always been elsewhere.

The door to the office opened, and his brother strolled in. 'Oh, so this is where you are. The old man's looking for you.'

Chris was about to get to his feet when he felt something push against the base of the chair. He looked down to see a pair of cold, angry eyes glaring up at him. 'Ah, for fuck's sake, Danny, how many times have I told you? Get that bloody dog out of here!'

Benjamin Tallow walked down by the harbour, smiling at the brightly coloured fishing boats, at the blueness of the sky, at just about everything he saw. He liked to think it was fate that had brought him here, that the resort of Ayia Napa had chosen him rather than the other way round. When he'd gone to Gatwick Airport with Kozlov's two grand in his pocket – sure, Terry Street had suggested a grand, but if you didn't ask, you didn't get – he'd been thinking more along the lines of Ibiza. It had been a noisy, tipsy gang of Peckham girls who'd made him change his mind, a hen party on their way out to Cyprus for the weekend. And now, all these months later, they were just a distant memory, and he was still here.

There were good opportunities for an ambitious boy in a place like this, plenty of deals to be made, plenty of customers to satisfy. Even over the winter months he'd managed to get work. And his scar had proved surprisingly useful, a don't-mess-with-me kind of symbol that gave him a peculiar kudos. Yeah, he loved it here all right: the sun, the cool music, the constant partying, but most of all the girls. Soon the season would be starting again, and the tourists would be flooding in. Yeah, life was good. For the first time since his mother had died, Benjamin could claim that he was truly happy.

It was seven o'clock when Hope left the cathedral and began the walk towards home. She loved this time of the evening, an hour before sunset, when the square was still bustling and the pungent smell of coffee drifted on the air. Perhaps she would take the longer way back and saunter along the old cobbled streets. She had no lessons tonight, so the time was her own.

She was barely halfway across the piazza when she felt a hand on her arm. She twisted round, startled, to find herself staring into the grey eyes of Michael Flint. Despite herself, her heart gave a tiny leap.

'What are you doing here?'

'Bad pennies,' he said, smiling. 'They always turn up in the end. How have you been?'

Hope didn't answer immediately. She was still trying to get over the shock of seeing him again, whilst simultaneously trying to work out how she felt about it. Happy? Angry? Resentful? Perhaps all of those things, but not, she noted, indifferent. No, she could never be indifferent to Flint.

'I'm all right,' she said finally. 'How did you know where I was?'

'Evelyn told me. And please don't be cross with her. I was very persuasive.'

'I'm sure.' Her voice sounded cooler than she felt. She stared at him for a moment. He seemed changed from when she'd last seen him, although she couldn't quite work out what that change was. Perhaps his hair was shorter. Or perhaps it was just the clothes he was wearing; he was dressed in a white shirt and cream trousers, with a pale blue sweater draped around his shoulders in the casual Italian way. Or maybe it wasn't anything physical at all. 'So what is it you want?'

'To talk. We could have a drink. Do you have the time?'

Hope had the opportunity to come up with an excuse, to claim that she was busy, that she had to be somewhere and soon. Her head was saying walk away from this, no good will come of it, but her heart refused to listen. Old feelings had started to stir, and no matter how hard she fought, there was nothing she could do about it. Anyway, she had questions of her own that needed answering.

'What about over there?' he said, pointing across the square towards a busy café on the corner.

Hope gave a small nod. 'A quick one, then.'

As they walked beside each other, neither of them spoke. She was overly aware of the closeness of his arm, of his hand almost brushing against her own. Smartly, she put her own hands in her pockets.

They found an empty table and sat down amongst the other couples. 'You're looking well,' Flint said. 'Florence must suit you.'

'I like it here.'

The waiter came over and they ordered two glasses of wine. Hope remembered the last occasion she'd had a drink with Flint, back in Albersea. She had a sudden vivid image of the bottle of Jack Daniel's, could almost feel the sour taste of the whiskey on her tongue. She gave a shiver and looked across the table at him. 'What are you really doing here?'

'Like I said, I wanted to talk, but most of all to apologise.'

'It's a long way to come to say sorry.'

Flint gave a shrug. 'Not after what I did.'

There was a short silence. The waiter came back with the Chianti. Hope lifted her glass to her lips and took a few fast sips.

'Evelyn told me about Jeff,' Flint said.

'They never found the body.' Her mouth twisted a little. 'It could just be another of his disappearing tricks. He always knew he'd be found out one day. He could have put some money aside, gone abroad. Jeff Tomlin could be anywhere.' Her eyes raked the square, as if the very mention of his name might summon him out of the ether.

'It's possible,' Flint agreed.

Hope looked back at him and took a breath. 'I still can't make sense of it. I mean, I can't reconcile the person I knew for all those years with the man he really was.'

'Jeff never liked to do things the easy way.'

'But I can't imagine what it's like to live like that, to be always looking over your shoulder, to know that every ounce of happiness you have has been gained at someone else's expense.' She took another quick sip of wine. 'And I think about my mother and wonder how much of it was her fault. If she hadn't wanted so much, if she'd been less demanding . . . ' She gave a shrug. 'I don't know.'

'Sometimes people just bring out the worst in each other. I think Jeff and Fay were like that. They were both obsessive and selfish, wrapped up in their own dramas and desires. I doubt if either of them really cared who else got hurt along the way.'

For a minute the surrounding chatter washed over them, the clink of glasses, the clatter of cutlery. Hope was the first to speak again. 'Connie never knew anything about me, did she.' It was a statement rather than a question.

Flint rested his chin on his hand and looked at her gloomily. 'No, it was Jeff who was always banging on about Albersea, about you and Fay. When Connie went missing, no one would talk to me, and that's when I got the idea of approaching you. It was a shot in the dark, but I thought it was worth a try.'

Hope gave a bitter laugh. 'And I was stupid enough to fall for it.'

'No, not stupid,' he said, with a vehemence that surprised

her. 'Don't ever think that. I gave you all the evidence, the birth certificate, the proof – you had no reason to doubt me. And you could still have refused.' He managed a small smile. 'I'm sure you wanted to, but you didn't. And that's to your credit.'

Hope decided to be honest. She'd heard too many lies to want to add to them. 'I did it because I felt I had to. I did it out of guilt and a sense of obligation.'

'At the beginning, perhaps, but not later. I know that you came to genuinely care about her.'

Hope couldn't argue with that. Her feelings for Connie had grown with every day she'd spent in Kellston.

'She would have liked you,' Flint said.

'Why do you say that?'

He tilted his head to one side, and examined her closely. 'Because you're like her. Inside, I mean. Because you're gutsy and principled and stand up for what you believe is right. And yes, I know that Connie wasn't the most law-abiding of citizens, but she had her own set of morals, her own ideas of what was right and wrong.' He paused. 'And she had a good heart.'

Hope thought about the vision she'd had on the beach. 'Yes, I think she did.'

'I lied to you, and I'm so sorry about that. God, I'm sorry about so many things. Jeff was right when he said that I wasn't prepared to take responsibility. After Paul died, I was a mess. I should have stepped up, offered to help Sadie raise the baby, but I didn't. I couldn't. And when she said that Jeff was willing to take Connie on as his own, I jumped at the opportunity. It was my get-out clause, my chance to walk free. I let Paul down, and then I let down Connie too.'

'You were young. You can't blame yourself for that.'

He flinched, and for a moment his face seemed to shut down, but then it swiftly cleared again, as if he too had decided that honesty was the only way forward. 'Except every time I saw

453

Connie, I was reminded of Paul. I should have come clean with her when she first got in touch again, told her who her father really was, who *I* really was. If I had, she might not have been so determined to track down Jeff Tomlin's killer. If she'd known the truth, she might never have gone to Danny Street, never got Derek Parr so worried, never been in a position where that bastard Gerald Grand could do what he did to her.'

Hope gave a sigh. The world was full of what ifs. She felt sorry for Flint. She couldn't help herself. He wasn't bad, he'd simply made mistakes. 'You can't know that.'

'So you don't hate me?'

Hope frowned at the question. 'No, I don't hate you. What you did, I mean what you did when you came to see me that first time at Albersea, was because you cared about Connie.' She paused, trying to get her thoughts in order before she continued. 'But no one likes being used.'

Flint nodded. 'Can I ask you something else?'

'What is it?'

After a long hesitation, he leaned forward, his expression more intense. 'Look, I'm not much good at this stuff, but there *was* something between us, wasn't there? Tell me to shut up if I've got this all wrong, but if there's one thing I've learned from all this mess, it's that sometimes, like Connie, you don't get second chances. You have to grab the ones you've got and hold on tight to them.'

It was what she'd wanted to hear, and yet Hope shrank back. Was he being serious? Was this for real? Her heart had started to thump out a drum beat in her chest. She was almost afraid of grasping for happiness, afraid that it would be cruelly snatched away from her again. 'I'm just getting my life back together. I'm not sure if—'

'There's no pressure,' he said. 'I don't mean right here, right now, but maybe some time in the future . . . '

Hope continued to gaze at him, wanting to say yes but too scared to make that leap of faith. She'd been hurt too much to put her emotions on the line again.

Flint reached out, took the glass from her hand and put it down on the table. Then he took her hands between his own. 'Okay, I'm not going to rush you. But do you think, eventually, you'll be able to forgive me?'

'Well, I suppose I understand why you did it.'

'You do?'

'I think so.'

Flint grinned. 'So is that a definite yes?'

Hope, feeling the warmth of his hands, gazed into those compelling grey eyes. Despite all her fears, all her caution, a smile tugged at the corners of her mouth. 'It's early days,' she said eventually. 'Let's take it one step at a time.'